Walter Hawken Tregellas

Cornish Worthies

Vol. 2

Walter Hawken Tregellas

Cornish Worthies
Vol. 2

ISBN/EAN: 9783337376628

Printed in Europe, USA, Canada, Australia, Japan

Cover: Foto ©Andreas Hilbeck / pixelio.de

More available books at **www.hansebooks.com**

CORNISH WORTHIES:

*SKETCHES OF SOME EMINENT CORNISH MEN
AND FAMILIES.*

BY

WALTER H. TREGELLAS.

IN TWO VOLUMES.—VOL. II.

'Cornubia fulsit
Tot fœcunda viris.'
JOSEPH OF EXETER (XIIIth century).

LONDON:
ELLIOT STOCK, 62, PATERNOSTER ROW, E.C.
1884.

CONTENTS OF VOL. II.

ERRATA AND ADDENDA.

Introduction, p. xiv., for *Dean Miller* read *Dean Milles*.

JOHN ANSTIS. (Vol. i., p. 33.)

His heraldic and other collections now form part of the Stowe MSS. in the British Museum.

See also p. 78 of that Catalogue.

THE ARUNDELLS.

'*Sir John Arundell*, the Vice-Admiral of Cornwall who took prisoner Duncan Campbell, the Scottish pirate, is said to have been a native of Truro.'—Lyson's 'Magna Britannia—Cornwall,' p. 313. (Vol. i., p. 84.)

'In Norden's time' (says Lysons), 'the Arundells had twelve seats in Cornwall.'

Sir Thomas (afterwards Lord) *Arundel* of Wardour, 1595, at Strigonium (Gran), says, 'being arrived at the camp at the very instant of that great and onlie Battaile between us and the Turks, unknown unto anie, and uncommanded of anie, I presented myselfe in the front of the armie, where, by reason of my plumes of feathers, of my armour, bases and furniture, all full of gould and silver (a thing there altogether unusual), I was presently marked by all men's eyes.'—*Vide* 'Count Arundell's Apologie to Lord Burghley.' (Vol. i., p. 58.)

THE BASSETS. (Vol. i., p. 107.)

Philip Basset was appointed Chief Justiciary of England by Henry III., in place of Hugh le Despenser, *circ.* 1260, after the attempt of the barons to seize the King's person at Winchester.— (Pat. 45 Hen. III., m. 8 ; and Rot. Claus., 45 Hen. III., m. 10 dors.)

The Royal Cornwall Infirmary, which dates from 1779, contains a tablet which records 'the establishment, permanency, and usefulness of the charity to be chiefly due to the munificent liberality and unwearied exertions of *Francis, Lord de Dunstanville.*' (Vol. i., p. 36.)

HENRY BONE, R.A. (Vol. i., p. 159.)

Many beautiful examples of his works are preserved at Mr. Hope's, Deepdene, near Dorking.

THE BOSCAWENS. (Vol. i., p. 199.)

The well-known non-juror, Bishop Trelawny, was a Dean of Buryan. See the seal of the Deans figured in Rev. W. Iago's paper, R. I. C. Journal, vol. viii., part i., March, 1884.

THE GODOLPHINS. (Vol. i., p. 378.)

There is a portrait of the celebrated Margaret Godolphin at Wotton, the seat of the Evelyns.

The letter signed 'Frances Godolphin,' vol. i., p. 173, should read as signed 'Frances St. Aubyn.'

THE GRENVILLES. (Vol. ii., p. 67.)

John Grenville (afterwards Earl of Bath) was Lieutenant-General of the Ordnance 1702-5.

SIR BEVILL GRENVILLE. (Vol. ii., p. 64.)

I am indebted to a recent very interesting biography of Sir Bevill by Mr. Alfred R. Robbins (which I did not see until the chapter on the Grenvilles had gone through the press) for information on the following points, which had escaped my notice.

Sir Bevill gave a silver cup to Exeter College.

He secured the success of Eliot's election, no doubt on account of strong personal friendship, as an anti-loan candidate about 1628. Bagg wrote to the Duke of Buckingham that he desired to have Eliot, Grenville, and John Arundell 'outlawed and put out of the House' . . . . 'for here we had Beville Grenville, John Arundell, and Charles Trevanion coming to the election with five hundred men at each of their heels.'

He was one of the executors named by Eliot in his will.

He was much encumbered with the debts of his ancestors, and sold (amongst other property) Brinn, his birthplace, to Sir William Noye, the Attorney-General.

He objected to the Bill of Attainder against Strafford, and wrote to his fellow Cornishman, Sir Alexander Carew, 'Pray, sir, when it comes to be put to the vote, let it never be said that any member of our country (county) should have a hand in this fatal business; and therefore pray ye give your vote against the Bill.' But this Carew stoutly refused to do.

He refused the summons of the Parliament 'to attend the service of the House,' pleading the King's special command to continue in his county to preserve the peace thereof; whereupon a resolution was passed disabling him from continuing to be a member.

His praises, after his death, were sung, not only by his old University of Oxford, but also by Sir Francis Wortley in his 'Characters and Elegies,' in 1646; by Robert Heath, in 1650; and by William Cartwright, in 1651.

THE KILLIGREWS. (Vol. ii., p. 119.)

The 1st Thos. Killigrew was buried at Gluvias, not at Budock.

THE ST. AUBYNS.

The letter signed 'Frances Godolphin,' vol. i., p. 173, should read as signed 'Frances St. Aubyn.'

THE GRENVILLES OF STOW,

HEROES BY SEA AND LAND.

THE GRENVILLES OF STOW,

HEROES BY SEA AND LAND.

'Tell me, ye skilful men, if ye have read,
In all the faire memorials of the dead,
    Of names so formidably great,
So full of wonder and unenvied love;
In which all virtues and all graces strove,
    So terrible and yet so sweete?'
From a 'Pindaric Ode' of 1686.

'The four wheels of Charles's wain—
Grenville, Godolphin, Trevanion, Slanning slain.'
Old Cornish Distich.

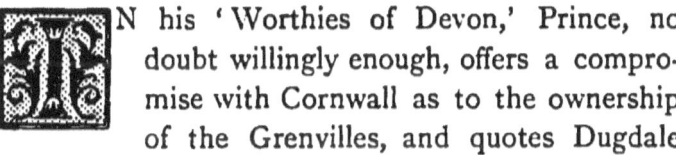N his 'Worthies of Devon,' Prince, no doubt willingly enough, offers a compromise with Cornwall as to the ownership of the Grenvilles, and quotes Dugdale and Fuller to the effect that both Cornwall and Devon are so fruitful of illustrious men, that each can spare to the other a hero or two, even if wrongfully deprived of her own; even Carew has a somewhat similar passage, in which he says, 'The merits of this ancient family are so many and so great, that ingrossed they would make one County proud, which, divided, would make two happy.'

But, as it appears to me, Cornwall *could* not, even

26—2

if she would, spare the Grenvilles—especially the
two most celebrated of them, Sir Richard and Sir
Bevill—from her roll of Worthies.   True it is that
the Grenvilles usually took the sea at Bideford (By-
the-ford), for it was their nearest port, though they
always kept a keen eye upon the possibility of utilizing
Boscastle, Tintagel and other North Cornwall ports;
true also that Sir Theobald Grenville (probably with
the assistance of a priest named Sir Richard Gornard,
or Gurney, and others), who flourished in the reign
of Edward III., mainly built the famous great Bideford bridge of twenty-four arches; doubtless, too,
they had lands and knights' fees, and a house or
houses at Bideford in which they occasionally
resided: but the *seat* of the Grenvilles was, from at
least the time of William Rufus, at Stow (which
even Prince calls 'their chiefest habitation'*), in the
parish of Kilkhampton, well within the Cornish
border, and separated, on the northern side, from
the fair sister county of Devon by the whole of the
broad parish of Morwenstow.†   For five centuries
or more their monuments were placed in Kilkhampton Church, on which they bestowed from time
to time many benefactions, and of which parish
many members of the family were Rectors.   Carew
says that one of the Grenvilles was parson of Kilkhampton, and that he lived so long as to see himself
uncle and great-uncle to more than 300 persons:

---

* Camden says they had four other seats, viz., Wolstan, Stanbury,
Clifton and Lanow.

† John Graynfylde was Vicar of Morwenstow, 1536; the church was
granted to Sir Richard Grenville, one of the Church Commissioners for
Cornwall, by Henry VIII.

this was probably John Grenville, temp. Edward IV.
Of another Rector of this parish the Rev. C. W. Boase,
in his ' Registers of Exeter College,' has recorded
that, shortly after the year 1316, Richard Grenfield
founded a chest of money for making loans to the
poor scholars of that Society. According to Lake's
' Parochial History of Cornwall,' the following
Grenvilles were Rectors of Kilkhampton, namely:
Richard, son of Sir Bart^w. Grenville, 1312; John
Grenville, 1524, who also held Week St. Mary;
Dennis Grenville, 10th July, 1661 ; Chamond Grenville, 1711. The Church Registers, as might be expected, abound in references to the family. Their
descent, too, is given in the ' Heralds' Visitations '
for *Cornwall** (p. 217) ; and Tuckett rightly omits
them from his edition of the 'Devonshire Pedigrees '
(p. 38, etc.). They commanded the *Cornish* forces
during the Civil War; and, from their earliest settle-
ment in the county, they intermarried with such old
Cornish families as Tregomynion, Trewent, Vivian,
Roscarrick, Killigrew, Arundell of Lanherne, Basset,
St. Aubyn, Bevill, Fortescue, Prideaux, and Tre-
mayne. That keen observer, the late Canon Kingsley,
has, moreover, not failed to detect, in the portrait of
the great Sir Richard, the thoroughly *Cornish* type
of face ; and, finally, they are rightly included in the
' Bibliotheca Cornubiensis.' It is, in view of all
these facts, probably unnecessary to dwell any
further on the supremacy of Cornwall's claims to
the Grenvilles.

* Harl. MSS. 1079; in which their shield has fifty-three quarterings
and three crests.

But it must be reluctantly confessed that they are, after all, not of strictly Cornish origin; for, though they lived for centuries in the county, they came in, like the Bevills (with whom they intermarried more than once), with the Conqueror; and, as an early form of their name suggests* had their first home in Normandy, and were descended from Duke Rollo, and from Hamon Dentatus, Earl of Carboyle (? Corbeil), and Lord of Thorigny and Granville in that country. Their name has been variously spelt Grenvill, Greenville, Grenvile, Greenvil, Granville, Grainvilla, Granaville, Greenvil and otherwise—it even occurs in one place as Grinfillde;† but it seems likely to be best known in history in the form prefixed to this chapter, and which has been adopted by the Poet Laureate in that stirring 'Ballad of the Fleet,' with which we have all of us lately been delighted, and to which we shall presently have occasion to refer more fully.

Younger branches of the family settled in Bucks and in Somerset, and preserved the favourite old Christian name of Richard, which was also perpetuated in the elder, or Cornish, branch: in fact it has

---

* George Granville, Lord Lansdowne, says, in a note to one of his poems, that the arms of his family—'gules, three clarions or'—carved in stone, had stood for nine centuries over one of the gates of the town of Granville. They also appropriately appear (as the arms of John Grenville, first Earl of Bath) over the principal gateway of Plymouth Citadel.

† In the fortieth year of Henry III. (1256), I find the name of Richard de Grenvile amongst the 'nomina illorum qui teñ : quindecim libratas terræ, vel plus, et tenent per servitium militare, et milites non sunt;' and in 1297 Richard Grenevyle, of Stow, was amongst those who had £20 a year, or more, in land. In later times the Grenvilles held Swannacote, Bynnamy, Ilcombe, Albercombe, and other places, as well as Stow, in the Hundred of Stratton.

been said that Cornwall was not without a Richard Grenville for 200 consecutive years. Among the earliest of them was one of the twelve knights amongst whom the Conqueror partitioned Wales : he built the monastery in South Wales, now known as Neath Abbey, the ruins of which are a familiar and picturesque object to the traveller by rail to Swansea. In 1653, a Mr. John Nichols, of Hartland, had in his possession 'a prophecy,' written in the year 1400, said to have been found in Neath Abbey, and which was kept in a curious box of jet. It referred to the founder ; and ran as follows :

'Amongst the trayne of valliant knights that with King William came,
  Grenvile is great, a Norman borne, renowned by his fame,
  His helmet rais d and first unlac'd upon the Cambrian shore,
  Where he, in honour to his God, this Abbey did decore
  With costly buildings, ornaments, and gave us spatious lands,
  As the first fruits which victory did give unto his hands.'

But the materials for the lives of the earlier Grenvilles are too scanty for our present purpose ; and— with one exception—we must therefore be content to dismiss them with the passing notice which has already been accorded to the builder of Bideford Bridge ; and with a reference to one of the family, William, who died in 1315, a distinguished statesman, and forty-first Archbishop of York. He was at Edward I.'s first Parliament at Carlisle ; and, according to some authorities, crowned Edward II. ; he also held several important councils at York relative to the dissolution of the Order of the Temple.*

'William de Grenefild' (says Carew), 'from the Deanery of Chichester stepped to the Chancellorship of England, and Archbishoprick of York, under

---

* Cf. the *Times*, 16th February, 1883.

King Edward the First. He was the son of Sir Theobald Grenvill, of Stow, and Jane Trewent, and was elected Archbishop of York in 1304, but not confirmed till 1306, at Lions in France, by Pope Clement the Fifth, who then held his Court in that city, subsisting chiefly by the money which he got of the Bishops for their confirmations. Of this Archbishop he squeezed out within one year 9,500 marks, besides his expenses whilst he lay there, which made him so poor that when he returned into England he was driven to gather money of the clergy within his province at two sundry times in one year; the first in the name of a benevolence, and the second by way of an aid. He much favoured the Templars, at that time oppresst by the Pope, and Philip, King of France, though more pitying them, says Fuller, as persons so stiffly opposed by the said Potentates, that there was more fear of his being suppressed by their foes, than hope of their being supported by his friendship. He was present in the Council of Vienna, where that Order was abolished, and his place assigned next to the Archbishop of Triers; which was very high, as only beneath the lowest Elector, and above Wurtzburg, or Herbipolis, and other German prelates, who were also temporal Princes. He died at Cawood (near Leeds, in Yorkshire), 1315, and was buried in the chapel of St. Nicholas*

* Drake figures the tomb (which represents him carrying the cross in his *left* hand) in his ' Eboracum ;' and it is also given in Waller's ' Sepulchral Brasses.' Cf. *Quarterly Review*, cii. 297 ; and Wright's ' Essays,' i. 134; Holinshed in 'Edward I.,' p. 315; and Le Neve's ' Fasti Eccl. Ang.,' vol. iii. p. 105.

(in York Cathedral)', leaving the reputation of an able statesman, and no ill scholar, behind him.' Tonkin also, in his notes to the 'De Dunstanville' edition of Carew, states, 'that the Archbishop was the son of Sir Theobald Grenville, of Stow, and Jane Trewent.'

But Dixon, in his 'Fasti Eboracenses,' says, 'that the birthplace and parentage of the Archbishop of York are uncertain—notwithstanding that both Carew and Fuller state that he was a Cornishman. He was undoubtedly, however, connected with several old and distinguished families, notably the Giffards. Now Richard de Grenville, the founder of the Grenville family, married a daughter of Walter Giffard Earl of Bucks, temp. William I.' Dixon speaks highly of the Archbishop's piety and zeal, and says that he was a most excellent and pains-taking diocesan. As to the ruby ring removed from the Archbishop's skeleton in 1735, and deposited in the Treasury, Grotius says:

'Annule, qui thecam poteras habuisse sepulchrum
Hæc, natalis erit nunc tibi, theca, locus.'

In Carew's 'Survey of Cornwall' (pp. 111, 112), under Trematon Castle, is the following reference to Sir Richard Grenville, Sheriff of Devon and Marshal of Calais* (grandsire of the more celebrated Grenville of that name), a man who 'enterlaced his home magistracy with martiall employments abroad,' and was a great favourite with bluff King Hal:

'At the last Cornish commotion Sir Richard

* Pole says that 'Sʳ Richᵈ. Grenvill, Kᵗ., served under th'erle of Hartford before Hamble Tewe, with 200 soldiers, and at Bolleyne, anno 38 of Kinge Henry 8.'

Greynuile the elder, with his Ladie and followers,
put themselves into this Castle, and there for awhile
indured the Rebels siege, incamped in three places
against it, who wanting great Ordinance, could
have wrought the besieged small scathe, had his
friends, or enemies, kept faith and promise: but
some of those within, slipping by night over the
wals, *with their bodies after their hearts*, and those
without, mingling humble intreatings with rude
menaces, he was hereby wonne, to issue forth at a
posterne gate for parley. The while, a part of those
rakehels, not knowing what honestie, and farre lesse,
how much the word of a souldier imported, stepped
betweene him and home, laid hold on his aged un-
weyldie body and threatened to leaue it liuelesse, if
the inclosed did not leaue their resistance. So prose-
cuting their first treachcrie against the prince, with
suteable actions towards his subjects, they seized on
the Castle, and exercised the uttermost of their bar-
barous crueltie (death excepted) on the surprised
prisoners. The seely (*i.e.* harmless) gentlewomen,
without regard of sexe or shame, were stripped from
their apparrell to their verie smockes, and some of
their fingers broken, to plucke away their rings,
& Sir Richard himself made an exchange from
Trematon Castle, to that of Launceston, with the
Gayle to boote.'

Sir Richard, who married Matilda Bevill, died in
1550; and I have been fortunate enough to find two
of his poetical effusions—apparently in his own
handwriting, now very indistinct in places—amongst
the 'Additional MSS.' in the British Museum.

They appear to me to be well worth inserting, notwithstanding their queer versification and grammar, and their odd orthography :

'IN PRAISE OF SEAFARINGE MEN IN HOPES OF GOOD
FORTUNE.

' Whoe seekes the waie to win Renowne
   Or flies with wyinges of ye Desarte
Whoe seekes to wear the Lawrell crowen
   Or hath the mind that would espire
Tell him his native soyll eschew
Tell him go rainge and seke Anewe

' Eche hawtie harte is well contente
   With euerie chance that shalbe tyde
No hap can hinder his entente
   He steadfast standes though fortune slide
The sun quoth he doth shine as well
A brod as earst where I did dwell

' In change of streames each fish can live
   Eche soule content with everie Ayre
Eche hawtie hart remaineth still
   And not be Dround in depe Dispaire
Wherfor I judg all landes a likes
To hawtie hartes whom fortune seekes

' Two pass the seaes som thinkes a toille
   Som thinkes it strange abrod to rome
Som thinkes it agrefe to leave their soylle
   Their parentes cynfolke and their whome
Thinke soe who list I like it nott
I must abrod to trie my lott

' Who list at whome at carte to drudge
   And carke and care for worldlie trishe
With buckled sheues let him go trudge
   Instead of laureall a whip to slishe
A mynd that basse his hind will show
Of carome sweet to feed a crowe

' If fasonn of that mynd had bine
   The gresions when they came to troye
Had never so the Trogians foyhte
   Nor neuer put them to such Anoye
Wherfore who lust to live at whome
To purchase fame I will go Rome

'FINIS—SUR RICHARD GRINFILLDE'S FAREWELL'

But Sir Richard feels bound to confess that there is another and quite a different aspect of the question ; and accordingly frames the following set-off to his former lines :

'ANOTHER OF SEA FARDINGERS DISCRIBING EVILL FORTUNES.'

'What pen can well reporte the plighte
  Of those that travell on the seaes
To pas the werie winters nighte
  With stormie cloudes wisshinge for daie
With waves that toss them to and fro
Their pore estate is hard to show

When boistering windes begins to blowe
  And cruel costes from haven wee
The foggie mysts soe dimes the shore
  The rocks and sandes we maie not see
Nor have no Rome on Seaes to trie
But praie to God and yeld to Die

When shoulders and sandie bankes Apears
  What pillot can divert his course
When foming tides draweth us so nere
  A las what fortenn can be worsse
The Ankers hould must be our staie
Or Ellse we fall into Decaye

We wander still from Loffe to Lie
  And findes no steadfast wind to blow
We still remaine in jeopardie
  Each perelos poynt is hard to showe
In time we hope to find Redresse
That long have lived in Heavines

O pinchinge werie lothsome Lyffe
  That Travell still in far Exsylle
The dangers great on Sease be ryfe
  Whose recompense doth yeld but toylle
O fortune graunte me mie Desire
A hapie end I doe Require

When freates and states have had their fill
The gentill calm the cost will clere
Then hawtie hartes shall have their will
That longe hast wept with morning chere
And leave the Seaes with thair Anoy
At whome at Ease to live in Joy.
'FINIS.'

The poetical Sir Richard's son Roger, a Captain in the Navy, lost his life at the sinking of the *Mary Rose* (commanded by Sir George Carew, a Cornishman), at Spithead in 1545. 'Thus the ocean became a bedde of honour,' as Carew says, 'to more than one of the Grenvilles.'

But it is time that we should turn to a greater Sir Richard—the son of Roger Grenville and Thomasin Cole of Slade.

My task will be on this occasion comparatively light;

' His praise is hymned by loftier harps than mine.'

The famous deeds of the great man to whom I have now to call attention have been celebrated by such writers as his kinsman Sir Walter Raleigh; by Carew; by that master of portraiture Lord Clarendon; by Charles Kingsley; and by Tennyson; and I shall of course offer no apology for not using any words of my own, where I can use theirs: for, as Fuller said of the Ashburnhams, 'My poor and plain pen, though willing, is unable to add any lustre to this family of stupendous antiquity.'

Sir Richard, then, was born in 1540; and, when only sixteen years of age, served in Hungary, under the Emperor Maximilian, against the Turks, and was present with Don John of Austria, at the battle of Lepanto. He afterwards assisted in the reduction

of Ireland; and, whilst there, filled the office of
Sheriff of Cork.   When Sheriff of Cornwall in 1577,
he arrested Francis Tregian for harbouring Cuthbert
Mayne, a recusant priest (see *sub* ' The Arundells ').
In 1571 he represented his native county in Parliament, and was knighted.   On 19th May, 1585, he
sailed from Plymouth with the first colonists, on a
voyage to the new-found land of Virginia, of which
voyage Thomas Hariot gave a ' Briefe and True
Report,' printed in 1588: on his homeward passage
he fell in with a Spanish ship of 300 tons, richly
laden, from St. Domingo, which he boarded on a raft,
his own boats being lost or disabled ; and in 1586
he made a second visit to Virginia, pillaging the
towns of the Spaniards, and taking many prisoners.
With Raleigh he seems to have made one or two
similar expeditions, gathering much experience, if
not much pecuniary advantage.*

When the Spanish invasion was projected, Sir
Richard was, almost as a matter of course, elected
on the Council for the defence of the country, and
he received the Queen's special commands not to
quit Cornwall during the peril.   On this occasion,
he is said to have provided ' 303 men at his own
cost, armed with 129 shot, 69 corsletts, and 179
bows.'   Of the result there is no need to speak here ;
but it has always been a matter of pride for West-

---

* Cf. 'A briefe and true report of the new found land of Virginia,'
1571 (?), fol.   Messrs. Boase and Courtney observe that a very limited
number of this, the rarest and most precious book relating to America,
has been executed in fac-simile by the photo-lithographic process, and
that an edition of 150 copies of this work has also been printed by the
Hercules Club.

country men to think how large a share in the
destruction of the Invincible Armada was performed
by the gallant sailors who quietly dropped out of
Plymouth Sound, and harassed their huge opponents
for days, till, what with shot, and storm, and tempest,
scarce one of the Spaniards was left to tell the tale
of their utter, and irretrievable defeat.

Kingsley has thus admirably described Sir Richard's
appearance :*

'The forehead and whole brain are of extraordinary loftiness, and perfectly upright; the nose
long, aquiline, and delicately pointed ; the mouth,
fringed with a short, silky beard, small and ripe, yet
firm as granite, with just pout enough of the lower
lip to give hint of that capacity of noble indignation
which lay hid under its usual courtly calm and sweetness ; if there be a defect in the face, it is that the
eyes are somewhat small, and close together, and the
eyebrows, though delicately arched, and without a
trace of peevishness, too closely pressed down upon
them ; the complexion is dark, the figure tall and
graceful; altogether the likeness of a wise and
gallant gentleman, lovely to all good men, awful to all
bad men ; in whose presence none dare say or do a
mean or a ribald thing ; whom brave men left, feeling

* I hardly know which portrait Kingsley is describing. One of the
finest that I have seen is a photograph of that now in the possession of
the Thynne family. It represents Sir Richard at about thirty years of
age, and with the most keen and determined expression imaginable.
Another is engraved in Prince's 'Worthies of Devon ;' and Crispin Pass
engraved a likeness of him for his ' Heroologia,' probably from the
same original as Prince's ; it bears the motto—

' Neptuni proles, qui magni Martis alumnus
Grenvilius patrias sanguine tinxit aquas.'

themselves nerved to do their duty better, while
cowards slipped away, as bats and owls before the
sun.   So he lived and moved; whether in the Court
of Elizabeth, giving his counsel among the wisest;
or in the streets of Bideford, capped alike by squire
and merchant, shopkeeper and sailor; or riding along
the moorland roads between his houses of Stow and
Bideford, while every woman ran out to her door to
look at the great Sir Richard; or sitting in the low,
mullioned window at Burrough, with his cup of
malmsey before him, and the lute to which he had
just been singing laid across his knees, while the red
western sun streamed in upon his high, bland forehead and soft curling locks; ever the same steadfast,
God-fearing, chivalrous man, conscious (as far as a
soul so healthy could be conscious) of the pride of
beauty, and strength, and valour, and wisdom, and
a race and name which claimed direct descent
from the grandfather of the Conqueror, and was
tracked down the centuries by valiant deeds and
noble benefits to his native shire, himself the noblest
of his race.   Men said that he was proud—but he
could not look round him without having something
to be proud of; that he was stern and harsh to his
sailors—but it was only when he saw in them any
taint of cowardice or falsehood; that he was subject,
at moments, to such fearful fits of rage, that he had
been seen to snatch glasses from the table, grind
them to pieces in his teeth, and swallow them—but
that was only when his indignation had been
aroused by some tale of cruelty and oppression;
and, above all, by those West Indian devilries of

the Spaniards, whom he regarded (and in those days rightly enough) as the enemies of God and man.'*

And the noble old house at Stow, with its chapel licensed by Bishop Brantingham of Exeter, in 1386,†

---

* An old Cornish song runs thus :

> ' Oh, where be those gay Spaniards
>   Which make so great a boast O ?
> Oh, they shall eat the grey goose-feather,
>   And we shall eat the roast O !'

† 'Stow,' says Carew, 'is so singly called, *per eminentiam*, as a place of great and good mark and scope, and the ancient dwelling of the Grenvile's famous family.' An indifferent picture of the second Stow is preserved at Haynes, Middlesex; and another is said to be in the possession of Mrs. Martyn, of Harleston, Torquay. Fragments of it may be seen in the cottages and gardens of Coombe, under the hill on which Stow once stood, and it is said that the staircase is at Prideaux Place, Padstow ; but it is believed that the greater portion of the materials were removed to South Molton, where the town-hall was erected with them ; and, according to Polewhele, traces of them were also to be seen at Star Hill and other places in that neighbourhood.

In the MS. diary of Dr. Yonge, F.R.S., a distinguished physician of the latter part of the seventeenth century, the following entry occurs in the year 1685 :

'I waited on my Lord of Bathe (then Governor of Plymouth) to his delicious house, Stowe. It lyeth on yᵉ ledge of yᵉ north sea of Devon, a most curious fabrick beyond all description.'

As regards the ruined mansion, well might Edward Moore exclaim :

> ' Ah ! where is now its boasted beauty fled ?
>   Proud turrets that once glittered in the sky,
> And broken columns, in confusion spread,
>   A rude misshapen heap of ruins lie.

> ' Where, too, is now the garden's beauty fled,
>   Which every clime was ransacked to supply?
> O'er the drear spot see desolation spread,
>   And the dismantled walls in ruins lie.

> ' Along the terrace-walks are straggling seen
>   The prickly bramble and the noisome weed,
> Beneath whose covert crawls the toad obscene,
>   And snakes and adders unmolested breed.

of which no vestige, alas! remains, was worthy of
being the abode of such a hero. It would be but
unprofitable labour to attempt a fresh description of
of it after the graphic account which Kingsley
gives:

' Old Stow House stands,' says he, 'or rather stood,
some four miles within the Cornish border, on the
northern slope of the largest and loveliest of those
coombes'—which he had just been describing in a
memorable passage of a preceding chapter (the sixth)
in ' Westward Ho !' ' Eighty years *after* Sir Richard's
time there arose a huge Palladian pile, bedizened
with every monstrosity of bad taste, which was
built, so the story runs, by Charles II. for Sir
Richard's great-grandson, the heir of that famous
Sir Bevil who defeated the Parliamentary troops at
Stratton, and died soon after, fighting valiantly at
Lansdowne over Bath. But like most other things
which owed their existence to the Stuarts, it rose
only to fall again. An old man who had seen, as
a boy, the foundation of the new house laid, lived
to see it pulled down again, and the very bricks
and timber sold upon the spot ; and since then the
stables have become a farmhouse, the tennis-court a
sheep-cote, the great quadrangle a rick-yard ; and
civilization, spreading wave on wave so fast elsewhere, has surged back from that lonely corner of
the land—let us hope only for awhile.*

* *Old* Stow House was pulled down in 1680, when it was rebuilt, and
again destroyed in 1720, the materials being sold by auction. The
carved-cedar work in the chapel was executed by Michael Chuke, an

'But I am not writing of that great *new* Stow House, of the past glories whereof quaint pictures still hang in the neighbouring houses ; . . . . I have to deal with a simpler age, and a sterner generation ; and with the *old* house, which had stood there, in part at least, from grey and mythic ages . . . a huge, rambling building, half-castle, half-dwelling-house. . . . On three sides, to the north, west and south, the lofty walls of the old ballium still stood, with their machicolated turrets, loopholes, and dark downward crannies for dropping stones and fire on the besiegers; . . . but the southern court of the ballium had become a flower-garden, with quaint terraces, statues, knots of flowers, clipped yews and hollies, and all the pedantries of the topiarian art. And, towards the east, where the vista of the valley opened, the old walls were gone, and the frowning Norman keep, ruined in the wars of the Roses, had been replaced by the rich and stately architecture of the Tudors. Altogether, the house, like the time, was in a transitionary state, and represented faithfully enough the passage of the old middle age into the new life which had just burst into blossom throughout Europe, never, let us pray, to see its autumn or its winter.

'From the house on three sides the hills sloped steeply down, and from the garden there was a truly English prospect. At one turn they could catch, over the western walls, a glimpse of the blue ocean

---

artist little inferior to Gibbons. The wood came out of a Spanish prize, and the carving was re-erected at the Duke of Buckingham's residence, Stow.

flecked with passing sails; and at the next, spread far below, range on range of fertile park, stately avenue, yellow autumn woodland, and purple heather moors, lapping over and over each other up the valley to the old British earthwork, which stood black and furze-grown on its conical peak; and, standing out against the sky, on the highest bank of the hill which closed the valley to the east, the lofty tower of Kilkhampton Church, rich with the monuments and offerings of five centuries of Grenvilles.'

Such were old Stow, and its gallant owner Sir Richard. And the women of the Grenville home seem, for the most part, to have been as fair and virtuous and accomplished as their husbands were sagacious and brave. Polwhele, in after-times, particularly noticed the remarkable beauty of Sir Richard's great-great-granddaughter Mary, the daughter of the Honourable Bernard Grenville, of Stow. Sir Richard married Mary, the daughter of Sir John St. Leger; but the lovely dame had, like the wife of her illustrious grandson, Sir Bevill, to give up what was dearest to her in the world, to the cruel necessities of the troubled times in which they lived.

Yet I cannot doubt that these women had the spirits of Roman matrons within them; and would have assented to Lovelace's lines had their husbands whispered the couplet to them:

'I could not love thee, dear, so much
Lov'd I not honour more.'

To return to Sir Richard:—In 1591 we find him acting as Vice-Admiral of a squadron sent out to intercept the richly-laden Spanish fleet on its return from the West Indies; a service of the utmost importance, as, in capturing or sinking the Indian supplies, observes Mr. Arber, England 'stopped the sources of Philip's power to hurt herself.' How the English ships were surprised in their lurking-place 'at Flores* in the Azores,' and how valiantly Sir Richard Grenville fought and died for Queen and country, let Raleigh and Tennyson tell.

It was towards the end of August, whilst the Admiral, Lord Thomas Howard,† with six of her Majesty's ships and a few smaller vessels and pinnaces, was at anchor at Flores, when news suddenly came of the near approach of the great Spanish fleet. Many of the Englishmen were ill on shore, while others were filling the ships with ballast, or collecting water. Imperfectly manned and ballasted as they were, there was nothing for it—at least so Lord Howard appears to have thought—in the face of so enormously preponderating a force as they found was close at hand, but to weigh anchor, and escape as they best could: and so it became a complete *sauve qui peut;*

* A modern American traveller has thus recorded his impressions of Flores as he passed the island : 'As we bore down upon it the sun came out and made it a beautifnl picture—a mass of green farms and meadows that swelled up to a height of 1,500 feet, and mingled its upper outlines with the clouds. It was ribbed with sharp, steep ridges, and cloven with narrow cañons, and here and there, on the heights, rocky upheavals shaped themselves into mimic battlements and castles; and out of rifted clouds came broad shafts of sunlight that painted summit and slope and glen with bands of fire, and left belts of sombre shade between.'

† Thomas Philippes, in a letter of 31st Oct., 1591, to Thomas Barnes, says : 'They condemn the Lord Thomas for a coward, and some say he is for the King of Spain.' He supposes his friend Barnes 'has heard of the quarrel and offer of combat between the Lord Admiral and Sir Walter Raleigh.'

some of the ships were even compelled to slip their cables. Sir Richard, as Vice-Admiral, was the last to start, delaying to do so till the final moment, in order to collect several of his sick crew who were on the island, and who, if he had left them there, must have been lost. This noble delay of his resulted in the safety of the remainder of the fleet; but it cost Sir Richard and his crew their lives; and the little *Revenge*, which had four or five times narrowly escaped shipwreck, her existence: but she was, as Admiral Hawkins described her, ' ever a ship loaden, and full fraught with ill successe.' Grenville refused to ' cut his mainsail, and cast about,' and so run from the enemy; but persuaded his crew that he would contrive to pass through the two great Spanish squadrons which intercepted him, ' in despight of them, and would enforce those of Sivil to give him way.' It was the story of the 300 Spartans at Thermopylæ acted over again. The huge *San Philip* of 1,500 tons (carrying ' three tier of ordinance on a side, and eleven pieces on every tier; she shot eight forth right out of her chase, besides those of her stern ports'), however, loomed to windward of the small English ship; and ' becalmed his sails in such sort as the *Revenge* could neither make way, nor feel the helm;' and then—

' Sir Richard spoke and he laughed, and we roared a hurrah, and so
    The little *Revenge* ran on sheer into the heart of the foe,
With her hundred fighters on deck, and her ninety sick below;
For half of their fleet to the right, and half to the left were seen,
And the little *Revenge* ran on thro' the long sea lane between.'

What end could there be, but one, to courage so chivalric, so desperate, and so devoted as this?

'After the *Revenge* was entangled with this *Philip*,' says Raleigh, 'four other boarded her—(*i.e.*, laid her aboard)—two on her larboard, and two on her starboard. The fight thus beginning at three o'clock in the afternoon, continued very terrible all that evening. But the great *San Philip* having received the lower tier of the *Revenge*, discharged with cross-bar shot, shifted herself with all diligence from her sides, utterly misliking her first entertainment. Some say that the ship foundered, but we cannot report for truth, unless we are assured. The Spanish ships were filled with companies of soldiers, in some two hundred, beside the mariners; in some five, in others eight, hundred. In ours there were none at all besides the mariners, but the servants of the commanders, and some few voluntary gentlemen only. After many interchanged vollies of great ordnance and small shot, the Spaniards deliberated to enter the *Revenge*, and made divers attempts, hoping to force her, by the multitudes of their armed soldiers and musketeers, but were still repulsed again and again, and at all times beaten back into their own ships, or into the seas.'

'And the rest they came aboard us, and they fought us hand to hand,
For a dozen times they came with their pikes and musqueteers,
And a dozen times we shook 'em off, as a dog that shakes his ears
When he leaps from the water to the land.'

'In the beginning of the fight,' Sir Walter Raleigh continues, 'the *George Noble*, of London, having received some shot through her, by the armadas, fell under the lee of the *Revenge*, and asked Sir Richard what he would command him, being but one of the victuallers, and of small force; Sir Richard bade him save himself, and leave him to his fortune. After the fight had thus, without inter-mission, continued while the day lasted, and some hours of the night, many of our men were slain and hurt, and one of the great gallions of the armada, and the admiral of the hulks both sunk, and in many other of the Spanish ships great slaughter was made.'

The marvel is how a fragment of the brave little craft was still afloat, for

'Ship after ship the whole night long, their high-built galleons came,
Ship after ship, the whole night long, with their battle-thunder and flame,
Ship after ship, the whole night long, drew back with her dead and her shame.
For some were sunk, and some were shattered, and some could fight us no more—
God of battles ! was ever a battle like this in the world before ?'

'Some write,' says Raleigh, 'that Sir Richard was very dangerously hurt almost in the beginning of the fight, and lay speechless for a time before he recovered. But two of the *Revenge's* own company brought home in a ship of Lime (Lyme Regis) from the islands, examined by some of the lords and others, affirm that he was never so wounded as that he forsook the upper deck, till an hour before mid-night; and then being shot into the body with a musket as he was a dressing, was again shot into the head, and withal his chururgion wounded to death. This agreeth also with an examination taken by Sir Francis Godolphin,* of four other

* Vice-Warden of the Stannaries, friend and contemporary of Richard Carew.

mariners of the same ship being returned, which examination the said Sir Francis sent unto Master William Killegrue,* of Her Majesty's Privy Chamber.'

But to return to the fight; 'the Spanish ships which attempted to board the *Revenge*, as they were wounded and beaten off, so always others came in their places, she having never less than two mighty gallions by her sides, and aboard her: so that ere the morning, from three of the clock of the day before, *there had been fifteen several armadas assailed her; and all so ill-approved their entertainment, as they were by the break of day far more willing to hearken to a composition than hastily to make any more assaults or entries.* But as the day encreased, so our men decreased; and as the light grew more and more, by so much more grew our discomforts; for none appeared in sight but enemies, saving one small ship called the *Pilgrim*, commanded by Jacob Whiddon, who hovered all night to see the success; but in the morning bearing with the *Revenge*, was hunted like a hare amongst many ravenous hounds, but escaped.

'All the powder of the *Revenge* to the last barrel was now spent, all her pikes broken, forty of her best men slain, and the most part of the rest hurt. In the beginning of the fight she had but one hundred free from sickness, and four score and ten sick, laid in hold upon the ballast. A small troop to man such a ship, and a weak garrison to resist so mighty an army. By those hundred all was sustained, the vollies, boardings, and enterings of fifteen

* Probably the brother of Sir Henry Killigrew, Kt., Queen Elizabeth's ambassador to France, the Low Countries, etc.

ships of war, besides those which beat her at large (*i.e.*, from a little distance off). On the contrary, the Spaniards were always supplied with soldiers brought from every squadron; all manner of arms and powder at will. Unto ours there remained no comfort at all, no hope, no supply either of ships, men, or weapons; the masts all beaten overboard, all her tackle cut asunder, her upper work altogether razed, and in effect evened she was with the water, but the very foundation of a ship, nothing being left overhead either for flight or defence.' Mr. O. W. Brierly's recently engraved picture of this stage of the fight, showing the little *Revenge* with her mainsail down and lying over her 'like a pall,' surrounded by her over-towering enemies, still afraid to approach the dangerous little barque, gives a vivid, and probably accurate idea of the tremendous odds against which the devoted Englishmen had to contend.

'Sir Richard, finding himself in this distress, and unable any longer to make resistance, having endured, in this fifteen hours' fight, the assault of fifteen different armadas, all by turns aboard him, and by estimation eight hundred shot of great artillery, besides many assaults and entries; and that the ship and himself must needs be possessed of the enemy, who were now all cast in a ring round about him, now gave the order to destroy his gallant craft:

'" We have fought such a fight for a day and a night
As may never be fought again !
We have won great glory, my men !

And a day less or more
At sea or ashore
We die—does it matter when?
Sink me the ship, Master Gunner—sink her, split her in twain!
Fall into the hands of God! not into the hands of Spain!"'

To this δαιμονίη ἀρετή (as Froude calls it) of the fiery Sir Richard the master-gunner readily assented; but, according to Raleigh's account, the captain and master pointed out that the Spaniards would doubtless give them good terms, and that there were still some valiant men left on board their little ship whose lives might hereafter be of service to England. Sir Richard was probably by this time too weak and wounded to contest the matter further; the counsels of the captain and master prevailed; and the master actually succeeded in obtaining for conditions *that all their lives should be saved, the crew sent to England, and the officers ransomed.* In vain did the master-gunner protest and even attempt to commit suicide: Tennyson has summed up the story in one sad line:

'And the lion lay there dying, and they yielded to the foe.'

Sir Richard was now removed to the ship of the Spanish admiral, ' the *Revenge* being marvellous unsavoury, filled with blood and bodies of dead and wounded men like a slaughter-house.'

And now—

'How died he? Death to life is crown, or shame—'

There, on the deck of Don Alfonso Bassano's ship, in the midst of the Spanish captains, who crowded round to wonder at the man who had so long defied their deadly attacks, two or three days

after the fight between ' the mastiffs of England and
the bloodhounds of Spain,' the grand old Cornish
warrior's spirit left the body, speaking his last words
thus—in Spanish, so John Huighen van Linschoten
(in ' Hakluyt's Voyages ') tells us :

' Here die I, Richard Grenville, with a joyful and
quiet mind ; for that I have ended my life as a true
soldier ought to do, fighting for his Country, Queen,
Religion and Honour : my soul willingly departing
from this body, leaving behind the lasting fame of
having behaved as every valiant soldier is in duty
bound to do.'

Lord Bacon says of the fight that it was ' Memorable euen beyond credit, and to the Height of
some Heroicall Fable.'

And well might Ruskin, in his ' Bibliotheca Pas-
torum ' (i. 33), class the Cornish hero with Arnold of
Sempach, Leonidas and Curtius as a type of ' the
divinest of sacrifices—that of the patriot for his country ' ! Well might the gentle Evelyn exclaim : ' Than
this what have we more ?   What can be greater ?'
And well might gallant old Sir John Hawkins wish
that this story might be ' written in our Chronicles,'
—as it has been, by Raleigh and by Tennyson,—in
' letters of Gold.'

The Spanish fleet were not permitted to enjoy the
fruits of this, their hard-earned and almost only capture during the war ; for, a few days after the battle,
a great storm arose from the west and north-west,
dispersing their battle-ships, and also the West
Indian fleet (the cause of the English Expedition)
which had now joined them ; and sinking, off the

coast of St. Michael, fourteen sail, together with the *Revenge*—which seemed to disdain to survive her commander—with 200 Spaniards on board her.

'So it pleased them,' says Raleigh, 'to honour the burial of that renowned ship the *Revenge*, not suffering her to perish alone, for the great honour she achieved in her life-time.' A noble elegy! which even Tennyson's genius has been unable to surpass.

This is not perhaps the time or the place to consider how it was possible for this one little English vessel with a crew of 100 men, to contend so long against 50 (or according to some accounts 53) Spanish galleons with 10,000 men, sinking four of the largest, and slaying 1,000 Spaniards; but it was no doubt owing to more causes than one:—to the low and short hull, which made her more manageable—to superior gunnery and seamanship—but mainly to the stoutest, freest, and fiercest *hearts* upon earth—the hearts of Englishmen. They *believed* they were more than a match for their foes, and confidence begat victory; and if ever there was an English victory, in the fullest sense of the word, it was the triumphant LOSS of the '*Revenge.*'

The Spanish proverb ran

'Guerra con todo il mondo;—y paz con Inghilterra;'

and it has well been said that the episode of the *Revenge* dealt a deadlier blow to the fame and moral strength of Spain, than even the defeat of the Armada itself.*

* In 1595 Gervase Markham wrote a poem entitled 'The most Honorable Tragedie of Sir Richard Grinuile, Knight. Bramo assai,

But Sir Richard was not left without a witness.
Passing over his son John, who, Carew says, followed
Raleigh, and was drowned in the ocean, which
'became his bedde of honour;' and also another son
Sir Bernard, who died in 1605, after having served as
Sheriff of Cornwall and M.P. for Bodmin—as not being
of such transcendent merit as either Sir Bernard's
father or son—we come to the 'immortal' Sir Bevill
Grenville, eldest son of the said Sir Bernard and his
wife Elizabeth Beville of Killigarth near Polperro—
(or, according to another account, of Brinn)—a man
no whit inferior in loyalty and courage to his illustrious grandsire.

Sir Bevill was born, somewhat unexpectedly, on
23rd March, 1595, at Brinn—probably Great Brinn,
the seat of the Bevills, but not a stone of the old
mansion is now standing—in the little Cornish parish
of Withiel; four years after the little *Revenge* went
down by the island crags,

'To be lost evermore in the main.'

He was doubtless carefully brought up at Stow—the
old Stow—which was in those days a sort of nursery for

---

poco spero, nulla chieggio :' a very rare book, only two copies of it being
known, but it has been reprinted by Arber.   It is a rather fantastic and
lengthy production, containing little that is quotable ; but perhaps this
verse may pass—
    ' Neuer fell hayle thicker then bullets flew,
    Neuer showr'd drops faster then show'ring blowes,
    Liu'd all the *Woorthies*, all yet neuer knew
    So great resolue in so great certaine woes ;
    Had *Fame* told *Cæsar* what of this was true,
    His Senate-murdred spirite would haue rose
      And with faire honors enuie wondred then
    Cursing mortalitie in mighty men.'

the better sort of young Cornishmen. The late Rev.
R. S. Hawker, vicar of Morwenstow, has given us the
following pleasant picture of it in Sir Bevill's days :

'On the brow of a lofty hill,* crested with stag-
horned trees, commanding a deep and woodland
gorge wherein "the Crooks of Combe" (the curves
of a winding river) urge onward to the "Severn
Sea," still survive the remains of famous old Stow,
that historic abode of the loyal and glorious Sir
Bevill, the Bayard of old Cornwall, "sans peur et
sans reproche," in the thrilling Stewart wars. No
mansion on the Tamar-side ever accumulated so
rich and varied a store of association and event.
Thither the sons of the Cornish gentry were accustomed to resort, to be nurtured and brought up with
the children of Sir Bevill Grenville and Lady
Grace ; for the noble knight was literally the "glass
wherein" the youth of those ancient times "did
dress themselves." There their graver studies were
relieved by manly pastimes and athletic exercise.
Like the children of the Persians, they were taught
"to ride, to bend the bow, and to speak the truth."
At hearth and hall every time-honoured usage and
festive celebration was carefully and reverently preserved. Around the walls branched the massive
antlers of the red deer of the moors, the trophies of
many a bold achievement with horse and hound.
At the buttery-hatch hung a tankard, marked with
the guest's and the traveller's peg, and a manchet,

* It commands a view of Lundy Island, which belonged to the Grenvilles.

flanked with native cheese, stood ready on a trencher for any sudden visitant who might choose to lift the latch ; for the Grenville motto was, "An open door and a greeting hand." A troop of retainers, servants, grooms, and varlets of the yard, stood each in his place, and under orders to receive with a welcome the unknown stranger, as well as their master's kinsman or friend.'

To Mr. Hawker's graceful pen we are also indebted for the following capital ballad:

SIR BEVILL—THE GATE SONG OF STOW.

'Arise, and away ! for the King and the land ;
 Farewell to the couch and the pillow :
With spear in the rest, and with rein in the hand,
 Let us rush on the foe like a billow.

'Call the hind from the plough, and the herd from the fold,
 Bid the wassailer cease from his revel ;
And ride for Old Stow, where the banner's unrolled
 For the cause of King Charles and Sir Bevill.

'Trevanion is up, and Godolphin is nigh,
 And Harris of Hayne's o'er the river ;
From Lundy to Loo, "One and all" is the cry,
 And "The King and Sir Bevill for ever !"

'Ay ! by Tre, Pol, and Pen, ye may know Cornish men,
 'Mid the names and the nobles of Devon ;
But if truth to the King be a signal, why then
 Ye can find out the Grenville in heaven.

'Ride ! ride with red spur ! there is death in delay,
 'Tis a race for dear life with the devil ;
If dark Cromwell prevail, and the King must give way,
 This earth is no place for Sir Bevill.

'So at Stamford he fought, and at Lansdowne he fell,
 But vain were the visions he cherished ;
For the great Cornish heart that the King loved so well,
 In the grave of the Grenville is perished.'

From Stow Bevill Grenville went to the famous old
West-country college, Exeter College, Oxford; where
he was placed under Dr. Prideaux (one, I fancy, of
the worthy family of Prideaux Place, Padstow). He
shortly afterwards entered Parliament, and going to
Scotland, in command of a troop of horse, with the
King, was knighted.*

The relations of Sir Bevill and Clarendon were
peculiar. Clarendon had quarrelled with Sir Bevill's
fiery brother, Sir Richard (created, according to
Whitelocke, Baron of Lostwithiel in 1644), a man of
high spirit and of considerable bravery and military
skill, but with an unlucky facility for getting into
scrapes and troubles of all sorts. He begins with a
squabble with his wife's brother-in-law, the powerful
Earl of Suffolk, which ends in Sir Richard's having
to pay a fine of £8,000, besides undergoing sixteen
months' imprisonment in the Fleet. He afterwards
served in Ireland, and on his return to England,
finding it a matter of considerable difficulty to get
his arrears of pay, resorted to the following questionable artifice for the purpose. He pretended to lend
a not unwilling ear to the Parliament's suggestion,
that in return for being paid the money due to him,
he should transfer his sword from the King's cause
to theirs. Indeed, he even went so far as to take the
command of a body of Roundhead horse, and marched
upon Basing. But on reaching Hounslow he, without much difficulty, persuaded all his officers and
men to proceed to Oxford instead, where he placed

* He is said to have been the first who attempted to smelt tin with
pit-coal.

the services of his whole party at the King's disposal, whereupon the Parliamentarians righteously enough dubbed him 'skellum' (scoundrel) and 'renegado.' He did yeoman's service for the King in Cornwall, and Charles left the blockade of Plymouth in his charge—a blockade which, as we know, was finally abandoned. The whole story is given in Llewellyn Jewitt's 'History of Plymouth,' together with a scornful letter to Sir Richard from the defenders. And I notice that in a letter from Sir R. Grenville to his nephew, the Earl of Bath, then only about sixteen years old, he is reported to have said, ' We have here made a stand with our forces and the garrisons of Salt Ash, Milbrooke and others considerable have come up and added to our former, and we hope well.' The letter is dated ' Truro, 29 July, 1644.'

There appears to have been no sufficient reason why he should have been asked to surrender his post of 'the King's General in the West '* in favour of Lord Hopton, but he was compelled to do so ; and on giving up his command he refused to serve under that officer, upon which he was forthwith 'clapped up' in Launceston Gaol, to the great dissatisfaction of many of the Cornish officers and soldiers, who attributed their ultimate discomfiture to the absence of Sir Richard from the field.†

* This is his designation inscribed on his tomb at Ghent.

† In November, 1645, according to Lysons, Launceston was fortified by Sir Richard Grenville, who, being at variance with Lord Goring (another of the King's generals), caused proclamation to be made in all the churches in Cornwall, that if any of Lord Goring's forces should come into the county the bells should ring, and the people rise and drive them out.

Clarendon (his foe), and the prejudiced and in-accurate Echard, give very unflattering accounts of Sir Richard; but his grand-nephew, George Lord Lansdowne, published a skilful and temperate vindi-cation of him against their aspersions; and Sir Richard printed his own 'Defence' in Holland, dating it 28th January, 1654. Whilst in Holland, by the way, he seems to have attempted reprisals upon the Earl of Suffolk; for we find that one of Milton's Latin 'State Letters' is addressed to the Archduke Leopold of Austria, Governor of the Spanish Netherlands undated), to the effect that Sir Charles Harbord, an Englishman, has had certain goods and household stuff violently seized at Bruges by Sir Richard Gren-ville. The goods had originally been sent from England to Holland in 1643 by the then Earl of Suffolk, in pledge for a debt owing to Harbord; and Grenville's pretext was that he also was a creditor of the Earl, and had obtained a decree of the English Chancery in his favour. Now, by the English law, neither was the present Earl of Suffolk bound by that decree, nor could the goods be distrained under it. The decision of the Court to that effect was trans-mitted, and his Serenity was requested to cause Grenville to restore the goods, inasmuch as it was against the comity of nations that anyone should be allowed an action in foreign jurisdiction which he would not be allowed in the country where the cause of the action first arose. The letter ends thus:

'The justice of the case itself and the universal reputation of your Serenity for fair dealing have

moved us to commend the matter to your attention;
and, if at any time there shall be occasion to discuss the rights or convenience of your subjects with
us, I promise that you shall find our diligence in
the same not remiss, but at all times most ready.'

Clarendon and Sir Richard both went into exile,
and more than once hurled reproaches at each other;
but the crowning misfortune of Grenville's life was the
refusal of Charles II., on Sir Richard's failing to
justify some statements which he had made against
Lord Clarendon, to let him appear at Court.   This
broke the old man's heart.   He let his beard grow
from that time; and died soon afterwards.*

Hals, delighting, as usual, to say anything sour and
disagreeable of his fellow-countymen, states in his
MSS. that when Sir Richard, at the death of
Charles I., 'for safe gaurd of his life fled beyond the
seas,' he passed most of his time 'in france and
Itally, sufferinge greate wants and necessities,' and
'was at Length comparitively starved to Death. . . .
His son Richard Grenvill, in the Interregnum of
Cromwell, was executed at Tyburne for robbinge
Passengers on the high way to Relieve his necessity.
Moreover Sir Thomas Grenvill Kt. at the same
tyme was Driven to such Extreame wants in his
owne Country that he was forced for Reliefe to
begge the Charity of his friends and Dyed in Great
want and penury—and his Lady also—though his
Daughter Jane, being a Servant to the Lady Robarts,

---

* He is said to have conceived the notable project of defending
Cornwall against the enemy by cutting a trench from Barnstaple to the
south coast, and filling it with sea-water.

was marryed to John Tregagle Gent. from whom the Tregagles of Treworder are Descended.'

Here is, perhaps, a convenient place to add that Polwhele thought that Henry Grenfield, Master of the Truro Grammar School in 1685, was one of this family. He wrote a charming 'Hymnus Vespertinus,' which is preserved in R. N. Worth's 'West Country Garland.'

A writer in *Notes and Queries* (5th Series, X. Sept. 14th, 1878) observes that, 'It is curious that, whereas the name of Grenville, as one of distinction, has long died out in Cornwall, it appeared suddenly in the registers of Fowey about a hundred years ago, the persons bearing it being in humble circumstances. As this is the only trace of the family name remaining in Cornwall or Devonshire, counties with which it was so intimately connected in local history, the matter may be of interest. There would, in fact, seem to be some mystery enveloping the extinction of the name, which is at the present moment borne *by right of birth* by very few persons, although some six creations of the title have been made to keep it in the peerage. Gilbert is believed to have entertained an opinion that the family still existed *in the direct line* in Cornwall or Devonshire, and had sunk out of sight by reason of poverty, when the never very flourishing condition of the Grenvilles became untenable. The Carterets, Thynnes, and Leveson-Gowers now jointly and severally represent the old family, but only indirectly, and solely in the line which Sir Bevill Grenville ennobled.'

But Clarendon, though he had quarrelled so utterly with Sir Richard, had nothing but good to say of 'the most generally beloved man of the county of Cornwall,' his brother, Sir Bevill*—' Sans peur et sans reproche '—of his mild and conciliatory character, his indefatigable activity, and his ardent courage—qualities which rendered him an invaluable adherent of the first Charles during the unnatural struggles of the Civil War—' the war without an enemy '—the black cloud ' which was to overspreade the whole kingdome, and cast all into disorder and darknesse.'

It will be within the memory of all readers of the noble historian that the King's cause suffered very much, from the first, from the superior promptitude of the Parliamentary leaders, who had actually appointed Militia Committees in the various counties—Cornwall included—long before the King's standard was raised. But the Cornish gentry, headed by our Sir Bevill, who had already in 1638 raised a troop of horse to serve with Charles against the Scots, were conspicuous for their loyalty, to which Charles's memorable letter of thanks from Sudeley Castle, 10th September, 1643 (copies of which still hang in many of the Cornish churches as commanded by the King) amply testifies. And at first Sir Bevill, 'the Mirror of Chivalry,' as he was called in the West, was more than a match for the Committees, which he speedily suppressed ; and at once, with the assistance of

* M.P. for Cornwall, 18 and 21 James I., and 15 Charles I. ; and for Launceston, 1, 3, and 15 Charles I.

Trevanion, Arundell, Basset, Godolphin, and others, set to work to raise a regular force.*

At this juncture, the following sweet and gallant letter, which Eliot Warburton quotes as an example of the romantic loyalty of the day, in his 'Memoirs of Prince Rupert and the Cavaliers,' was addressed to Sir John Trelawny, the first baronet of that name —evidently in reply to a communication from Sir John urging the Knight of Stow not to embark in so perilous an enterprise:

'MOST HONOURABLE SIR,

'I have in many kinds had trial of your nobleness, but in none more than in this singular expression of your kind care and love. I give also your excellent Lady humble thanks for respect unto my poor Woman, who hath been long a faithful much obliged servant of your Ladyes. But, Sir, for my journey, it is fixed. I cannot contain myself within my doors, when the King of England's standard waves in the field upon so just occasion. The cause being such as must make all those that die in it little inferior to martyrs. And for my own part,

* In 1643, according to a very curious old tract (E.$\frac{1}{1}\frac{0}{0}\frac{4}{7}$ Brit. Mus.), the Cornish forces lay at Liskeard, Saltash, Launceston, Bridgerule and Stratton. Lord Mohun was at Liskeard, Slanning at Saltash, Trevanion at Launceston; Sir Bevill Grenville was at Stratton, with 1,200 men. Sir Bevill was described as colonel of one foot regiment, Basset of another, Trevanion, the elder, of a third—he had Arundell for a lieutenant-colonel, and Trelawny for his sergeant-major, two of his captains were Burlacy and Boskoyne (? Borlase and Boscawen)— Trevanion, the younger, of a fourth, with Edgecombe as his lieutenant-colonel, and Carew as his sergeant-major; and Godolphin colonel of a fifth. The Cornish gave out that they were 10,000 to 12,000 strong—but 'of fighting men in pay,' says the writer of this interesting tract, ' we know for certaine not full 6,000.'

I desire to acquire an honest name or an honourable grave. I never loved my life or ease so much as to shun such an occasion; which if I should, I were unworthy of the profession I have held, or to succeed those ancestors of mine, who have so many of them in several ages sacrificed their lives for their country.

'Sir, the barborous and implacable enemy, notwithstanding His Majesty's gracious proceedings with them, do continue their insolencies and rebellion in the highest degree, and are united in a body of great strength; so, as you may expect, if they be not prevented and mastered near their own homes, they will be troublesome in yours, and in the remotest places ere long.

'I am not without the consideration, as you lovingly advise, of my wife and family; and as for her, I must acknowledge, she hath ever drawn so evenly in the yoke with me, as she hath never prest before, or hung behind me, nor ever opposed or resisted my will. And yet truly, I have not, in this or anything else, endeavoured to walk in any way of power with her, but of reason; and though her love will submit to either, yet truly my respect will not suffer me to urge her with power unless I can convince with reason. So much for that, whereof I am willing to be accomptable unto so good a friend.

'I have no suit unto you in mine own behalf, but for your prayers and good wishes; and that if I live to come home again, you would please to continue me in the number of your servants.

'I shall give a true relation unto my very noble friend Mr. Moyle, of your and his Aunt's loving respect to him, which he hath good reason to be thankful for. And so, I beseech God to send you and your noble family all health and happiness, and while I live, I am, Sir,

'Your unfeigned loving and faithful Servant,

'BEVILL GRENVILE.'

Writing to his ' Deare love ' and ' best friend,' from Bodmin on the 12th October, he says : ' My neighbours did ill that came not out, and are punishable by the law in high degree ; and although I will do the best I can to save some of the honester sort, yet others shall smart.' Nevertheless he was a staunch friend of Sir John Eliot (who was godfather to one of his children), and was mainly instrumental in procuring Sir John's release from the Tower. Forster quotes many of Sir Bevill's letters, in his ' Life of Eliot,' all of which are in the highest degree noble, patriotic, and affectionate. But by far the most charming are the following delightful letters to his graceful, affectionate, and accomplished wife :*

' To my best Frend—the Lady Grace Grenvile— these.

Plimp. (Plympton), Feb. 20, 1642.

' MY DEARE LOVE,

' Y^r great care and good affection, as they are very remarkable, so they deserve my best thankes,

---

* She was the daughter of Sir George Smith, of Maydford, Heavitree, near Exeter, was born in 1598, and married Sir Bevill in 1620. Her portrait is said to be preserved at Haynes, Middlesex, ' Ætatis suæ 36 —1634.' And there was another (in a red dress) belonging to the late Rev. Lord John Thynne, dated two years later ; in this the likeness to her son is very striking. Her sister, Lady Elizabeth Monk, was the mother of George Monk, Duke of Albemarle.

and I could wish that the subject which you bestowe them upon could better requite you.

'I shall returne ye messenger with but little certainty concerning our present condition.'

(Here follows a description of the positions of the contending forces.)

'The Queene is coming with good Ayde to the King. The Parl. did attempt to force severall quarters where the King's army lay, and were beaten off with great losses to themselves in all places. We have advertiz^{mt} that some ayde is coming from his Matie to us, but it is so slowe as we shall need it before we see it, but God's will be done, I am satisfied I cannot expire in a better cause. I have given some directions to Jack' (his son John Grenvile) 'for his study, pray cause him to putt them in execution, and to make some exercise in verse or prose every day. Intreat my cos.' (imperfect) 'and Bar. Geal. to take a little paines (with) him. I have released the Prisoners that Bar. Geal. wrote for. Let Cap. Stanb. know, it is all one to me whither he goe by Byd' (Bideford), 'or Pads. (Padstow) so he make haste and now to conclude, I beseech you take care of your health, I have nothing so much in my prayers. Y^r Phisiton Jennings is turned a Traytor with the rest—whereby he hath lost my love, and I am doubtfull to trust you with him. Present my humble duety and thanks to your mother and I beseech God to blesse your young People.

'I rest y^r owne ever,

'BEVILL GRENVILLE.

' My new cap is a little to straight. I know not what forme of a certifficate it is that Jo. Geal. desires, but if he will send it to me drawne, I will get it sign'd.'

Then comes the account of the victory over the Parliamentary forces on Braddock Down, half-way between Lostwithiel and Liskeard:

' MY DEARE LOVE,

'It hath pleas'd God to give us a happie victory this present Thursday being ye 19th of Jan^y, for which pray join with me in giving God thanks. We advanced yesterday from Bodmin to find ye enemy which we heard was abroad, or if we miss'd him in the field we were resolved to unhouse them in Liskeard or leave our boddies in the high-way. We were not above 3 miles from Bodmin, when we had view of two troops of their horse to whom we sent some of ours, which chased them out of the field while our foot march'd after our horse; but night coming on we could march no further than Boconnocke Parke,* where (upon my co. Mohun's kind notion) we quartered all our army by good fires under the hedge. The next morning (being

---

* In Boconnoc Park, near the gate of Rookwood Grove, was an ancient oak, under which, according to tradition, an attempt was made to assassinate the King whilst receiving the sacrament. A hole, (made by woodpeckers) used to be shown in support of the tradition. Pol-whele fancies the story must have arisen from the King's having really been shot at whilst in the Hall walk, Fowey, when a fisherman, who was gazing at his Majesty, was killed. On this occasion it is said that on 8th Aug., 1644, King Charles 'lay in the field all night in his coach' on Boconnoc Down, having been 'affrighted by the Militia' out of Lord Mohun's house at Boconnoc.

this day) we marched forth, and about noone came in full view of the enemies whole army upon a fair heath between Boconnocke and Braddocke Church. They were in horse much stronger than we, but in foot we were superior, as I thinke. They were possest of a pretty rising ground which was in the way towards Liskeard and we planted ourselves upon such another against them with in muskett shot, and we saluted each other with bulletts about two hours or more, each side being willing to keep their ground and to have the other to come over to his prejudice; but after so long delay, they standing still firm, and being obstinate to hould their advantage, Sir Ra. Hopton resolved to march over to them, and to leave all to the mercy of God and valour of our side. I had the Van; so after solemne prayers in the head of every division,* I led my part away, who followed me with so good courage both down one hill and up the other, as it strooke a terror in them, while the seconds came up gallantly after me, and the wings of horse charged on both sides, but their courage so failed them as they stood not our first charge of the foot, but fled in great disorder and we chast them divers miles; many were not slain because of their quick disordering, but we have taken above 600 prisoners among which Sr Shilston Calmady is one, and more are still brought in by the soldiers; much armes they have lost, and colours we have won, and 4 pieces of ordinance from them,

---

* An interesting illustration of a fact, sometimes apt to be overlooked, that reliance on the 'God of Battles' was not confined to the Puritan side in this memorable struggle.

and without rest we marched to Liskeard, and tooke
it without delay, all their men flying from it before
we came, and so I hope we are now againe in ye way
to settle the country in peace. All our Cornish
Grandies were present at the battell with the Scotch
Generall Ruthen, the Somersett Collonels and the
horse Captains Pim and Tomson, and but for their
horses' speed had been all in our hands; let my
sister and my cossens of Clovelly, with ye other
friends, understande of God's mercy to us, and we
lost not a man. So I rest

'Yours ever,

'BEVILL GRENVILE.

'Liskeard, Jan. 19, 1642.
    'For the Lady Grace Grenvile
      at Stow. d. d.

'The messenger is paide, yet give him a shilling
more.'

As a result of the battle, Saltash was now relieved,
many prisoners, guns, and a frigate were taken there,
and the Parliamentary leaders were reduced to propose (ineffectually, however) the neutrality of Cornwall and Devon in the conflict. We next hear of Sir
Bevill's being, in conjunction with Sir Ralph Hopton,
after a sudden and forced march from Plymouth,
attacked at Launceston; but the Cornish forces
repulsed their assailants and drove them back
into Devonshire. Such was the reputation of this
gallant little force that it was now determined to
send an army of 7,000 men against them, and the
battle of Stratton, almost within sight of the old
Grenville seat at Stow, ensued; in which the Parlia-

mentarians, though two to one, were again defeated.
Sir Bevill once more led the van of the King's army;
and Clarendon thus describes the engagement in language so vivid, that we almost see the cavaliers as
they dashed, all plumed and crimson-scarfed, through
fields of blood :

> ' Then "Spur and sword !" was the battle-word, and we made their
>   helmets ring,
> Shouting like madmen all the while, "For God and for the King !"
> And, though they snuffled psalms, to give the rebel dogs their due,
> When the roaring shot poured thick and hot they were stalwart men and
>   true.'

Thus Clarendon :

' In this manner the fight begun : the King's
forces pressing, with their utmost vigour, up the
hill, and the enemies as obstinately defending their
ground. The fight continued with very doubtful
success, till towards three of the clock in the afternoon; when word was brought to the chief officers
of the Cornish that their ammunition was spent to
less than four barrels of powder; which (concealing
the defect from the soldiers) they resolved could
only be supplied with courage ; and therefore, by
messengers to one another, they agreed to advance
with their full bodies, without making any more
shot, till they reached the top of the hill, and so
might be upon even ground with the enemy;
wherein the officers' courage and resolution was so
well seconded by the soldiers, that they begun to get
ground in all places ; and the enemy, in wonder of
the men, who out-faced their shot with their swords,
to quit their post. Major-General Chudlegh, who

ordered the battle, failed in no part of a soldier;
and when he saw his men recoil from less numbers,
and the enemy in all places gaining the hill upon
him, himself advanced, with a good stand of pikes,
upon that party which was led by Sir John Berkley
and Sir Bevil Grenville, and charged them so
smartly that he put them into disorder; Sir Bevil
Grenville in the shock being borne to the ground,
but, quickly relieved by his companion, they so
re-inforced the charge that having killed most of the
assailants, and dispersed the rest, they took the
Major-General prisoner, after he had behaved himself with as much courage as a man could do. Then
the enemy gave ground apace, inasmuch as the four
parties, growing nearer and nearer as they ascended
the hill, between three and four of the clock, they all
met together upon one ground near the top of the
hill, where they embraced with unspeakable joy,
each congratulating the other's success, and all
acknowledging the wonderful blessing of God; and
being there possessed of some of the enemy's
cannon, they turned them upon the camp, and
advanced together to the perfect victory. But the
enemy no sooner understood the loss of their Major-
General but their hearts failed them; and being so
resolutely pressed, and their ground lost, upon the
security and advantage whereof they wholly depended, some of them threw down their arms, and
others fled, dispersing themselves, and every man
shifting for himself.

'This victory,' pursues the historian, 'was in
substance, as well as circumstance, as signal a one

as hath happened to either party since the unhappy
distraction; for on the King's party were not lost in
all above four score men, whereof few were officers,
and none above the degree of a captain; and though
many more were hurt, not above ten men died
afterwards of their wounds.   On the Parliament side,
notwithstanding their advantage of ground, and that
the other were the assailants, above three hundred
were slain on the place, and seventeen hundred
taken prisoners with their Major-General and above
thirty other officers.   They took likewise all their
baggage and tents, all their cannon, being, as was
said before, thirteen pieces of brass ordnance, and
a brass mortar-piece: all their ammunition, being
seventy barrels of powder, and all other sorts of
ammunition proportionable, and a very great magazine of bisket and other excellent provisions of
victuals; which was as seasonable a blessing as the
victory, to those who for three or four days before
had suffered great want of food as well as sleep, and
were equally tired with duty and hunger.'

Perhaps I may be excused for mentioning here
that Camden quotes approvingly from Johannes
Sarisburiensis a tribute to Cornish valour, and that
Michael Cornubiensis has also referred to the
subject in the following lines:

> ' Rex Arcturus nos primos Cornubienses
> Bellum facturus vocat, ut puta Cæsaris enses
> Nobis non aliis, reliquis, dat primitus ictum
> Per quem pax lisque, nobis fit utrumque relictum
> Quid nos deterret, si firmiter in pede stemus,
> Fraus ni nos superet, nihil est quod non supremus.'

Charles   was   not   unmindful   of   the   gallant   Sir

Bevill's share in the fight, as will be seen from ' His Majestie's letter to Sir Bevill Granvill after the great victory obtained over the Rebels, at the Battle of Stratton :'

'To our Right Trusty and Well beloved Sir Bevill Granvill at our Army in Cornwall.

   'CHARLES R.

     'Right Trusty and Well beloved wee greet you Well. Wee have seen your Letter to Endymion Porter Our Servant: But your whole conduct of Our Affairs in the West, doth speak your Zeal to Our Service and the Public Good in so full a Measure; as Wee Rest abundantly satisfy'd with the Testimony thereof. Your labours and your Expenses Wee are graciously Sensible of, and Our Royall Care hath been to ease you in all that Wee could. What hath fallen short of Our Princely Purposes, and your Expections, Wee know you will attribute to the great malignity of the Rebellion Wee had, and have here to wrestle withall ; And Wee know well, how effectually a diversion of that mischievous strength you have made from us at your own hazzards. Wee assure you Wee have all tender sense of the hardness you have endured and the State wherein you stand : Wee shall not fail to procure you what speedy relief may be : In the mean space Wee send you Our most hearty thanks for some encouragement, and assurances in the Word of a Gracious Prince, that (God enabling us) Wee shall so reflect upon your faithfull Services, as you and yours shall have cause to acknowledge Our

Bounty and Favours: And so Wee bid you heartily farewell. Given at Our Court at Oxford the 24th March, 164⅜.'

Cornwall was thus cleared of the enemy, and secured for the King; and the Cornish infantry were available for service elsewhere: they were accordingly re-inforced by a body of cavalry under Prince Maurice, and the combined troops met at Chard. Clarendon pauses to praise the loyal spirit evinced by the Cornishmen, who, notwithstanding their late gallant victories, now found themselves—both officers and men—overshadowed by the superior military rank allotted to their new associates. Nor were they less remarkable for their discipline and conduct. 'The Chief Commanders of the Cornish army,' says the great historian, 'had restrained their soldiers from all manner of licence, obliging them to frequent acts of devotion; insomuch that the fame of their religion and discipline was no less than of their courage.'

A junction with the King's troops at Oxford was the next object of the Royalists in the west; and they accordingly advanced through Taunton and Bridgewater upon Wells, where they fell upon the advanced guard of Waller's forces, which they routed and drove back upon Bath. Here the Par-liamentarian General awaited, upon Lansdowne Hill, the advance of the victorious and elated troops of the King. We cannot do better than once again listen to the tale of the fight as told in Clarendon's own words:

'It was upon the 5th of July, 1643, when Sir Wm. Waller, as soon as it was light, possessed himself of that hill; and after he had upon the brow of the hill, over the highway, raised breast-works with faggots and earth, and planted cannon there, he sent a strong party of horse towards Marsfield; which quickly alarmed the other army, and was shortly driven back to their body. As great a mind as the King's forces had to cope with the enemy, when they had drawn into battalion, and found the enemy fixed on the top of the hill, they resolved not to attack them upon so great disadvantage, and so retired again towards their old quarters: which Sir Wm. Waller perceiving, sent his whole body of horse and dragoons down the hill, to charge the rear and flank of the King's forces; which they did thoroughly, the regiment of cuirassiers so amazing the horse they charged, that they totally routed them; and, standing firm and unshaken themselves, gave so great terror to the King's horse, who had never before turned from an enemy, that no example of their officers, who did their parts with invincible courage, could make them charge with the same confidence, and in the same manner they had usually done. However, in the end, after Sir Nicholas Slanning, with 300 musqueteers, had fallen upon, and beaten their reserve of dragooners, Prince Maurice, and the Earl of Carnarvon, rallying their horse, and winging them with the Cornish mus-queteers, charged the enemy's horse again, and totally routed them; and in the same manner received two bodies more, and routed and chased them to the hill; where they stood in a place almost inaccessible. On the brow of the hill there were breast-works, on which were pretty bodies of small shot, and some cannon ; on either flank grew a pretty thick wood towards the declining of the hill, in which strong parties of musqueteers were placed ; at the rear was a very fair plain, where the reserves of horse and foot stood ranged, *yet the Cornish foot were so far from being appalled at this disadvantage, that they desired to fall on, and cried out ," That they might have leave to fetch off those cannon."** In the end order was given to attempt the hill with horse and foot. ' Two strong parties of musqueteers were sent into the woods, which flanked the enemy ; and the horse and other musqueteers up the roadway, which were charged by the enemy's horse and routed ; then Sir Bevil Grenville advanced with a party of horse on his right hand, that ground being best for them, and his musqueteers on his left, himself leading up his pikes in the middle ; and in the face of their cannon, and small shot from the breast-works, gained the brow of the hill, having sustained two full charges of the enemy's horse ; but in the third charge his horse failing, and giving ground, he received, after other wounds, a blow on the head with a poll-axe, with which he fell, and many of his officers about him ;†

---

* It will be remembered how the eagerness of the Grenville, Godolphin, Basset, and Trevanion troops of Cornishmen at the siege of Bristol precipitated the attack on 26th July, 1643, and greatly contributed to the capture of that city for the King.   Here, and at Lansdowne, fell the flower of the Cornish chivalry.

† Sir John Hinton, M.D., in his 'Memorial to Charles II.,' writes : ' In his extremity I was the last man that had him by the hand before he dyed.'   His body was brought to Stow, and deposited in the family vault in Kilkhampton Church, July 26th, 1643 ; and the remains of his ' deare love and best friend,' the Lady Grace, were laid by his side four years afterwards.

yet the musqueteers fired so fast on the enemy's horse, that they quitted their ground, and the two wings who were sent to clear the woods, having done their work, and gained those parts of the hill, at the same time beat off their enemy's foot, and became possessed of the breast-works, and so made way for their whole body of horse, foot, and cannon, to ascend the hill, which they quickly did, and planted themselves on the ground they had won; the enemy retiring about demy-culverin shot, behind a stone wall upon the same level, and standing in reasonable good order.

'Either party was sufficiently tired and battered, to be contented to stand still. The King's horse were so shaken, that of 2000 which were upon the field in the morning, there were not above 600 on the top of the hill; so that, exchanging only some shot from their ordnance, they looked upon one another till the night interposed. About twelve of the clock, the night being very dark, the enemy made a show of moving towards the ground they had lost; but giving a smart volly of small shot, and finding themselves answered with the like, they made no more noise; which the Prince observing, he sent a common soldier to hearken as near the place where they were, as he could; who brought word, That the enemy had left lighted matches in the wall behind which they had lain, and were drawn off the field; which was true; so that as soon as it was day, the King's army found themselves possessed entirely of the field, and the dead, and all other ensigns of victory: Sir Wm. Waller being marched into Bath, in so much disorder and apprehension, that he had left great store of arms, and ten barrels of powder, behind him, which was a very seasonable supply to the other side, who had spent in that day's service no less than four score barrels, and had not a safe proportion left.'

It is believed in the West that Sir Bevill was attended at the Battle of Lansdowne by one of his servants from Stow—Anthony Paine, the Cornish Giant, of whom Mr. Stokes tells us that

> ' His sword was made to match his size,
> As Roundheads did remember ;
> And when it swung 'twas like the whirl
> Of windmills in September.'

And there is a further tradition that, on seeing his master fall, Anthony at once clapped John Grenville (afterwards first Earl of Bath), then a youth of sixteen, on his father's steed in order to prevent the Royalist troops from being discouraged. Anthony measured, so it is said, seven feet two inches in height. He was present, not only at Lansdowne, but at the fight on Stamford Hill, and remained on the field that night to assist in burying the dead, after his master had returned home to Stow. At the 'Tree' Inn, Stratton (said to have been the headquarters of the Royalists on the night preceding that battle), the hole in the ceiling is still shown through which, years afterwards, the corpse of poor Anthony was removed from the room in which he died—his coffin being too long to be taken out of the window or down the stairs in the usual way.

Thus did the worthy retainer write to his mistress

on the terrible day of Lansdowne fight; at least so
Mr. Hawker assures us :

'Honored Madam. Ill news flieth apace. The
heavy tidings no doubt hath already traveled to
Stow that we have lost our blessed master by the
enemy's advantage. You must not, dear lady,
grieve too much for your noble spouse. You know,
as we all believe, that his soul was in heaven before
his bones were cold. He fell, as he did often tell us
he wished to die, in the great Stewart cause, for his
Country and his King. He delivered to me his last
commands, and with such tender words for you and
for his children as are not to be set down with my
poor pen, but must come to your ears upon my best
heart's breath. Master John, when I mounted him
upon his father's horse, rode him into the war like
a young prince, as he is, and our men followed him
with their swords drawn and with tears in their
eyes. They did say they would kill a rebel for every
hair of Sir Bevill's beard. But I bade them remember their good master's word when he wiped
his sword after Stamford fight : how he said, when
their cry was " Stab and slay !"—" Halt, men ! God
will avenge." I am coming down with the mourn-
fullest load that ever a poor servant did bear, to
bring the great heart that is cold to Kilkhampton
vault. O ! my lady, how shall I ever brook your
weeping face ? But I will be trothful to the living
and to the dead.

'These, honoured Madam, from thy saddest,
truest Servant,

'ANTHONY PAYNE.

Anthony was, at the Restoration made 'Halberdier of the Guns' at Plymouth Citadel, and Sir Godfrey Kneller was commissioned by the King to paint Anthony's portrait. It was engraved as a frontispiece to the 1st vol. of C. S. Gilbert's 'History of Cornwall,' and the picture itself was afterwards sold for £800. And here it may perhaps be added that at the siege of Plymouth another Cornish man, John Langherne, of Tregavethan, of huge strength and stature, being seven feet six inches high, 'Rid up,' as Tonkin tells us, 'to one of the gates of the Town, and stuck his sword in it so deep that two strong men could not possibly pull it out.'—(Borlase's Additional MSS.)

It is gratifying to learn that the Cornishmen demeaned themselves so well at Lansdowne; but the victory was far too dearly bought. Clarendon goes on to say:

'In this battle, on the King's part, there were more officers and gentlemen of quality slain, than common men; and more hurt than slain. That which would have clouded any victory, and made the loss of others less spoken of, was the death of Sir Bevil Grenville. He was indeed an excellent person, whose activity, interest, and reputation was the foundation of what had been done in Cornwall; and his temper and affection so publick, that no accident which happened could make any impressions in him; and his example kept others from taking anything ill, or at least seeming to do so. In a word, *a brighter courage, and a gentler disposition*, were never married together to make the most chearful and innocent conversation.' 'Clarendon's immortals,' says Forster, 'still lie unwithered' on Sir Bevill's grave.

A monument, erected by his grandson George Lord Lansdowne, marks the spot where our hero fell.* On the north side of the monument was inscribed:

> 'Conquest or death was all his thought, so fire
> Either o'ercomes, or does itself expire.
> His courage work'd like flames, cast heat about,
> Here, there, on this, on that side, none gave out;
> Nor any pike in that renowned stand,
> But took new force from his inspiring hand.
> Soldier encourag'd soldier, man urg'd man,
> And he urg'd all, so much example can.

---

* A writer in 'Notes and Queries' says that Sir Bevill did not die on the spot, but that he expired next day at Cold Aston (Ashton) Parsonage, some four or five miles to the north of the battle-field.

Green, in his 'History of the English People,' thus refers to the event:

'Nowhere was the Royal cause to take so brave or noble a form as among the Cornishmen. Cornwall stood apart from the general life of England : cut off from it not only by differences of blood and speech, but by the feudal tendencies of its people, who clung with a Celtic loyalty to their local chieftains, and suffered their fidelity to the Crown to determine their own. They had as yet done little more than keep the war out of their own county; but the march of a small Parliamentary force under Lord Stamford upon Launceston, forced them into action. A little brave band of Cornishmen gathered around the chivalrous *Sir Bevil Greenvil,* "so destitute of provisions that the best officers had but a biscuit a day," and with only a handful of powder for the whole force ; but, starving and out-numbered as they were, they scaled the steep rise of Stratton Hill, sword in hand, and drove Stamford back to Exeter, with a loss of two thousand men, his ordnance and baggage train. Sir Ralph Hopton, the best of the Royalist generals, took the command of their army as it advanced into Somerset, and drew the stress of the war into the west. Essex despatched a picked force under Sir William Waller to check their advance ; but Somerset was already lost ere he reached Bath, and the Cornishmen stormed his strong position on Lansdowne Hill in the teeth of his guns.'

> Hurt upon hurt, wound upon wound did call,
> He was the mark, the butt, the aim of all ;
> His soul this while retired from cell to cell,
> At last flew up from all, and then he fell ;
> But the devoted stand enrag'd the more
> From that his fate, played hotter than before ;
> And proud to fall with him, sworn not to yield,
> Each sought an honour'd grave, and won the field,
> Thus he being fall'n, his actions fought anew
> And the dead conquer'd, whilst the living flew.'

The remaining lines are those quoted as Sir Bevill's epitaph on the fine monument to his memory,* and to that of the great Sir Richard, at the old Church of Kilkhampton, where both of them must have often worshipped. The epitaph runs as follows :

. 'To the immortal memory of his renowned grandfather this monument was erected by the Right Honorable George, Lord Lansdowne, Treasurer of the Household to Queen Anne, and one of her Majesty's Most Honorable Privy Council, &c., in the year 1714.

> 'Thus slain thy valiant ancestor did lye,
> When his one bark a navy did defy,
> When now encompass'd round the victor stood,
> And bath'd his pinnace in his conquering blood,
> Till, all his purple current dried and spent,
> He fell, and made the waves his monument.
> Where shall the next famed Grenville's ashes stand ?
> Thy grandsire fills *the seas*, and thou the land.
>   MARTIN LLEWELLYN.

(*Vide also Oxford University Verses, printed* 1643.)

Mrs. Delany has stated that Sir Bevill had the

---

* Sir Bevill Grenville was forty-eight years of age at the time of his death, as appears by the following record of his birth in the parish register at Kilkhampton :
'Bevell, the sonne of the worshipful Bernarde Greynville, Esquire, was borne and baptized at Brinn in Cornwall, Ao. Dni. 1595.'
In the margin, 'Marche 1595, borne the 23d day ; baptized the 25th day of Marche.'

patent for an Earldom in his pocket on the day of the fatal fight at Lansdowne; and in this there seems nothing improbable, as his youngest daughter, Joan, or Johanna, had a patent of precedence as an Earl's daughter.

We have seen something of Sir Bevill's epistolary productions; and, if we are to accept the testimony of the Rev. S. Baring-Gould, the writer of the biography of the Rev. R. S. Hawker, some specimens of Lady Grace's were preserved under the following singular circumstances:

One day, he tells us, Mrs. Hawker, the first wife of the Vicar of Morwenstow, when lunching at Stow in the farmhouse, noticed that a letter in old handwriting was wrapped round the mutton bone that was brought on the table. Moved by curiosity, she took the paper off, and showed it to Mr. Hawker. On examination it was found that the letter bore the signature of Sir Bevill Grenville. Mr. Hawker at once instituted inquiries, and found a large chest full of letters of different members of the Grenville family in the sixteenth and seventeenth centuries. He at once communicated with Lord Carteret, owner of Stow, and the papers were removed, but by some unfortunate accident they were lost! The only ones saved were a packet removed from the chest by Mr. Davis, Rector of Kilkhampton, previous to their being sent away from Stow. These were copied by Miss Manning, of Eastaway, in Morwenstowe, and her transcript, together with some of the originals, was said to be in the possession of Ezekiel Rous, Esq., of Bideford.

The following, from Lady Grace to her husband, was probably another of the letters in the collection said to have been found by Mr. Hawker, and afterwards so mysteriously lost.

'For My Best Friend, Sir Bevill Grenville.

'My ever Dearest,

'I have received yours from Salisbury, and am glad to hear you came so farr well, with poore Jack. Ye shall be sure of my prairs, which is the best service I can doe you. I canott perceave whither you had receaved mine by Tom, or no, but I believe by this time you have mett that and another since by the post. Truly I have been out of frame ever since you went, not with a cough, but in another kinde, much indisposed. However, I have striven with it, and was at Church last Sunday, but not the former. I have been vexed with diverse demands made of money than I could satisfie, but I instantly paid what you sent, and have intreated Mr. Rous his patience a while longer, as you directed.

'It grieves me to think how chargeable your family is, considering your occasion. It hath this many years troubled me to think to what passe it must come at last, if it run on after this course. How many times what hath appeared hopefull, and yet proved contrary in the conclusion, hath befalen us, I am loth to urge, because tis farr from my desire to disturbe your thoughts; but this sore is not to be curd with silence, or patience either, and while you are loth to discourse or thinke of that you can take little comfort to see how bad it is, and I was un-

willing to strike on that string which sounds harsh in
your eare (the matter still grows worse, though). I
can never putt it out of my thoughts, and that makes
me often times seeme dreaming to you, when you
expect I should sometimes observe more complement
with my frends, or be more active in matters of
curiousity in our House, which doubtlesse you would
have been better pleasd with had I. been capable to
have performd it, and I believe though I had a naturall
dullness in me, it would never so much have appeard
to my prejudice, but twas increasd by a continuance
of sundry disasters, which I still mett with, yet never
till this yeare, but I had some strength to encounter
them, and truly now I am soe cleane overcome, as
tis in vaine to deny a truth. It seems to me now tis
high time to be sensible that God is displeased,
having had many sad remembrances in our estate
and children late, yet God spard us in our children
long, and when I strive to follow your advice in
moderating my grieffe (which I praise God) I have
thus farr been able to doe as not to repine at God's
will, though I have a tender sence of griefe which
hangs on me still, and I think it as dangerous and
improper to forgett it, for I cannott but think it was
a neer touched correction, sent from God to check
me for my many neglects of my duty to God. It was
the tenth and last plague God smote the Egyptians
with, the deathe of their first borne, before he utterly
destroyed them, they persisting in their disobedience
notwithstanding all their former punishments. This
apprehension makes me both tremble and humbly
beseech Him to withdraw His punishments from us,

and to give us grace to know and amend whatever is
amisse. Now I have pourd out my sad thoughts
which in your absence doth most oppresse me, and
tis my weakness hardly to be able to say thus much
unto you, how brimfull soever my heart be, though
oftentimes I heartely wish I could open my heart
truly unto you when tis overchargd. But the least
thought it may not be pleasing to you will at all times
restraine me. Consider me rightly, I beseech you,
and excuse, I pray, the liberty I take with my pen in
this kinde. And now at last I must thanke you for
wishing me to lay aside all feare, and depend on the
Almighty, who can only helpe us; for his mercy I
daily pray, and your welfare, and our poore boys;
so I conclude, and am ever your faithfully and
only

'GRACE GRENVILLE.

'Stow, Nov. 23, 1641.'

'I sent yours to Mr. Prust, but this from him
came after mine was gone last weeke. Ching is
gone to Cheddar. I looke for Bawden, but as yet
is not come. Sir Rob. Bassett is dead.

'I heard from my cosen Grace Weekes, who writes
that Mr. Luttrell says if you could meete the liking
between the young people, he will not stand for
money you shall finde. Parson Weekes wishes you
would call with him, and that he might entice you
to take the Castle in your way downe. She says
they enquire in the most courteous maner that can
be imagind. Deare love, thinke how to farther this
what you can.'

The following is said to have been an earlier letter by many years, written when Grace was a wife of six years' standing :

'SWEET MR. GRENVILE,

'I cannott let Mr. Oliver passe without a line though it be only to give you thankes for yours, which I have receaved. I will in all things observe your directions as neer as I can, and because I have not time to say much now I will write againe to-morrow (. . . something torn away) and think you shall receave advertizment concerning us much as you desyre. I can not say I am well, neither have I bin so since I saw you, but, however, I will pray for your health, and good successe in all businesses, and pray be so kinde as to love her who takes no comfort in anything but you, and will remayne yours ever and only

'GRACE GRENVILE.

'Fryday night, Nov. 13, 1629.'

The superscription of this letter is :

'To my ever dearest and best Friend, Mr. Bevill Grenvile, at the Rainbow, in Fleet Street.'

The other letters in this collection—alleged to have been so strangely discovered—will be found enumerated in the Appendix to Mr. Gould's 'Life of Hawker.'

There are many portraits of Sir Bevill Grenville. One is in Prince's 'Worthies of Devon;' another in Lloyd's 'Worthies;' and one, by Dobson, is in the fine collection at Petworth Park. Here also is a group described as Sir Bevill Grenville, Anne St.

Leger (his grandmother!) and John Earl of Bath, their son—after Vandyck.

What can be added to such tributes as those which we have just read but that, in Sir Bevill Grenville's case at least, 'the good was *not* interred with his bones;'* his valiant spirit continued to animate his friends and followers, and prompted their valour on Roundway Down, at the siege of Bristol, and—when one of the last gleams of success shone upon the Royal cause—when Essex's infantry surrendered to the King in person, at Fowey. On the latter occasion Sir Richard, brother of Sir Bevill, held and fortified Hall House, on the eastern side of the harbour, for the King: he had previously captured Restormel Castle near Lostwithiel.

Then there soon came a time when, as Macaulay says, England had to witness spectacles such as these: 'Major-Generals fleecing their districts—soldiers revelling on the spoils of a ruined peasantry—upstarts, enriched by the public plunder, taking possession of the hospitable firesides and hereditary trees of the old gentry—boys smashing the beautiful windows of cathedrals—Fifth-Monarchy men shouting for King Jesus—Quakers riding naked through the market-place—and agitators lecturing from tubs on the fate of Agag.'

'Where,' asked Dr. Llewellyn, the Principal of

* Sir Bevill's name and memory were of course long revered in the family. Mrs. Delany was particularly anxious that it should be always borne by some member of it, and it may be convenient to note here that his grandson, Sir Bevill Grenville, was Governor of Barbadoes, in 1704 (cf. Rawlinson, A 271, Bodleian Library), a major-general in the army, and M.P. for Fowey, 1685-89.

St. Mary Hall, Oxford, in the stilted style of the day
in which he wrote :

> ' Where shall next famous Grenvil's ashes stand ?
>   Thy grandsire fills the sea—and thou the land.'

The answer to which question must be that the
next famous Grenville—Sir Bevill's eldest son, Sir
John—was destined to become a conspicuous figure
in the field of Diplomacy.   He even attained to
a higher rank than his father, soon after the Stuart
cause became once more triumphant.   Leaving
Gloucester Hall, Oxford,—where he was a Gentleman Commoner,—when only fifteen years of age,
he commanded his father's regiment in the west;
and at the second battle of Newbury (to which he
brought his Cornish troops) he was wounded, and
left for dead on the field.   He had received a dangerous wound in the head from a halberd, and was
carried to the King and Prince of Wales, who
ordered him to be taken care of in Donnington
Castle hard by.   The Castle was soon after besieged,
and the bullets constantly whistled through his
sick-room ; but the boy-warrior at last came safely
off.   When the Scilly Isles revolted from the Parliament and became the last rallying-point of the
Royalists, he it was who (like one of his ancestors)
was made Governor, for the King—taking up
his quarters at Elizabeth Castle on St. Mary's
Island.   But the Parliamentary Admirals, Blake
and Ayscough, appeared before Scilly with so over-
whelming a force, that Sir John Grenville thought it
best to capitulate ; extorting, however, such favour-

able terms that, until Blake represented to what an extent his own honour was involved in their confirmation, the Parliament refused to recognise them. It is said that Sir John had with him commissioned officers enough to ' head an army.'

Sir John Grenville, although he now returned quietly to Stow, was by no means unmindful of his royal master, and soon opened négotiations with his cousin George Monk (afterwards Duke of Albemarle), who became the well known chief instrument in the restoration of Charles II. A brother of Monk's (afterwards Bishop of Hereford), who was at this time in Cornwall, having been appointed by the Grenvilles to the living of Kilkhampton, seems to have been the medium of this dangerous intercourse; but our Sir John managed matters with such loyalty, courage, and discretion, that all ultimately went well for the Royal cause.* He had at one time accompanied Charles into exile, and was one of the Commissioners, known as the ' Sealed Knot ' from their secrecy, appointed to conduct the affairs of the King in England during his absence; and though Sir John Grenville could not obtain from Monk (who was determined upon being supreme in the transaction) the stipulations which even Charles's most loyal friends thought desirable for the future, events proved that it would have been well if more weight had been attached to the suggestions of the sagacious Cornish Knight and his colleagues.

---

* Echard gives some interesting details respecting the conduct of this delicate business; and Masson refers to it in his ' Life of Milton ' (vol. v.)

So highly, however, were his fidelity and wisdom esteemed, that he was selected to present to Parliament the King's proposals from Breda : an office which he discharged with such efficiency as to obtain the thanks of both Houses, and a jewel worth £500, as well as a ring worth £300 from the Common Council, for his services at this important crisis. (Cf. also Thurloe's ' State Papers,' Grammont's ' Memoirs,' Clarendon's Correspondence and Diary, and Dr. John Price's ' Mystery and Method of His Majesty's Happy Restoration,' dedicated to the Earl of Bath.) Pepys describes the circumstances, and tells us how, on 2nd March, 1660, Parliament continued bareheaded whilst the King's letter was being read.*

The favours of royalty were also showered upon Grenville—though Charles II. was apt to be unmindful of his friends in the past—and Sir John was made a Secretary of State, and was created Lord Grenville, of Kilkhampton and Bytheford, Viscount Grenville of Lansdowne, and Earl of Bath ; with a pension of £3,000 a year to be paid out of the Stannaries, of which he was made Lord Warden, and a reversion to the Dukedom of Albemarle. He also received the Royal Licence to use his titles of Earl of Corboile, Thorigny, and Granville. Of the architectural merits of his ' new house' at Stow,

---

* The following extract from Pepys is so amusing that I cannot forbear inserting it : ' This afternoon Mr. Ed. Pickering told me in what a sad, poor condition for clothes and money the King was, and all his attendants, when he came to him first from my Lord, their clothes not being worth forty shillings the best of them. And how overjoyed the King was when Sir J. Greenville brought him some money : so joyful, that he called the Princess Royal and Duke of York to look upon it as it lay in the portmanteau before it was taken out.'

built for him, it is said, by the King, Kingsley writes
in disparaging terms, as we have seen. He married
Jane, the daughter of Sir Peter Wiche or Wych, by
whom he left a noble offspring. The eldest son,
Charles, second Earl of Bath, died in 1701,—twelve
days after his father; the second son, John, who
was created Baron Grenville of Potheridge in 1703,
died in 1707; and the male line became extinct on
the death, from small-pox, of his son William Henry,
third Earl of Bath, in 1771.

James II., however, seems to have shown the Earl
of Bath — who was a staunch Protestant — little
favour. So Grenville declared for the Prince of
Orange; and, having first seized Plymouth citadel,
admitted the Dutch fleet into that harbour; his
nephew Bevill performing a similar service with his
uncle's own regiment at Jersey. King William III.
consequently created him a member of his Privy
Council, and continued him in his previous offices.

The Earl's eldest son, Charles, was accidentally
killed by the discharge of a pistol at his father's
funeral; and the title consequently devolved upon
his son William Henry, thus giving rise to the observation that at one time there were 'three Earls of
Bath above ground at the same time.' From the
first Earl descended, in the female line, the present
representatives of the family—the Thynnes, not unknown to fame.

And Sir Bevill had another son, Dennis, who was
by no means undistinguished in his own walk of life.

Born in 163⅞, and educated probably at Eton,* he
was entered a Gentleman Commoner of Exeter College, Oxford, on 22nd Sept., 1657 ; took his degree
of M.A. on 28th Sept., 1660, and that of D.D. on 20th
Dec., 1670. Kilkhampton was his first preferment,
though he does not appear to have taken up residence
there. He was Chaplain in Ordinary to Charles II. ;
and in 1684 was made Archdeacon and Dean of
Durham. But he was a true Grenville in his attachment to the Stuarts ; and early in 1690 went into
exile with James II., residing at Corbeil, in France
(near the place whence his family are supposed to
have sprung), rather than acknowledge William III.
as his sovereign. He left several works behind him,
and died in Paris in 1703.

There are many incidents, however, connected
with his career which seem to require a fuller notice
of the Cavalier Dean. The command, ' Fear God,'
scarcely commended itself more forcibly to his con-

---

* This appears the more probable from the following passage, which
occurs in Lyte's 'History of Eton College ' (p. 269): ' The keen competi-
tion for Fellowships, which we have noticed at the period of the Restoration, continued almost throughout the reign of Charles II. Sir John Grenville was not satisfied with having procured the Provostship for his kinsman, Nicholas Monk, and applied to the King for a Fellowship for his
own brother. The vacancy caused by the death of Grey had just been
filled up, but it was arranged that Denis Grenville should have the
next. But, though the letter in his favour was confirmed sixteen
months later, the Fellowship which Meredith resigned on his promotion
to the Provostship, was granted by the forgetful King to Dr. Heaver,
of Windsor. The Grenvilles were naturally indignant at such treatment, and the King had to write to the Provost and Fellows, explaining
that the late appointment had been made in consequence of Laud's
decree of 1634, which annexed a Fellowship at Eton to the Vicarage of
Windsor, and once more bidding them reserve the next place for Grenville, whose family had rendered such eminent services to the Royalist
cause.

science than its complement 'Honour the King;' and, although he was in a *very* small minority, his high-minded consistency and loyalty were such, that, whatever we may think of his prudence, or of the practicability of his views, we are bound, I think, to honour the man who chose rather to sacrifice the highest preferments than to swear allegiance to one whom he, at least, regarded as an invader and a usurper.

There are full details of the latter part of his career preserved in the library of the Dean and Chapter of Durham, from which I have gathered most of the following accounts.

He married Ann, daughter of Bishop Cosin (an unhappy union, for her husband—and two physicians confirmed his statement—alleged that the lady was subject to fits of temporary insanity), at a time when the Church of England was in sad disorder, and when vigorous, earnest spirits were wanted to remedy the listless slovenliness of many of her clergy.

Dennis Grenville was equal to the trying occasion. He found that the Church services were often either curtailed or omitted altogether ; many of the churches were 'altogether unprovided of ministers'; and the fabrics themselves were 'ruinous and in great decay.' Not only the minor Canons and singing men, but even many of the highest dignitaries were guilty, according to Cosin,* of sluttish and disorderly habits, even in the cathedrals themselves ; and the Rubrics and Canons were almost ignored. But, as Parish Priest, as Prebendary, and as Archdeacon, and after-

---

* 'Comperts and Considerations.'

wards, especially in securing a weekly celebration of the Holy Communion in his own cathedral, Dennis Grenville laboured so earnestly and so conscientiously, as to warrant his promotion, young as he was, to the post of Dean.

His rapid advancement, however, seems to have almost turned his head; he became ambitious and extravagant, was frequently absent from his post, and fell into pecuniary troubles (aggravated by the non-payment of an expected marriage portion with his wife) which, almost to the last, hung like a mill-stone round his neck. On the 8th of July, 1674, on returning from public prayers and Captain Foster's funeral, he was actually arrested 'in his Hood and Surplice' for debt, within the cloisters; and although he was afterwards released as a Chaplain in Ordinary of the King, and though the bailiffs and the Under Sheriff who were responsible for his arrest were reprimanded before the Council Board at Hampton Court, yet the indignity seems to have entered into the Dean's very soul, producing, however, more than one good result, viz. the more economical manage-ment of his resources, and salutary counsels to his nephew at Oxford, published in 1685. He was a capital preacher, but a bad man of business: ' " I cannot manage nor mind these money affairs," is his own candid confession,' observes the Rev. George Ormsby, in his interesting memoir.

Of the Dean's management of his own household full details are preserved; they will probably be found interesting here as showing how a Church dignitary lived two hundred years ago : one who was always at work on the scheme of reformation to which he had laid his hands, and who seems to have taken for his model George Herbert's 'Country Parson.' This book he recommended to his curates, and to all the clergy in his jurisdiction, 'for their rule and direction in order to the exemplary discharge of their functions, having always made it mine.' The Diocese of Durham, under such auspices as those of Cosin and Grenville, (notwithstanding the incapacity of the latter to properly manage his money affairs,) accordingly improved rapidly in tone, until the Dean was at length able to report to the King that it was 'without dispute the most exemplary county for good order and conformity of any in the nation.'

These, then, were amongst Dean Grenville's thirty-two Home Rules :

'1. That all persons should labour to contrive their businesse soe as to be present at God's service in the Church, as often as possible, not only on publick daies but private ones ; never staying at home (any one) but in cases of infirmity, or of some necessary lawfull impediment.'

'3. That as soon as the bells of the Church begin to ring or toll, all persons who intend to goe to the Church at that time shall begin to put themselves in readinesse, and wait for mee in the parlour and the hall, that they may all goe forth with mee at the same time (for which purpose there shall be given one toll of my House bell) and accompany mee to the Church, not dropping in one after another after service is begun.'

'5. That all persons of my family shall carry their

Bibles and Common Prayer-books to the Church with them, and use them in the performance of the Service and Lessons.

'6. That when I keep daily labourers in the summer time, or have any number of servants imployed without doores, that must goe to their worke abroad, before the houre of morning prayers, that they repaire to my house, and have some short prayers in my hall at five of the clock, or at such houre and in such manner as I shall appoint.'

'11. That in case the worke and imployment of my house bee too much to bee dispatched in the forenoon or before Evening Prayers on such daies, I doe allow of the hiring one, two or three women for the spedier dispatch of the same.'

'12. That I allow all my domesticks some time every day for private prayer and reading of the Scriptures (nay, doe in the Name of God injoyne every person to imploy some to that purpose), and that every person may have some reasonable time and liberty for devotion, and not be oppressed with too much businesse, I am willing to keep a servant or two more than would bee other wise necessary.'

'14. That all persons playing at any game (tho' they are in the middle of a game) shall breake it off and cease their play, soe soon as the bell tolls for prayers, either in church or chaple, or as soon as the Butler appears with the things to lay the cloth for dinner or supper.'

'15. That there shall bee noe playing in my family at any game on the Vigills and other fasting daies of the Church, nor on Fridaies and Saturdaies (unlesse

within the 12 daies of Christmasse), but that what
time shall be gained from necessary businesse bee
better imployed in devotion, reading, good conference
or the like.

'16. That to the former end and purpose I doe
order my chesseboard, bowles, and all other things
relating to such games (as I doe allow) to be locked
up on Thursday night till Monday morning, as alsoe
on other daies before mentioned.

'17. That I allow of noe great game for any considerable summe to bee played in my family, nor
indeed of any at all when my poor box is forgotten,
which I doe recommend more earnestly than my
Butler's.

'18. That at nine o'clock, our family prayers being
ended, all persons shall repair to their chambers ;
and are desired to dismisse the servants soe soon as
possible, that they may put the house in order,
and go to their beds near ten of the clock or by
eleven at farthest. . . . .'

'20. That my house bell be rung every morning at
5 in the winter, and about 4 in the summer to
awaken my family, and alarume my servants to arise,
and to give opportunity and incouragement to early
risers, who are alwaies the most welcome persons to
my family.'

'25. That there shall bee no dinners on Wednes-
daies and Fridaies in Lent.'

*   *   *   *   *

But James II.'s 'Second Declaration of Indulgence,' 7th April, 1688, an attempt to divide the Protestant party, and to secure the favour of the Non-

conformists after having failed to seduce from their
allegiance the leaders of the Church of England,
placed the Dean in a most trying position. His
loyalty to his Church was in conflict with his loyalty
to his Sovereign ; and the latter prevailed : ' If the
King goes beyond his Commission, he must answer
for it to God, but I'le not deface one line thereof.
Let my liege and dread Sovereign intend to do what
he pleases to me or mine : yet my hand shall never
be upon him, so much as to cut off the skirt of his
garment.' Not only (to the Dean's intense grief) did
his elder brother, the Earl of Bath, now desert the
Stuart cause, but another Cornish Church dignitary
of this period—Bishop Jonathan Trelawney—took
the bolder course of opposing the King's views,
thus exemplifying the old Cornish saying that
a *Trelawny never wanted courage, nor a Grenville
loyalty.* It is needless to repeat that the Dean of
Durham found himself in a *very* small minority.

His loyalty was about to undergo another and a
severer test. In the autumn of 1688 news arrived
of the projected 'invasion and usurpation,' as our
Dean would always call it, of the Prince of Orange :
at once he summoned his Chapter, prevailed
upon them to assist the King's cause 'with their
purses as well as their prayers,' and £700 were
accordingly subscribed forthwith. But Lord Lumley
pounced upon Durham on the 6th of December in
that year, whilst the Dean was in his pulpit preaching
a sermon, still preserved in the Surtees Collection,
on ' Christian Resignation and Resolution, with
some loyal reflexions on the Dutch Invasion '; and

Dr. Grenville was, on his refusal to deliver up his arms and horses, confined within the walls of his own Deanery during the occupation of the city by the friends of King William III. Another similar sermon, however, did he, with undaunted courage, preach on the following Sunday, notwithstanding his now almost solitary position amongst his brother clergy. But James's cause was entirely lost; and our Dean had to fly from Durham to Carlisle at midnight on the 11th of December, with the help of two faithful servants. At Carlisle he learned that all was over, and made up his mind to follow his King into France, if only he could make good his escape by way of Edinburgh. On his way thither he was roughly handled by a mob, who took him for a Popish priest and Jesuit, and at eleven at night ' pulled me out of my bed, rifling my pockets and my chamber, and carrying away my horses (two geldings worth £40) and my portmantoe, and mounting me on a little jade not worth 40s.' Once more he was plundered on the road, and returned to Carlisle, where he preached on Christmas Day, when he says he hoped that he convinced the people that he was no Romanist.

In the following month, however, he made another attempt—this time successfully—to reach Edinburgh; and after a long and tedious voyage, arrived at Honfleur on the 19th March—the very day after James had left Brest for Ireland, 'a great mortification and disappointment to mee,' adds Dean Grenville. Rouen was the place which he had fixed upon for his abode, and thither he removed a few days afterwards, forthwith setting about writing remonstrances to his Bishop, his brother, and his ' lapsed assistants,' his Curates; printing his sermons, to which reference has just been made, and also his ' Loyall farewell Visitation Speech,' delivered on 15th November, 1688.*

Little remains to be told of him, but that he was formally deprived on the appointed date of 1st February, 169$\frac{0}{1}$, and his goods and chattels were distrained by the Sheriff, in consequence of his continued pecuniary embarrassments; his library, also, which was very rich in Bibles and Prayer-books, was purchased by Sir George Wheeler; and the Chapter had to grant the unhappy Mrs. Grenville an allowance of £80 a year 'in compassion to her necessities.' She died twelve years before her husband, and was buried in Durham Cathedral.

Nor did James, to whose Court at St. Germains Dennis Grenville shortly afterwards repaired, by any means console his faithful servant for the troubles and trials he had undergone in his King's behalf. ' He was slighted,' says Surtees, in his ' History of Durham,' ' by the bigoted Prince, for whom he had forfeited every worldly possession, because he would not also abandon his religion.'† In fact, the Dean

---

* He had also published previously some other sermons; a letter written to the Clergy of his Archdeaconry ; and 'Counsel and Directions, Divine and Moral, in plain and familiar Letters of Advice to a Young Gentleman' (his nephew, Thomas Higgons), 'soon after his admission into a College in Oxon ;' and his Memoirs, some of them of a painfully personal character, were edited by the Surtees Society in 1865.

† It is indeed said that James promised him, on his restoration, the Archbishopric of York (a post which, as we have seen, was once before filled by a member of the Grenville family).

was at length compelled to retire from the Court to Corbeil, his ancestral home, about twenty miles from Paris, in consequence of the indignities heaped upon him there by his ecclesiastical opponents, and by their persistent, though vain, attempts to draw him into polemical discussions. Whilst in France, he sometimes went by the name of Corbeil—sometimes by the name of Stotherd; and here it may be added, that Mr. H. R. Fox Bourne, in his 'Life of John Locke,' mentions that the illustrious metaphysician and Dean Grenville were old friends, and that they corresponded in 1677-78 on the subjects of Recreation and Scrupulosity. Copies of the letters are in the British Museum, Additional MSS. 4290. Mr. Bourne states that James II. actually appointed Dean Grenville Roman Catholic Archbishop of York.*

Two furtive journeys did he make to England, in disguise—one in February, 1689-90, 'whereby he got a small sum of money to subsist while abroad . . . . tho' with much trouble and danger occasioned him by an impertinent and malitious post master, who discovered him in Canterbury;' and once again in 1695, probably with the same object. In 1702 he wrote an amusing letter to his nephew, Sir George Wheeler, acknowledging 'a seasonable supply' of £20, from which it may be gathered that he preserved to the last his unbroken and cheerful spirit. But, in the following year, on Wednesday, the 8th April, 1703, at six in the morning, the exiled, supplanted,

* Cf. Wood's 'Athenæ Oxonienses,' vol. iv., col. 498; and the 'Fasti Oxonienses,' part ii., cols. 229-326.

and childless Dean of Durham died—as he asserts, himself, in the preamble of his will—a true son of the Church of England, at his lodgings at the Fossée St. Victoire, in Paris, in the sixty-seventh year of his age.

His portrait, admirably engraved by Edelinck, was painted by Beaupoille when Dean Grenville was fifty-four years of age ; a print of it is prefixed to the copy of his 'Farewell Sermons' preserved in the Bodleian Library, and there is another copy in the British Museum. His character may almost be gathered from what we have seen of his life and works; and it should be added that he was not only of good natural abilities, but also no mean scholar. His kinsman, Lord Lansdowne, may have drawn a some-what too eulogistic account of the Dean ; but, over-shadowed as his fame undoubtedly is by the greater names of his ancestors, Sir Richard and Sir Bevill, it should never be forgotten that he was an ener-getic reformer, in very difficult times, of the Church and the clergy ;—though, as he says, ' *his* religion and loyalty were not of the new cutt, but of the old royall stamp ;'—yet he was the friend of such men as Beveridge and Comber—and, above all, it should be remembered that, whatever we may think of his judgment, he undoubtedly performed that rare act of moral heroism, the sacrifice of his dignities and honours, his ample revenues, all the comforts of his native land, and, in fact, all his worldly interests, to his *conscience*.

Well might it have been said of Dennis Grenville that his

> ' Loyalty was still the same
> Whether it won or lost the game ;
> True as the dial to the sun,
> Altho' it be not shone upon ;'

and truly might he have exclaimed, whilst in exile
and poverty paying the penalty of his loyal attachment to the House of Stuart, in the words of one
of the Roxburgh Ballads :

> ' Then hang up sorrow and care,
> It never shall make me rue ;
> What though my back goes bare ?
> I'm ragged and torn and TRUE.'

He wrote to his elder brother—the Earl of Bath
—a reproachful letter, in November, 1689, wherein
he says, evidently hoping against hope, that
nothing 'shall convince him that it is possible for
one descended from his dear loyall father Sir Bevill
Grenville to dye a rebell ;' but I confess that the
sentiment of Dean Grenville's which I prefer
treasuring in my own memory, is the noble
and tolerant one with which he concludes his
'Third Speech' to his clergy :

' My fourth and last counsell is, to be just to all
men, both to the Romanist and Dissenter. That
your aversion to the doctrine of any party (tho'
never soe contrary to your owne) should not, in any
manner, exceed youer love and concerne for the
Religion you profess.'*

To one more only of the Grenvilles does it seem
necessary to refer, as with him the connexion of

---

* A Mr. Beaumont, a Durham clergyman, is believed to have
written a ' Narrative of the Life of Dean Grenville.'

that illustrious family with Cornwall ceases: viz., to George Baron Lansdowne, the poet, who was a nephew of the Dean and a grandson of Sir Bevill. His father's as well as his brother's name was Bernard. It is true that he did not live at Stow, which, as we have seen, was no longer the family mansion; but he comes within our scope: for, in a defence of his grand-uncle, Sir Richard ('Skellum') against some anonymous author who took the side of the Parliament, I find him writing thus: ' *Like an old staunch Cornishman* I tell you that we, who had before beaten two of your generals into the sea, might as well have beaten the third :' and again, in a letter, in 1718, to his 'dearest niece,' Mrs. Delany, he calls Cornwall 'his country.'

He was entered at Trinity College, Cambridge, in 1667, and was about the Court of James II., much smitten, it was said, with the charms of his Queen, Mary of Modena—the Myra, in all probability, of some of his amatory lines. He wrote both poems and plays, many passages in which are of a somewhat licentious character: amongst the plays are the 'British Enchanters' (for which Addison wrote the Epilogue); the 'She Gallants, or once a Lover always a Lover;' and the 'Jew of Venice,' imitated from Shakespeare. He was Member of Parliament successively for Fowey, Lostwithiel, Helston, and finally for the county of Cornwall itself; and was at length made by Queen Anne a Privy Councillor, and Treasurer of the Household, but, on some silly suspicion of plotting against the Government, was, in 1715, committed to the Tower, from which place of confinement, however, he was shortly released. In 1722, his affairs becoming embarrassed through his somewhat extravagant mode of life, he went abroad to retrench his expenses; and, returning to England, died at his house in Hanover Square on the 30th January, 1735. He had married the widow of Thomas Thynne,* and was celebrated for his tender devotion to his family.

A curious story about his remains is told in Lady Llanover's 'Life of Mrs. Delany.' No tomb or tablet of any kind marks (in St. Clement Danes Church) the site of their sepulchre; and when inquiries on this point were made in 1859, it was found that a short time previous to that date an order to close a vault under the Church had been put in force. The coffins in the vault were placed in the centre of the chamber, a quantity of quicklime was thrown in, and the whole then filled with rubbish. There were two bodies in the vault which had always been called 'My Lord and my Lady,' and which were in extraordinary preservation. They were not skeletons, although the skin was much dried, and they were very light; they were set upright against the wall, and it had always been the custom whenever a new clerk was appointed, to take him down into the vault and introduce him to 'My Lord and my Lady.' It seems not at all improbable that these were the corpses of Lord and Lady Lansdowne; and that their remarkable preservation was due to their having been embalmed. Lord Lansdowne's portrait may be seen in the 'Life of Mrs. Delany,' vol. i., p. 418. She says of him:

* Many of the Grenville portraits are in the possession of this family.

'No man had more the art of winning the affections where he wished to oblige . . . he was magnificent in his nature, and valued no expense that would gratify it, which in the end hurt him and his family extremely.'

Of his character, as a man and as a poet, Anderson thus writes in his ' Poets of Great Britain :'

'The character of Granville seems to have been amiable and respectable. His good nature and politeness have been celebrated by Pope, and many other poets of the first eminence. The lustre of his rank no doubt procured him more incense than the force of his genius would otherwise have attracted; but he appears not to have been destitute of fine parts, which were, however, rather elegantly polished than great in themselves.

' There is perhaps nothing more interesting in his character than the veneration he had for some, and the tenderness he had for all of his family. Of the former his historical performances afford some pleasing proof; of the latter, there are extant two letters, one to his cousin, the last Earl of Bath, and the other to his cousin, Mr. Bevil Granville, on his entering into holy orders, written with a tenderness, a freedom, and an honesty which render them invaluable.

' The general character of his poetry is·elegance, sprightliness and dignity. He is seldom tender, and very rarely sublime. In his smaller pieces he endeavours to be gay, in his larger to be great. Of his airy and light productions the chief source is gallantry, and the chief defect a superabundance of sentiment and illustrations from mythology. He seldom fetches an amorous sentiment from the depth of science. His thoughts are such as a liberal conversation and large acquaintance with life would easily supply. His diction is chaste and elegant, and his versification, which he borrowed from Waller, is rather smooth than strong.

'Mr. Granville,' says Dr. Felton, 'is the poetical son of Waller. We observe with pleasure, similitude of wit in the difference of years, and with Granville do meet at once the fire of his father's youth, and judgment of his age. He hath rivalled him in his finest address, and is as happy as ever he was in raising modern compliments upon ancient story, and setting off the British valour and the English beauty with the old gods and goddesses !'

'Granville,' says Lord Orford, 'imitated Waller, but as that poet has been much excelled since, a faint copy of a faint master must strike still less.'

The estimate of his poetical character, given by Dr. Johnson, is, in some respects, less favourable :

'Granville,' says the Doctor, 'was a man illustrious by his birth, and therefore attracted notice ; since he is by Pope styled " the polite," he must be supposed elegant in his manner, and generally loved ; he was in times of contest and turbulence steady to his party, and obtained that esteem which is always conferred upon firmness and consistency. With these advantages, having learned the art of versifying, he declared himself a poet, and his claim to the laurel was allowed.'

Pope, in a courtier-like passage in his 'Windsor

Forest '—a poem which he dedicated to Lord Granville—says of him :

> ' Here his first lays majestic Denham sung ;
> Here the last numbers flowed from Cowley's tongue.
>   *   *   *   *   *   *
> Since fate relentless stopped their heavenly voice
> No more the forest rings, or groves rejoice ;
> Who now shall charm the shades where Cowley strung
> His living harp, and lofty Denham sung?
> But hark ! the groves rejoice, the forest rings—
> Are these reviv'd ? or is it GRANVILLE sings ?'.

adding,

> ' The thoughts of gods let GRANVILLE's verse recite,
> And bring the scenes of opening fate to light.'

With one more extract from the praises of his contemporaries, and this the weightiest and most poetic of them all, we will conclude.

Dryden said of him—àpropos of his tragedy of ' Heroick Love '—

> ' Auspicious poet, wert thou not my friend,
> How could I envy what I must commend ?
> But since 'tis Nature's law, in love and wit,
> That youth should reign, and with'ring age submit ;
> With less regret these laurels I resign,
> Which, dying on my brow, revive on thine.'

INCLEDON,

THE SINGER.

INCLEDON,

THE SINGER.

'The British National Singer.'

HIS MAJESTY KING GEORGE III.

N artist might have a worse subject for a picture than the interview to which we are about to refer. The Vicar of Manaccan, the Rev. Richard Polwhele, of Polwhele, ever busy in gathering information about Cornwall and Cornishmen, one day near the beginning of the present century, rides over to the quaint and pretty little fishing-cove of Coverack, near the Lizard, to have a chat with old Mrs. Loveday Incledon, the mother of the ' rantin' roarin' blade ' (the youngest, I fancy, of a somewhat numerous family) who forms the subject of this memoir. Polwhele probably passed through the quiet little village of St. Keverne (with—that unusual sight in Cornwall—a tall *spire* and a large church), where our hero was born. Reaching Coverack, the worthy Vicar doubtless opened the siege in due form, and with regular approaches, to the old lady ; but all his skill and blandishments were in vain. She would tell him plenty about the rebellion of '45, and repeat many

scraps of old ballads referring to it; but not one word would she say about her *son*, then in the meridian of his fame. It was, however, probably she who told Polwhele that all the Incledons were musical, and that her boy Benjamin's aunt was cele- brated for her rendering of ' Black-eyed Susan ;'— but in the end the Vicar had to remount his nag, and return to his snug Vicarage of Manaccan, not much wiser than when he left it in the morning.

Whether Incledon's mother's reticence was due to old age, or to the almost invariable reluctance of elderly people in the country to discuss family affairs with '*strangers*,' it would be hard to say; but it could scarcely be because the mention of her son's name and career gave her pain ; for in her declining years he was the main source of her support till she died, after her husband, in 1808, eighty-one years of age. Incledon's father was a member of the medical pro- fession, but probably not entitled to be described, as he was in some of the books of the day, as 'a respectable *physician*.' There is, however, a cosy little inn at St. Keverne, and on one of the stone posts of the back-door I have seen, deeply cut, the letters ' MICHAEL INCLEDON.' This would seem to give us perhaps the only clue now left to the home, during his boyhood, of the finest English singer of his day.

Cornwall has always been celebrated for the rich quality of its bass voices, but is not remarkable for the number or excellence of those of the tenor register. Incledon may almost be said to have possessed both; for, in his prime, his natural voice ranged from A to G (fourteen notes), and his singularly sweet and powerful falsetto from D to E or F (ten notes). It is not difficult to ·understand that, even more than a hundred years ago, the fame of a fine voice might travel eastward as far as Exeter Cathedral, where Jackson, whose once popular ' Te Deum ' and many pleasing ballads and duets are familiar to most of us, then held the post of organist ; and accordingly, under him was little Incledon placed about the year 1772, when eight years old. His voice delighted everybody, and he became 'a little idol.'

Bernard, who wrote the ' Theatrical Retrospections,' made Incledon's acquaintance whilst he was under Dr. Jackson's care, and says he did not at that time perceive anything remarkable in his voice or style. The boy was then a tall, lanky lad of fifteen, chiefly noticeable for his ' courage, gratefulness, and love of the water '—in fact, adds Bernard, more Newfoundland dog than boy. A gentleman of Exeter offered a money reward to any lad who would swim out to a certain moored boat, with a rope on his shoulders, and swim back with it again. The task, however, baffled all the Exeter boys, till young Incledon made the attempt, and, when he had earned the prize, handed the money immediately to a poor widow who had been kind to him. Bernard seems to have been a good friend of Incledon's through life; and Davy, the composer, whose acquaintance was also made about this time, was another. He, too, was a Cornishman, according to some writers,* and was Incledon's ' coach ' when

* He was, however, christened on Christmas Day, 1763, at Upton-Helions, near Crediton, Devon.

any new part or song had to be prepared. It was through Bernard that Incledon got his first start in life, at Bath, to which event reference will shortly be made.

But Incledon has not yet left Exeter (although it is not altogether improbable that he had already attempted* to do so), and here he continued his duties as chorister for awhile. It is said that when Judge Nares attended service at Exeter Cathedral, he was so entranced by the boy Incledon's singing 'Let the Soul live,' that he burst into tears, and at the end of the service sent the little fellow a present of five guineas. After having failed altogether to trace this piece of music, I am indebted to my friend, Mr. W. H. Cummings, the eminent tenor, and the biographer of Purcell, for the suggestion that it is probably part of one of Jackson's unpublished anthems.

Either the imposed restraint, and the punctuality and decorum of the Cathedral services, were too much for him, or (according to another suggestion) he was witness of some Cathedral scandal which it was thought desirable to keep quiet; at any rate, when about fifteen years old, Master Incledon at length successfully broke his fetters, and went as a sailor in his Majesty's navy, on board the *Formidable*, Captain Cleland, with whom he sailed to the West Indies. There he afterwards changed his ship,

---

* When he first ran away to Plymouth, to go to sea, it was with a fellow-chorister—all their property 'tied up in a blue and white pocket-handkerchief;' but on this occasion they were overtaken at Ivy Bridge, and brought back to Exeter.

and joined the *Raisonnable.* He remained in the navy for about four years, and was present in more than one action; notably, whilst on board the *Formidable* of 90 guns, in the famous fight of 12th April, 1782, between Lord Rodney (then Sir Geo. Brydges Rodney) and the French Admiral, Comte de Grasse, in the West Indian Archipelago,—when, after a fight which lasted the livelong day, and during which 9,000 French and Spaniards were killed and wounded, the British victory saved Jamaica from the enemy, and revived the then drooping fortunes of England.

Incledon seems to have made himself a great favourite amongst all classes on board the fleet, who were not only delighted by his magnificent singing, but also welcomed a boon companion. Admirals Pigot and Hughes were almost always singing glees and catches with the lad. The atmosphere must have been very congenial to him; and it was probably during this period of his life that he not only contracted the low tastes and hard-drinking habits which disfigured his career, yet, doubtless, he also now acquired that sea-faring style which enabled him to sing ' The Storm,'* ' Cease, rude Boreas! blustering railer,' etc., in such a way as they have never been sung before or since,

> ' In notes with many a winding bout
> Of linkèd sweetness long drawn out
> With wanton heed and giddy cunning,
> The melting voice through mazes running.'

---

* There is an engraved portrait of him, in which he is represented as singing this song.

Admiral Lord Hervey became one of his chief patrons; and, in conjunction with Lord Mulgrave, Admiral Pigot, and others, on Incledon's return to England in 1783, these officers introduced him to Sheridan and to Colman—'the modern Terence,' as the latter was called—with a view to Incledon's appearing on the stage. It was not usual in those days for managers to fail to carry out the wishes of noble and influential patrons; but neither Sheridan nor Colman, whose practised eyes probably at once discovered that Incledon was no actor,—nor ever likely to make one—that his pronunciation was coarse, and that moreover his face and figure were somewhat sailor-like and ungainly,—could be prevailed upon to give the aspirant for histrionic honours, then in his nineteenth year, even a *trial*.

Not to be balked, however, in his intentions, our hero proceeded to Southampton, where Collins's itinerant dramatic company was then performing; and here he made his *début* as Alfonso in 'The Castle of Andalusia,' with what result I have been unable to discover, though it would be interesting to learn; his salary (very acceptable, small as it was) was only some ten or fifteen shillings a week. He remained with this company for about a year, travelling with them to Winchester, and thence on foot to Bath, where he arrived 'with his last shilling in his pocket.' At Bath his great musical talents seem first to have been recognised—yet even there tardily, as he was for a long time engaged merely as a chorus singer, and was still miserably paid accordingly; though his salary was now raised to thirty

shillings a week.   His first appearance as a soloist is
said to have been as Edwin, in ' Robin Hood.'

But one night Incledon had to sing a song ' between the acts'—an old practice, now fallen into dis-
use, but then prevalent at many theatres, and which
afforded amusement to the audience whilst the
cumbrous scenes were being slowly shifted by
few and clumsy hands.   One of the audience
happened to be Rauzzini, an Italian singer and
teacher at the fashionable watering-place ; and he
(notwithstanding his usual contempt for English
singers) instantly detected the exceptional range
and quality of Incledon's voice.   He is said to have
rushed behind the scenes, exclaiming : ' Incledon !
Sare ! I tank you for the pleasure you af give me :
you vas de fus Engleesh singer I have hear vat can
sing.   Sare ! you af got a voice—you af got a voice !'
On another occasion, Incledon, at the conclusion of
one of his ballads, made a roulade in a way altogether his own—rolling his voice grandly up like the
surge of the sea, till, touching the top note, it died
away in sweetness—causing Rauzzini to ejaculate :
' Coot Cot ! it vas vere lucky dere vas some roof dere,
or dat fellow vould be hear by de ainshels in hev'n.'
Rauzzini at once became his friend ; and, for six
or seven years, his instructor ; and Incledon, who
now joined the ' Noblemen's and Gentlemen's Glee
Club,' was at length on the high-road to success.

The London stage was, however, still the object of
his ambition ; and in the summers of 1786 to 1789, he at
length succeeded in procuring engagements at Vauxhall Gardens, which resulted in a great triumph.   His

singing of 'The Lass of Richmond Hill' was, especially, so popular, that copies of the song were sold at one shilling each, instead of the usual sixpence. Still, Vauxhall was not 'the stage;' and, indeed, the regular actors looked down upon the Vauxhall performers as being artists of an inferior rank, so that poor Incledon's engagement there rather retarded than hastened the gratification of his wishes. At length actors' jealousies and managers' reluctance all had to give way to the sheer force of Incledon's unsurpassable voice and growing fame; and on the 20th January, 1790,* he made his *début* at Covent Garden in the character of Dermot in 'The Poor Soldier.' His engagement was for three years, at £6, £7, and £8 a week. The applause with which he was received was general and sincere; his success was assured; and he became, from his rollicking, generous, sailor-like disposition, a favourite, both before and behind the scenes. He was always either playing off practical jokes upon others, or becoming the butt of them himself; and the latter was notably the case whenever Incledon was about to take his 'benefit.' On these occasions he was always very anxious about his success, and so credulous, that he believed all that the theatrical wags told him. Inquiring on one occasion as to how the list of his patrons was progressing, he was informed that 'the Marquis of Piccadilly' had just taken some tickets, and that 'the Duke of Windsor' had written for a

* Other authorities say October, but I have followed Parkes in the above dates; and this is a point on which he ought to have been accurate.

box. 'Ah!' says Incledon, 'he must be one of the
Royal Family, I suppose.' He was further delighted
—or seemed to be so—when he was told that ' Lord
Highgate' and the ' Bishop of Gravesend' were also
coming.

But the author of the ' Records of a Stage
Veteran' asserts that Incledon was not so silly or
unlearned as he pretended to be, and could give a
Roland (often coarse enough) for an Oliver. When
some of the poorer actresses, relying upon his open-
handed generosity, used to besiege him in the cold
weather for donations to purchase flannel, they
always got some money from him; but they not
unfrequently repaired forthwith to the ' Brown
Bear,' and invested it in egg-flip, which in consequence, it is said, soon came to bear the *alias* of
' flannel' in the green-room. When Incledon found
this out, he took his revenge by sprinkling some
' flannel' with ipecacuanha, and so saved his pocket
from similar forays for the future. In 1804, he joined
the Duke of Cumberland's sharp-shooters; but, being
so fat, the story goes that he and Cooke were
generally last of the skirmishers. On one occasion
he gave a butcher-boy a shilling to carry his gun
for him, and, on another, a shilling to a little girl to
carry his sword, which was always getting between
his legs; and he thus appeared with his two young
subalterns on parade.

On the 26th February, 1791, Shield's operetta of
' The Woodman' was brought out at Covent Garden;
and Incledon, now earning a salary of £16 a week,
or £2 more than was then paid to any other English

singer, enraptured all his hearers by the way in which he sang 'The Streamlet.' 'The Cabinet,' in which operetta he sang during the winter of 1804, with Braham and Storace, was also, like 'The English Fleet,' highly popular with the public; but Incledon's favourite part was Captain Macheath in the 'Beggar's Opera'—to play which he used to say he would always willingly get up in the middle of the night. And here it may be observed, that Braham gradually delegated to Incledon most of his younger *rôles ;* but Dibdin tells us that, as Incledon's fame advanced, he had to be very cautious, in writing for the stage, to allot equally prominent parts to Incledon and to Braham. 'If one had a ballad, the other was also to have one; each a martial or a hunting song ; each a bravura ; and if they were to have a duet, each one was to lead alternately.' As an illustration of the relations which existed between the singer and the librettist, I may quote a letter which, about the year 1807, Incledon wrote to Dibdin from Norwich :

'DEAR TOM,

'You have on many occasions expressed a wish to serve me: you have it now in your power. I am much distressed for two comic songs for my new entertainment : one to be sung by an Irishman, and I should wish it complimentary to that country; the other to be sung by a funny tailor. Mr. Horn, a very clever young man now with me, will set them. We opened here on Saturday—receipts £103 ; and I expect nearly as much this night. I shall be at

Bury St. Edmund's on Saturday and Sunday next: if you can let me have them by that time, I shall be greatly obliged to you; if not, I shall be at Lynn on the following Wednesday. With best compliments to Mrs. Dibdin,

'I am, dear Tom,

' Your friend,

' C. INCLEDON.

' P.S. D—n such paper.'

Incledon seems to have been at this time devotedly attached to his profession, and was perfectly furious when hoarseness or any other form of illness prevented his appearing in public. He was now in the zenith of his fame, and a musical critic of the period has thus described his voice and style :

' His natural voice was full and open, neither partaking of the reed nor the string, and was sent forth without the smallest artifice; such was its ductility, that when he sang pianissimo, it retained its original quality. His falsetto was rich and brilliant, but totally unlike the other. He took it without preparation, according to circumstances, either about D, E, or F; or, ascending an octave, which was his most frequent custom, he could use it with facility, and execute in it ornaments of a certain class with volubility and sweetness. His shake was good, and his intonation much more correct than is common to singers so imperfectly educated. His pronunciation of words, however, was thick, coarse, and vulgar. His forte was ballad; and ballad not of the modern cast of whining or rant or sentiment, but the original, manly, energetic strain of an earlier and better age of English poesy and English song-writing : such as "Black-eyed Susan," and "The Storm," the bold and cheering hunting-song, or the love-song of Shield, breathing the chaste, simple grace of genuine English melody.'

Nearly all accounts agree in saying that (notwithstanding Incledon's own very decided opinion to the contrary) he was no *actor*. Not even his friend and biographer Parkes, the oboe-player, who, with Shield the composer, lived much with Incledon, would allow him to have possessed *this* merit. Indeed, the story is told that when Incledon was on one occasion enraged at hearing that, on the performance of one of the oratorios at a certain cathedral, the bishop had determined that neither Incledon nor any other *actor* should sing in such a place, and on such an occasion, Bannister said to our hero, with mock seriousness, 'Incledon, if I were you I should make him *prove his words*.' Notwithstanding, however, Incledon's obtuseness on some points, he must have possessed a fund of genuine humour, as the following anecdote will show : When he and the elder Mathews (who, by the way, was singularly successful in imitating his friend, notwithstanding their great difference in person) were once playing together at Leicester, Incledon was much in want of a drab suit in which to appear in the character of 'Steady,' a Quaker ; so, seeing a portly member of the Society of Friends, a druggist, standing at his shop-door, Incledon entered, consumed some quack medicine or other, and laid his hard case before the Quaker. This he did with such admirable tact that he actually succeeded in persuading the good-natured druggist not only to lend him the desired clothes, but also to appear secretly (against his convictions, of course) at the performance. Truth, however, compels me to add that the roguish songster's success was partly due to his unblushing statement that he and his family were themselves formerly Quakers !

Incledon used also, during Lent, to appear in oratorio, though apparently not with so much success as in performances of secular music. He was not so vain of his own voice as not to be very fond of concerted vocal music. His singing of ' All's Well ' with Braham may perhaps be remembered by a few who are still alive ; but probably all those who heard Incledon at the old ' Glee Club,' singing with Shield, Johnstone, Bannister the elder, Dignum, C. Ashley, and Parkes, have ' gone over to the majority.' The jolly fellows used to meet every alternate Sunday night at the Garrick's Head Coffee House, in Bow Street.*

He retired from Covent Garden in 1815—when he took a parting benefit at the Italian Opera House ; but, like so many other public favourites, he made several ' last appearances ' on the boards : one of the really last ones being at Southampton, where he commenced his career as a singer.

During the summer months, when the theatre

---

* For minuter details of the singer's professional career, an article entitled ' Leaves from a Manager's Note-Book,' in the *New Monthly Magazine*, for 1838, may be advantageously consulted.

was closed, and, indeed, during most of the latter
part of his career, it was Incledon's practice to visit
the provinces, giving entertainments, one of which
he called ' Variety,' and the other ' The Wandering
Melodist,' very much after the style of Dibdin's; and
for the nonce styling himself also ' The Wandering
Melodist.'   It will be readily understood that these
performances were highly appreciated in the days
when locomotion was so much more difficult than it
is nowadays, and when to have ' been to London '
was the exception rather than the rule.   It was
probably on one of these occasions that H. C. Robinson fell in with him, on the top of a coach, and thus
records his impressions, in his diary of 4th April,
1811. After noting that Incledon was just the man
he expected to find him, with seven rings on his
fingers, five seals on his watch-ribbon, and a gold
snuff-box in his pocket, Robinson goes on to say:

' I spoke in terms of rapture of Mrs. Siddons.
He replied, " Ah ! Sally's a fine creature.   She has
a charming place on the Edgware Road.   I dined
with her last year, and she paid me one of the finest
compliments I ever received.   I sang " The Storm "
after dinner.   She cried and sobbed like a child.
Taking both my hands, she said. " All that I and my
brother ever did, is nothing compared with the effect
you produce !"   Incledon spoke with warmth, and
apparent knowledge, of Church music, praising
Purcell especially, and mentioning Luther's simple
hymns.   I was forced to confess that *I* had no ear
for music ; and he, in order to try me, sang in a sort

of song-whisper some melodies, which I certainly enjoyed more, I thought, than anything I had heard from him on the stage.'

But in order to show that Incledon did not himself exaggerate the effect which the fire of his manner and the sweetness of his singing sometimes produced, let the following story testify. William Robson, in the ' Old Playgoer,' says :

' I remember when the *élite* of taste, science, and literature were assembled to pay the well-deserved compliment of a dinner to John Kemble, and to present him with a handsome piece of plate on his retirement. Incledon, on being requested, sang, as his best song— on what he, I am sure, considered a great, though melancholy event—" The Storm." The effect was sublime, the silence holy, the feeling intense ; and, while Talma was recovering from his astonishment, Kemble placed his hand on the arm of the great French actor, and said in an agitated, emphatic, yet proud tone, " *That* is an English singer." ' Munden adds that Talma jumped up from his seat, and embraced Incledon *à la Française.*

A list of his favourite songs at these entertainments, preserved at the British Museum, may not be unacceptable, as showing the musical tastes of the day ; some of them are still sung occasionally, but most are long since forgotten. The songs in the ' Variety ' entertainment, which was in three acts, were an introductory recitation and song entitled ' Variety ;' ' The Thorn ;' ' Jack Junk ;' ' The Glasses Sparkle on the Board ;' ' Black-eyed

Susan ;' ' The Post Captain ;' ' Charming Kitty ;'
' The Irish Phantasmagoria ;' ' The Captive to his
Bird ;' ' The Storm ;' ' Inconstant Sue ;' ' Irish Hunting-song ;' A new loyal and national song ; ' The Maid
with the Bosom of Snow ;' and, for a finale, ' Loud
let the merry, merry welkin sound.'

' The Wandering Melodist' comprised : ' The
Married Man ;' ' Patrick O'Stern ;' ' The Farmer's
Treasure ;' ' Mr. Mullins and Miss Whack ;' ' Mad
Tom ;' ' The Despairing Damsel ;' ' The Sea-Boy on
the Giddy Mast' (which, by the way, must have
reminded him of old times) ; ' Fortune's Wheel ;'
' Tom Moody ;' ' The Siege ;' ' Sally Roy ;' ' Mariner's
Compass ;' ' Hail to the Beam of Morning ;' ' The
Italian Count and English Captain ;' ' The Finale ; or
The Rose, Shamrock, and Thistle.'

Incledon's last benefit at Drury Lane—when Ellis-
ton engaged him in 1820, at £15 a week—is said to
have brought him £1,000 ; but, as we have seen,
towards the latter part of his career he did not often
appear in London, and on 8th October, 1824, he
sang, for the last time in public, at Southampton.
His voice was observed to falter as he sang the final
verse of ' Then Farewell my trim-built Wherry ;' and
he thus took leave of his audience :

' Ladies and Gentlemen,—It is with the sincerest
feelings of gratitude that I acknowledge this evening
the distinguished favour you have ever conferred upon
me. In this town, and on these boards, I first
appeared as a singer ; and the encouragement I then
received from you was, I may say, the passport to

my fame. Since that time I have passed through many vicissitudes. I have served His Majesty in many engagements : there is not a ship in the navy, nor many towns in the country, that I have not sung in ; but still your early liberality has never been effaced from my memory. It is now six years ago since I left the stage, but it has always been my wish to appear once more before you. Age, sickness, and infirmities have altered me much from what I once was, but I have always done my best to please; and, I repeat it, while I live I shall never forget the kindly support I have received from the inhabitants of Southampton.'

Another authority (Donaldson) adds that on this occasion Incledon also referred to his darling wives, saying : ' I have had three—the first was the sainted Jane [Miss Lowther, of Bath]; the second the angel Mary [Miss Howell, of Bath—she died May, 1811]; and the third, still living, is the divine Martha.'*

It will be seen that each of the entertainments referred to above consisted of fifteen songs, and must have taxed the singer's powers severely. I was a little surprised at not finding either ' The Heaving of the Lead,' or ' My bonny, bonny Bet, sweet Blossom,' on either list ; for the latter especially was a great favourite, and Incledon always had to sing it twice, often three times ; but probably this was the very reason why he omitted it from these programmes.

I have not been able to put my hand upon more than one example of his talents as a composer,

---

* His third wife's name has not been traced by me.

namely, a song called 'Soft as the Morning's blush-
ing Hue,' which he used to sing in 'Family Quarrels'
(but Shield used to say that Incledon generally
managed to improve *his* composition). The song
mentioned above is a rather pretty, flowing melody,
eminently adapted to the remarkable compass and
flexibility of Incledon's voice; there is a copy of it at
the British Museum, with the initials 'C.I.,' in faded
ink, sprawling over the first page. And here it may
be well to observe that having added 'Charles' to
his Christian name Benjamin, he at length dropped
the latter name altogether.

Incledon did not confine his musical experiences
to England; but occasionally made trips to Ireland,
where 'no singer was ever more caressed.'

R. W. Procter, in his 'Manchester in Holiday
Dress,' says: When Incledon was returning home
from Dublin, on one occasion, the vessel in which he
embarked was upset in passing the bar. Several of the
passengers were drowned, but the singer saved himself by climbing, in sailor fashion, to the round top,
with his wife lashed to him; Incledon all the while
uttering a strange mixture of oaths, prayers, and
confessions. They remained in that perilous position
for several hours, until rescued by some fishermen.'

Once, towards the close of his career, when his
powers, enfeebled by his careless manner of life, were
on the wane, he even ventured across the Atlantic.
In America, however (notwithstanding that a writer
in the *New Monthly Magazine*, for 1838, asserts that
he made £5,000 by this trip), he is said to have been
a failure; though Incledon himself would insist upon

it, to the last, that his want of success there was merely an example of the caprice of the public.

On his return to England he went to Brighton, where, by a slight attack of paralysis, he received his first warning that his career was nearly closed. The 11th of February, 1826, found him, now sixty-four years old, at Worcester, organizing one of his entertainments. Here he attended a meeting of a local glee-club, but declined, for some reason, to take his part in the music. At his inn, however, 'The Reindeer,' he did sing in the kitchen*—to gratify the servants—his last song :

> 'Then farewell, my trim-built wherry !
> Coat, and oars, and badge, farewell !'

and a few nights afterwards, on the 19th February, he bade farewell to a world which had often hung upon his lips for the sweetest and manliest strains that any English singer had ever warbled forth. 'The hunting-song, the sea-song, and the ballad,' observes C. R. Leslie, in his autobiography, ' may be said to have expired with Incledon.'

All contemporary accounts agree as to his vocal merits. Parkes says that in twenty-four years he never knew Incledon sing out of tune : indeed, it has been observed that he *could* not have done so if he had tried, for whilst his ear was marvellously accurate, his knowledge of music was slight. Parkes

---

* The kitchen seems always to have had attractions for poor Incledon. One night, whilst at a friend's house, he was missed for a time, but was at length discovered helping the servants to ' pick parsley ' for supper. Another of his peculiarities was a fondness for all sorts of quack medicines, and cough-drops, lozenges, and the like, of which he never failed to carry a large assortment in his pocket.

speaks of his friend's memory being quick and retentive, for melodies ; but Incledon seems to have had
the greatest difficulty in recollecting any ' part ;' and
more than once, when he had forgotten it, he has
been known to give an impromptu turn to the dialogue in order to introduce some ballad appropriate
to the occasion, whilst cudgelling his brains for the
lost ' cue.'

The few glimpses we have had of his private
character do not prepare us to expect much ele-
gance or refinement in Incledon, off or on the stage.
Indeed, it must be confessed that he was vain,
coarse, irritable at times, and dissipated ; but he had
the redeeming traits of frankness and generosity ;
and allowances must be made for his having lived in
' three-bottle ' days. Cyrus Redding tells an amusing
story of Incledon's having been invited to a dinner
at ' The Pope's Head ' Inn, Plymouth, in order that he
might be induced to entertain the company afterwards. The wine of course circulated freely, and
Incledon, as was his wont, freely partook of it. He
attempted a recitation of the lines from ' Samson
Agonistes,' beginning ' Total eclipse !' but the good
cheer had proved too much for his wits, his head
sank upon his shoulders, and he became for a time
totally eclipsed himself :—he had been ' dining out '
daily, for a week before. It was, however (though
he drank hard), very rarely that he succumbed like
this. And Fitz Ball (Edward Ball)—who, by the
way, mentions that latterly Incledon got very fat—
tells a story which may be fitly inserted here. Being

once at Bury St. Edmund's, whilst some military ball was going on, Incledon, well in his cups, said something to a young officer about 'feather-bed captains,' which the military hero chose to regard as a personal affront, and accordingly, accompanied by some friends (so the story goes), besieged Incledon's room the next morning, and demanded satisfaction. In the first place, there was great difficulty about waking the singer from his deep, vinous slumbers; and when at last he did awake, he was quite at a loss to know why his privacy had been invaded. On learning, however, that 'satisfaction' was what was wanted, he sat up in bed and sang, in his most exquisite manner, ' Black-eyed Susan,' so that there was at last not a dry eye in the room. When he had finished, 'There, my fine fellow!' said Incledon blandly, '*that* has satisfied thousands—let it *satisfy* you ;' and, putting out his hand, it was as generously taken as it was offered.

Some accounts give Incledon three wives, others two ; but those who are at all acquainted with the history of the stage, seventy or eighty years ago, will admit that this is a point upon which Incledon himself might possibly not have been very clear. There was one ' Mrs. Incledon,' however, who, like the songster himself, was very fond of good living ; and there is a story that once, when Incledon was entertaining at dinner, at his house, No. 13, Brompton Crescent, his friend and medical adviser, Dr. Moseley of Chelsea Hospital, and two or three others, the dish of fish was artfully so arranged that

a fine dory (to which the host and hostess were both
very partial) was completely overlaid by herrings;
and it was not until the guests had all been helped
to the humbler fish, that the gourmands' favourite
was—as if by accident—discovered. On this memorable occasion we hear that 'pink *and* white cham-
pagne' were handed round; that on its production,
the trio 'Beviamo tutte tre' was sung by Shield,
Parkes, and Incledon, with appropriate action; and
that, when the conversation turned upon the sort of
deaths which the Chelsea veterans died, Incledon,
delighted with Dr. Moseley's satisfactory account of
them, got up and persuaded all who were present to
join in singing Dr. Callcott's noble glee, ' Peace to the
Souls of the Heroes !'

Incledon, though he made plenty of money, was
often pecuniarily embarrassed, owing no doubt to
that 'lax and sailor-like twist of mind' which, as
Leigh Hunt says, always hung about him.   An
instance of this occurs in a letter preserved among
the Egerton MSS., in which Incledon, writing to the
magniloquent George Robins, from Ipswich, in
February, 1816, tells how he had been arrested a few
days before, at Colchester, for £19, by a Mr. Marriot
of Fleet Street, for the balance of a bill of over
£100. The singer had recently taken a house, and
had been put to great expense in furnishing it; and
his object in writing to Robins was to get him to
contradict, in London, the report that 'Incledon
was about to fly from the kingdom.'   He adds that
he was then going on to Norwich, Aberdeen, Edin-

burgh, and Dublin, and finishes by saying that his wife was with him, and that his being 'arrested has given my Poor Little Woman so great a Shock that she will not soon get over. She is now very Ill, and continually in Tears.' He nevertheless was supposed* to have been worth £8,000 when he died, leaving this third wife a widow with three children. He was buried in Hampstead churchyard, on the 20th February, 1826, aged sixty-four, by the side of his first and second wives, and five of their children.

So lived and so died Charley Incledon—'generous as a prince,' as Charles Mathews wrote of him, 'never ashamed of his antecedents;' and as Dowton says,

> 'Unrivalled in his native minstrelsy.'

One of his sons, Charles, who had been unsuccessful as a farmer near Bury St. Edmund's, attempted, under Braham's auspices, to succeed as a singer: he made his *début* either as Hawthorn in 'Love in a Village,' or as Young Meadows, at Covent Garden, on the 3rd October, 1829; but in this attempt, too, the poor fellow (who had a large family, and who had, moreover, a strong objection to the stage on moral and religious grounds) failed. Another son, Frank, became a well-to-do London tradesman; and a daughter married well, and settled in Sunderland.

* 'Era Almanac,' 1870.

THE KILLIGREWS;

DIPLOMATISTS, WARRIORS, COURTIERS, AND POETS.

THE KILLIGREWS;

DIPLOMATISTS, WARRIORS, COURTIERS, AND POETS.

'Fuimus.'

 LITTLE ploughed field in the parish of St. Erme, about five miles north of Truro, on a farm still called Killigrew, is the site of the old residence of this distinguished family. Their place knows them no more; and even their own name is, with the sole exception just referred to, and in one or two instances where it appears as a Christian name of some of their remote descendants, 'clean blotted out.' Yet it was once—as the old Cornish word implies—'a grove of eagles'; for we shall find that their race soared high, and produced examples of each of the distinguished classes noted above; and that their memory is worthy of their tombs in Westminster Abbey, and of a local monument—the pyramid which one who married into the family and assumed the name, in the latter part of the seventeenth century, erected at Falmouth in 1737-38.*

* This monument was originally placed on a site which overlooked on the one hand the remains of the family mansion, and on the other

33—2

There is some reason to believe that the family was of royal descent. The first of the name whom I have been able to trace, is one Ralph Killigrew, said to have been a natural son of Richard, Earl of Cornwall, and King of the Romans, by his concubine Joan de Valletort. Hence, so it is said, the double-headed spread eagle and the ' border bezanty ' of the family arms.† Henry, Otho, Simon, Thomas, John, and Maugan are other Christian names of very early Killigrews.

Lysons gives the following instances of their being at an early date possessors of lands in Cornwall : John de Killigrew, of Killigrew, had £20 a year or more in land in 1297 ; Henry de Killigrew held a military feu in Orchard Marries (? Marrais) in the hundred of Stratton in 3rd Henry IV. (1402) ; Rad. de Killigrew held a 'feod. parv.' at some place in the hundred ot Powder ; Henry, son of Maugi de Killigrew, had a similar tenure in Trewyn, in the same hundred—and they retained the Manor of Killigrew till 1636, so Lysons says. I may add, as an early instance of the name being mentioned, that there was a Richard (or Michael) Killigrew, one of a riotous lot of junior scholars at Merton College, Oxon, about the year 1350.

---

the little lake—formerly an arm of the sea, and known in Leland's time as ' Levine Prisklo,'—which was once the well-filled swannery of the Killigrews.   It was moved in 1836 to make way for the houses now known as ' Grove Place ;' and again in 1871, to its present appropriate site opposite the Arwenack Manor-office.

† The town arms of Falmouth, modified of course, are derived from those of Killigrew.   The arms of the *Devonshire* Killigrews are gules, three mascles or.   This latter coat appears on some woodwork in St. Budock Church, and on the brass of Thomas Killigrew, to which reference will presently be made.

After the lapse of about a century and a half from the time of Ralph, one of the Killigrews married the heiress of Arwenack, near Falmouth—a lady of broad lands, for her estates extended, it is said, from Arwenack (an old Cornish name which is said to signify either ' the beloved, still cove,' or 'upon the marsh ') to the mouth of the Helford river, a distance along the coast of some five or six miles. To this place, overlooking the beautiful waters of Falmouth Haven, then a deeper and far more important har-bour than it is at present, the Killigrew of the day, Simon by name, moved from his ancestral abode in St. Erme sometime during the reign of Richard II., probably about 1385 ; and here the Killigrews remained for nearly four centuries, acting as governors of Pendennis Castle for a great part of that period, intermarrying with many of the oldest Cornish families, and attending at the Courts of Henry VIII., Elizabeth, the first and second James, the first and second Charles, and William III.— loyal, able, and trusted adherents.

The earliest monument to any member of the family is, so far as I can ascertain, the brass in Gluvias Church, near Penryn, to Thomas Killigrew and his two wives Joan and Elizabeth, and all their children.* On the brass Thomas Killigrew is de-

* I am somewhat inclined to think that this *may* be the Thomas Killigrew who died at Biscay, in Aragon. He married twice — Johanna Herry and Jane Darrell ; possibly there may be some mistake in the Christian name of the latter lady. Perhaps the same Thomas who is mentioned in the Journals of Roger Machado, of an embassy to Spain and Portugal, in 1488, as having entertained the traveller, whom stress of weather drove into Falmouth harbour ; and as having bequeathed, in the year 1500, one hundred marks for the rebuilding of

scribed as a gentleman ('generosus'); he is represented in the costume of the latter part of the fifteenth century, in a long handsome robe trimmed with fur, and carries on his right shoulder his hat, after the fashion of the time—a wealthy merchant, in all probability. Thus far and no further, I regret to say, can I trace anything of interest respecting the early Killigrews.

But we now approach comparatively modern times, and are soon bewildered by the number of more or less illustrious names from which to select examples. A genealogical table, which I compiled for my guidance, offers at least fifty names not unknown in history, and of whose possessors accounts, not without interest, might be given.* But to do this would be to write a book instead of a chapter; and a far smaller number must suffice.

The Killigrew family seems naturally to divide itself into two classes, roughly speaking, complementary to each other: viz., the elder branch, which was on the whole the steadier and the more prosperous, whose present representative (by marriage) is the Earl of Kimberley, Secretary of State for India; and the younger branch (now also extinct in the male line) more fertile than the former in statesmen, soldiers, and wits. This division it is proposed to

St. Budock Church. In the autumn of 1882, whilst restoring St. Gluvias Church, the workmen came upon some leaden coffins in good preservation, which were supposed to contain the remains of members of the Killigrew family. The coffins were not opened.

* Since doing this I have had the advantage of consulting Colonel J. L. Vivian's elaborate pedigree in his recent annotated edition of the 'Herald's Visitations to the County of Cornwall.'

adopt in the following notices of both branches of the family.

Seniores priores. Let us commence with the first John Killigrew, of importance, upon record. His brass, like that of the first Thomas, is to be found in another little village church—St. Budock by name— near Falmouth. Evidently a grim warrior, covered *cap-à-pied* with plate armour, and associated in the representation with his wife—one of another good old Cornish family (now also extinct)—Elizabeth, daughter of James Trewinnard of St. Erth. This John was a rich man, his estate being worth no less than £6,000 a year; and he was the first Captain of Pendennis Castle, built on his own ground, under his own superintendence, and with the co-operation of Thomas Treffry of Place (who, by the way, married Elizabeth Killigrew, John's sister), in the reign of our castle-building King, Henry VIII. The same John Killigrew was appointed in 1551, together with Sir William Godolphin and Francis Godolphin, to survey the Islands of Scilly, and to build a fort there; no doubt that which stands on St. Mary's Isle, and is now known as Elizabeth Castle, with its inscription, ' E.R. 1593,' over the principal entrance. He was, moreover, sheriff for the county, and in that capacity wrote a letter, dated at Truro, to Cardinal Wolsey, on the subject of a threatened French invasion. Not content with building a castle for his King, John built (or rather rebuilt) for himself (about 1571, according to Hals), Arwenack House, in such a style that it was reputed the finest

and most costly in the county at that time. Little
did he think that one of his descendants was to see
it almost entirely destroyed, either by Waller, or by
the owner himself, to prevent its falling into the
enemy's hand, nearly a century later. Some part of
the structure still stands, and is used as a manor-
office; and here is preserved a conjectural restoration
of Arwenack House in its long-since-departed glory.

To him succeeded his son, Sir John Killigrew,
Knight, as second captain of the fortress. I find
nothing further recorded of him, save that he
married one Mary Wolverston,* and that when he
died on the 5th March, 1584, he too was buried at
St. Budock.

His son John—third of the name—seems to have
been, according to some contemporary accounts,
a man of no very high character; in fact, he has
been stigmatized as 'a pirate,' an 'avoider of his
debts,' 'a gamester,' and 'spendthrift.' Amongst
the Lansdowne MSS., in the British Museum,
are preserved accounts of his misconduct. One,
dated 7th March, 158⅞, is a 'Complaynte against
John Killigrew of yᵉ County of Cornwall, of many of
his ill demeners.' First comes a list of his 'knowen
debtes' to Her Majesty and others. Then the
document sets forth that, notwithstanding many
judgments obtained against him, he 'satisfieth no

---

* This lady seems to have been the real heroine of an exploit
accredited by Hals to Dame Jane Killigrew, one of her successors (*see
post*). Mr. H. Michell Whitley has drawn attention to Hals's mistake,
or confusion, in the *Journal of the Royal Institution of Cornwall,* 1883.
But in those high-handed days there may have been more than one
culprit, and more than one misdemeanour — and Hals is curiously
circumstantial

man;' but rides abroad, attended by armed servants, defies the bailiffs, and commits all sorts of high-handed irregularities. It concludes with the statement that he endeavours to satisfy his wealthier creditors with vain promises, and the poorer ones with blows and threatening words; and in fact, the complainants say it would require 'a hole quire of pap^r ' to sum up all his misdeeds. His boarding and pillaging a Danish ship, and some similar acts of violence, are set forth by Sir Julius Cæsar in other documents of this series; and our hero, together with one William Ewens, are set down as 'notorious pirates.' That he did not obtain the honour of knighthood under such circumstances is hardly to be wondered at.

I cannot, however, help thinking that he has been debited with many of the misdeeds of one Peter Killigrew, who lived a century before him, but whose exact connexion with the family I have been unable to trace satisfactorily. Perhaps the one mentioned in Strype's ' Memorials of Edward VI.,' of whom it is observed, in 1552, that one ' Strangwich ' (? Restronguet), 'and two Killigrews with him, were such notable sea-rovers, that, in the month of February of that year, the King sent a letter to the French King, that he would do his endeavour for the apprehension of them.' And yet, in 1592, a Mr. Killigrew, according to the same authority, was appointed, at Sir Walter Raleigh's request, on a commission to inquire into the matter of the distribution of the spoil of a certain richly-laden Spanish carrack, ' *The Mother of God* ' taken by some of Sir Walter's ships on her return from the East Indies.   Indeed, there is considerable difficulty in identifying some of the Killigrews of the sixteenth and early in the seventeenth centuries. But the fact is, that not only were the Killigrews concerned in exploits of this nature, but there were many others amongst the west - countrymen who, under Sir Peter Carew, slipped over to France, and did a little privateering against Spain on their own account, being anxious to do all in their power to prevent the marriage of Mary with Philip of Spain. A Killigrew of this date had three ships under his command, according to the Calais MSS. 'Wild spirits of all nations,' says Froude—'Scots, English, French, whoever chose to offer—found service under their flag. They were the first specimens of the buccaneering chivalry of the next generation, the germ out of which rose the Drakes, the Raleighs, the Hawkinses, who harried the conquerors of the New World.' Ultimately the Godolphins and Killigrews were threatened with prosecution, but nothing came of it.   By his wife Dorothy, daughter of Thomas Monck of Potheridge, Devon, John is said to have had nine sons and five daughters, though I can only trace ten children altogether.   She was the sister of General Monck, Duke of Albemarle, whose exploits on behalf of his royal masters, and especially the prominent part he took in the restoration of Charles II., are well-known matters of history.   I have referred somewhat more fully to this in the chapter on the Grenvilles.

This John (whom we have called the third) had two brothers, Thomas and Simon, both of whom

were Court favourites. Some other Cornish gentlemen of the time seem to have been equally popular
with the Queen, as Elizabeth said of them that they
were all 'born courtiers, and with a becoming confidence.' Queen Elizabeth sent Thomas on an
embassy to the Count Palatine of the Rhine; and
I find that he was also commissioned to seize a
certain ship of Brittany at 'Pensans' (Penzance),
and to 'distribute the spoil among such as by
certain Britaines have been heretofore spoiled of
their goods and wronged.' Rough and ready justice
this, seemingly, and a lesson from which some subsequent Killigrews, as we shall find, did not fail to take
a hint. John's younger brother, Simon, was, to some
extent, a herald, as appears by a letter from him on the
subject of the Manaton coat of arms, preserved
amongst the Harleian MSS. (1079), in the British
Museum. The two younger brothers added to the
family estates by purchases of a property, with a
town-house at Lothbury; a country seat at Kineton
(? Kempton) Park, near Hampton Court; besides
sundry lands and manors in East Cornwall, Devon,
and Lincolnshire. Of their two sisters, Mary and
Katherine, I can learn nothing, except that the
latter married twice.

To return, therefore, to the main line—Sir John,
the fourth and last of that name (for Sir William,
the eldest son, who was made a baronet in 1661,
and was buried in Westminster Abbey in 1665,
would seem to have led an uneventful life, and
need not detain us), was knighted at Whitehall
on 8th November, 1617; he was 'a good, sober

man,' and was likewise, I fancy, a Captain of Pendennis. He seems, moreover, to have been the chief promoter, at great pecuniary loss, of the first beacon-light on the Lizard, for which he obtained a patent from King James I., in 1619.* But he had the misfortune to marry an unsuitable partner—Jane, the daughter of Sir George Fermor—about whom Hals tells the following story (the credibility of which Davies Gilbert thought was at least questionable; but the tradition is still locally extant).†

Towards the close of Elizabeth's reign, two Dutch ships of the Hanse Towns League, and therefore under special protection, sailed into Falmouth Harbour, driven there either by the Spaniards or by stress of weather. They had scarcely arrived before Dame Killigrew, accompanied by some ruffians, boarded the Dutch ships, slew the owners, and seized two hogsheads of pieces of eight, which she took ' for her own use.' This high-handed proceeding of course produced remonstrances on the part of the rightful proprietors of the money, and led to the trial, conviction, and execution of all the offenders, save the lady herself, at Launceston, She barely escaped, and not without the utmost interest having been made for her with the Queen by Sir John Arundell, of Tolverne, and Sir Nicholas Hals, of Pengerswick.

Nor was this the only irregularity for which the authorities of Pendennis were complained of. In 1631

* Cf. Mr. Howard Fox's article on the ' Lizard Lighthouses,' *Journal of the Royal Institution of Cornwall*, No. XXII., March, 1880, p. 319. Sir William Killigrew vainly endeavoured to obtain a renewal of the patent in 1631.

† Dame Mary Killigrew seems to have been the true heroine of this story. *See ante.*

the Castle guns were fired upon the King's ships!
and on the 2nd November in that year a Captain
Kettleby writes thus : ' None disturb the free trade
in those parts more than the Captain of Pendennis
Castle—he is at peace with neither King's ships, nor
others—both the Admiral and the writer have been
twice shot at by him in going in and out. The last
shot fell in the town of St. Mawes, but only hurt one
woman.' Possibly the explanation of such apparently wanton mischief as this is to be found in the
rivalry which existed for precedence between the
two castles, Pendennis and St. Mawes, on opposite
sides of the harbour mouth—a rivalry so intense as
to have finally rendered a compromise indispensable.

Whether the details of the story of Dame Mary, or
Dame Jane (an 'old Jezebel,' as her enemies called her)
be true or not ; whether it be a distorted reproduction
of some of the misdeeds of her father-in-law, the third
John ; or whether the real cause of the misunder-
standing between her husband and her faithless self
was the now fast-growing rivalry between the ports of
Penryn and Falmouth—this much at least is certain :
that in the year 1633 Dame Jane gave to the mayor
of ' Permarin,' and his successors in office for ever, a
handsome silver chalice, still used as a loving-cup at
the mayor-choosings, on which it is recorded that
the Penryn mayor succoured her when she was ' in
greate miserie.'* The unhappy pair were divorced,
without issue ; the husband dying in 1632 or 1636,
and his wife twelve years afterwards.

A few words may be added here on the subject of

* The cup is figured in the *Journal of the Royal Institution of
Cornwall.*

the harbour. Penryn, the more ancient port, lies at the head of a long, tortuous creek; more secure, doubtless, from its position, and its once stockaded channel, from an enemy's ships than Falmouth was before the erection of Pendennis and St. Mawes Castles; and to Truro the same remark applied with still greater force. The rivalry between the two more ancient ports, Penryn and Truro, and the comparatively modern Falmouth, was, as may be supposed, of the keenest; but the natural advantages of Falmouth—at length defended by two forts, and aided by the powerful interest of the Killigrews—prevailed; and Falmouth, too, became 'a port.' A town—now one of the largest, busiest, and gayest of the quiet towns of Cornwall—accordingly sprang up around the once lonely site of Arwenack.*

Failing issue of the eldest brother, Sir William, the first baronet—and also of Sir John—Sir Peter, first knight of that name, now becomes the representative of this, the elder branch of the family: 'a merry youth, bred under the Earl of Bristol,' says one authority—and known as 'Peter the Post,' as another tells us, from the alacrity with which he despatched 'like wild-fire' all the messages and other commissions entrusted to him in the King's cause. On him was laid the important duty of conveying from Oxford the King's proposals to the Parliament in January, 1645. Like Rupert himself, he seems to

---

* Arwenack is so shown on a chart preserved in the British Museum, and engraved by Lysons in his 'Mag. Brit.' (Cornwall). St. Mawes Castle is shown as half built, Pendennis not yet commenced, and two other works—one at Gillyngvase Bay, the other at Trefusis Point—as *contemplated.* There is another and still finer coloured map, with Lord Burghley's handwriting on it, in the National Collection.

have been in perpetual motion; and on one occasion, during 'Oliver's usurpation,' Sir Peter rode from Madrid, through France, and having passed the sea, got to London in seven days. Like Sir Tristram in the 'Monks and Giants,'

> 'From realm to realm he ran, and never staid.'

He was one of those who very nearly succeeded, it is said, in enabling Charles I. to effect his escape into France; and it was in his time that (as it is said) in revenge for his attachment to the Stuart cause, the mansion of Arwenack was ruined by Waller during the memorable operations of the siege in the time of the Civil War. It is, however, not improbable that its destruction was commenced by its patriotic owner in order to prevent its occupation by the enemy. Pendennis was the last castle (except Raglan) which held out for the King's cause;* but on the 16th August, 1646, it too was forced to surrender (though with flying colours, and all the honours of war) to Fairfax, after a terrible five months of siege 'and famine and harsh wounds,' endured gallantly by old John Arundell of Trerice, then nearly eighty years of age.

> 'Lady Penelope, fair Queen, most chast,
> Pendennis, of all Royall Forts the last,
> The last, the only, Fort ne'er conquered was,
> Ne'er shall be; who in constancy doth passe
> The rest of all thy sisters, who to thee
> (The eclipse of all thy kinde) but strumpets be.'

The author of these verses, after the surrender, significantly, and not unnecessarily, added the ensuing note:

* The *negotiations* for the surrender of Raglan were begun before those for Pendennis. Cf. the Chapter on the Arundells.

'Penelopen ipsam (persta modo), tempore vinces,
Capta vides sero Pergama ; capta tamen.'

The family estates, worth, at one time, £6,000 a
year, had sadly dwindled away by the time they came
into the second Sir Peter's possession ; indeed, they
are said to have been worth no more than about £80
a year ; yet he contrived to become elected M.P.
for Camelford, and by 1630 had married Mary, the
sister of Lord Lucas, of Colchester, Earl Pembroke
giving the marriage portion of ' a good £300 a
year ;' and the *Mercurius Politicus* for 15th March,
1660, informs us that in that month he was
made Governor of Pendennis by General Monk.
This Sir Peter continued, like his predecessors, a
sturdy champion of Falmouth.   He got the Custom
House removed from its old place at Penryn, to his
own more modern town ; carved the parish of Falmouth out of that of St. Budock (15 Charles II.) ;
and, with the assistance of the King and others, built
and endowed the church, dedicated to the memory
of King Charles the martyr,* where his own bones
first, and then those of other Killigrews after him,
were laid.   Some accounts give 1670 as the date
of his death ; others say—probably more accu-
rately—that he died on the road to Exeter, in 1667:
possibly killed on one of his break-neck rides ; for,
as we have seen, he was a man of no common

* Sir Peter measured out the ground for the church, churchyard, and
minister's house, on 29th August, 1662.   The first sermon was preached
in the church on 21st February, 1663, by Mr. John Bedford, of Gerrans,
from Genesis xxiii. 20, ' And the field, and the cave that is therein,
were made sure unto Abraham for a possession of a buryingplace by
the sons of Heth.'

energy and daring. He left three children : Peter, William, and Elizabeth.

Of the sister it seems unnecessary to say more than that she married a Count de Kinski, a title which, I believe, still survives. William, who died unmarried in 1678, became a soldier of fortune, and ultimately a general officer; and he was commander-in-chief of some Danish forces, sent by the Spaniards against the Swedes. After one of his successful engagements, he sold certain captured horses (his share of the spoil) to His Majesty of Denmark for some £3,000. But failing to get his money from his royal employer, the general executed the military movement known as 'right-about-face,' and transferred his sword to the Dutch, by whom his valour was more honourably rewarded. I have failed to trace the details of his career; but he seems to have been recalled to England at the Restoration, and had a regiment of foot. His nephew succeeded to his estate, which Martin Lister says was 'composed more of honour than of substance.'

It is, however, with the elder son of this generation that we have chiefly to deal, for through him the succession was kept up. Sir Peter, the second baronet (inheriting that title from his uncle, the foregoing Sir William, the first), was born in 1634, and was educated, notwithstanding his father's reduced estate, first at Oxford, and afterwards in France. Whilst he was at Oxford, the horrible execution of Anne Green, for murdering her infant illegitimate child, took place. After hanging for half an hour, she recovered her life in consequence of judicious medical treatment ; and full particulars of the event are given in a rare little volume published at Oxford in 1651, and entitled 'News from the Dead.' To this work many of the members of the university contributed short sets of verses, some in Latin, some in English. The following lines were those supplied by the Cornish baronet :

> 'Death, spare your threats, we scorne now to obey ;
> If Women conquer thee, surely Men may.
> How came this Champion on I cannot tell,
> But I nere heard of one *come off* so well.
> 'PET. KILLIGREW, Eq. Aur. fil. Coll. Reg.'

And here is a specimen of his powers as a writer of Latin verse, on a very different subject :

[PRO REGE SOTERIA.]

> ' Funera funeribus commiscens, bustaq̃ ; bustis
> Ira avidæ, nato Principe, pestis abit.
> Filius an regis potuit dum vagijt infans
> A tôta rabidam gente fugare luem ?
> Nec valet, Antidotas sibi Rex, depellere varos
> Cujus Apollinea est tam benè nota manus ?
> Tantane *Carolidæ* potuêre crepundia ? plebem
> De tumulo redimet qui modò natus erat ?
> Et res usque ; nova est ? morbum miramur abortum,
> Depulsum sceptro, Carole magne, tuo ?'

In 1662, Sir Peter, who had been made Governor of Pendennis on the Restoration, married the handsome, virtuous, and accomplished Frances Twysden, daughter of Sir Roger, the well-known judge of that name;* and the union appears to have been a happy

---

* One of the most scathing letters of reproach ever written was addressed by this lady to Rev. Mr. Quarme, the Incumbent of Falmouth, for his ingratitude after Sir Peter's decease. It is preserved amongst the archives in the manor-office at Arwenack.

one in every respect, save as to the offspring. Peter, the eldest, died young ; George, the second son, was killed in a tavern brawl at Penryn (at the house of a Mr. Chalons, says Tonkin), by ' a stab in the back ' from a barrister named Walter Vincent. Another account states that the skull, which was found in 1861, showed that the hole made by the rapier was clearly visible in the forehead. Frances, the elder daughter, married a Cornish gentleman named Richard Erissey,* who ' cast her off' three years after their marriage. Ann, the youngest, who died without issue, married Martin Lister, a Staffordshire gentleman and soldier of fortune, who assumed the name of Killigrew, and managed the estates for many years. Clearly the main stem of the great race of Killigrew was rapidly decaying !

On the death, or murder, of his son George, old Sir Peter, who had gone to live at Arwenack in 1670, disappointed at having no male issue, and sick of the innumerable squabbles in which he found himself involved with the Falmouth folk, retired, first to London, and then, in 1697, to Ludlow, where he passed his time in scientific pursuits of a speculative character, the results of which appear to have died with him. His portrait, by Sir Godfrey Kneller, now in the possession of Mrs. Boddam

---

* Probably a descendant of that Erissey whose nimble dancing delighted James I. so much that he inquired what was his name. The King admired the gentleman, but ' liked not his name,' to which some one had possibly prefixed the letter ' h ' in pronouncing it. Some remains of the ancient mansion of this old Cornish family are still to be seen on the estate of that name in the parish of Ruan Major : the dates on an old doorway and on some lofty gate-posts are, respectively, 1603 and 1671.

Castle, of Grove House, Clifton (a descendant of the Killigrews), fully harmonizes with what we know of his character. One practical thing, however, he did : viz., to build the public quay at Falmouth; and to that old town, endeared to him by so many pleasant memories of the past, were his remains conveyed to be interred in the parish church, among those of his more immediate ancestors. The monuments are not, at present, to be seen ; perhaps they are hidden under the raised floor of the chancel : but there were laid, in 1704, the remains of Sir Peter Killigrew,—the last male in the main* line.

George, his son, though, as we have seen, he died young, was not unmarried. He gained for his wife an offshoot of another old Cornish family, Ann, daughter of Sir John St. Aubyn, Bart., by whom he had issue one daughter (Ann), married to a Major John Dunbar. To the heiress of the ill-starred Erissey match—Sir Peter's youngest grand-daughter, Mary—the bulk of the remaining Killigrew property seems to have descended; and through her the present representative of the family (the Earl of Kimberley) holds it. She married, in 1711, a Colonel John West.†

There are few things more amusing in its way than the account which Mr. R. N. Worth has pre-

---

* It was this Sir Peter who, finding that, in 1689, Pendennis Castle required some repairs, visited the Collector of Customs at Penryn, at ten o'clock at night, and carried off the Collector and the money (some £200 odd), 'for the good of the King's castle.'

† Both their daughters, Frances and Mary, took the name of Killigrew ; the former married the Hon. Charles Berkeley, the latter John Merrill, Esq. ; but from both marriages there was female issue only.

served for us in the *Journal of the Royal Institution of Cornwall*, of the arrangements which Martin Killigrew (Lister) requested should be made for Colonel West's reception at Arwenack. They are as follows :

' MR. ABRM. HALL,

*   *   *   *   *

' It is but by guess I have to tell you that you are not to expect to see ye Col^n. till about ye end of ye first week in May, who bringing with him ye young gentleman* in question, must add considerably to ye flurry you will be put in from his being a person of great consideration as I hear, tho' I know not so much as his name and as Little any particular of his circumstances. But suppose you must be advised by the Col^n. as to your providing accommodation for their Retinue : Two bed chambers for ye gentlemen you will put in ye best order you can ; a room for ye servants to Eat in : The best Cook your Town affords ; some choise good Hambs and a provision of fatt chickens : Wine you must leave Mr: James to provide ; and if any fine green Tea† be to be had, you must secure some of it, as what ye Col^n. is most Nice in, and drinkes much off. Two of ye largest Tea potts you can borrow, He using them both at a time. Nice and knowing beyond ye comon in providing a Table, so that your Mother will only have to receive his orders every morning on

---

* The young gentleman is apparently Mr. Merrill, subsequently the husband of the Colonel's eldest daughter.

† When this letter was written the price of tea was—Bohea, 12s. to 14s. ; Pekoe, 18s. ; and Hyson, 35s. per lb.

that head.   The stable put in ye best order you can, provided with Hay and Corne.

'If I do not greatly mistake, this flurry cannot continue above three weeks, for that their impatience will be greater to get back to Bath than it is to see Falmouth.

'You are still in time to see that your Closett and Books be put in ye best Order you can, and nothing to be seen there belonging to other people's business, but only to ye Estate.   You will finde ye Col^n. quick of comprehention and as ready at figures as can be supposed.

'*At ye same time you observe to them ye great sums I have raised from ye Estate you will do me Justice to note ye improvements I have made upon it.   And that tho' times are now dead as thro'out ye kingdome, yet as they have been good it may reasonably be hoped they will be so again, & that in ye main you doubt not of giving a yearly demonstration (by ye Rentall) of ye increase of ye Estate;* when Diner is over you get back to your Closet, and as you see it proper, you returne with your pen in your ear, making ye Col_n sensible he is wanted above, whereby he may git rid of impertinant Comp^n. if such be with him.   Nor can I see in respect to time ye Col^n. can do more in business than from day to day, he giving you orders which you will take in writing, and at parting take his hand to them, you giving him a duplicate.

'You will be able to borrow glasses, knives, forks, and spoons, with some handsome pieces of plate, in everything to make ye best figure you can; and if you can borrow a better horse than your own, you ought to do it. Relying upon ye Col^n. generosity (His greatest fault), you will be nothing out of pocket upon this occasion. As from me pray your Mother to trouble ye Col^n. with as Little of her conversation as her business will admit off. I thinke enough at a time to a man of your accute parts—

'Yours

'MART. KILLIGREW.

'St. James's, 16th April, 1737.'

It will be seen from the above that Martin was a man of some mettle, and able to manage the affairs of his stewardship adroitly, though far away from the scene. He was always at war with the Corporation of Falmouth, of which borough he was for some time Recorder, and he died in St. James's Square, London, on 7th March, 1745.*

Amongst the latest notices of any member of the family that I have met with, one is contained in the sprightly pages of Mrs. Delany's 'Life and Correspondence;' the subject of her remarks seems to have been a true Killigrew, at least so far as his dramatic talent affords any indication. On the 26th January, 1752, at Mr. Bushe's (near Dublin), at a dinner-party, she met a Mr. Killigrew, who was 'a very entertaining, charming man, well-bred, good-humoured, and sings in a most extraordinary manner; has a fine voice, fine taste, no knowledge of music, but the exactest imitation of Senesino and Monticelli that you can imagine. He

---

* To a copy of a MS. history of the family, written by him in 1737-38, I have been indebted for some interesting particulars.

sings French songs incomparably, with so much humour that in spite of my gloom he made me laugh heartily.'

Of another, the last male of his name, Thomas Guildford Killigrew, I find from *Notes and Queries*, 1873, p. 224, and also from other sources, including information * with which I have been favoured by Mrs. Boddam Castle, that he married Miss Catharine Chubb, a distant relative, after having much impoverished himself in the Stuart cause in 1745, and that he settled in Bristol for the sake of economy. He died in 1782 without issue. At his death Mrs. Killigrew adopted her great niece, Mary Iago, afterwards married to Daniel Wait, Mayor of Bristol, in 1805. On the death of Mrs. Killigrew, in 1810, the family plate and portraits (one of the latter, Sir Peter Killigrew, by Sir Godfrey Kneller, and another, of Thomas Guildford Killigrew himself) passed to Mrs. Wait by will, and from her to Mrs. Boddam Castle, wife of Mr. Boddam Castle, barrister-at-law, now residing at Clifton. Some of the plate is more than 150 years old ; the crest a demi-griffin, with ' T. C. K.' over it.

The last who bore the surname of Killigrew was Frances Maria (daughter of George Augustus Killigrew, of Bond Street), who died in Portman Street, London, on 20th July, 1819, aged seventy-one.

And here let us pause, after having exhausted (so far as I am aware) all the sources of information, and

---

* The statement in *Notes and Queries* is on the authority of Mr. William Killigrew Wait, who still, I believe, lives in or near Bristol.

having, I believe, at least set down all that was note-worthy, of the *elder* branch of the Killigrews.

THE SECOND BRANCH.

JOHN KILLIGREW, the first Captain of Pendennis, had three brothers, James, Thomas, and Bennet, of whom I can learn nothing of interest. And he also had other sons than John the second knight, his successor at Pendennis Castle, of whom we have already heard. One son—Thomas—died young. Another, the fourth son, was the famous Sir Henry Killigrew, Knight, who sat as Member of Parliament for Launceston in 1552-53, and for Truro about twenty years later. Him let us take as our first representative of the younger branch of the family. He is described as a Teller of the Exchequer, Com-mander of ' Newhaven ' (Nieuwport), and Ambassa-dor to Germany, France (where he temporarily relieved Sir Francis Walsingham), Scotland, the Palatinate, Frankfort, and the Low Countries.* Of a man of such mark—one whom Emerson would have called ' a bright personality '—traces would as-suredly be forthcoming; and we do not seek them in vain amongst the Lansdowne, the Cottonian, the Egerton, and the ' Additional ' Manuscripts in the

* He was taken prisoner at Rouen, in Nov. 1562, and, according to Wright's ' Queen Elizabeth and her Times,' was to be ' redeemed for young Pegrillion.' And here it may be conveniently observed that this work contains Killigrew's letters to Burghley on the state of Scotch affairs—perhaps the most important business which he had to manage in the course of his diplomatic career.

British Museum; amongst the Scotch MSS.; and in
the Public Record Office. Moreover, the Yelverton
MSS. contain references to him, as also do the collections in Lambeth Palace Library. Most of these
are Letters, Instructions, and Memorials, referring to
the diplomatic functions which he was called upon
to discharge, and partaking rather too much of the
'Dryasdust' character to be interesting to the
general reader. There are some verses by him to
'My Ladye Cecylle' (his wife's sister), preserved in
the Cambridge University Library; but I propose to
omit these in favour of some Latin lines addressed to
the same lady by Sir Henry's wife; not only because of the courteous maxim, '*Place aux dames*,'
but also because the lady's verses are really charming.
In lieu of any specimen of Sir Henry's *poetic* vein,
an extract from a letter which he wrote from Edinburgh, on 6th October, 1572, descriptive of John
Knox—towards the close of his life—and some other
fragments of his prose, will probably be more acceptable. 'John Knox,' he says, 'is now so feeble as
scarce can he stand alone, or speak to be heard of
any audience, yet doth he every Sunday cause himself to be carried to a place where a certain number
do hear him, and preacheth with the same vehe-
mency and zeal that ever he did.' This account is
fully confirmed by another contemporary description
of him, which is so graphic that I cannot refrain
from giving it.

From May, 1571, to August, 1572, Knox lived in
St. Andrews, and frequently preached there. 'I
haid my pen and my little book,' says James Mel-

ville, 'and tuk away sic things as I could compre-
hend. In the opening upe of his text he was
moderat the space of an halff houre ; bot when he
enteret to application, he maid me sa to grew &
tremble, that I could nocht hald a pen to wryt. . . .
He was verie weak. I saw him everie day of his
doctrine go hulie and fear, with a furring of mar-
triks about his neck, a staff in the an hand, and
guid godlie Richart Ballanden, his servand, halding
upe the uther oxtar, from the Abbay to the paroche
kirk; and be the said Richart and another servant,
lifted upe to the pulpit, whar he behovit to lean at
his first entrie; bot or he haid done with his sermont,
he was sa active and vigorus that he was lyk to ding
that pulpit in blads, and fly out of it !' But his work
was nearly done ; weary of the world, and 'thirsting
to depart,' in a few months he entered into his rest.

We learn of Sir Henry, from Heppe, that
Queen Elizabeth being very desirous of concluding a sincere alliance, or 'Common League,'
between herself and the Evangelical Princes of the
Empire, sent to the Elector Palatine and other the
Electors of the Holy Roman Empire and the States,
Henry Killigrew—her 'approved and faithful servant '—and her 'orator,' Dr. Mount, with a view to
counteracting 'the pernicious and sanguinary plots
of certain persons against all the professors of the
Holy Gospel in every place.' The Congress to
which they were accredited met at Frankfort, in
April, 1569, but Killigrew and Mount arrived too late
for it.

These, and other of his diplomatic missions are

referred to in the following extract from a memorial
in Leonard Howard's 'Collection of Letters of
Princes, Great Personages, and Statesmen.' After
recounting his many* diplomatic missions for his
Queen to France, 'to discover theire intents there
against this Realme;' to Germany, 'to sound the
Princes of Germanye touching a League defensive
for Religion' (for which he had 'but Fortye Pounds
allowance for all manner of Chardges; which coste me
as muche more with the least'); and again several
times to those Countries, as well as to Scotland in
1573, and to Newhaven, where he was hurt and im-
prisoned—Sir Henry thus concludes:

'Now for all these Journeys, Chardges, Daungers,
Hurtes and Losses, in the meanwhile, and the
Tyme used only in her Majesties' service, without
any Proffitt of my owne, I have only to lyve by, of
Her Majesties' Goodness, the Tellershippe, which
was given me before I went to Newehaven. . .' In
consideration of all which—by way of a provision
for his family—he prefers a 'Suite for the said
Firme of the Manor of Sarrake (?) in Cornwall . . .';
adding, 'The Rent is somewhat great, I confess;
but truly the Proffitt nothinge equall.'

Let us hope that services so long, so faithful, and
so important, at length received their reward. That

---

* Thus summarized by F. S. Thomas in his 'Historical Notes,' and
by other authorities : Ambassador to Scotland, 1566; negotiating in
1569 for fresh ports to be opened in the Baltic; to France, when
Walsingham was sick, 1571; Scotland again, 1572, to negotiate for
the surrender of Edinburgh Castle; again, 1573; and at Berwick,
1574; in London, 1575, and back to Scotland the same year; in the
Low Countries in 1586; and to France with the Earl of Essex, to
assist the King of France, in 1591.

they probably did may be surmised from the following account of the close of his active career, given by the Cornish historian Carew: 'After ambassades and messages, and many other profitable employments of peace and warre, in his prince's service, to the good of his country, (Sir Henry Killigrew) hath made choyce of a retyred estate, and, reverently regarded by all sorts, placeth his principal contentment in himselfe, which, to a life so well acted, can no way bee wanting.'

Lord Burleigh's instructions to him,* on the subject of his Scotch mission, written with his own hand, dated 10th September, 1572, especially as to getting Mary Queen of Scots out of the kingdom, and delivering her to the Regent's party, form a most interesting document. The letter closes thus: 'Herein yow shall, as Comodite shall serve yow, use all good Spede, with the most Secresy that yow can, to understand their Mynds; *and yet so to deale to your uttermost, that this Matter might be rather Oppened to yow, than yourself to seme first to move it. . . .*'

Another object of his momentous mission to Scotland, as to which Elizabeth gave him her instructions with her own mouth, was to impress upon Mary Queen of Scots a sense of her faults, her duties, and her danger—a vain task! Froude gives an account of the interview, which took place after Darnley's murder. 'The windows at Holyrood were half-closed, the rooms were darkened, and in the profound gloom the English Ambassador

* Murdin.

was unable to see the Queen's face, but by her words she seemed very doleful.' And at length, having extorted from her a promise that Bothwell should be put upon his trial, Killigrew went back to London in less than a week, after having carried out his difficult and delicate duty 'like a loyal servant.'

The 'Cabala' states that when Henry Killigrew went to France, he was considered 'in livelihood much inferior to Walsingham;' but Leicester's opinion of him was subjected to revision. He says he found our hero 'a quicker and stouter fellow than he tooke him for.' I have often wondered whether this impression was derived from Sir Henry's bearing when the question of his pay was mooted. ' 60/ a pece, per dyem' had been set down, complains Leicester, writing to Walsingham on 15th December, 1585, as the pay of Killigrew and his colleague, whereas *he* had understood it was to be only 40s. The Earl's impression proved to be correct, and heart-burnings doubtless arose; with what result I know not, but Leicester's revised estimate of his man may point to the event. Sir H. Killigrew was at the siege of St. Quentin, in 1557; and Sir James Melville says how he met at La Ferre (? La Frette) 'Maister Hary Killygrew, an Englis gentleman, my auld frend, wha held my horse till I sate down in ane barbour's buith, to be pensit of the hurt in my head.'*

* According to Froude, there was a Killigrew of Pendennis, who was one of the 500 forlorn hope who cut their way through Guise's lines at Rouen, in October, 1562. On the capture of that place, and after the garrison had been cut down almost to the last man, he was taken, half-dead, but eventually recovered. I cannot help thinking this must be the same Killigrew.

He is found described, amongst the strangers resident in London in 1595 ('Nichols' Collections,' viii. 206), as living then in 'Broad Street Warde;' and he died on the 16th March, 160¾. The character of this 'Admirable Crichton' has been so well drawn by David Lloyd in his 'State Worthies,' that I cannot refrain from giving it, in the words of Whitworth's translation.

'Travellers report, that the place wherein the body of Absalom was buried is still extant at Jerusalem, and that it is a solemn custome of pilgrims passing by it to cast a stone on the place; but a well-disposed man can hardly go by the memory of this worthy person without doing grateful homage thereunto in bestowing upon him one or two of our observations.

'It's a question sometimes whether diamond gives more lustre to the ring it's set in, or the ring to the diamond; this gentleman received honour from his family, and gave renoun to it. Writing is the character of the speech, as that is of the mind. From Tully (whose orations he could repeat to his dying day) he gained an even and apt stile, flowing at one and the selfsame height. Tully's Offices, a book which boys read, and men understand, was so esteemed of my Lord Burleigh, that to his dying day he always carried it about him, either in his bosome or his pocket, as a compleat piece that, like Aristotle's rhetorick, would make both a scholar and an honest man. Cicero's magnificent orations against Anthony, Catiline and Verres; Cæsar's great Commentaries that he wrote with the same spirit that he fought; flowing Livy; grave, judicious and stately Tacitus; eloquent, but faithful Curtius; brief and rich Salust; prudent and brave Xenophon, whose person was Themistocles his companion, as his book was Scipio Affricanus his pattern in all his wars; ancient and sweet Herodotus; sententious and observing Thucidides; various and useful Polybius; Siculus, Halicarnasseus, Trogus, Orosius, Justine, made up our young man's retinue in all his travels where (as Diodorus the Sicilian writes) he *"sate on the stage of human life, observing the great circumstances of places, persons, times, manners, occasions, etc, and was made wise by their example who haue trod the path of errour and danger before him."* To which he added that grave, weighty and sweet Plutarch, whose books (said Gaza) would furnish the world, were all others lost. Neither was he amazed in the labyrinth of history, but guided by the clue of cosmography, hanging his study with maps, and his mind with exact notices of each place. He made in one view a judgement of the situation, interest, and commodities (for want whereof many statemen and souldiers have* failed) of nations; but to understand the nature of places, is but a poor knowledge, unless we know how to improue them by art; therefore under the figures of triangles, squares, circles and magnitudes, with their terms and bounds, he could contrive most tools and instruments, most engines, and judge of fortifications, architecture, ships, wind

---

* As Cyrus at Thermopylæ, Crassus in Parthia : therefore Alexander had exact maps always about him to observe passages, streights, rocks, plains, rivers, etc.

and water-works, and whatever might make this lower frame of things useful and serviceable to man-kinde; which severer studies he relieved with noble and free Poetry-aid, once the pleasure and advance-ment of the soul, made by those higher motions of the minde more active and more large. To which I adde her sister Musick, wherewith he revived his tired spirits, lengthened (as he said) his sickly days, opened his oppressed breast, eased his melancholy thoughts, graced his happy pronunciation, ordered and refined his irregular and gross inclinations, fixed and quickened his floating and dead notions; and by a secret, sweet and heavenly Vertue, raised his spirit, as he confessed, sometime to a little less than angelical exaltation. Curious he was to please his ear, and as exact to please his eye; there being no statues, inscriptions or coyns that the Vertuosi of Italy could shew, the antiquaries of France could boast off, or the great hoarder of rarieties the great duke of Tuscany (whose antic coyns are worth £100,000) could pretend to, that he had not the view of. No man could draw any place or work better, none fancy and paint a portraicture more lively; being a Durer for proportion, a Goltzius for a bold touch, variety of posture, a curious and true shadow, an Angelo for his happy fancy, and an Holben for works.

'Neither was it a bare ornament of discourse, or naked diversion of leisure time; but a most weighty piece of knowledge that he could blazon most noble and ancient coats, and thereby discern the relation, interest, and correspondence of great families, and thereby the meaning and bottom of all transactions, and the most successful way of dealing with any one family. His exercises were such as his employments were like to be, gentle and man-like. Whereof the two most eminent were riding and shooting that at once wholesomely stirred, and nobly knitted and strengthened his body. Two eyes he said he travelled with; the one of wariness upon himself, the other of observation upon others. This compleat gentleman was guardian to the young Brandon in his younger years, agent for Sir John Mason in king Edward the sixth's time, and the first embassador for the state in Queen Elizabeth's time. My Lord Cobham is to amuse the Spaniard, my Lord Effingham to undermine the French, and Sir Henry Killigrew is privately sent to engage the German princes against Austria in point of interest, and for her majesty in point of religion : he had a humour that bewitched the elector of Bavaria, a carriage that awed him of Mentz, a reputation that obliged them of Colen and Hydelberg, and that reach and fluency in discourse that won them all. He assisted the Lords Hunsdon and Howard at the treaty with France in London, and my Lord of Essex in the war for France and Britain. Neither was he less observable for his own conduct than for that of others, whose severe thoughts, words and carriage so awed his inferiour faculties, as to restrain him through all the heats of youth, made more than usually importunate by the full vigour of a high and sanguine constitution; insomuch that they say he looked upon all the approaches to that sin, then so familiar to his calling as a souldier, his quality as a gentleman, and his station as a courtier, not onely with an utter disallowance in his judgement, but with a natural abhorrency and antipathy in his very lower inclinations. To which happiness it conduced not a little, that though he had a good, yet he had a restrained appetite (a knife upon his throat as well as upon his trencher) that indulged itself neither frequent nor delicate entertainment; its meals, though but once a day, being its pressures, and its fast, its only sensualities; to which temperance in diet, adde but that in sleep, together with his disposal of himself throughout his life to industry and diligence, you will say he was a spotless man, whose life taught us this lesson, (which, if observed, would accomplish mankinde; and which King Charles the first would inculcate to noble travellers, and Dr. Hammond to all men), viz.: *To be furnished always with something to do;* a lesson they proposed as the best expedience for innocence and pleasure; the foresaid blessed man assuring his happy hearers, "*That no burden is more heavy, or temptation more dangerous, then to have time lie on one's hand: the idle man being not onely* (as he worded it) "*the Devil's shop, but his kingdome too; a model of, and an appendage unto Hell, a place given up to torment and to mischief.*"'

He left four daughters only, Anna, Dorothy, Elizabeth, and Mary, by his wife Katherine, fourth of the erudite daughters of Sir Anthony Cooke, of Giddy Hall, Essex, the accomplished Preceptor of Edward VI.—'vir antiqua serenitate,' according to

Camden—from whom (as Strype tells us) his 'daughter Killigrew' inherited, amongst other things, 'a nest of white bowls.'

Dame Katherine was skilled, after the manner of the learned ladies of her time, in Hebrew, Greek, and Latin, and in poetry; and both Sir John Harrington and Thomas Fuller commend and quote her compositions. But that, with all her learning, she had, what was even better, a devotedly affectionate heart, let the following lines testify, which she addressed to her sister Mildred, who had married Cecil, Lord Burghley.* The Lord Treasurer was about to send his young relative on a diplomatic mission to France, at a dangerous juncture—whether before or after the death in that country of Thomas Hobby, who married her sister Elizabeth, and who also went to France as an ambassador, I am uncertain—while the loving Katherine thought her husband would be safer and happier with her in Cornwall—probably either at Arwenack, or at Rosmeryn in Budock, or at Trevose in Mawgan, or at Penwerris, at all of which places were estates of the Killigrews. The dauntless wife thus threatens Elizabeth's solemn First Minister :

> 'Si mihi quem cupio cures Mildreda remitti
> Tu bona, tu melior, tu mihi sola soror :
> Sin male cessando retines, et trans mare mittis,
> Tu mala, tu pejor, tu mihi nulla soror.
> Is si Cornubiam, tibi pax sit et omnia læta,
> Sin Mare, Ciciliæ nuncio bella. Vale.'

Of which, for the benefit of (some few at least of) my

---

* Another sister, Anne, married Nicholas Bacon, Lord Chancellor, and became the mother of Sir Anthony and of Francis Bacon—Lord Verulam.

lady readers in these later days, I have appended Fuller's harsh translation :

> ' If, Mildred, by thy care, he be sent back whom I request,
>   A sister *good* thou art to me, yea *better*, yea the *best.*
>   But if with stays thou keep'st him still, or send'st where seas
>   . may part,
>   Then unto me a sister *ill*, yea *worse*, yea *none* thou art.
>   If go to Cornwall he shall *please*, I *peace* to thee foretell ;
>   But, Cecil, if he set to Seas, I *war* denounce.   Farewell.'

Fortunately, thanks to the poetic skill of my friend Mr. H. G. Hewlett, I am able to give his smoother and more classical rendering of the lines :

> ' Mildred ! if truly my sister, the best, the one of all others,
>   Make it thy care to send back him whom I love to my arms.
> If by neglect thou withholdest thine aid, and art cause of his exile,
>   Wicked, the worst, wilt thou be, sister in nowise of mine.
> Should he to Cornwall return, all is peace with the Cecils and
>   kindness ;
>   If o'er the sea he depart, count on my hatred !   Farewell !'

I do not know the exact date of Dame Katherine Killigrew's death; but she was alive on the 22nd May, 1576. She was buried in the Church of St. Thomas the Apostle, in the Vintry Ward of the City of London, where there is—or rather was, for the church is destroyed—'her elegant monument ;' and many Greek and Latin verses were addressed to her memory by her sister Elizabeth and others. She thus wrote her own epitaph :

> ' Dormio nunc Domino, Domini virtute resurgam ;
>   Et σωτηρα meum carne videbo meâ.
> Mortua ne dicar, fruitur pars altera Christo :
>   Et surgam capiti tempore tota meo.'

By his second wife, Jael de Peigne, the friend and hostess of Isaac Casaubon, our Sir Henry left two sons, Sir Joseph and Sir Henry Killigrew, and

one daughter; but nearly all traces of Sir Joseph and
his sister Jane are lost, save what is interesting to
the genealogist alone.

But Henry was a man of some mark. He was
one of those loyal Members of the House of
Commons who refused to join the Parliament
against the Crown, and is described by Clarendon
as 'a person of entire affections to the King,' and
as commanding a troop of horse on Charles I.'s
march from Shrewsbury to London in 1642.* The
Lords Capel and Hopton were particular friends of
his; and with such Royalist connexions and predi-
lections, one is not surprised to learn that, together
with Messrs. Coryton, Scawen, and Roscarroth, he
was elected one of the Royal Commissioners for the
County of Cornwall; and that, when Pendennis
Castle was besieged, he was one of its stout defenders, remaining in it to the very last, and striving,
both by sword and pen, to shake off the grip of the
Roundhead bulldogs; all in vain, as we have already
seen. The following letter from Lord Jermyn, who
had married his cousin Katherine, serves to show, at
once how sore were the straits of the besieged, and
how highly their efforts were rated by Queen Henrietta Maria. (It will be remembered that Harry
Jermyn was commander-in-chief of the army which

---

* When he was called upon in Parliament to profess his adherence to
'The Good Cause,' as the Parliamentarians termed it, Sir Henry
bluntly and bravely declared, 'When I see occasion, I will provide a
good horse, a good buff coat, and a good pair of pistols : and then I
make no question but I shall find a "good cause." ' Very shortly after
this speech he found it necessary for his safety to leave London for
Cornwall, with the results about to be described.

marched from York to Oxford for the relief of
Charles I., under the Queen, who used to style herself, 'She Majesty Generalissima over all.' It is
believed that relations of too intimate a character
existed between the Queen and *her* commander-in-
chief.)

' MY DEAR COUSIN HARRY,

'I have received yours, and truly do, with all
the grief and respect that you can imagine to be in
any body, look upon your sufferings and bravery in
them; and do further assure you that the relief of
so many excellent men, and preservation of so important a place, is taken into all the considerations
that the utmost possibility, that can be in the Queen
to contribute to either, can extend to. The same
care is in the prince, from whose own hand you will
particularly understand it.

' I have now only time to tell you, that I am confident those little stores that will give us and you
time to stay and provide for more, will be arrived
with you; and I do not so encourage you vainly,
but to let you know a truth that cannot fail, that if
you, as I do no way doubt, have rightly represented
the state of the place, and of the minds that are in
it, you shall be enabled to give the account of it you
wish beyond your expectations; and already some
money is at the sea-side for this purpose, and more
shall daily be sent. I entreat most earnestly of you
that the Governor, Sir John Digby, and those other
gentlemen that did me the honour to write to me,
may find here that I shall not fail to give them

answer by the next. In the mean space, God of
heaven keep you all, and give us, if he please, a
meeting with you in England. I have no more to
add.

    ' I am, most truly,
        ' Your most humble and most faithful Servant,
                    ' HE. JERMYN.'

On the surrender of the Castle,* Sir Henry appears
to have gone to St. Malo, where he died on 27th
September, 1646, from splinter-wounds received in
the forehead by the explosion of a firearm whilst
he was discharging it in the air after the capitulation
of Pendennis. Clarendon sums up his character for
us as being ' a very gallant gentleman, of a noble extraction, and a fair revenue in land; he was of
excellent parts and great courage, and was exceedingly beloved. He was a passionate opposer of the
extravagant proceedings of the Parliament;' and,
when it came to blows, though he ' was in all actions,
and in those parts where there was most danger,
yet he would take no command in the army, yet he
was always consulted; he was of great courage, and
of a pleasant humour, but was a sharp reprover of
those who neglected their duty. His loss was much
lamented by all good men.' The Rev. Lionel
Gatford (who acted as chaplain to the Royalists
during the siege of Pendennis) preached Sir Henry
Killigrew's funeral sermon, which is described in a
MS. in the possession of S. Elliott Hoskins, M.D.,

* Cf. the chapter on the Arundells for an account of the siege of
Pendennis.

F.R.S., Guernsey, as 'une perle de grand prix, lequel ravissoit le cœur de ses auditeurs.'

Whilst he lay dying of his wound at St. Malo, some priests tried to convert him to the Roman faith; but he would have nothing to say to them, and sent for a clergyman of his own Communion forthwith. By his own wish his body was taken across to Jersey. It lay in state at the Constable's house at St. Helier's, guarded by his exiled soldiers. The funeral was performed with all military honours, on 3rd October, 1646, and the corpse was laid in a vault in the church or 'Temple' of St. Helier's, near that of Maximilian Norys. His income had been about £800 a year before the troubles of the Civil War; but he had lost it all.

Sir Henry married a lady named Jemima Bael, and by her had one son, Henry. He too was a warrior; and fell, a Major in the King's army, at Bridgewater in 1644, whilst defending a magazine of provisions against an attack by the Parliamentary troops: 'a very hopeful young man,' says Clarendon, 'the son of a gallant and most deserving father.'

As we have already seen, three daughters only were the fruit of old Sir Henry's first marriage with Katherine Cooke.

Sir William Killigrew, Knight, the first Sir Henry's next brother, now claims a short notice. He too—Killigrew-like—was about the Court, for he was a Groom of the Privy Chamber to James I., and was sworn in Chamberlain of the Exchequer on 28th November, 1605. He married Margaret Saundars of Uxbridge, a widow lady; and they seem to have been a steady-going old couple, to whom, it may be mentioned, John Fox and Robert Some dedicated a volume of their sermons. There is some correspondence about Sir William in the Lansdowne MSS. touching his 'farming' the Seals of the Queen's Bench and Common Pleas, to which the Chief Justice of the latter court objected; and Sir William, who was appointed to his post by Burghley, seems to have ultimately compromised matters by receiving the sum of £3,000. The Additional MSS. contain other references to him; but hardly anything of sufficient interest to warrant our lingering over his share in the family history. He died at Lothbury on 23rd November, 1622; and his portrait, with that of Thomas Carew, by Van Dyck, is preserved in the collection of Her Majesty Queen Victoria. Richard Carew says that he was 'the most kind patron of all his country and countrymen's (county) affairs at Court.'

But from this Sir William and 'Mystresse Margarye' descended Killigrews who have made some noise in the world, as we shall presently find. Besides two daughters, Katherine and Elizabeth—both of whom married, but make no figure in our story—they had a son, Sir Robert Killigrew of Hanworth, a wealthy man, and Chamberlain to two Queens of England, viz., Elizabeth and the hapless consort of Charles I. He too kept up the old family connexion with Pendennis Castle—of which he was made Governor in succession to Sir John Parker, on 11th June, 1632, towards the close of his life; and

he further served the Crown by going, in 1625, as an
Ambassador to the United Provinces. Sir Robert
was an original shareholder in the New River Company (incorporated in 1619) ; and was a great stickler
for his rights in the matter of the reclaimed lands
in Lindsey Level, Lincolnshire (as to which, see
Dugdale's 'History of Embanking') ; moreover,
Farnaby, the celebrated schoolmaster, dedicated to
him the 1624 edition of his translations of ' Martial's
Epigrams.' He was once ' sequestered ' for a manual
scuffle in the House, in 1614, as appears in Spedding's
' Works of Francis Bacon ;' and he was mixed up in
the story about the poisoned powder administered to
Sir Thomas Overbury, though it was clearly proved
that Killigrew was not to blame in that matter ; but it
is nevertheless true that he was sent from the Council
Table to the Fleet Prison for talking with Overbury
at his prison-window, after having paid a visit to Sir
Walter Raleigh in the Tower of London.

Sir Robert gave Whitelocke ' a place for Helston,'
whereupon Whitelocke caused his brother-in-law
Bulstrode to be returned for that place. He
must have had a fine seat at Hanworth ; for Conway,
writing to Buckingham on 3rd May, 1623, says that
on that day the King passed Sir Robert Killigrew's,
' and there saw the designment of a fine ground : a
pretty lodge, a gracious lady, a fair maid, the
daughter, and a fine bouquet. He saw the pools,
the deer, and the herondry ; which was his errand.'

When he took to himself a wife, he went to a
good stock, for he selected Mary Wodehouse, a
daughter of Sir Henry Wodehouse, of Kimberley,

Norfolk,* known as the 'young' or the 'French'
Lady Killigrew. She was a niece of one whose name
(erroneously as we apply it) is familiar to every
Englishman—I mean Lord Bacon. Of Sir Robert
himself, little more need be said here than that he
died on the 26th November, 1632 ; but his offspring
will detain us much longer.

Sir Robert had six daughters and five sons ; and
it may be as well to offer first the slight result of
my inquiries into the careers of the former.

They were about the Court of Charles II. ; and
one of them, Elizabeth, who married Viscount
Shannon, became one of the dissolute King's mis-
tresses. She died at her house in Pall Mall on 28th
July, 1684, and was buried in Westminster Abbey,
' having no Coat-of-arms of her own, as the King
had assigned her none.' Mary married Sir John
James, Knight ; and has a monument at the east end
of the north choir aisle in Westminster Abbey. Of
the others, I can only learn that they married men of
title—one the Earl of Yarmouth ; another Berkeley,
Lord Fitz-Hardinge ; and one married into a grand
old Cornish family — the Godolphins. Another,
Anne, ' a beauty and a poetess,' was the first wife of
George Kirk, and the unhappy lady was drowned at
London Bridge, in the Queen's barge, in July, 1641 ;
like so many others of her race, she was interred
in Westminster Abbey.

Robert, the eldest son, died young. The only

---

* It will be seen, further on, that these two families intermarried again ;
and that the house of Kimberley now represents that of Killigrew.

trace I can find of him is the following college exercise on the birth of Charles II. :

> ' Dum Solis radios abscondit Luna, videmus
>   Reginæ ex utero surgere Solem alium :
>   Quid tu, Phœbe, redis ? et cur te pœnitet umbræ ?
>   Non deerit, vel te deficiente, dies.'

His brother William, next in age, succeeded him as
the representative of the family—a position which
he must have held for about seventy years; for he
was nearly ninety when he died, in or about 1694.
When a Gentleman Commoner of Oxford he wrote
some verses, which Henry Lawes thought good enough
to set to music ; he also wrote four plays ; and when
he left the University (where he afterwards took
the degree of D.C.L.), he was forthwith welcomed
at Court, and became a Gentleman Usher of the
Privy Chamber, and afterwards Vice-Chamberlain
to Queen Katherine. About 1661 he was made a
Baronet, probably on account of his loyal attachment to the late King, whose body-guard he often
commanded. At York, when the Civil War broke
out in 1642, he commanded a troop of cavalry, composed of servants and retainers of the 1st troop of
Life Guards, under Lord Bernard Stuart ; and at
Edgehill he was one of the foremost in Prince
Rupert's fiery charge—a charge which at once began
and had almost ended the battle.

Old Sir William kept up the Killigrew connexion
with the West-country, by being, in his turn also,
made Governor of Pendennis ; but he is best known
and remembered by two little books which he wrote
very late in life, and especially by his ' Artless Mid-

night Thoughts,' written when he was eighty-two years old, and described by himself as the reflexions ' of a gentleman at Court, who for many years built on sand, which every Blast of Cross Fortune has defaced ; but now he has laid new Foundations on the Rock of his Salvation, which no Storms can shake ; and will outlast the Conflagration of the World, when Time shall melt into Eternity.'*

This curious little work is full of pious reflexions and thoughts, both in prose and verse.   It was dedicated first to Charles II., and afterwards to James II., who had made his old age much happier than ever his youth was, ' when I shared in all the glories of this Court, and splendour of Four great Kings for three score years.'   He himself describes the book as ' a small parcel of such fruit as my little cell in White Hall doth naturally produce from the barren brains of 82 years old.'   He also wrote some plays of a very different stamp from those of his younger brother, as may be judged from the following lines :

' COMMENDATORY VERSES BEFORE THREE PLAYS† OF
SIR WILLIAM KILLIGREW.—(By T. L.)

> ' That thy wise and modest Muse
> Flies the Stage's looser use ;
> Not bawdry *Wit* does falsely name,
> And to move laughter puts off shame :—

---

* The first edition, a little duodecimo, was published in 1684, a third edition was published at Winchester (where, it will be remembered, Charles sometimes kept his Court), on 7th Aug., 1686.

† ' Selindra,' ' Pandora,' and ' Ormasdes.'   Printed in 1665, London, 8vo.

'That thy theatre's loud noise
May be virgin's chaste applause ;
And the stoled matron, grave divine,
Their lectures done, may tend to thine :—

'That no actor's made profane,
To debase Gods, to raise thy strain ;
And people forced, that hear thy Play,
Their money and their *souls* to pay :—

'That thou leav'st affected phrase
To the shops, to use and praise ;
And breath'st a noble Courtly vein,—
Such as may Cæsar entertain,

'When he wearied would lay down
The burdens that attend a crown ;
Disband his soul's severer powers,
In mirth and ease dissolve two hours ;—

'These are thy inferior arts,
These I call thy second parts ;—
But, when thou carriest on the plot,
And all are lost in th' subtle knot,

*   *   *   *   *

'Th' easy and the even design ;
A plot, without a God, divine !—
Let others' bold pretending pens
Write acts of Gods, that know not men's ;
In this to thee all must resign ;
Th' Surprise of th' Scene is wholly thine.'

He was buried at the Savoy some time between
1693 and 1695, and left by his wife, Mary Hill, a
Warwickshire lady, one son, Sir Robert, Vice-
Chamberlain to Queen Anne of Denmark, and some
time Lord of the Manor of Crediton, in Devon,
whose only son Sir Henry died in St. Giles'-in-the-
Fields, without issue. Of his two daughters, one,
Elizabeth, married Sir Francis Clifton ; the other,
Mary, married Frederic de Nassau, Lord of Zule-
stein. Their son William Henry was in great

favour with our William III., who, in 1695, created him Baron Enfield, Viscount Tonbridge, and Earl of Rochford ; but, as we have seen, the descent, in *the male line*, from old Sir William became extinct.

The venerable author of the ' Artless Thoughts ' had, however, two brothers—Thomas* and Henry— and of these we have now to speak. Of the former, ' Tom Killigrew, the King's jester,' as he is sometimes inaccurately styled—probably more persons have heard than of any other member of this family ; and for his fame he is indebted, perhaps, in as great a degree to his being enshrined in the pages of that delightful gossip, Samuel Pepys, as to his printed plays.

Tom was Sir Robert's fourth son, and was born in 1611. Very early he became, through the family influence, a Page of Honour to Charles I. ; and he followed into exile that monarch's dissolute son, to whom, on the Restoration, he became a Groom of the Bedchamber and Master of the Revels, with a salary of £400 per annum. He seems to have added to his income by taking fees from those who were silly enough to offer them for using his interest in procuring for the gullible candidates the post of ' King's physic-taster,' or His Majesty's ' curtain-drawer.' Doubtless Killigrew was sometimes a minister to the profligacies of the ' merry ' monarch ; yet he was also one who could venture to tell a home-truth to the King when, it was absolutely necessary, and when no one else durst do it. The following story

* A Thomas Killigrew, whom I cannot quite identify, was in the Queen's Bench prison in 1642-43 on a suspicion of having raised arms against the Parliament.

may serve as an example. One day, Tom Killigrew came into the King's presence, clothed in pilgrim's weeds, and with a staff in his hand, evidently prepared for some long journey. 'Whatever are you about now, Killigrew?' cried the King; 'where are you going?' 'To hell, sir!' replied Tom, 'to fetch back one Oliver Cromwell to this unfortunate country; it was governed badly enough in his time, but infinitely better then than it is now.' An engraved portrait of him, dressed as a pilgrim, and another after Wissing, representing him with a beard, and armed with a sword, are preserved in the Print Room of the British Museum. Another instance of his adroitness in recalling Charles to a sense of his duty may be mentioned. The King found councils tedious; and would often leave them before the business was concluded,

> To sport with Amaryllis in the shade,
> Or with the tangles of Neæra's hair,

greatly to the disgust of (amongst others) Lauderdale. Accordingly, on a certain day, Tom Killigrew —between whom and the Chancellor no love seems to have been lost—offered to bet £100 that *he* could bring the King to the council, though the minister himself could not. The bet was concluded, and Killigrew started off after His Majesty, knowing probably better than anyone else where he was likely to be found. At once he disclosed to Charles what had happened, and urged the King to let him win the bet, whereby he, Tom Killigrew, would be £100 (sorely wanted, perhaps) in pocket; whilst Lauderdale, who was remarkable for the tight grip

with which he held his money, would be mulct in
that amount. Charles could not resist the double
pleasure of annoying Lauderdale and gratifying
Killigrew, and so granted the latter's request, and
won his bet for him.

Thomas Killigrew was sent—not without some
misgivings, as it would seem—by Charles II., whilst
in exile, as ' Resident ' to Venice ; and his instructions
from the King (with many other papers, some of
which are in Killigrew's own writing, are preserved
among the Harleian MSS., in the British Museum)
throw an amusing light upon the circumstances of
the Ambassador and his Royal Master. They were,
amongst other things, 'to presse the Duke to furnish
Us with a present Some of Money and We will
engage Ourself by any Act or Acts to repay with
Interest, and so like wise for any Armes and Ammunition hee shalbe pleased to furnish Us withall.
The summe you shall moue him to furnish Us with
shall be Ten thousand Pistolls.'

Killigrew's first paper was presented to the
Duke and Senate in Venice, 14th February,
1649-50.   It consists of five closely-written folio
pages in Latin, and he quotes in it King James's
saying of ' Sublato Episcopo tollitur Rex,' in support of his arguments against the cause of ' the
Rebels,' who, Charles feared, might be sending an
ambassador of their own, on a similar errand, to
that Court.

This mission does not seem to have proved very
successful ; and Tom Killigrew and his servants got
into sad disgrace at Venice with the Doge, Francis,

Erizzo, and other authorities, for their riotous
behaviour, the result being that the whole party
were dismissed ; deservedly perhaps, but somewhat
informally. On Thomas Killigrew's return to the
English Court, Sir John Denham addressed him in
these lines:

'Our Resident Tom
From Venice is come,
And has left all the statesmen behind him ;
Talks at the same pitch,
Is as wise, and as rich,
And just where you left him you'll find him.

'But who says he's not
A man of much plot
May repent of this false accusation ;
Having plotted and penned
Six plays, to attend
On the farce of his negotiation.'

The last three lines naturally lead us to a consideration of the 'Resident's' dramatic works,
written, as he says, to beguile the tedium of exile.
Thomas Killigrew wrote eleven plays in all; and,
according to Genest, strictly speaking wrote but two
at Venice; but the four written at Naples, Rome,
Turin and Florence, were probably completed before
his return to Paris. Dibdin, in his 'History of the
Stage,' points out that these plays are by no means
original, tracing some of them to their sources, and
calling them 'paste-and-scissors' affairs. But this
is not their chief defect. I have, as I thought myself
in duty bound, read one of them, and intend never
to read another. How it was possible, even
in that dissolute age—'never to be recalled,' as
Macaulay says, 'without a blush '—for a man to sit
down and deliberately write such obscene buffoonery,

and dedicate it to ladies—some of whom were his own relations—I cannot imagine. Plays too, of which one, at least, 'The Parson's Wedding,' was to be performed wholly by women! and in which the words assigned to those who played the women's parts are scarcely less offensive than those supposed to be spoken by men!* We find ourselves indeed 'surrounded by foreheads of bronze, hearts like the nether millstone, and tongues set on fire of hell.' I must add that they have scarcely a sparkle of that witty wickedness which one meets with in the writings of Sir Charles Sedley;—luckily they are dead, and they deserved to die! It is difficult to find an extract which is now presentable; and I can put my hand on no better specimen, on the whole, than this:

WALKING.

'*Fine Lady.* I am glad I am come home, for I am weary of this walking; for God's sake whereabouts does the pleasure of walking lie? I swear I have often sought it till I was weary; and yet I could ne'er find it.'

Not all of the plays were performed; though 'The Parson's Wedding' certainly was, at the King's House, and Luellin told Pepys that it was 'an obscene, loose play.' 'Claracilla,' a 'tragi-comedy,' Pepys himself went to see on 4th July, 1661; he merely says, however, that when he first saw it, it was 'well acted.' On a second occasion, when he saw it performed at the Cockpit, he thought it 'a poor play.' He might, in my opinion, have said the same of them all; but they were nevertheless sump-

* Women did not appear on the stage until after the Restoration.

tuously printed. King Charles II.'s own copy is in the British Museum (644, m. 11), and a portrait of the author contemplating the huge pile of his precious productions is prefixed to the volume. The original of this portrait was painted by W. Sheppard, and splendidly engraved by William Faithorne ; another portrait (also by Sheppard, according to Redgrave) is in the possession of Mr. J. Buller East, to whom it was presented, shortly before her death in 1819, by Frances Maria Killigrew, the last of her name. There is yet another portrait of Thomas Killigrew, which represents him, not, as Walpole says in his 'Anecdotes of Painting,' 'in a studious posture,' but stooping, worn out with his vicious life, with a gibbering monkey at his side, and clad in a tawdry dressing-gown, on which are represented the portraits of a host of the wantons of his acquaintance. The lines at the foot of this rare engraving by Bosse (British Museum, 009. f. 4) are an even more savage caricature than the picture itself.

Of Tom Killigrew's early fondness for plays, Pepys' story will serve as an illustration. 'I would not forget,' he writes, 'two passages of Sir J. Minne's at yesterday's dinner, one being Thomas Killigrew's way of getting to see plays when he was a boy. He would go to the Red Bull, and when the man cried to the boys, "Who will go and be a devil, and he shall see the play for nothing?" then would he go in, and be a devil upon the stage, and so get to see plays.' Would it be going too far to say that throughout his connection with the stage he stuck to his youthful part ?   He talked, however, much better than he wrote ; with Cowley the case was the reverse ; hence Denham's epigram :

> 'Had Cowley ne'er spoke, Killigrew ne'er writ,
> Combined in one they'd make a matchless wit.'

Pepys describes him as 'a merry droll, but a gentleman of great esteem with the King ; he told us many merry stories ;' again, that Killigrew was 'a great favourite with the King on account of his uncommon vein of humour ;' though on one occasion, when the King went to the Tower of London, to see the Dunkirk money, the conversation of Killigrew and the others was but 'poor and frothy.'   More than once, however, Tom Killigrew, to his credit, spoke out, and to the point, in a tone of which we have already heard something ; and Pepys himself has thus chronicled it :

' Mr. Pierce did also tell me as a great truth, as being told it by Mr. Cowley (Abraham Cowley the poet), and who was by and heard it, that *Tom Killigrew* should publickly tel the King that his matters were coming into a very ill state ; but that yet there was a way to help all. Says he, "There is a good, honest, able man that I could name, that if your Majesty would employ, and command to see all things well executed, all things would soon be mended ; and this is one Charles Stuart, who now spends his time in employing his lips about the Court, and hath no other employment ; but if you would give him this employment, he were the fittest man in the world to perform it." '

On another occasion, when even Charles reproached the 'chartered libertine' with his many 'idle words,' Killigrew did not shrink from retorting, with special significance, on the King, that, after all, '*idle promises* and *idle patents*' were even worse.

But something should be said of the domestic affairs of the subject of these observations. He lived, I believe, near that part of the old Court of Whitehall where Scotland Yard now stands; and, whilst there, married his first wife, Cecilia, daughter of Sir James Croft—a maid of honour to Henrietta Maria, and a lady whose portrait by Vandyck is in her present Majesty's collection.

The weather was rude and boisterous on the wedding-day, which gave rise to the following lines by Thomas Carew:

> ' Such should this day be ; so the sun should hide
> His bashfull face, and let the conquering bride
> Without a rivall shine, whilst he forbeares
> To mingle his unequall beames with hers ;
> Or if sometime he glance his squinting eye
> Betweene the parting clouds, 'tis but to spye,
> Not emulate her glories ; so comes drest
> In vayles, but as a masquer to the feast.'

I fear their wedded life must have been stormy throughout; the very first thing we hear of their courtship is a dispute in which they became engaged; and by-and-by we hear of Madam Killigrew's 'Case,' which sets forth that she brought her husband a fortune of £10,000, which Tom, writing from the Hague

in 1654* (the year in which his wife died of small-
pox), solemnly promised not to waste or otherwise
dispose of.   Two houses in Scotland Yard were built
with the money, or part of it.   Francis Quarles thus
bemoaned the hapless lady's fate: ' Sighes at the
contemporary deaths of those incomparable Sisters
—the Countesse of Cleaveland and Mistrisse Cicily
Killegreue.'   (They appear to have been buried in
the same tomb, and to have died within twice two
days of each other.)   The little poem ends
thus :

> ' My pen,
> Thou hast transgrest ;
> Archangels, and not Men
> Should sing the story of their Rest :
> But we have done, we leave them to the trust
> Of heaven's eternall Towre, and kisse their sacred Dust.'

About this time we come across a characteristic
little story about Tom Killigrew in Evelyn's
' Diary.'

Sir Richard Browne, writing from Nantes, 1st
November, 1653, to Hyde, then Chancellor of the
Exchequer, says that he has sent to him, carriage
paid, three barrels of canary wine to Mr. Thomas
Killigrew's care.   But Hyde does not seem to have
got them, at any rate for a very long time.   He heard
of the arrival of the consignment at Paris, and that
it was there 'conceaved to be Mr. Killigrew's own
wyne'!—very possibly, it may be feared, from the use
to which the consignee was putting it.

---

* About this time we find Elizabeth, Queen of Bohemia, interceding
with the Court on Thomas Killigrew's behalf, for a commission in
' Captaine Morgan's companie, who is dead.'

Thomas Killigrew was associated with Dryden, Sir William Davenant, and others, in obtaining a license (which, by the way, Sir Henry Herbert, his predecessor in the office of Master of the Revels, vainly endeavoured to get revoked) for a company of players, and a playhouse which was called the Theatre Royal, and which was situated somewhere between Drury Lane and Bridge Street.*

In fact, Killigrew was playhouse mad, as may be further seen by this extract from Pepys, date 1664:

' To King's playhouse: saw Bartholomew Fayre. I chanced to sit by Tom Killigrew, who tells me that he is setting up a nursery: that is, is going to build a house in Moorefields, wherein he will have common

---

* On April 8th, 1663, at the New Theatre in Drury Lane, the prices of admission were: boxes, 4s.; pit, 2s. 6d.; middle gallery, 1s. 6d.; upper gallery, 1s. The play began at 3 p.m., the prices not so very different from those at present, except that the pit seems to be proportionately dearer. The company at first consisted, so Mr. Froude says, of actors from the old ' Red Bull,' with additions from Rhodes's. Nell Gwynne and Mrs. Knepp (Pepys' Knip) were amongst them. I am indebted to my friend, Dr. G. Fielding Blandford, for the following information as to the site of the building:—' Killigrew converted Charles Gibbons' Tennis Court into a theatre in 1660. It was in Bear Yard, Vere Street, Clare Market, and was opened 8th November, 1660, with the play of "Henry IV." Pepys was there November 20th, and saw the play of " Beggar's Bush," and, for the first time, Mohun (known as Major Mohun), " said to be the best actor in the world." Here (January 3rd, 1661) he, for the first time, saw women on the stage. He calls it in other places the New Theatre, and says "it is the finest playhouse, I believe, that ever was in England." The names of the actors are given in the rate-books of St. Clement Danes for 1663. This theatre is not to be confounded (as it often is) with the one subsequently built in Portugal Row, and known as the Duke's Theatre. This is now the site of the Hunterian Museum. I believe the first theatre of that name only existed a few years.'

plays acted. But four operas it shall have in the year, to act six weeks at a time, where we shall have the best scenes and machines—the best musique, and everything as magnificent as is in Christendome, and to that end hath sent for voices and painters, and other persons from Italy.'

'It might naturally have been supposed' (observes Genest in his ' History of the Stage ') ' that Killigrew, on becoming patentee of the Theatre Royal, would have brought out some of his own plays; it does not, however, appear that any of them were ever acted, except " The Parson's Wedding " and " Claricilla." On the contrary, the silence of Langbaine and Downes does not amount to a proof that none were acted; as Langbaine did not frequent the theatres till several years after the Restoration, and Downes's account of the Theatre Royal is very imperfect. " The Pilgrim " is a good T. (theatre) play, with judicious alterations it might have been made fit for representation. " Cicilia " and " Clarinda," " Thomaso " and " Bellamira's Dream," are, each of them, rather one play in ten acts, than two distinct plays. When a play is written in two parts, there ought to be some sort of a conclusion at the end of the fifth act, but in these plays there is no more conclusion at the end of the fifth act than at the end of the first; improprieties occur in numberless plays, but perhaps no author ever made such strange jumbles as Killigrew has made in " The Princess," and " Cicilia " and " Clarinda." All his plays are in prose—most of them

are of an enormous and tiresome length—verbosity
is his perpetual fault—there is scarcely a scene in
which the dialogue might not be shortened to advantage.'

But to return to Killigrew's domestic affairs. Tom
married a second time—one Charlotte Van Hess, who
is described as first Lady of the Queen's Privy
Chamber in 1662, and as also holding the apparently
delectable appointment of Keeper of Her Majesty's
Sweet Coffer. By this marriage there were three
sons—Thomas, Robert, and Charles, of whom more
hereafter.

Tom Killigrew must have been nearly sixty years
old when he narrowly escaped assassination in St.
James's Park. He had had an intrigue with Lady
Shrewsbury, but found a dangerous and more successful rival in the Duke of Buckingham; whereupon the disappointed rake turned upon the lady a
stream of foul and venomous satire. The result
was that one evening, on his return from the Duke
of York's, some ruffians, probably hirelings of the
inconstant fair one, set upon Tom's chair, through
which they made no less than three passes with
their swords, one of them wounding him in the arm.
The assassins fled, leaving Tom Killigrew in danger
of death, and his man quite dead.*

* As regards the well-known story of his flippant tongue having
brought him into collision with Rochester—for which, according to
Pepys, Rochester never apologized—it may be observed that Rochester
did apologize to Tom's son, Harry, before going to France (7th
Report Dep. Keeper of Records, p. 531*a*).

This brings nearly to a close all that needs be said about Thomas Killigrew, who died thirteen or fourteen years after the foregoing event, on the 19th March, 168⅔, and was buried in Westminster Abbey.

Notwithstanding his vices, it may at least be recorded to his credit that he was faithful to the Stuart cause which he adopted ; was never ambitious, or avaricious ; and that it was said of him when he died, that ' he was bewailed by his friends, and truly wept for by the poor.'

His will is dated on the 15th March, and was proved in the Prerogative Court on the 19th of the same month by his son Henry, his executor, and residuary legatee. He left some houses in Scotland Yard, and he mentions a pension from the King. ' In the will,' says my authority, ' *there is no jest.*' That his pecuniary affairs were not in a very satisfactory condition would seem to be the case from a statement of ' Secret Money Services Charles II. and James II.,' ' Payd to several persons for the respective causes, uses and purposes und^r-menc'oned, as by divers acquittances & a particular accompt signed & allowed in the like manner on the 14th day of June, 1683, doth appear, several sumes amounting to £4,743 4½d.—amongst others To James Gray, for and towards the funeral charges of Thos. Killigrew, deceased, £50.' This supposition would also appear to be confirmed by the following autograph letter, written when Tom Killigrew must have been about seventy years old (Harl. MSS. 2, 7005, art. 42) :—

' For Mrs. Francesse Frecheville, Thes :

' DEAR MRS. FRECHEUILLE,

'You may imagen your letter was very well come to me for I receved it att a time when I needed all the kindnes you expresse to me in it and all the consolation it brought me, for I was halfe dead, but I am of the opinion that the greatest cordiall in the world, and that which will bring one allmost from death to life, is the kindnes of a person for whome one has a great estime, and I am, sure you cannot doubt but I have as much for you as it is possible, since I could never desemble in my life nor neuer make an expressione that I did not meane sencerly from my hart, I hope you doe beleeue this and that you will allwayes continue affectione to me since you can bestow it upon nobody that is more sencible of it and that will more reioyce in it than my selfe pardon this most horible scribble and beleeve I am with as much trewth as tis possible

' Ddear Mrs. Frechevill

' Your most affectionate

' humble Servant,

' T. KILLIGREW.

' My Lady Anne is Your humble Servant.'

Of his three sons by his second marriage, Thomas, generally known as Tom Killigrew the younger, was Gentleman of the Bedchamber to George II., when Prince of Wales, and was somewhat of a playwright, like his father. He wrote a piece called 'Chit-Chat' (in which, by the way, the mercurial Colley

Cibber played the principal part—'Alamode, a fop').
It was produced at Drury Lane shortly before the
author's death, an event which took place at Kensington, in July, 1719. This play is said to have been
very successful—was one of 'the four taking plays
of the season'—and on its production the Prince
made Killigrew a present of 100 guineas, to which
the Princess added another fifty. As far as I can
make out—though the matter is involved in great
obscurity—the lady to whom reference has already
been made as the possessor of the elder Tom Killigrew's portrait, and as dying, the last of her name,
in 1819, must have descended from this branch of
the family.

Robert, brother of the foregoing Thomas the
younger, was a soldier. 'Militavit annos 24' is
recorded on his monument in the north aisle of the
nave of Westminster Abbey;* and he had risen to the
rank of Major-General, when he fell on the plains of
Almanza, near Chinchilla, on 25th April, 1707, being
then forty-seven years old. This battle was fought,
during the Spanish war of succession, between the
Spanish and French, commanded by the Duke of
Berwick (a natural son of James II.), and the allied
English and Dutch forces under the incompetent
General Ruvigny, Earl of Galway; on which occasion
the latter were defeated; the fate of Spain was
decided; and the Bourbon line was practically restored to the Spanish throne, in the person of Philip V.

---

* 'It was considered remarkable as being cut out of one stone ; and it
has been reckoned one of the best pieces of sculpture in the whole
church.'—(*Royal Magazine*, 1763, p. 22.)

Galway—

> 'Deep versed in books, but shallow in himself'

(a red-tapeist general, who fought always according to rule),—'drew up his troops agreeably to
the manner prescribed by the best writers, and, in a
few hours, lost 18,000 men, 120 standards, all his
baggage, and all his artillery.' 'Do you remember,
child,' says the foolish woman in the *Spectator* to her
husband, 'that the pigeon-house fell the very afternoon that our careless wench spilt the salt upon the
table?' 'Yes, my dear,' replies the gentleman,
'and the next post brought us an account of the
battle of Almanza.'*

This battle is further remarkable as having been the
first occasion on which the Union Jack was used as the
British Ensign; and from its being almost the first
time when British troops used the bayonet; it is
also noteworthy, because at Almanza English and
Dutch troops, commanded by a Frenchman, were
defeated by French and Spaniards, commanded by a
British General. The battle was fought on a plain
about a mile in front of the town; and, I believe, an
obelisk still marks the site.

Colonel Townshend Wilson, in his 'Memoir of the
Duke of Berwick' (1883), gives a vivid description of
the stubbornly contested three hours' conflict — in
which 'never did Briton and Dutch face the foe more
steadily.' They were however out-numbered and
out-generalled—and on this day the old Das Minas
might have been seen, accompanied by a young lady,
his mistress, in a gay riding-habit, cantering to and
fro among the allied troops under fire; but an un-

* See Macaulay's review of Lord Mahon's 'War of the Succession.'

mannerly shot emptied her saddle.   The end of the battle is thus described :

'From stern resistance the cosmopolitan infantry suddenly changed to brilliant attack. With a tremendous effort they beat down all opponents.   Two battalions, irresistible in might, trampled down the enemy's double line, pressed even to the walls of Almansa. Superb audacity in front of well-led soldiers is sometimes foolishness.   Don José de Amezaga, with two squadrons, charging the enemy, blown and in disarray, cut them to pieces. . . . Then the wondrous English and Huguenot foot, quite *en l'air*, deprived of support, most of their superior officers laid low, thought of retreat.   The manœuvre was impracticable.   Hundreds of men were trampled under the hoofs of exulting cavaliers.   Six battalions, crushed into a crowd, had to lay down their arms.   But thirteen battalions (five of which were English), holding grimly together, under Count Dhona, and Major-General Shrimpton of the Guards, retired in fine order to a hill about a league from the field.' Being, however, without provisions, these gallant fellows were compelled on the following day to surrender to their antagonists.   The Spanish loss was 2,000 ; that of the Allies double that number, and eighty-eight British officers, including Brigadier Killigrew and Colonels Dormer and Roper, were amongst the slain.

Among Brigadier Robert's small effects were twenty-two pistoles, a bay horse, a pair of gold buttons, and his watch and seal—as appears from some family letters preserved among the ' Additional

MSS.' in the British Museum. He seems to have found life a 'fitful fever,' for in his very last letter to his brother—as ' T. K.' has endorsed it—he says that he is ' verre wery of sarvin in this Hott Contre.' But he was a courageous soldier ; for his nephew, Major Henry Killigrew, of the Irish Carabineers, who seems to have also been present at the battle, writes that 'no man there gave up his life with greater bravery' than his uncle did. General Robert Killigrew, in fact, appears to have deserved the place which he attained amongst the Worthies of England at Westminster.

Charles, the third brother, was born in 1650, and was buried in the Savoy in 1725. He succeeded his father in the post of Master of the Revels* in 1680, with a fee of £10 per annum ; and he was made a Commissioner of Prizes in 1707. J. T. Smith tells us that he used to license, ' in black and red print,' all ballad-singers, mountebanks, rope-dancers, prize-players, 'and such as make shew of motions and strange sights.' He also succeeded to the ownership of the play-house in Drury Lane; and is said to have done much to correct the profaneness of the stage.

Amongst the Lord Chamberlain's Records of the Reign of Charles II. is a volume marked ' Players

---

* The post of Master of the Revels was created in 1546, and, though the salary was small, the office entitled the holder of it to a seat in any part of the theatres. The seal of office, which was engraved on wood, was in the possession of Francis Douce, Esq., F.S.A., in 1815. Cf. ' Chalmer's Apology ' (title-page), for the arms of the revels. Much information as to this office will be found in Warton's 'History of Poetry,' ii. 405, iii. 307, note; 'Archæologia,' xv. 225; ' British Critic'; Brand's ' Popular Antiquities,' etc.

Booke,' which contains many curious entries, such as regulations against persons forcing their way into the theatre without payment at the beginning of the last acts of the piece. No actor to leave the theatre without giving three months' warning. No visitor to come between the scenes, or sit or stand upon the stage during the time of acting. It also appears that certain of the actors had entered into a bond of £500 with Charles Killigrew for the theatrical properties, and a regulation was made that thenceforth none of the actors or actresses should 'presume to go out of the House in theire acting Clothes.' The well known Mohun, who was one of the parties to this bond, had served as Major of a regiment in Flanders.

But Harry, who seems to have been a son of Tom the elder, by his first wife Cecilia Crofts, took most after his father. He was Groom of the Chamber to James II., when Duke of York; and was the scapegrace of the family. Pepys was more than once shocked at his conduct, and speaks of him as a 'rogue newly come out of France.' Before he did this he had earned a bad character abroad; for on 21st July, 1660, the Prince Palatine wrote of a duel which Master Harry fought at Heidelberg, and adds, ' He will never leave his lying as long as his tongue can wagg.' There were ugly suspicions of his having, in a drunken fit, stabbed his own servant; and of his having committed other outrageous misdeeds. In 1666 he was banished from the Court, 'for raw words spoken against a lady of pleasure.' Yet he seems to have contrived to find his way back again; for in 1667 occurred the memorable squabble between him and Buckingham, which Pepys thus relates, and to which Charles II. also referred in a letter to Prince Rupert:

'Creed tells me of the fray between the Duke of Buckingham at the Duke's play-house the last Saturday (and it is the first day I have heard that they have acted at either the King's or Duke's houses this month or six weeks), and Henry Killigrew, whom the Duke of Buckingham did soundly beat and take away his sword, and make a fool of, till the fellow prayed him to spare his life; & I am glad of it, for it seems in this business the Duke of Buckingham did carry himself very innocently & well, & I wish he had paid this fellow's coat well.'

The quarrel seems to have originated in some insulting words used by Harry Killigrew towards the Duke from an adjoining box, and to these the Duke replied in like fashion; whereupon a quarrel ensued, which ended in a challenge from Killigrew. This the Duke refused to accept, and a personal encounter was the consequence—the two combatants chasing each other round the house, to the great annoyance of the rest of the audience, as may be supposed. Killigrew seems to have lost his character as a man of courage—whilst the Duke lost—his wig! as well as his temper. I have not been able to discover what became afterwards of this 'ne'er-do-weel,' except that in 1698 he contrived to get a free grant of £200 from the Treasury. He married Lady Mary Savage, had two sons (Henry and James), and was buried on 16th December, 1705, at St. Martins-in-the-Fields.

37—2

We have thus completed, so far as seemed desirable, our sketches of all the sons and grandsons of Sir Robert Killigrew of Hanworth, except that of his fifth son, Henry; to him and to his career and progeny we now turn.   He was born at Hanworth the year after his brother Tom, viz. in 1612; and was at first educated, as Wood tells us, by that celebrated schoolmaster, Farnaby, at St. Giles's, Cripplegate.   Thence he went to Christ Church, Oxford, when sixteen years of age, and at that University obtained his degrees of M.A. in 1638, and D.D. four years afterwards.   Of his Latinity when at college, the following example, amongst others, has been preserved :—

ΠΡΟΤΕΛΕΙΑ.

ANGLO-BATAVA.

'Lævis adhuc, nec dum Vir constituende Marite ;
  Tuque Uxor Virgo, Virgo futura diu ;
Tam Castos Dilatus Hymen colit ipse Pudores,
  Nec tantum Cœlis Pinus Adulta placet.
Ne jactet plures Amor hoc ex Fœdere Tœdas,
  Et ludat Ritus, Pronuba Diva, Tuos
Præcipitata celer diffundat Tempora Currus,
  Hanc Matrem facias, Hunc citò, Juno, Virum.

'Hic Fratri Lucem, dedit hic Tibi, Sponsa, Maritum,
  O Quantum Mensis Munus Utrumq ; juvat !
Quære Mihi Niveos, Puer Officiose, Lapillos
  Ut Gemmâ Festum Candidiore notem.
Si tamen has vincant magè Lactea corpora gemmas,
  Pulchrior Ipse Suum Signet, et Ipsa Diem.'

He, too, received a Court appointment, and was Preceptor to James II. and a Chaplain to the King's Army and to the Duke of York.   In 1660, he was made Prebendary of the Twelfth Stall at West-minster, and about the same time Rector of Wheat-hampsted, where are some of the family tombs.   But it was not until 1667, when he was between fifty and sixty years of age, that he obtained the post in connexion with which his name is most generally known—that of ' Master of the Savoy and Almoner to His Royal Highness.'

Whilst still a youngster of seventeen, he wrote a tragedy which he called ' The Conspiracy,' intended for performance at the celebration of the ' Nuptialls of the Lord Charles Herbert and the Lady Villers.' It was played at the Blackfriars Theatre in 1638, and was received with great applause—obtaining high praise from ' rare Ben Jonson ' himself. One critic, indeed, objected that the sentiments expressed by the hero of the piece, Cleander, were far beyond his age —seventeen—until he was reminded that that was the age of the author himself. Here is a specimen of the youthful writer's powers :

'(*The Rightful Heir to the Crown kept from his inheritance: an angel sings to him sleeping.*)

' SONG.

' While Morpheus thus does gently lay
 His powerful charge upon each part,
Making thy spirits ev'n obey
 The silver charms of his dull art ;

' I, thy Good Angel, from thy side—
 As smoke doth from the altar rise,
Making no noise as it doth glide,—
 Will leave thee in this soft surprise ;

' And from the clouds will fetch thee down
 A holy vision, to express
Thy right unto an earthly crown ;
 No power can make this kingdom less.

' But gently, gently, lest I bring
 A start in sleep by sudden flight,
Playing aloof, and hovering,
 Till I am lost unto the sight.

'This is a motion still and soft,
    So free from noise and cry
  That Jove himself, who hears a thought,
    Knows not when we pass by.'

The play appears to have been printed without
the writer's consent, in 1638, in an imperfect form;
but it was not until fifteen years afterwards that he
published an amended copy of it under the title of
'Pallantus and Eudora.' He also wrote another
play, 'The Tyrant King of Crete,' which was never
acted. Many of his sermons too were printed; one of
them, Pepys—who seems to have gone almost everywhere, and heard almost everything—listened to in
1663: 'At Chapel I had room in the Privy Seale
pewe with other gentlemen;' but he has left no
record of the impression produced. Probably, therefore, it was not very deep or lasting; and, in fact,
the sermons have no special excellence: yet there
is something true and pathetic in this saying:
'Misery lays stronger bonds of love than Nature;
and they are more than one, whom the same *misfortune* joined together, than to whom the same womb
gave life.'

The Rev. W. J. Loftie, in his 'History of the
Savoy,' tells us that Henry Killigrew succeeded
Sheldon as Master, and that he was no more careful
and economic in the management of the decaying
establishment than was his predecessor; yet King
William III.'s Commissioners tell a somewhat
different story, and describe him as 'a man of generous and public spirit, as his expenses in the Chapel
of the said Hospital, and of King Henry VII. at

Westminster, who was the founder of the said Hospital, do sufficiently testify.'

In the Savoy itself Henry Killigrew lived, paying £1 a year for his lodgings. No pleasant neighbourhood was that ' Sanctuary '* which Macaulay thus describes :

'The Savoy was another place of the same kind as Whitefriars; smaller indeed, and less renowned, but inhabited by a not less lawless population. An unfortunate tailor, who ventured to go thither for the purpose of demanding payment for a debt, was set upon by the whole mob of cheats, ruffians, and courtezans. He offered to give a full discharge to his debtor, and a treat to the rabble, but in vain. He had violated their "franchises," and this crime was not to be pardoned. He was knocked down, stripped, tarred, and feathered. A rope was tied round his waist. He was dragged naked up and down the street amidst yells of " A bailiff! a bailiff!" Finally he was compelled to kneel down, and curse his father and mother—and then " to limp home without a rag upon him." '

The Master of the Savoy married twice, it is said; but I have failed to trace the maiden name of either of his wives. It would have been interesting to know who the first was, especially; for she was the mother of the fairest and brightest of all the Killigrews—Mistress Anne. The second wife con-

* It will be remembered that, before Chelsea Hospital was built, Charles II. turned out many of the denizens of the Savoy to make room for the soldiers and sailors wounded in the wars.

tinued to live in the Savoy after her husband's death, which took place the 14th March, 1699.

He had two sons and two daughters. The sons, both of whom were sailors, were Henry and James; and the daughters, Elizabeth and the incomparable ANNE. Clutterbuck, in his 'History of Hertford-shire,' says that Elizabeth married Dr. J. Lambe, Dean of Ely, who succeeded to the Rectory of Wheathampstead; and that they had five sons and five daughters. Her epitaph records that she was 'a most intirely beloved wife,' and that 'to mencon some of her virtues only (though very great ones) would lessen her character, who was a most eminent example of all those virtues whatsoever that adorn her sex.'

Henry, the elder son, appears to have been, on the whole, a successful man in his profession; he entered the navy in 1666, and for the next twenty years sailed in almost as many different ships; he was made Vice-Admiral of the Blue in 1689, and finally was created a Lord of the Admiralty under King William III. He died at his seat at St. Albans (for which place he had been elected M.P.) on the 9th November, 1712, eighteen years after his retirement from the Admiralty. Many MS. letters by him are in the Bodleian Library, and at All Souls' College, Oxford. In the British Museum is preserved a broadside entitled—

'GOOD NEWS FROM THE ENGLISH FLEET:

being an Account of a great and bloody Engagement which happened yesterday between Their Majesties'

Fleet commanded by Admiral Killigrew, and the French Fleet near the Beachy—with a particular account of the Taking Six of their Ships, and Sinking Three.'

It was printed 17th September, 1690 ; on which date the final result was not known, but enough had been learnt to describe the engagement as a victory ; the battle was fought three leagues off the shore, and lasted from 10 a.m. till night.

Macaulay does not refer to this exploit ; but, writing of the year 1693, he tells us that ' Killigrew and Delaval *were Tories*, and that the Whigs carried a vote of censure upon the Government in consequence of the late naval miscarriages, but failed to fix it on Killigrew and Delaval themselves, the Admirals.' The facts seem to have been that Killigrew and Delaval were appointed to convoy seventy ships of the line and thirty smaller vessels—the richly-freighted Smyrna fleet—past Brest to the Mediterranean; Rooke was to take them on afterwards. But the French fleet lay in wait for them near Gibraltar, and Rooke fell into the trap, with dire results. Macaulay thinks that Killigrew and Delaval ought to have been sharper, and not to have returned to England so soon. On hearing of the news in England, many of the merchants went away from the Royal Exchange ' pale as death.' There is, however, in the British Museum a rare ballad which somewhat conflicts with Macaulay's views, and I am tempted to refer to it, without being able to reconcile the discrepancy. It is entitled—

' The Seamen's Victory, or *Admiral Killigrew's* glorious conquest over the French Fleet, in the Streights, as they were coming from Thoulon towards Brest. With the manner of Taking Three of their French Men of War, and sinking Two more; although the French Admiral vainly boasted he would recover Brest or Paradice, yet he shamefully run from the English Fleet. (*To the Tune of The Spinning Wheel.*)'

The ballad is illustrated with rough wood-cuts, three of which represent ships, and a fourth, it is to be presumed, the Admiral himself. It begins thus:

> ' Here's joyfull news came late from Sea,
> 'Tis of a gallant Victory,
> Which o'er the French we did obtain,
> Upon the throbbing Ocean Main.
> As soon as e'er they found our Rage,
> The Rogues was glad to disengage.'

The defeat of the attempt made by the Toulon fleet to join that at Brest is then described, in the same rude sort of lines eminently adapted for the roystering choristers who frequent seaside taverns; and the poet thus continues:

> ' Now while we did maintain the Fight,
> Two French Ships there we sunk down right,
> And likewise have we taken Three,
> This Crown'd our Work with Victory;
> The noble, valiant KILLEGREW,
> After the rest do's still pursue.'

And the ballad concludes with the hope—

> ' That we hereafter may advance
> To shake the very Crown of France.'

Possibly it refers to an episode of the fight which

may have escaped the notice of the illustrious historian. This much, however, is certain, that the exploits of the British Admiral were caricatured in a street play, probably got up for political purposes.

Admiral Killigrew has been described in the following terms by one G. Wood, his clerk, who sailed with him to the Mediterranean :

' A young man in the flower of his age but a man of great experience and to add to his experience he's a man of undaunted Courage Prudence and Conduct, making it his study in all his actions to doe nothing (though never so much to his own advantage) but that which is truely honorable and altogeither tending to the honor and advantage of his King and Country. Hee likewise carry'd his comand wth so much gravity and wisdome that he was both belov'd and fear'd by all y^e squad^n from y^e highest to y^e lowest ; and for his Prudence and Dilligence in managing of his Ma$^{tie's}$ affairs. . . . . I might inlarge much more and speak nothing but truth of this hono^{ble} comand^s yett fear I should be look't upon as a flatterer by those y^t knows him not.'

Whilst serving in the Mediterranean, in chase of a *Salletine* frigate, he was severely wounded by the bursting of a gun in his own ship, the splinters breaking both bones of his right leg, and frightfully wounding his head.

I have been unable to ascertain whom Admiral Henry married; but he had a son who bore the same name as himself, and who settled at St. Julian's in

Hertfordshire. I think it must have been he who
was a Major in Lord Strafford's Royal Regiment of
Dragoons, the composition of which corps and the pay
of its members are set forth in the Add! MSS. 22,231
in the British Museum. It would, however, be un-
interesting to trace farther the descent of this branch
of the family.

James, the younger brother, when only twenty-one
years of age, and unmarried, was killed in a sea
engagement off Leghorn, in January 169$\frac{4}{5}$, on board
the *Plymouth;* like Nelson, 'in the arms of victory.'*
His ship was a fast sailer, and outstripped her companions, so that when Captain James Killigrew
came up with the French he had to engage two
ships at once, both bigger than his own, one of
which, however, he sunk, and the other he took. He
sustained the unequal combat, it is said, for four
hours. Besides losing his own life, fifty of his men
were killed and wounded when the remainder of the
British ships at length came up to his assistance.
' Characters like his need no encomium,' observes
Charnock. Some accounts attribute cowardice to
his comrades on this occasion.

We have now nearly completed our task, and have
come to the last of the Killigrews whose history is
likely to be entertaining, or instructive. ANNE,

'quæ stabat ubique victrix forma, ingenio, religione,'

as her epitaph (now destroyed) in the chancel of St.
John the Baptist, in the Savoy Chapel, once described

---

* He entered the navy on 5th Sept., 1688, and served successively in
the *Portsmouth,* the *Sapphire,* the *York,* the *Crown,* and the *Plymouth.*

her ; * and most gratifying it is to close our account of the Killigrews with the story of this admirable woman.

She was born in 1660, in St. Martin's Lane; and, the Restoration not having then been effected, was (according to Cibber's 'Lives of the Poets') christened in a private chamber, the offices of the Common Prayer-book not being at that time publicly allowed. Early distinguished for her skill in poetry and in painting, and for her learning, taste, and purity of life, for her fame she is not indebted to that which alone would have been sufficient to perpetuate it—I mean Dryden's renowned ode. This, exaggerated as its terms may appear, is nevertheless said, by those who knew her, to be hardly too strongly expressed. Even the ascetic Anthony Wood wrote of her the well-known line,

'A Grace for beauty, and a Muse for wit ;'

and he assures us that 'there is nothing spoken of her which she was not equal to, if not superior.' That she was an accomplished artist Dryden's verse records, and that this was a talent possessed by at least one of her ancestors we have seen in the account of Sir Henry Killigrew, the diplomatist; but I am not aware that any of her paintings remain to us; but Walpole saw her portrait by herself, and thought more highly of her painting than of her poetry. The portrait has been admirably engraved in mezzotint by Becket and by Blooteling. She painted James II. and his Queen, as well as several

---

* Ballard says on the north side. Mr. Loftie tells us that it stood on the eastern side of the chapel, not far from the vestry-door and pulpit.

'history-pieces,' landscapes, and still-life subjects,
which Dryden mentions in the poem that Dr. Johnson pronounced 'the noblest ode that our language has
produced.' I am aware that Warton somewhat differs
from the great critic as to this; but it would be difficult
to point to a finer English threnody; and, notwithstanding the probability of its being familiar, if not
to all, yet to most of my readers, I venture to think
that the reproduction here of such parts as particularly refer to Anne Killigrew may not be unacceptable.   The noble strain thus opens :

> 'Thou youngest virgin daughter of the skies,
> Made in the last promotion of the blest :
> Whose palms, new plucked from Paradise,
> In spreading branches more sublimely rise,
> Rich with immortal green, above the rest ;
> Whether, adopted to some neighbouring star,
> Thou roll'st above us in thy wandering race ;
>   Or, in procession fixed and regular,
>   Mov'st with the heaven's majestic pace ;
>   Or, call'd to more superior bliss,
> Thou tread'st, with seraphims, the vast abyss :—
> Whatever happy region is thy place,
> Cease thy celestial song a little space ;
> Thou wilt have time enough for hymns divine,
> Since heaven's eternal year is thine.
> Hear then a mortal muse thy praise rehearse,
>   In no ignoble verse,*

---

* A touching apology for much 'ignoble verse' of Dryden's own
majestic muse—

> 'Licentious satire, song and play.'

Elsewhere in this ode he laments :

> 'Oh wretched we ! why were we hurried down
> This lubrique and adulterous age—
> Nay, added fat pollutions of our own !'

But such as thy own voice did practise here,
When thy first fruits of poesy were given,
To make thyself a welcome inmate there ;
    While yet a young probationer
    And candidate of heaven.'

Exaggerated language perhaps, but sincerely meant. And the master of the 'long-resounding line' concludes :

'When in mid-air the golden trump shall sound,
To raise the nations under ground ;
When in the Valley of Jehoshaphat,
The judging God shall close the book of fate,
And there the last assizes keep
For those who wake, and those who sleep ;—
When rattling bones together fly
From the four corners of the sky ;
When sinews o'er the skeletons are spread,
Those clothed with life, and life inspires the dead ;
The sacred Poets first shall hear the sound,
And foremost from the tomb shall bound,
For they are covered with the lightest ground ;
And straight, with inborn vigour, on the wing,
Like mounting larks, to the new morning sing.
There thou, sweet Saint ! before the choir shalt go,
As harbinger of heaven, the way to show,
The way which thou so well hadst learnt below.'

The allusion to the grief of her brother Henry, the Admiral, then at sea, is very fine :

'Meantime her warlike brother on the seas,
His waving streamers to the wind displays,
And vows, for his return, with fond devotion pays.
Ah, generous youth ! that wish forbear,—
The winds too soon will waft thee here !
Slack all thy sails ! and fear to come ;—
Alas ! thou know'st not—*thou art wrecked at home.*'

Her skill as a painter he depicts in the following happy lines :

'Her pencil drew whate'er her soul designed,
And oft the happy draught surpass'd the image in her mind.

> The sylvan scenes of herds and flocks,
> The fruitful plains, and barren rocks ;
> Of shallow brooks that flowed so clear
> The bottom did the top appear :
> Of deeper, too, and ampler floods,
> Which, as in mirrors, showed the woods :
> Of lofty trees with sacred shades,
> And perspectives of pleasant glades,
> Where nymphs of brightest form appear,
> And shaggy satyrs standing near,
> Which them at once admire and fear.
> The ruins, too, of some majestic piece
> Boasting the power of ancient Rome or Greece ;
> Whose statues, friezes, columns, broken lie,
> And, though defaced, the wonder of the eye ;
> What Nature, Art, bold Fiction e'er durst frame,
> Her forming hand gave feature to the name.'

Dryden then alludes to her portraits of the royal family—and first of the King :

> ' For, not content to express his outward part,
> Her hand called out the image of his heart.'

Of his Consort's likeness the poet gracefully observes :

> ' Our phœnix Queen was pourtrayed, too, so bright,
> Beauty alone could beauty take so right.'

And, with a grand hyperbole, the poem ends with the above prediction that at the last day the Poets shall first awake at the sound in mid-air of the golden trump :

> ' For they are covered with the lightest ground.'

Mistress Anne Killigrew, as the virgin poetess and paintress was called, after the fashion of the time, was, like so many others of her family, attached to the Court. She was Maid of Honour to the Duchess of York; and, even in those loose days, was unspotted by the contaminating influences amongst which she found herself. One other taint, however, she did not escape—the contagion of small-pox, of which horrible malady this 'cynosure' died at her father's prebendal house in the Cloister of Westminster Abbey, on the 16th June, 1685, in the twenty-fifth year of her age.*

To her 'Poems,' now a rare book—a thin quarto, which appeared shortly after her death—are prefixed Dryden's ode, and the mezzotint by Becket, after her portrait of herself. Sir Peter Lely also painted her likeness.

It has already been said that none of her paintings remain; but of her poetical powers we may still judge from the following extracts. They will, of course, fall somewhat flat after the lofty lines which have just been cited; yet I venture to think that they will be found worthy of perusal. At any rate, Dryden writes,

> 'Thy father was transfused into thy blood,
> So wert thou born into a tuneful strain;'

and they were at least considered at the time sufficiently good for the insinuation that they were not her own—a calumny to which the gentle Anne replied:

* Mr. Loftie says that the entry in the Savoy Register is dated 15th April, 1685.

'UPON THE SAYING THAT MY VERSES WERE MADE
BY ANOTHER.

  *   *   *   *   *   *

' Th' envious Age, only to Me alone,
Will not allow, what I do write, my Own,
But let 'em rage, and 'gainst a Maide Conspire,
So Deathless Numbers from my Tuneful Lyre
Do ever flow ; so Phebus I by thee
Divinely Inspired and possest may be ;
I willingly accept Cassandra's Fate,
To speak the Truth, although believ'd too late.'

The following lines also are, I venture to think, far
from commonplace :

'AN ODE.

' Arise, my Dove, from midst of Pots arise,
Thy sully'd Habitation leave,
To Dust no longer cleave ;
Unworthy they of Heaven that will not view the Skies.
Thy native Beauty reassume,
Prune each neglected Plume
Till, more than Silver white,
Than burnisht Gold more bright,
Thus ever ready stand to take thy Eternal Flight.'

Notwithstanding her modesty, she was not without
some confidence that her poetry would survive her,
as it has, in fact, already done for two centuries; for
thus she wrote her own epitaph :

' When I am Dead, few friends attend my Hearse ;
And for a Monument I leave my *Verse ;*'

a monument, perhaps, *ære perennium*, and which
certainly remains longer than the marble cenotaph
which was destroyed by the fire in the Savoy.*

* Alexander Pendarves, M.P. for Launceston, and first husband of
Mary Granville (Mrs. Delaney) ; Wm. Vivian, ' son and heir of Michael
Vivian of Cornwall ' (1520) ; and Richard Lander (the well-known
traveller), were other Cornish folk, to whom monuments were erected in
the Savoy. The tablets were all destroyed in the fire of 7th July, 1864 ;
but, in the case of Lander, a stained-glass window has been substituted
for the destroyed monument.

Epitaphs, indeed, seem to have had a charm for her, as if she had a foreboding of her early death; and the following lines in praise of Mrs. Phillips may serve for a fair description of herself, and as a finish to these extracts from her compositions :

> 'Orinda (Albion's and her sex's grace)
> Owed not her glory to a beauteous face,
> It was her radiant *soul* that shone within ;
> Which struck a lustre through her outward skin ;
> That did her lips and cheeks with roses dye,
> Advanced her height, and sparkled in her eye.
> Nor did her sex at all obstruct her fame,
> But higher 'mong the stars it fixed her name ;
> What she did write, not only all allowed,
> But every laurel to her laurel bowed.'

Perhaps too much has been said of the virtues and graces of this chaste and accomplished lady; but it must be remembered that women such as she were rare in the days in which she lived and wrote. Nor must we forget that we are far removed from the sphere of that *personal* influence, the attractions of which are so powerful, and which probably contributed in no small degree to the fame of this fair scion of the Killigrews.

It was written on her epitaph, according to Ballard :

> 'Abi, Viator, et plange,
> Si eam plangi oporteat
> Cui, tam pié morienti,
> Vel Cœlites plauserint.'

Even at this distance of time, it is delightful to think that she left a wicked world and age before a single spot had dimmed the lustre of her widely admired, but unsullied, fame :

> 'Wearing the white flower of a blameless life.'

RICHARD LANDER,

THE EXPLORER.

RICHARD LANDER,

THE EXPLORER.

'Les fleuves sont de grands chemins qui marchent.'—*Pascal.*

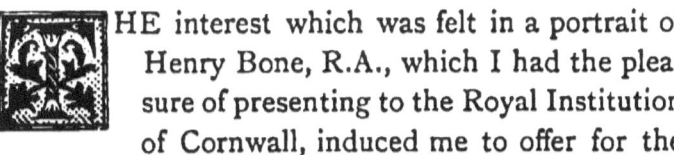HE interest which was felt in a portrait of Henry Bone, R.A., which I had the pleasure of presenting to the Royal Institution of Cornwall, induced me to offer for the acceptance of that Society the portraits of two other Truro worthies; which I thought (though the engravings possess no great merit as works of art) might at least serve as reminders of the energy, skill, and determination possessed by two Truro men—half a century ago;* and, almost as a matter of course, Richard Lander's name found a place among the Cornish Worthies, whose stories I am attempting to write. I am just old enough to remember the commencement, on the 16th June, 1835, of the erection of the column designed by P. Sambell, jun., to the memory of Richard Lander, which stands at

---

* There is a portrait of Richard Lander in the possession of the Royal Geographical Society, painted by W. Brockedon, F.R.S., and it was engraved by C. Turner, A.R.A.

the top of Lemon Street, and (owing to bad work-
manship) the fall of a considerable portion of it on
the 21st of May, 1836. Amongst other reminis-
cences I may perhaps also mention that my father
has told me that, on the occasion of laying the
foundation-stone of the column, he was one of those
who formed the procession, and that he and the late
Mr. Humphry Willyams, of Carnanton, then led by
the hand Richard Lander's child. On that occasion, as on a more recent one of higher importance
at Truro, viz., the laying of the foundation-stone of
the new Cathedral, the Masonic ceremony was
followed by a religious service.

Although generally spoken of as the Brothers
Lander, it should be borne in mind that to Richard,
the elder brother, the world is mainly indebted for
the discovery of the course of the lower portion of
'the lordly Niger' (as Longfellow calls the river).
John, the younger brother, had considerable powers
of observation and some poetic taste, and was by
trade a printer. He accompanied Richard simply
from affectionate motives (and certainly without
promise of any pecuniary reward), on the *second* of
Richard's three expeditions to Africa, from which
the brothers returned safely ; but John will appear no
further (except incidentally) in the remarks which I
have to offer. He was born in 1807, and died in
1839 in consequence of illness contracted during his
one voyage to Africa.

Richard Lemon Lander, the heroic but unfortunate
traveller, whose name will ever be associated with
the splendid discovery of the course and termination

of that mysterious and fatal river, which some of
the ancients confounded with the Nile, and which
the Moors of Northern Africa still call 'the Nile
of the Negroes,'* was the fourth of six children,
and was born at his father's house, the 'Dolphin
Inn,' Truro (then called 'The Fighting Cocks'), on
the 8th February, 1804, the day on which Colonel
Lemon was elected M.P. for the town. Hence his
second name ; and hence also a certain appropriate-
ness in the site which was chosen at the top of
Lemon Street for his statue, the work of a Cornish
sculptor, the late N. N. Burnard. In the midst of
his unfeigned humility in his account of his parents,
he nevertheless boasts that, as his father's name
began with a *Lan* and his mother's maiden name
(Penrose) with a *Pen*, no one could deny his claim
to being a right *Cornishman.* But Colonel J. Lam-
brick Vivian informs me that Lander came from an
older and a better stock than he was himself aware
of. The family can be traced, in St. Just at least, as
early as 1619, at which time a Richard Lander
married Thomasine Bosaverne, one of a good old
Cornish family. The Polwheles and Landers also

---

* The Niger, so Herodotus heard, flowed from the west *eastward*—
ἀπὼ ἑσπέρης πρὸς ἤλιον ἀνατέλλοντα.

Pliny first uses the word Niger or Nigris. He seems to have thought
that the *Niger* and Nile were somehow united ; and Claudian seems to
have fallen into the same mistake :

' Gèr notissimus amnis
Æthiopum, simili mentitus gurgite Nilum.'

The French have a notion that the Senegal and the Niger may be
connected by a cutting, by which means Timbuctoo might be conveniently approached, and trade opened up with the interior of Africa.

intermarried.   Richard's grandfather, a noted
wrestler, lived near the Land's End.

Of Lander's early life in Truro I can learn little
further than that he went to "old Pascoe's" school
in Coomb's Lane, and was one of those few
favourites of his master, who was thought worthy to
receive one of the then newly-coined 1s. 6d. pieces.
Richard seems to have been a merry, bright-eyed
lad, somewhat below the usual height,* but he was
always of a roving, adventurous spirit, and, when
only eleven years old, accompanied a merchant to
the West Indies, whence, after a residence there of
three years, and having been attacked by fever in St.
Domingo, he returned to England in 1818, and lived
as a servant in various wealthy families, with some
of whom he visited the continent of Europe.

In 1823 he went with Major Colebrook (one of
the Royal Commissioners of inquiry into the state
of the British Colonies) to the Cape of Good
Hope, and returned to England in the following
year.   In 1825, when Captain Clapperton and
Major Denham returned from their travels in the
interior of Africa, Lander, charmed, as he says, by
the very sound of the word 'Africa,' and impelled
by his inborn love of adventure, offered to accompany the former officer in a second expedition to
that continent, notwithstanding the efforts of all his
friends to dissuade him.   Amongst these may be
mentioned Mr. George Croker Fox, who offered
Lander, by way of a counter-temptation, a more

---

* On account of his short stature he was generally called by the
natives in Africa ' Nasarah Curramee,' or Little Christian.

lucrative post in South America. However, Lander's proposal was gladly accepted by Clapperton, and the adventurous youngster remained with his employer up to the hour of the Captain's death at Soccatoo, in the interior, in April, 1827. · He then made his homeward-way, alone, by land to Badagry on the coast, and arrived at Portsmouth with Clapperton's papers in April, 1828, much debilitated by fevers contracted during his long sojourn in a pestiferous climate.

In the December of the following year Richard Lander published a most entertaining account of his travels, dating the first part of the introduction to the book, 'Truro, Oct. 29th, 1829.' To this work is prefixed his portrait, in his Eastern travelling costume.

Now comes his most important voyage of discovery. Having arranged, under the auspices of the Government, a second expedition to West Africa, not only with a view to commerce, but also in the hope of doing something which should lead to the suppression of the slave-trade and of human sacrifices, he embarked with his brother John in the merchant-vessel *Alert* at Portsmouth, on the 8th January, 1830. He says the party went out 'with the fixed determination to risk everything, even life itself, towards the final accomplishment of their object. Confidence in ourselves and in the natives will be our best panoply, and an English Testament our best fetish.' The Colonial Secretary granted an allowance of £100 a year to Mrs. Richard Lander during her husband's absence, and the

traveller was himself to receive a gratuity of £100 on
his return to England.   The little expedition arrived
at Cape Coast Castle on the 22nd February, 1830,
and was conveyed thence on board H.M.'s Brig
Clinker to Accra, where they landed on the 22nd
March.   On the 17th June, after a toilsome and
dangerous journey overland, they reached Boussa on
the West bank of the Niger, the place where, it will
be remembered, Mungo Park met with a similar
fate to that which was ultimately to befall Lander.
Thence they ascended the river to Yaoorie, a distance of about 100 miles; and this place, the
extreme point of the expedition, they reached on the
27th June.   On the 2nd August they returned to
Boussa, where they embarked in canoes in order to
descend the stream—considering that such a method
must at last solve the mighty problem somehow—
though of course in utter uncertainty as to whither
the stream might lead them.

As they proceeded, difficulties and dangers increased.   At Kirree they were plundered and cruelly
ill-treated; and at Eboe they were made prisoners by
the Negro King, who demanded a large sum for their
ransom, which, after long delay, was procured.   At
length they reached the mouth of the Nun branch of
the Niger; and on the 1st December, 1830, they
were put on shore at Fernando Po; and ultimately,
after first visiting Rio Janeiro, they reached Portsmouth on the 9th June, 1831.

So triumphant a result naturally excited the public
interest; and it is stated that Murray, the eminent
publisher, offered the Landers 1000 guineas for their

papers; the offer was accepted, and the task of blending the brothers' two journals into one, and of constructing a map of their route, having been performed by Lieutenant Beecher, R.N., the work, in three volumes, was published in 1832 as No. 28 of the Family Library, and has been translated into French, German, Dutch, and Swedish. For his valuable discoveries Richard Lander received from the Royal Geographical Society its first annual premium of fifty guineas, presented by King William IV.

It may be interesting to note here the following description of the scenery of the lower Niger, translated from a recent work by a Belgian traveller— Adolphe Burdo :—

'It is a grand and beautiful river, as it rolls majestically along, widening at every step, while its banks display all the splendours of the African flora. The birds have re-appeared, and enliven us with their songs or cries; in the distance the proud cocoa-nut palms lift their superb heads against the azure sky; the dwarf date-palms bathe their curious foliage in the waters; sitting motionless on the young green trunks the pale blue kingfishers keep watch for incautious fish or wandering flies ; a thousand birds with variegated plumage, some yellow with a black necklace, others with gay crests, flutter joyously among the trees; great *bombax* or cotton-trees sway to and fro, their thick foliage forming clusters; manchineels, whose red blossoms set off the verdure ; and finally the bananas, whose large leaves reveal the existence of a negro village behind the screen which they form.'

Commerce with the rich interior of Africa now at length seemed practicable; and accordingly, with this view, early in 1832 several Liverpool merchants formed a company, and arranged a trading expedition up the Niger, which was placed under the direction of Richard Lander. This expedition consisted of two iron steam-vessels, the *Quorra* (' Shining River '), of 145 tons, and the *Alburka* (' Blessing ') measuring only 55. They were accompanied as far as the Gulf of Guinea by a brig laden with coals for the steamers, and a variety of articles for presents or barter. The little squadron sailed from Milford Haven on 25th July, 1832, and reached Cape Coast Castle on 7th October. After innumerable mishaps, and fearful prostrations by illnesses caused by the unhealthy climate, but having succeeded in tracing the Niger (this time *upwards*) for a considerable portion of its course, Lander returned for a short time to Fernando Po for further supplies of cowries,* etc., leaving the steamers in charge of Surgeon Oldfield.

Having obtained what he required, he started on his return and final voyage, of which the following is a summary.

Early in 1834 Lander left Fernando Po in the *Craven* cutter with four hundred pounds' worth of goods to rejoin the *Alburka*. On arriving at the Nun mouth of the Niger he quitted the *Craven*, and with his companions began ascending the river in two canoes of different sizes. All the party were in excellent spirits. With them were two or three negro

---

* Cowries are small shells, the medium of exchange with the natives: their present value is about one shilling per thousand.

musicians, who, when the labours of the day were over, cheered their countrymen with their instruments, to the sound of which they danced and sang in company, while the few Englishmen belonging to the party amused themselves with angling on the banks of the stream; thus, stemming a strong current by day, and resting from their toil at night, Lander and his little band, totally unapprehensive of danger, and unprepared to overcome or meet it, proceeded slowly up the stream. At some distance from its mouth they met King Jacket, a relation of King Boy, one of the heartless and sullen chiefs who ruled over a large tract of the slimy, poisonous marshes which border the Brass River. This personage was hailed by our travellers, and a present of tobacco and rum was offered him: he accepted it with a murmur of dissatisfaction, and his eyes sparkled with malignity as he said in his own language: "White man will never reach Eboe this time." This sentence was immediately interpreted to Lander by a native of the country (a boy, who afterwards bled to death from a wound in the knee); but Lander made light of the matter, and attributed King Jacket's prophecy (for so it proved to be) to the petulance and malice of his disposition. Soon, however, he discovered his error; but too late to evade the danger which threatened him. On ascending the river sixty or seventy miles further, the Englishman approached an island near Ingiamma, near where the progress of the larger canoe was effectually obstructed by the shallowness of the stream. Amongst the trees and underwood which grew on this island, and on both banks of the river in its vicinity, large ambuscades of the natives had previously been formed, and shortly after the principal canoe had grounded, its unfortunate crew, busily occupied in endeavouring to get it into deeper water, were saluted with irregular but heavy and continued discharges of musketry. So great was Lander's confidence in the sincerity and goodwill of the natives that he could not at first believe that the destructive fire by which he was literally surrounded was anything more than a mode of salutation they had adopted in honour of his arrival. But the Kroomen who had leaped into the boat, and who fell wounded by his side, convinced him of his mistake, and plainly discovered to him the fearful nature of the peril into which he had fallen so unexpectedly, as well as the difficulty he would experience in extricating himself from it. But, encouraging his comrades with his voice and gestures, the traveller prepared to defend himself to the last ; and a loud and simultaneous shout from his little party assured him that they shared his feelings, and would follow his example. Meanwhile, several of the savages having come out from their concealment, were brought down by the shots of the English ; but Lander, whilst stooping to pick up a cartridge from the bottom of the canoe, was struck near the hip by a musket-ball. The shock made him stagger ; but he did not fall, and he continued cheering on his men. Soon, however, finding his ammunition expended, himself seriously wounded, the courage of his Kroomen beginning to droop, and the firing of his assailants instead of diminishing become more general, he resolved to attempt getting into the smaller canoe, afloat at a short distance, as the only remaining chance of preserving a single life. For this purpose, abandoning their property, the survivors threw themselves into the stream, and with much difficulty (for the strength of the current was enormous) most of them succeeded in accomplishing their object. No sooner was this observed by the natives in ambush than they started up and rushed out with loud and hideous yells; some Bonny, Brass, and Benin canoes that had been hidden behind the luxuriant foliage which overhung the river were, in an instant, pushed out into the middle of the current, and pursued the fugitives with surprising velocity; while numbers of savages, with wild antics and furious gesticulations, ran and danced along the beach, uttering loud and startling cries. The Kroomen maintained on this occasion the good reputation which their countrymen have deservedly acquired: the lives of the whole party depended on these men's energy and skill, and they impelled the slender barque through the water with unrivalled swiftness.

The pursuit was kept up for four hours; and poor Lander, with only wet ammunition, and with no defensive weapons whatever, was exposed to the straggling fire, as well as the insulting mockery of his pursuers. The fugitives, however, outstripped their pursuers, and when they found the chase discontinued altogether, Lander stood up, *for the last time*, in the canoe; and, being seconded by his re-

maining associates, he waved his hat and gave a last
cheer in sight of his adversaries. He then became
sick and faint from loss of blood, and sank back
exhausted in the arms of those who were nearest
to him. Rallying shortly afterwards, the nature of
his wound was communicated to him by Mr. Moore,
a young surgeon from England, who had accompanied him up the river, viz., that the ball could not
be extracted; it had worked its way into the left
thigh, and Lander felt convinced that his career
would soon be terminated. When the state of
excitement to which his feelings had been wrought
gave place to the languor which generally succeeds
powerful excitement of any kind, the invalid's wound
pained him exceedingly, and for several hours afterwards he endured, though with calmness, the most
intense sufferings. From that time he could neither
sit up nor turn on his couch; but while he was
proceeding down the river in a manner so melancholy, and so very different from the mode in which
he was ascending it only the day before, he could
not help indulging in mournful reflections: he talked
much of his wife, his child, his friends, his distant
home, and his blighted expectations. It was a
period of darkness, distress, and sorrow to him; but
his natural cheerfulness soon regained its ascendency
over his mind, and, freely forgiving all his enemies,
he resigned himself into the hands of his Maker.
At length, having succeeded in escaping down the
stream, Lander reached Fernando Po on the 27th of
January. After his arrival he was doing so well,
that, on the very day previous to his death, which

occurred on the 6th of February, 1834,* he took food with appetite, and no doubt was entertained of his recovery. But mortification of the wound suddenly set in, and all hope was abandoned. So rapid was his prostration, that he died soon after midnight ; having given such directions respecting his affairs as the shortness of the last fatal warning permitted. While on his sick-bed, every needful and possible aid was afforded him. In the airiest room of Colonel Nicholl's residence, receiving the unremitting attention of that humane and gallant officer (the Governor of Fernando Po), with the best medical assistance, and the most soothing services, his pains were alleviated and his spirits were cheered. He was conscious of his approaching dissolution, talked with calmness to those around him, and anticipated the termination of his career with composure and with hope. His body was laid in the grave at the Clarence Cemetery amid the vivid regrets of the whole population, who accompanied the funeral.

An account of this voyage, which Lander had promised should be his *last*—though he did not anticipate its *fatal* termination—was published by Messrs. Laird and Oldfield, the only surviving officers of the expedition, in 1835 ; but I have been obliged to obtain the foregoing account of the attack at Ingiamma, and the death of Richard Lander, from other sources. Messrs. Laird and Oldfield's work is illustrated by another, containing

* The 2nd of February is the date given by S. Tissington as that which was on the monument erected to Lander's memory in the Savoy Chapel by his widow and child.

eleven views and maps by Commander W. Allen, R.N., published by Murray in 1840.

Though the subject of these notes seems to have been in every sense the life and soul of the expedition, yet, as the French writer Lanoye tartly pointed out, at the time of his writing poor Lander's grave in the cemetery of Fernando Po was undistinguished by any monument; nor do I know whether or not this omission has even yet been rectified. 'A solitary palm tree,' says Baikie,* 'marks the spot where this heroic traveller and most intrepid pioneer of civilization fell;' but the village itself from which the attack was delivered has, I believe, been moved about a quarter of a mile farther up the river.

The Royal Geographical Society, however, has not been unmindful of Lander's claim to a place in the front rank of discoverers, and have fixed in the Chapel Royal, Savoy, a stained glass memorial window, the subjects of which are the Transfiguration and the Last Supper, with the following inscription :

'In memory of Richard Lemon Lander, the discoverer of the source of the Niger, and the first Gold Medallist of the Royal Geographical Society.† He was born at Truro, in 1804, and died in the Island of Fernando Po in 1834, from wounds inflicted by the natives. This window is inserted by her Majesty's permission by some of his relations and friends, and by some of the Fellows of the Royal Geographical Society.'

This was in substitution for the tablet erected in 1834, and destroyed by the fire of 7th July, 1864.

* Baikie's ' Niger,' 1854.   † Namely, in 1832.

His native place has not forgotten his fame, as the Doric column at Truro surmounted by his statue testifies. The plate on the foundation-stone bore this inscription : 'To honour the enterprise and sufferings of the brothers Richard and John Lander, natives of this town, and to commemorate the early fate of Richard, who perished on the Quorra, Ætat. 30.' And his name has been given to two places on the Niger. That he did not himself forget his Cornish home is clear from his having named an island on the river *Truro* Island,' and one of the high hills on its banks, '*Cornwall* Mountain.'

A writer in the 'Annual Biography and Obituary' for 1834 says of him that 'Richard Lander was of short stature, but he possessed great muscular strength, and a constitution of iron.' No stranger could help being 'struck (as Sir Joseph Banks was with Ledyard) with the breadth of his chest, the openness of his countenance, and the restlessness of his eye.' He was gifted in an eminent degree with that passive courage which is so requisite a qualification in an African traveller. His manners were mild, unobtrusive, and highly pleasing, which, joined to his cheerful temper and ingenuous handsome countenance, rendered him a favourite with everyone that knew him, by most of whom he was beloved in the fullest sense of that word.'

So greatly was Richard Lander beloved by the untutored Africans, that at various places in the interior where he had remained some time, as at Katunga, Boussa, Yaoorie, numbers of the inhabitants ran out of their huts to embrace him on his leaving, and with hands uplifted, and eyes filled with tears, they blessed him in the name of their gods.

The *Literary Gazette* for 3rd May, 1834, had the following observations on Lander's death : ' Thus has another sacrifice to African discovery been made : a man whose character was of the highest human stamp. Calm and resolute, steady and fearless, bold and adventurous, never did there exist a more fit instrument for the undertaking of such exploits as those which have shed a lustre over his humble name. We cannot express the sorrow with which the sad calamity has filled us—it is a deep *private* affliction, and a lasting *national* regret.'

A pension of £70 a year was granted by the Government to Lander's widow, and a donation of £50 to his daughter ; and a sum of 80 guineas which had been collected in Truro (with a view to presenting the Landers with a piece of plate) was diverted towards the cost of erecting the Lander column. An infant son of the same name died the same year as his father, and was buried in the churchyard of the Savoy.

I do not know that I can more suitably conclude these imperfect remarks than by quoting the following touching letter—I believe the last he ever wrote— as an illustration of his amiable, unselfish character :

                              ' River Nun,
                                ' Jan. 22, 1834.
' DEAR SIR,

        ' Having an opportunity of writing to you by King Boy (who will give it to King Obie to forward to you) I will avail myself of it. I was coming up to you with a cargo of cowries and dry goods worth

£450, when I was attacked from all quarters by the natives of Hyammah off the fourth island from Sunday Island (eighty-four miles from the mouth of the Nun). The shot were very numerous both from the island and shore, Mrs. Brown and child were taken prisoners, whom I was bringing up to her husband, as well as Robert the boy. I have advanced King Boy money to go and purchase them; the vessel will call here immediately, as I am going to Fernando Po to get *the people's* wounds attended to.

'We had 3 men shot dead: Thomson, second mate of the cutter, one Krooman, and one Cape Coastman. I am wounded, but I hope not dangerously, the ball having entered close to the "bottom of the spine," and struck the thigh bone: it is not extracted yet. Thos. Oxford is wounded in the groin, two Kroomen wounded dangerously and one slightly. I am sorry to say I lost all my papers and everything belonging to me, the boat and one canoe; having escaped in one of the canoes barely with a coat to our backs, they chasing us in their war-canoes; and all our cartridges being wet, we could not keep them off. They attacked us at 3 p.m. on the 20th January, and left us at 8 at night. We pulled all night and reached the cutter on the 21st. We are now under weigh for Fernando Po.

'I remain,

'Your most affectionate Friend,

'R. L. LANDER.

' To Surgeon Oldfield,
' *Alburka* Steamer,
' River Niger.'

Such was the fate of one who may be not unfairly described as one of the chief, if not the chief, of the pioneers of West African exploration. It is evident that access to the interior of the Dark Continent continues to engage the attention of travellers; for, according to the comments of a recent writer on the meeting of the Royal Geographical Society in May, 1883:

'Africa has at no period of its history been so flooded with eager seekers after the unknown as at the present hour. Apart from the explorations for commercial and political purposes that are being carried out by French officers in Senegambia and on the Upper Niger and Congo, a Russian expedition under Rogozinzki, and an Italian one under Bianchi and Licata, have been planned to enter the country at the Bight of Biafra. These expeditions will probably be absent several years, for they are organized with the object of crossing through the unknown region between the Congo, the Benueh, and Lake Tchad, and of so eventually reaching Abyssinia. Numerous other travellers are either in the interior or making for the goal as best they can; and Mr. Stanley, in pursuance of his mission on the Upper Congo, is understood to have made a voyage up one of its greatest tributaries, and discovered a hitherto unsuspected lake of considerable magnitude. Another such sheet of water is believed to be not far from the Welle; and now that Mr. Joseph Thomson and Dr. Fischer are far on their way to examine the country between the sea and the northern end of Lake Nyassa, the snow-capped Mounts Kenia and Kilimandjaro promise before long to be removed from the region of myth. Messrs. O'Neill, Johnson, and Stewart's explorations in the same quarter are adding much to our acquaintance with a country hitherto little known, and as soon as the steamer can be carried in sections across the road cut between Nyassa and Tanganyika, the latter lake will become almost as well surveyed as Lakes Huron or Superior. Holub intends boring from one end of Africa to another, and without doing more than mentioning a few of the names which most readily suggest themselves, Böhm, Kaiser, Stecker, Giraud, Aubrey, Hamon, Revoil, and Schuver are among the many eager, and in most cases tried, explorers whose efforts or achievements in different parts of Africa during the past year deserve special remark. The scheme of international stations, started and carried out by the committee presided over by King Leopold, is rapidly joining the East and West Coast by a chain of civilized settlements, where the rude tribes can learn the arts of peace, and the weary explorers find the succour and assistance denied to their predecessors from the hour they entered the Dark Continent. Africa must before long become permeated with what Europeans call light, and, though the accounts of later travellers do not confirm the sanguine estimates of the earlier pioneers, the resources of its great forests, rich valleys, and mineral veins are at least capable of supporting a vastly greater trade than the country at present enjoys.'

Whatever may be the future of Africa, Richard Lander's name will always be remembered as that of one of the earliest and bravest of her explorers.

THE REV. HENRY MARTYN, B.D.,

THE CHRISTIAN MISSIONARY AND ORIENTAL SCHOLAR.

THE REV. HENRY MARTYN, B.D.,

THE CHRISTIAN MISSIONARY AND ORIENTAL SCHOLAR.

'Atque opere in medio defixa reliquit aratra.'

'Hopes have precarious life;
They are oft blighted, withered, snapped sheer off
In vigorous youth and turned to rottenness;
But faithfulness can feed on suffering,
And know no disappointment.'

Spanish Gypsy.

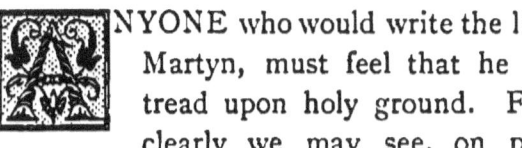NYONE who would write the life of Henry Martyn, must feel that he is about to tread upon holy ground. For, however clearly we may see, on perusing his 'Journals and Letters,'* that his introspection was morbidly minute, his temper naturally irritable, and his religious views generally of the gloomiest as well as of an almost impracticable character, yet his ardent zeal, his saint-like devotion, his self-denial, and his deep humility, afford such an example of

* Edited by Bishop Wilberforce, while Rector of Brighstone, Isle of Wight, 1839. It is truly wonderful how so sincerely good a man as Martyn should have entertained such desponding thoughts; and still more wonderful how he could have so long continued writing them down.

earnest piety as is rarely to be met with in the annals
of the Church, since the days of the Apostles themselves. His very faults were but 'the shadows of
his virtues,' and of Henry Martyn it might truly be
said that to him—without religion—

> 'The pillared firmament was rottenness,
> And earth's base built on stubble.'

How much of this was due to that frequent corre-
lation which, as Mr. Galton points out, frequently
exists between an unusually devout disposition and a
weak constitution, it would of course be hard to say.

I cannot help thinking that Martyn has been a
little unfortunate in his biographer, the Rev. John
Sargent, jun., although that writer's 'Memoir' has
been so popular that I believe it has run through
about a score of editions. There was a tardy apology
for the tone of the book in the preface to the tenth edition—and an explanation to the effect that Martyn's
religion was really by no means of a desponding character, and that few persons 'have equalled him in
the enjoyment of that "peace which passeth all
understanding."' If such were the case it is unfortunate that the extracts made by Mr. Sargent from
Martyn's 'Journals' should have left so wide-spread an
impression to the contrary—an impression which it
is probably as fruitless to attempt to counteract as
Mr. Sargent expected it would be.

Sargent appears to have sympathized chiefly
with one side of Martyn's character, namely, the
gloomy and self-torturing one, and the result is
that to read the 'Memoir' harrows one's feelings. Very similar remarks apply to the 'Journals

and Letters,' but in the latter, at least, we have only
the man himself, and are spared the somewhat com-
placent tone in which his mental anguish and physical
sufferings are depicted by his friend and biographer.
Charles Kingsley used to say of Martyn : ' My mind
is in a chaos about him. Sometimes one feels inclined to take him at his own word, and believe him,
as he says, a mere hypochondriac; then the next
moment he seems a saint. I cannot fathom it. Of
this, however, I am certain, that he was a much
better man than I am.' One great lesson, however,
of this learned, brave, and good man's life—crowned
as it surely was with the crown of the martyr, if
ever mortal's brow were so adorned—appears to
me to be this: that a life of seclusion, nay, almost
isolation, such as his, defeats its own object, if that
object be, like Martyn's, to influence our fellow-men.
' It is miserable,' he used to say, when thinking of
the vast amount of sin there was in the world, ' it is
miserable living with men ;' and, again, ' a dried leaf
or a straw makes me feel in good company.' And
herein seems to lie a great difference between Martyn,
notwithstanding his learning, his piety, and his
dauntless courage amidst incessant perils, and such
heroic Christian missionaries as were St. Paul and
Bishop Heber, who had learnt to mix more freely with
their fellow-men, and to combine the wisdom of the
serpent with the harmlessness of the dove.

But to turn to the life itself. Henry Martyn, like
Martin Luther, sprang from a family of mine captains,
and was born at Truro, on Feb. 18th, 1781—the
third child of a family of four. His father, who lived

at first near Gwennap Church-Town, had been an Accountant at Wheal Virgin ; and being, like many others of his calling, an ingenious and self-reliant man, taught himself arithmetic and some mathematics ; his abilities attracted the attention of Mr. Daniell, one of the Truro merchants, and ultimately John Martyn became his chief clerk. 'The elder Martyn,' Polwhele says, 'was a tall, erect man, used to take his daily exercise under the Coinage Hall, which was opposite his house.' The house was pulled down to make room for the new Town Hall ; it occupied the site of the present Police Station, as I am informed. Henry's great-uncle, Thomas Martyn, was the author of the large and excellent Map of Cornwall, known by his name.* He was a surveyor, and his map is said to have been the result of fifteen years' labour—the survey having been made on foot. He died in 1752-53. Henry's mother, from whom he seems to have inherited his delicate constitution, was a Miss Fleming of Ilfracombe ; she died the year after he was born.

Henry Martyn—' little Henry Martyn,' as his schoolfellows used tenderly to call him—was sent at Midsummer, 1788, to that capital nest of so large a number of our most distinguished Cornishmen—the Truro Grammar School—and he is thus described by one of his fellow-pupils, the late Clement Carlyon, M.D., Fellow of Pembroke College, and thrice Mayor of Truro, in his ' Early Years and Late Reflections :' ' A good-humoured, plain little fellow, with red eyelids devoid of eye-lashes, and indicative of a scrofu-

* Son of a John Martyn of Gwennap, alive in 1695.

lous habit; and with hands so thickly covered with warts that it was impossible for him to keep them clean, or for his respected master,* who borrowed a large leaf out of Dr. Busby's book, to inflict on him, when idle, stripes over the back of his hand.' He seems to have improved in appearance as he grew older; but was always "rather low in stature, and plain in person, though not disagreeably so;† whilst his amiable disposition‡ and sociability ensured him the esteem and friendship of all who were acquainted with him.' Though all his life long he was particularly fond of laughing and playing with little children, at school he seldom played with the other boys; and seems to have evinced no precocity, nor was he very

---

* The Rev. Cornelius Cardew, D.D., Rector of St. Erme and Vicar of Uny Lelant, was one of the most distinguished masters of Truro Grammar School. He was born on 27th Feb., 1748, and died at St. Erme, 18th Sept., 1831, eighty-three years of age. He was buried in the chancel of that church, and his monument records that

> ' Per annos triginta quatuor
> Scholæ Grammaticæ apud Truronenses
> præsidebat Archididasculus.'

† An engraved portrait of him will be found in the Rev. Hy. Clissold's ' Lamps of the Church,' London, 1863. Mrs. Sherwood, in the *Christian Remembrancer* for October, 1854, thus refers to Martyn's appearance when in India : ' He was dressed in white, and looked very pale ; his hair, a light brown, was raised from his forehead, which was a remarkably fine one. His features were not regular, but the expression was so luminous, so intellectual, so affectionate, so beaming with divine charity, as to absorb the attention of every observer ; there was a very decided air of the gentleman, too, about Mr. Martyn, and a perfection of manners arising from his extreme attention to all minute civilities. He had, moreover, a rich, deep voice and a fine taste for vocal music.'

‡ He used to say *of himself,* that his temper was satirical and arrogant, and that his heart was ' of adamant.'

studious, like his friend and school-fellow Kempthorne*
(Senior Wrangler of 1796, and afterwards vicar of
a church in Gloucester) : nor did Martyn display the
poetic vein of another of his colleagues, Humphry
Davy.

At the Truro Grammar School, having failed in
1795 to obtain a Scholarship at Corpus Christi
College, Oxford, he remained till 1797, in which
year he took up residence at St. John's College,
Cambridge, where, from his assiduity, he was
known as 'the man who had never lost an hour,'
and was at once fortunate in securing the advice and
friendship of his old acquaintance Kempthorne, who,
as well as Martyn himself, soon came within the
influence of a very earnest Low Church Divine, the
Rev. Charles Simeon, a fellow of King's College, of
whom it is only right to add that he more than once
warned Martyn, whilst in the East, that he was over-
taxing his strength and energies. To this clergyman
Martyn was afterwards to become curate.

The death of his father in 1800 led Martyn to
study the Bible most seriously; and he so read its
pages as to determine upon basing his whole life
upon its promises. He says, for instance, of his
magnificent success in becoming the Senior Wrangler
of his year (and that year was a distinguished one
in the annals of the University) : ' I obtained my
highest wishes, but was surprised to find I had

* Though Exeter College, Oxford, was the usual Cornish College,
yet many Cornishmen have gone to Cambridge ; where they have not
failed to distinguish themselves. Besides the two Senior Wranglers
named above, may be mentioned Mr. Adams, the eminent astronomer,
born at Lidcott, Laneast, Senior Wrangler in 1843; and the late
Bishop Colenso, 2nd Wrangler in 1836, who was born at St. Austell.

grasped a shadow!' Indeed, it is said that, when he entered the Senate House for the examination, and saw the unusually large number assembled there, he ejaculated, with apparently some inconsistency, the text: 'Seekest thou great things for thyself? seek them not, saith the Lord.' In 1802 he became Fellow and Tutor of his college, and gained the first prize for Latin prose composition, thus compensating amply for his lack of success in 1799, when he failed to obtain the prize for themes in his college, and came out second instead of first, as was expected, at the examination.

He now returned to his native place for a short time, for much-needed rest and change; not, however, staying much at Truro, but passing most of his holiday at Woodbury, just below Malpas, on the Fal, the residence of his brother-in-law, Rev. Mr. Curgenven (curate of the parishes of Kenwyn and Kea). These were amongst the happiest moments of his life. He says, either of this place or Lamorran (and the description is applicable to either): 'The scene is such as is frequently to be met with in this part of Cornwall. Below the house is an arm of the sea flowing between the hills, which are covered with wood. By the shore I walk in general, in the evening, out of the reach of all sound but the rippling of the water and the whistling of the curlew.'

On his return to Cambridge in the following October, conversations with Mr. Simeon, instigated by a perusal of the 'Life and Labours of David Brainerd among the North American Indians,' gave rise to Martyn's intense desire to become a missionary; and, notwithstanding his alleged appreciative enjoyment of a literary and social life at home, he offered his services to a Missionary Society. They were not, however, accepted; and after having been ordained at Ely in October, 1803, he became Mr. Simeon's curate—preaching sometimes at Lolworth, a church six miles from the University, on the Huntingdon road, and sometimes at Trinity Church, Cambridge. Simeon always continued a friend and admirer of Martyn, and had his portrait hung up over his fireplace. He often used to look up at it with affectionate earnestness: 'There!' he used to say, 'see that blessed man! What an expression of countenance! No one looks at me as he does—he seems always to be saying, "Be serious, be in earnest; don't trifle—*don't* trifle."' Then he would smile at the picture, and gently bow, and add: 'And I won't trifle—I won't trifle.'

Early in 1804, Martyn, as well as his younger sister, Sally (Mrs. Pearson), to whom he seems to have been fondly attached, had the misfortune to lose all their patrimony; an event which, in addition to the causes already referred to, probably led to his making a second effort (which was also at the time unsuccessful) to procure an appointment as a missionary—this time in the form of a 'chaplaincy' to the East India Company. This year was further memorable from Martyn's making the acquaintance of a kindred spirit—the poet, H. Kirke White (also a Johnian), 'a religious young man of seventeen, who wants to come to college, but has only £20 a year.'

Another visit to his solitary retreat in Cornwall refreshed him during the summer, and whilst there he preached to a crowded congregation at Kenwyn Church from 2 Cor. v. 20, 21: 'Now we are ambassadors,' etc. (a very favourite text of his), and availed himself of the opportunity, before returning to Cambridge on 18th of September, 1804, to take leave of his county and friends, in view of the probability of his soon getting the desired appointment under the East India Company. On his way back to the University, as his journals testify, with characteristic zeal and devotedness, though, apparently, not always with tact and skill, he lost no opportunity, in season or out of season, of turning the conversation of his fellow-travellers to religious topics.

At this period of his life his usual routine seems to have been to rise every morning at about half-past five (and, if he failed to do so, his self-reproaches are most bitter); to work hard, either with his pupils, his flock, or his books; to pray at least four times a day, and to write at least one sermon a week. The Scriptures he doubtless read daily; and the spirit in which he read them may be seen from the following extract from his Journals, written when on board ship, on his way to India: 'Read Isaiah the rest of the evening—sometimes happy and at other times tired, and desiring to take up some other religious book; *but I saw it an important duty to check this slighting of the Word of God.*' And here it may be interesting to note the other works which seem to have been amongst Martyn's favourites. Of course, he kept up his mathematics and science; but the references to these in his Journals are slight and few. He often read the Greek plays, but his chief reading was, as might be expected, divinity; and especially St. Augustine, Grotius, Paley, Baxter, Hooker, Pearson, Fletcher's ' Portrait,' Flavel's 'Saint Indeed,' Searle's ' Christian Remembrancer,' Thomas à Kempis, Law's ' Serious Call,' Lowth, Bishop Hopkins, Jonathan Edwards's ' Original Sin,' and his work on the Affections, Whitfield's Journal, Leighton, Milner's ' Church History,' etc., etc. ; and these were interspersed with the study of Hindostanee and other Oriental languages.

Martyn's religious position and views have been thus described in the *Edinburgh Review* for July, 1844, by a writer who traces their origin to the well-known Clapham School of ' Evangelical ' religion :

' From that circle he adopted, in all its unadorned simplicity, the system called Evangelical—that system of which (if Augustine, Luther, Calvin, Knox, and the writers of the English Homilies may be credited) Christ Himself was the author, and Paul the first and greatest interpreter.

' Through shallow heads and voluble tongues, such a creed (or indeed any creed) filtrates so easily, that, of the multitudes who maintain it, comparatively few are aware of the conflict of their faith with the natural and unaided reason of mankind. Indeed, he who makes such an avowal will hardly escape the charge of affectation or of impiety. Yet if any truth be clearly revealed, it is, that the Apostolic doctrine was foolishness to the sages of this world. If any unrevealed truth be indisputable, it is, that such sages are at this day making, as they have ever made, ill-disguised efforts to escape the inferences with which their own admissions teem. Divine philosophy divorced from human science—celestial things stripped of the mitigating veils woven by man's wit and fancy to relieve them—form an abyss as impassable at Oxford now, as at Athens eighteen centuries ago. To Henry Martyn the gulf was visible, the self-renunciation painful, the victory complete. His understanding embraced, and his heart reposed in, the two comprehensive and ever-germinating tenets of the school in which he studied. Regarding his own heart as corrupt, and his own reason as delusive, he exercised an unlimited affiance in the holiness and the wisdom of Him, in whose person the divine nature had been allied to the human, that, in the persons of his followers, the human might be allied to the divine.

'Such was his religious theory—a theory which doctors may combat, or admit, or qualify, but in which the readers of Henry Martyn's Biography, Letters, and Journals, cannot but acknowledge that he found the resting-place of all the impetuous appetencies of his mind, the spring of all his strange powers of activity and endurance. Prostrating his soul before the real, though the hidden Presence he adored, his doubts were silenced, his anxieties soothed, and every meaner passion hushed into repose.'

On the 2nd of April, 1805, having previously been
ordained priest at St. James's Chapel Royal, London,
and having taken his degree as Bachelor of Divinity,
he preached his last sermon at Cambridge, and
came to London to prosecute his studies in Hindostanee, and to preach occasionally at St. John's
Chapel, Bedford Row.   It was about this time that
he made the acquaintance of Wilberforce, dining
with him and going afterwards to the House of
Commons, where he was much struck with the
eloquence, great seriousness, and energy of Pitt
' about that which is of no consequence at all.'

He at length, on the 24th April, 1805, obtained
the long-wished-for chaplaincy, with a salary of
£1,200 a year, and was fervently longing to enter
upon his labours, exclaiming on one occasion,
from the very depths of his soul: 'Gladly shall this
base blood be shed, every drop of it, if India can be
benefited in one of her children !'

This would seem to be the proper occasion to
advert to a passage in Martyn's Life which must
possess for any 'genial reader a most touching
interest.   The enthusiastic clergyman had become
deeply smitten with the attractions of Miss Lydia
Grenfell, of the parish of St. Hilary, three or four
miles from Marazion.   His affection for this lady
appears to have been both profound and sincere;
but he feared that its indulgence might prove a bar
to the higher aims which he had set before him.
His mental conflicts on this subject, as on all others,
were most severe; and under such circumstances,
and with his gloomy and excitable religious views,

he may have appeared, what the lady herself (some
few years his senior) undoubtedly was, a somewhat
languid and vacillating lover. That the lady never
married him—although her final refusal did not
reach him till 1807, when he was in India—was
perhaps fortunate for both parties; but, undoubtedly,
Martyn continued to love her and to correspond
with her to the last. The peculiar circumstances
of this attachment gave rise to Holme Lee's (Harriet
Parr's) story of 'Her Title of Honour;' that title
consisting of the honour done to Eleanor Trevelyan
by being beloved by so good and great a man as
Francis Gwynne (Martyn). Miss Grenfell never
married. Her sister Emma became the wife of the
Rev. T. M. Hitchins,* of Devonport, Martyn's
cousin; and some interesting letters to her from
Martyn, mostly bearing upon the subject of his love
for Lydia, will be found in a supplement to the
'Journal of the Royal Institution of Cornwall' edited
by Mr. Henry Martyn Jeffery, F.R.S. (vol. vii. pt. 3,
December, 1882, No. 26).

The ship in which he was to sail for India left
London on the 8th of July, 1805. Martyn joined
her at Portsmouth on the 17th, after having had
'a convulsion fit' on the road down. The *Union*
called (unexpectedly) at Falmouth, where she was
detained for three weeks by unfavourable winds, and
Martyn thus had opportunities of returning to St.
Hilary, about twenty miles off, and again enduring
the 'pleasing pain' which he found in his loved

---

* His father, the Rev. Malachi Hitchins, Vicar of St. Hilary and
Gwinear, was Assistant Astronomer at Greenwich, and first Computer
of the Nautical Almanac.

one's society. But whilst there the wind suddenly shifted, and Martyn had the narrowest possible escape from missing the ship. His self-reproaches on such an occasion as this may be imagined !

On the 10th of September the *Union* at length sailed from Falmouth, and our devoted hero's dejection on contemplating the Cornish cliffs fading away in the distance was very deep. He longed to die, so he says, on the way out. A storm arose as they left Ireland behind them, and added to his sufferings. But at length, after touching at Madeira, and at San Salvador in Brazil, they safely reached Calcutta on the 14th of May, 1806, after a tedious and dangerous voyage of nine months.

On the passage Martyn's usual zeal, and, it might be added, want of tact, had ample opportunities of displaying themselves. Nothing could exceed his devotion to the men when sick, or whenever the slightest opportunity presented itself of speaking to any of them on the subject which was ever uppermost in his own soul. And his courage was admirably displayed in landing almost *with* the troops when the successful attack was delivered by the British under Sir David Baird upon the French and Dutch troops at the Cape of Good Hope in January, 1806. Nor was he unmindful of the welfare of the cadets on board, to whom he imparted instruction in a variety of subjects, with all the force of his powerful intellect. But his religious ministrations were, for the most part, unappreciated, owing to the excessively gloomy tone with which they were pervaded, and to his tendency to 'scold his congregation,' a fault of which it may be remembered even Cowper complained in Mr. Scott, the curate of Olney. The captain dared not allow him to preach more than once on Sundays, and all the officers made a point of standing near the cabin-door, so as to make good their retreat whenever the sermon became too miserably painful. ' Mr. Martyn,' they once said, '*must* not damn us to-day, or none will come again.'

After a stay of about four months in Calcutta, during which, notwithstanding a sharp attack of fever, he went on with his lingual studies, occasionally preached to somewhat unsympathetic audiences, and had opportunities of witnessing Suttee and the Juggernaut procession, he was, on the 13th September, at length appointed to Dinapore, and on the 15th October proceeded up the Ganges to his post, in a budgerow, passing most of his time in translating portions of the Scriptures into the native tongues. He reached Dinapore on 26th November, and met with but a very cold reception from the Europeans there, as well as from the natives; and, worst of all, there was no church or church furniture at his disposal. But he soon got to work, and gave his most special attention to the native children, who appeared to have been very apt and tractable, and for whom he is said to have built, at his own cost, whilst in India, five schools. He now obtained, for the purposes of his translations, the assistance (such as it was) of two natives—Mirza Fitrut, who is described as being guileful and hypocritical, and the vain and furious-tempered Nathanael Sabat, who seem to have entertained a very cordial jealousy and hatred of each other. Sabat had served both in the Turkish and Persian armies. He had a free and haughty manner, and a fierce look, and signed himself 'Nathanael Sabat, an Arab who was never in bondage.' He used to contend with Martyn so violently at times that Martyn had to order his palanquin and be off to his friends, the Sherwoods.

Part of the Prayer Book was, under conditions such as these, translated into Hindostanee; to this his 'dear friend and brother chaplain' Corrie added; but it was not completed until 1829, seventeen years after Martyn's death. In 1807 Martyn finished, in Hindostanee, his 'Commentary on the Parables;' and, by the end of 1809, a plain and idiomatic version of the four Gospels. The following year saw the New Testament completed. His translations into the Persian were not considered quite so successful; but about this time he appears to have first definitely conceived the desire of evangelizing Persia, and it was always with regret that he went on with his translations, dreading lest they might interfere with his strictly ministerial duties. He was at this time so strict a Sabbatarian that he thought he was doing wrong in translating even the Prayer Book into Hindostanee on a Sunday.

Signs of breaking health were now becoming too painfully apparent; in fact, he may be said to have been constantly ill. His friend Corrie (afterwards Bishop of Madras) paid Martyn two visits in 1808, and saw that 'there was small prospect of his long continuance in this vale of tears.' But the tone of

Martyn's people towards him had somewhat improved; and in April, 1809, he was moved to Cawnpore, a distance of 240 miles—the journey being performed in a fierce heat. He was kindly received by
Captain and Mrs. Sherwood; but here again he
found no church. He first preached at Cawnpore in
the native tongue, and remained at his post until the
30th September, 1810, when, notwithstanding his
'bright invincibility of spirit,' his health utterly
gave way, and he went back to Calcutta, arriving
there with pallid countenance and enfeebled frame.
' Fortia agere Romanum est, fortia pati Christianum,'
wrote an old author; and, surely, if ever the
courage of the Roman, and the calm brave endurance of the Christian met, they met in Henry
Martyn.

But returning after a while to Cawnpore, he
resumed his correspondence with Miss Grenfell,
now *as a friend;* and tells her that this was his
daily routine : ' We rise at daybreak, and breakfast at six.. Immediately after breakfast we pray*
together ; after which I translate into Arabic with
Sabat, who lives in a small bungalow on my ground.
We dine at twelve, and sit recreating ourselves with
talking about dear friends in England. In the afternoon I translate with Mirza Fitrut into Hindostanee ; and Corrie employs himself in teaching some
native Christian boys, whom he is educating with
great care, in the hopes of their being fit for the
office of catechists. I have also a school on my pre-

---

* Martyn used finely to speak of prayer as 'a visit to the invisible
world.'

mises for natives ; but it is not well attended. At
sunset we ride or drive, and then meet at the
church, where we often raise the song of praise with
as much joy, through the grace and presence of our
Lord, as you do in England. At ten we are all
asleep. . . . My work at present is evidently to
translate ; hereafter I may itinerate.'

By the spring of 1810 his church, converted from
its former use as a heathen temple, was ready,* and
his friend Corrie came to visit and assist him ; but
he preached in it for the last time on 30th September, 1810, and shortly afterwards went back to
Calcutta.

Persia now finally became the object of Martyn's
pious yearnings ; and, on the 9th January, in the
following year, he set out on his memorable, but, it
is much to be feared, slightly rewarded, journey—a
journey accomplished with so much fatigue, and
under such sudden and excessive changes of tem-
perature, as to have been, doubtless, the proximate
cause of the destruction of his frail body. He
stopped at Goa on the route, and travelled *viâ*
Bombay, landing at Muscat, in Arabia Felix, on the
22nd April. On the 30th he set out for Shiraz, 'the
City of the Rose'—the Athens of Persia, where he
arrived on the 9th June, and met with a most insulting reception from the people. But Martyn thought
that even such a reception as this was better than so
unworthy a sinner as he merited ! Referring to this
episode in Martyn's career Dean Alford writes :

* It was destroyed in the mutiny of 1857.

'The pale-faced Frank among them sits : what brought him from afar?
Nor bears he bales of merchandise, nor teaches arts of war.
One pearl alone he brings with him—the Book of life and death.
One warfare only teaches he—to fight the fight of faith.'

Matters, however, improved after a while ; the Armenian ladies came to kiss his hand, and the priest incensed him four times over at the altar. Here, on the 24th February, 1812, he completed, under most discouraging circumstances, his translation of the New Testament into Persian.* After labouring ' for six weary moons,' a similar version of the Psalms was finished in the following month ; and on the 24th May, ' the meek missionary of the Cross' left Shiraz in order to present the precious documents himself to the Shah. Much difficulty and delay intervened on account of the diplomatic formalities considered necessary on such an occasion ; and eventually, after visiting Ispahan and Teheran, Martyn was disappointed in the object he had in view, having been struck down by illness, increased by the hardships of travel and climate, before his desires were accomplished. For two months he was completely laid up—weeping many 'tears from the depths of a divine despair '—at the house of Sir Gore Ouseley, the British Ambassador at Tabriz, who afterwards had the gratification of showing Martyn's manuscript to the Shah, and it was sent to St. Petersburg to be printed.

This renewed illness caused Martyn to determine

* The late lamented Professor Palmer, the well-known Oriental scholar, who perished in the attempt made during the recent Egyptian campaign to detach the native supporters of Arabi from their leader's cause, superintended, with Dr. Bruce, a new edition of Martyn's Persian Version of the New Testament.

on returning to England, for his health's sake. But it was too late. On his homeward way (*viâ* Constantinople), seeing Mount Ararat on the journey, and passing through Erivan, Kars, Erzeroum, and Tokat—'hardly knowing how to keep his life in him '—he succumbed near the latter place, to hunger, thirst, sunstroke, fever and ague, aggravated by his desperate gallop for life across the scorching plains, and beneath a rainless sky, untempered by a single cloud, on the 6th October, 1812, in the thirty-second year of his age. Here the last entry, commencing 'Oh! when shall Time give place to Eternity?' appears in his sad, self-searching diary. Ten days afterwards he was no more.

He was buried in the Armenian burial-ground at Tokat, with the honours usually accorded by Armenian Christians to an Archbishop; and a marble slab, which the Tokat Christians were wont to keep clear of weeds, covers his remains. Sir R. K. Porter, in his 'Travels in Persia' (vol. ii., p. 703), after eulogizing Martyn's self-devotion and zeal beyond the strength of a naturally delicate constitution, adds that 'exhausted nature sank under the apostolic labour, and in this place he was called to the rest of heaven. His remains sleep in a grave as humble as his own meekness.'

Would it be too much to say of him

> 'Heaven scarce believed the conquest it surveyed ;
> And Saints with wonder heard the vows he made '?

Wordsworth's lines, at least, on another devoted son of the Church, are clearly appropriate to Martyn :

' He sought not praise, and praise did overlook
    His inobtrusive merit; but his life,
    Sweet to himself, was exercised in good
    That shall survive his name and memory.'

His tomb is still, I believe, piously regarded by the natives, and it has been adorned by Lord Macaulay with the following lines :

' Here Martyn lies ! In manhood's early bloom
    The Christian hero finds a Pagan's tomb :
    Religion sorrowing o'er her favourite son,
    Points to the glorious trophies which he won.
    Eternal trophies, not with slaughter red,
    Not stained with tears by hapless captives shed ;
    But trophies of the Cross ! For that dear Name
    Through every form of danger, death, and shame,
    Onward he journeyed to a happier shore,
    Where danger, death, and shame assault no more.'

A Hall, dedicated to his memory, and designed to provide a place of meeting for the different Religious Societies in Cambridge, is about to be erected in Market Street; and on the centenary of Martyn's birth, viz., 18th February, 1881, special services in his memory were held at the pro-Cathedral at Truro. In the evening Bishop Benson delivered a lecture on Martyn at the Town Hall, at the close of which he proposed that subscriptions should be invited towards the construction of a portion of the new Cathedral, as for instance an aisle or transept, to be dedicated to the cause of Missions in honour of his name. A Baptistry was finally decided upon ; and about £1,250 had been collected up to June, 1883. By the attainment of these objects, this distinguished Cornishman, whose motto was, ' To believe, to suffer, and to love,' will be provided with fitting memorials.

OPIE,

THE PAINTER.

OPIE,

THE PAINTER.

'A wondrous Cornishman, who is carrying all before him! He is Caravaggio and Velasquez in one!'—*Sir Joshua Reynolds to Northcote.* (*Redgrave's 'Century of Painters.'*)

ORNWALL—so far as I am aware—has contributed only two members to the Royal Academy of Arts, since its foundation on 10th December, 1768.* Henry Bone, of Truro, and John Opie,† born in May, 1761, at Harmony Cot (once known as Blowing House‡),

---

* On an examination of the list of the members, it will be found that Cornwall has produced about the usual average of the English counties.

† Opie painted Bone's portrait, and presented it to him, 1795; also one of Bartolozzi, the engraver, which is preserved in the National Portrait Gallery.

‡ A blowing-house is a building where tin ore was smelted prior to the construction of the larger smelting-works. The first Mrs. Opie had the name changed to one more consonant with her notions of connubial felicity. Opie's second wife thus sketched it in a letter dated 'St. Agnes, 11th mo. 26th, 1832:' 'Yesterday I dined at Harmony Cot, where my husband and all the family were born and bred. It is a most sequestered cottage, whitewashed and thatched; a hill rising high above it, and another in front; trees and flower-beds before it, which in summer must make it a pretty spot. *Now* it is not a tempting abode; but there are two good rooms, and I am glad I have seen it.'

near the hamlet of Mithian, in the out-of-the-way parish of St. Agnes. The bleak desolate moors, saturated by frequent hissing rain-storms, and scarred with mine-heaps, the jagged cliff-coast, and the dark rolling Atlantic waves of the neighbouring sea, have a savage grandeur of their own which cannot have been without its effect on the youthful mind of the future professor of painting. For, though he rose to the high position of a Royal Academician when only about twenty-seven years of age, we shall seek, I think, in vain amongst his works for that delicate, airy grace of many of his more courtly contemporaries, which no one admired more than himself; and we shall find instead an original, broad, and manly, though somewhat grim and sombre style, which may well have been inspired by the wildness and gloom of his surroundings when a child on this remote 'bench of the world-school.' Allan Cunningham says well of him that he was not 'the servile *follower* of any man, or of any school;' and, as a matter of fact, his self-reliance early showed itself. On seeing a butterfly painted by one Mark Oates, an officer of Marines, an amateur artist of some merit (whose portrait Opie afterwards painted),—Jan Oppie (as his name was sometimes pronounced) exclaimed : '*I* can paint it as well as Mark Oates.'

Opie's father, Edward Opie, who died while John was quite young, and his grandfather were both of them carpenters and builders, though a writer in the *Fine Arts Magazine* has striven to show that the family was really of old and gentle descent. *Tonkin* (who, as a St. Agnes man, ought to have known) says the Opies came from Ennis, or De Insula, in St. Erme.

Jno. Opie, sr. (lived here temp. Eliz.).

Robt. Opie⊤Jane, daur. of Agnes Jago.

Robt. (sold the Barton to Jago).

(? descended from the Opies of Pawton, in St. Breock.)

Arms : Sa. on a chev. between three garbs or, as many hurtleberries proper.

Other authorities also say the Opies originally came from St. Breock. One thing, at least, from the genealogical point of view, is clear : namely, that the genius for painting still remains in the family of Opie: for 'the great nephew of a great uncle'—as Mr. Edward Opie is pleasantly called in the recently published memoirs of Caroline Fox—has for many years past been a highly successful portrait and genre-painter in the West-country, and a constant exhibitor at the Royal Academy for more than a quarter of a century.

Whatever may have been the origin of the family, John's father was considered an unusually skilful craftsman ; and his son was apprenticed to him. His mother, a woman of very high principle and singularly sweet disposition, was forty-eight when the son of her old age was born ; and she lived till she was ninety-two, dying in May, 1805. Her maiden name was Mary Tonkin, of Trevaunance, near St. Agnes Porth ; a family whom Polwhele classes amongst his 'little gentry' of Cornwall. While on this point, it may be well to state that Oppy, a Cornish artist with whom the subject of this memoir has frequently been confused, was a member of another and quite distinct family.

The fire of genius having been kindled by the butterfly episode, was soon fanned into a flame by the intense and daring spirit of thé boy. Going with his father to carry out some repairs to the house of Mr. B. Nankivell, at Mithian, the boy discovered that in one of the rooms hung a painting of a farm-place. What its merits were it would be difficult now to say, for the accounts of it are conflicting; but the picture excited the most ardent admiration of young Opie, and he made more than one furtive visit to the room in order to gaze upon the object of his emulation, of which he was endeavouring to make a copy from memory, as he feared to ask permission to inspect. Being detected, however, on one of these occasions, the boon of a loan of the picture was granted, in order that it might serve him as a model. His delight knew no bounds; the much-wished-for copy was made, and was sold to a Mrs. Walker* (whose son was Vicar of St. Winnow, on the banks of the Fowey) for five shillings—a sum the magnitude of which so astonished the youngster that he ran about the house shouting: ' I'm set up for life! I'm set up for life !' Upon this his father is said to have cynically observed : ' That boy'll come to hanging, as sure as a gun ;'—in fact, the father did all in his power to keep the son close to a handicraft which for two generations had been a sure, if small, means of support.

* When Polwhele wrote, some seventy or eighty years ago, this picture was in the possession of Richard Hoskins, Esq., of Carennis.

John's temperament seems to have always been excitable. Another instance of his exuberant joy at ,an early success was when he returned with twenty or thirty guineas in his pocket (which he presented to his mother) from painting some of the Prideaux portraits, still preserved at Place House, near Padstow ; he threw the glittering coins on the floor, and himself upon them, twisting about in his fine new coat, lace ruffles, and silk stockings, and exclaiming with humorous glee, 'See ! see ! I'm walving [wallowing] in gold !' But he was as easily depressed. He used to tell how he once went to the neighbouring town of Redruth, with half-a-crown in his pocket, to buy himself some colours, but was so attracted by the gilded gingerbreads and other delights of the fair that in a very short time his money was all wasted, and he had to trudge his weary way homewards without the painting materials, and so overcome by the miserable plight to which his thoughtlessness had reduced him that he said he seriously meditated suicide by the way.

There was nothing enervating in the way in which young Opie was reared. Not only was his fare frugal and his clothing and lodging of very simple sort, but his religion and morals were doubtless very strictly looked after by his parents, who seem to have been of the old Puritanical school. But the spirit of the artist broke out one summer Sunday afternoon, when Opie—then eleven years old—was left in the cottage with his father, whilst old Mrs. Opie went to church, or meeting-house. The old man had fallen fast asleep, and his hopeful offspring seized the

golden opportunity of painting his portrait, hitherto
a forbidden operation ;—the way in which the
'Sabbath-breaking' young rogue was reviled by his
progenitors may be imagined better than I can describe it. Yet the likeness was so good, and the motive
so affectionate, that the offence was condoned, and
the portrait exhibited to all the neighbours with
parental pride, notwithstanding the boy's having
irritated his father during the progress of the work
by awakening him from his nap in order to 'get his
eyes lightened up.'   One of his uncles, however, is
said to have fostered John's talents, both as a
mathematician and as an artist ; at any rate his love
of art was not to be quenched, and the cottage-walls
were ere long decorated with portraits of most of his
relations and playfellows, painted with singular force
and brilliancy for so young and untaught an artist.
Wolcot says that Opie used often to get up at three
in the morning to go to work on his painting.

From his thraldom in Mithian, Jan Opie was no
doubt glad to get the chance of escaping, when it was
offered to him by Dr. Wolcot (' Peter Pindar '), then
living at Truro ; a man who added to a strong satiric
vein of poetry a considerable amount of artistic
taste, sufficient at any rate to recognise that his
protégé was no common lad.   It has been said that
Wolcot employed 'Jan' in some menial capacity
about his house on the Green ; but this is not the
case. He certainly did give Opie the opportunity of
copying his pictures, some of which were very good ;
adding the sound advice to study hard from the life.
It was perhaps also whilst under the old doctor's roof

that he continued his mathematical studies with such success that he is said to have mastered his Euclid when only twelve years old. William Sandby, in his 'History of the Royal Academy,' says that Opie had a very good knowledge of Euclid when only ten years of age; and that, about this time, spending his scanty pocket-money in candles and writing materials, he set up an evening school at St. Agnes, in which most of his pupils were twice as old as himself. His uncle loved to call him 'little Sir Isaac.'

Dr. Wolcot did his best to get the rising young artist commissions from his patients and acquaintances, and Opie's services were soon in great request as a local portrait-painter. Many an old Cornish house still possesses specimens of his early skill, as may be seen from the long and elaborate account of his works prepared by the late Mr. J. Jope Rogers. Sir Rose Price, of Trengwainton, had a portrait of an old beggar by Opie, which was considered at the time a *chef-d'œuvre;* and the Truro families of Daniell and Vivian, who were liberal patrons of his skill, also had some of the best examples of his rapid, vigorous brush. Viscount Bateman, who was for some time quartered at Pendennis Castle, Falmouth, with his regiment, the Hereford Militia, was another of his early patrons, and gave Opie several commissions to paint beggars, old men, and similar subjects. His usual price for a portrait, when he was sixteen years of age, was seven shillings and sixpence.

But John Opie was getting a little too big for his remote native county; and, instigated by ' Peter

Pindar,' resolved on trying his fortunes in London. The story goes—and it is not without some sort of foundation—that the doctor (who had met with some pecuniary losses) and his *protégé* (or *pupil*, as Wolcot preferred calling him) were to share profits; but that this arrangement only lasted for a year. However that may be, either in 1780 or 1781 they both came to Town, when 'the Cornish wonder' was forthwith introduced to Sir Joshua Reynolds, then President of the Royal Academy; and in 1782, Opie, now twenty-one years of age, exhibited (for the first time) on the walls of that institution pictures of an old man's head, an old woman, and three portraits.*

He now, with Wolcot, took apartments, which he himself furnished out of the thirty or forty guineas which formed his capital, in Orange Court, Leicester Fields—near Sir Joshua Reynolds' studio. The court itself is demolished, but it stood at the back of the present National Gallery, on the site of St. George's Barracks. Here John soon got to work with his painting—copying the old masters, and studying diligently the best English authors, whose wit and wisdom his powerful mind and retentive memory

---

* Mr. Rogers, in his 'Opie and his Works,' has thus classified the 760 works catalogued:

Portraits (counting each head in family groups) .	508
Sacred Subjects	22
Historical	17
Shakespeare	11
Poetical and Fancy	134
Landscape	5
Supplementary and addenda (various). . .	63
	760

He exhibited altogether 143 pictures at the Royal Academy.

enabled him to easily assimilate and retain. Milton, Shakespeare, Dryden, Pope, Gray, Cowper, Butler (Hudibras), Burke, and Dr. Johnson seem to have been his special favourites. The last-named he idolized, and painted his portrait twice. He now also added French, Italian, and a little Latin to his attainments. Sitters gradually thronged round him ; he ' trembled at his terrific popularity ' and his many flatterers; and, having been introduced to the King and Queen, his fame spread like wild-fire, and he used merrily to say that he thought of keeping a loaded cannon at his door to frighten off the crowds by whom he was besieged. Wolcot says that Jan answered ' George ' with St. Agnes intrepidity, that the King bought some of his pictures, and wished Opie every success.

The following is a letter to his mother on the memorable occasion of his reception at the Palace. The MS., much tattered and torn, was communicated to the Rev. Richard Polwhele by the present Mr. Edward Opie :

' DEAR MOTHER,

' I received my brother's two last letters, and am exceedingly sorry to hear that my father is so poorly ; don't let him work any more, I hope he will be better before this arrives. I have all the prospect of success that is possible, having much more busi-ness than I can possibly do. I have been with the King and Queen, who were highly pleased with my work, and took two of my pictures, and they are hung up in the King's collection at the Queen's palace. As to the £200 business, it is entirely false, for I was but paid my price and no more. I could have had more money for the pictures if I had sold them to several noblemen. . . . There is no work stirring at this time, and it is a very improper time to see the town, as it is cold and very dirty, and so full of smoak and fog that you can hardly see the length of your nose, and I should not be able to stir anywhere out by day nor keep them company in-doors, by reason of the quantity of business. I would advise them to come up in June, when they may see everything in fine weather; and probably I shall not be so busy then as I am now, because most of the quality go out of town at that time, and then also they may see all the great houses, &c., but now the familys are in town, they'd not be able to see one. As to my stay here, it will depend on circum-stances, as the continuation of employ and the encouragement I may meet with. If I have time and money I shall certainly come down in the summer. . . . Many have been in town, years, and have had nothing to do, whilst I, who have been here but two or three months, am known and talked of by everybody. To be known, is the great thing in London. A man may do ever so well, if nobody knows it, it will signify nothing; and among so many thousand and ten thousand people, it is no easy matter to get known. I cannot think what gave rise to the report which you heard, as I have never had a present from anybody in my life. Money is very scarce among everybody, and I only desire to get paid for what I do. I have a new method, and

make them all, or most of them, pay half as soon as
I begin the pictures, which is a very good method.
Brother E. and his wife are very well and will be
very glad to see Brother and Betty up at the time I
mentioned ; they join in their duty to you and Father,
and love to Uncle, Brother and sisters, &c., with
your affectionate son,

'J. OPIE.

'Direct to me at Mr. Riccard's, Orange Court,
Leicester Fields, London.

'March 11, 1782.'

In the following year he removed to Great Queen
Street, Lincoln's Inn Fields; and somewhere about
this time became infatuated with the black eyes and
arch smiles of a City solicitor's daughter, one Mary
Bunn, of St. Botolph's, Aldgate, who brought him
some money on his marriage with her at St. Martin's-
in-the-Fields, 4th December, 1782. It was a foolish
union—she, pretty and giddy, and her husband a
blunt, strong-minded, hard-working artist. He tried
to gloss over her follies, being placable to a degree ;
but in vain. She at last crowned her faithless
career by eloping with a Mr. John Edwards in 1795,
and an Act of divorce left Opie a free and a happier
man. It was *à propos* of this miserable affair that
Opie once uttered the following grim *bon-mot*. He
was passing the above-named church one day
with his quondam friend Godwin, who was an infidel,
when Godwin exclaimed : 'Ah ! I was christened at
that church.' 'And I was married in it,' replied
Opie ; 'they make unsure work there, for it neither
holds in wedlock nor in baptism.'

But at length the crowds of sitters and callers who used to annoy both Opie and his neighbours began to dwindle away, as the novelty of seeing that ' nine days' wonder '—a great artist—in

> ' The Cornish boy in tin-mines bred
> Whose genius, like his native diamonds, shone
> In secret, till chance gave them to the sun,'

began to wear off; and gave Opie the much-desired opportunity of pursuing the higher branches of his art. Henceforth he painted less portraits and more historical compositions ; but amongst the former, even up to the end of his career, we still find some notable subjects, such as a whole-length of Charles James Fox (which West thought his best), William Siddons (the husband of the great actress), Fuseli, Southey, the Poet Laureate,* and many others. In 1784 he exhibited his ' School,' of which Horace Walpole remarked that it was ' Great nature—the best of his works yet.'

His first great work of the ' historical ' school, and one of his very best, ' The Assassination of James I. of Scotland,' was produced in 1786; as to which a writer in the *Quarterly Review* for 1866 tells the following amusing story of Northcote's jealousy of Opie. When the latter was engaged at Hampstead on this picture (the story is, by the way, also told of the Rizzio picture), Northcote became alarmed at the reports which reached him of its extraordinary merit,

---

* Writing to Southey, from Norwich, 3rd June, 1806, William Taylor says, ' Opie is soon to be knighted ;' and in 1807 he says that Opie had been at the point of death from abdominal paralysis—probably caused by the absorption into his system of lead-vapours from his paints.

and accordingly he paid a visit to Opie's studio in order to judge for himself. 'When I entered the room,' he said, ' I was astounded. The picture had the finest effect I ever witnessed; the light on the figures gleamed up from a trap-door by which the murderers were entering the King's chamber. " Oh!" said I to myself; "go home, go home; it is all over with you !" I did go home, and brooded over what I had seen. I could think of nothing else; it perfectly haunted me. I could not work on my own pictures for thinking of his. At last, unable to bear it any longer, I determined to go there again, and when I entered the room I saw, to my great comfort, that Opie had rubbed all the fine effect out.'

In the following year his next great work, ' The Assassination of David Rizzio,'* was painted, and Opie's claim to be elected an Associate of the Royal Academy was established, the full honours being accorded to him the year after. His diploma picture, ' Age and Infancy,' still hangs on the Academy's walls.

Amongst his other more important works may be named, ' The Presentation in the Temple,' ' Jephthah's Vow,' ' Young Arthur taken Prisoner,' 'Arthur with Hubert,' ' Belisarius,' ' Juliet in the Garden,' ' The Escape of Gil Blas ' (his last historical work), and ' Musidora.' A very large proportion of these, and others of Opie's paintings have been engraved. It may be here mentioned, as an illustration of the prices which some of Opie's best works fetch, that at the sale of Mr. Jesse Watts Russell's pictures,

---

* Mrs. Gilbert says that her father got 250 guineas for engraving this picture.

at Christie and Manson's, in July, 1875, 'The School-mistress,' from the collection of Mr. Watson Taylor, a large and important work of several figures—an old lady schoolmistress and her pupils—painted in emulation of Rembrandt, fetched £787 10s.

Pursuing his career at the Royal Academy, in 1789, on the expulsion of Barry, the Professor of Painting, on account of his impertinent remarks upon his brother Academicians, and his generally unsatisfactory con-duct, Opie preferred his claims ; but was induced to waive them in favour of the elder artist, Fuseli. The latter, however, resigned in 1805, and the indis-putable claims of Opie to the post were at once fully and honourably recognised.

Before, however, that event took place, one which had still greater and happier influence on our artist's professional career and domestic happiness occurred : in 1798 he had the good fortune to fall in love at first sight, and, after much coy reluctance on the lady's part, to secure the heart and hand of the amiable, sprightly, and accomplished Amelia Alderson, the only child of a Norwich physician, and a relative of H. P. Briggs, R.A. They were married on the 8th of May ('Flora Day,' as it is called in Cornwall), she being then twenty-nine years of age, and her husband thirty-seven. She was much courted in the fashionable circles of London for her literary and conversational talents, and numbered Sir Walter Scott, Sir James Mackintosh, Wordsworth and Sydney Smith among her friends and acquaintances.

When she became a Quakeress (and I fancy that

at heart she was always more or less of one) in 1825, she endeavoured to recall her novels; but copies of them are still to be met with in many of our libraries. Indeed, she tells us that she would never have published at all had it not been for the strong wish of her husband that she should do so.

As regards her novels, or tales, as they should rather be called, 'She can do nothing well,' says Jeffrey, 'that requires to be done with formality, and therefore has not succeeded in copying either the concentrated force of weighty and deliberate reason, or the severe and solemn dignity of majestic virtue. To make amends, however, she represents admirably everything that is amiable, generous and gentle.'

Of her poetic vein, the following specimen may perhaps be admitted here :—

LINES WRITTEN IN 1799, BY MRS. OPIE TO HER HUSBAND, ON HIS HAVING PAINTED THE POR-TRAIT OF HER FRIEND, MRS. TWISS.

' Hail to thy pencil ! well its glowing art
Has traced those features painted on my heart ;
Now, though in distant scenes she soon will rove,
Still shall I here behold the friend I love—
Still see that smile, "endearing, artless, kind,"
The eye's mild beam that speaks the candid mind,
Which sportive oft, yet fearful to offend,
By humour charms, but never wounds a friend.

' But in my breast contending feelings rise,
While this loved semblance fascinates my eyes ;
Now, pleased I mark the painter's skilful line,
And now, rejoice the skill I mark is *thine :*
And while I prize the gift by thee bestow'd,
My heart proclaims, I'm of the giver proud.
Thus pride and friendship war with equal strife,
And now the *friend* exults, and now the WIFE.'

She died on the 2nd December, 1853, eighty-four years of age (forty-seven years after her husband's death), and was buried in the same grave with her father, in the Friends' burial-ground, at the Gilden Croft, Norwich. Her life has been written by her friend, Miss Brightwell; and a portrait of 'la charmante Madame Opie' (as she was called in Paris), in her Quakeress's cap and with uplifted eyes full of gentle ardour, after a medallion by David, is prefixed to that work. Haydon also (who, by the way, was indebted to Opie for much sound practical advice in his art) painted her, in her tall black Quakeress's bonnet, in his great group of the 'Anti-Slavery Convention,' now in the National Portrait Gallery; and her husband painted her portrait more than once: an engraving after one of these portraits is prefixed to a later edition of Miss Brightwell's 'Life.'

To her more refined taste were said to be due not only a superior delicacy and grace sometimes thought to be found in the female portraits painted after Opie's second marriage, but also some of the finer touches in his lectures as Professor of Painting, to which reference will presently be made. But Mrs. Opie disclaimed the latter suggestion with all the energy and indignation of which her tranquil spirit was capable, observing that 'the slight texture of muslin could as easily assume the consistency of velvet.' About half of Opie's sitters were ladies; and one of his best early works is a portrait of Mrs. Delany,* now at Hampton Court; it used formerly to hang in the Royal bedchamber at Windsor. The

* Opie painted a *replica* of Mrs. Delany's portrait for the Countess of Bute, for which Horace Walpole designed a frame; and I confess these paintings appear to me to refute entirely the statement that Opie's female portraits were unsuccessful.

following contemporary criticism by a Cornish lady on Opie's work will be interesting to at least some of my readers:

The Honble. Mrs. Boscawen to Mrs. Delany.

'26th Sept., 1782.

*   *   *   *   *

'Your favoured Opie is still in raptures at the thoughts of Bulstrode (the residence of the Duke of Portland). His portrait of Lady Jerningham did not *quite* satisfy me, for I concluded it wou'd be perfect, and her *person, hands, posture, spinning-wheel,* all *are so;* but the face (or rather countenance) does not *quite* please me.'

To his wife Opie was indebted for the graceful and affectionate memoir—her 'dearest and last duty'—which was prefixed to his 'Lectures,' which she edited after his death, in 1809. It is said that he used always to keep in his studio an unfinished portrait of his wife, with her abundant waves of auburn hair, constantly working on it in order to obtain that power of delineation of female delicacy and beauty in which he thought himself deficient. Opie was devotedly attached to her, and they were most happy in each other's love; the only point of difference between them being her liking for a gayer social existence than suited her husband's tastes. Yet he was always fond of a dinner-party when there was *good talk*, and many such noteworthy gatherings are described in Holcroft's 'Memoirs.' They had a memorable trip to Paris together in 1802; the only occasion on which Opie ever left England,

except once before, in 1786, for a short trip to
the picture-galleries in Belgium and Holland. Mrs.
Opie was very fond of sketching in profile all her
friends' portraits, of which she made a large collection, and was altogether a lady of refined tastes as
well as of the most active benevolence. Southey
has sketched her in his ' Colloquies,' vol. ii., p. 322 ;
and her friend and biographer has told us that
' her cheerful heart shone through her bright face,
and brought comfort and pleasure into every house
she entered.'   Miss Thackeray (Mrs. Richmond
Ritchie) has also included Amelia Opie in her recent
' Book of Sibyls ;' and Harriet Martineau has admirably described her in the ' Biographical Sketches.'

In 1791 Opie had moved to the house in which he
resided for the last sixteen years of his life, No. 8,
Berners Street, Oxford Street ;* and here he passed
what was probably his serenest and happiest days,
overshadowed with only one cloud, and that was one
which scarcely disturbed him, for he attributed it to
causes over which he had no control.   I mean his
decreasing popularity, which for a short time waned ;
but, as we shall see, was at length recovered. Public
caprice no doubt had, as Opie thought, much to do
with this ; but the novelty had gone off, and the
London world is always on the look-out for new
wonders.   His pencil was, notwithstanding, as ever,
busy. Alderman Boydell had formed the idea of a
Shakespeare Gallery—a collection of pictures which
should illustrate the works of our greatest dramatist.

---

* Lonsdale the painter afterwards occupied it : it now forms part of
an hotel.

Now Shakespeare was, as we have seen, a favourite author with Opie; and the painter accordingly set to work with a will, adding five pictures to the series, to which many other eminent artists also contributed. Amongst them are the following:

Juliet on her Bed	Romeo and Juliet.
Antigonus sworn to destroy Perdita .	Winter's Tale.
Talbot and the Countess of Auvergne ⎫	Henry VI.
The Incantation Scene . . . ⎭	
Timon with Phryne and Timandra .	Timon of Athens.

To Macklin's 'British Poets and Bible,' and to Bowyer's 'Hume's History of England,' he also contributed largely. 'The Death of Sapphira' is a remarkable example of his artistic power.

About this period he must have written the following letter to his sister, which is perhaps worth inserting—being, as it were, a peep behind the scenes, affording us a glimpse of his rough, affectionate nature:

'Nov. 20, 1800.

'DEAR BETT,*

'What the devil is the reason that thou art in such a fright, indeed what should make thee suspect the contrary? My not having written is the very thing that ought to have kept thee quiet, for if any accident had happened to me thou certainly wouldst have heard of it by me and by many others, henceforth I desire thou wilt remember the old saying "no news is good news," and not fret thyself

* Betty Opie was a remarkably shrewd and sagacious old lady. She gave my father most entertaining accounts of her visit to London, when she went up to see 'Jan,' as she called her illustrious brother, and especially of an escapade of hers at the British Museum, where, having accidentally broken off the finger of a mummy, she brought it home to her brother, who ground it down into a fine brown paint.

because I am lazy and don't like to write when I have nothing to say.

'My dearest Amelia was not so fortunate in coming to town as myself; she was overturned in the mail about 30 miles from town, and so bruised as to cause her to be lame for a fortnight or three weeks after, but she is now I hope perfectly recovered : she desires me to give her kindest love to you and mother, and to thank you for your presents. . . . Keep up Mother's spirits and tell her I am very well and hope to see her again next summer, and my wife hopes the same. Give my love to Mary James,* &c., &c., and believe me ever

'Affectionately yours,

'JOHN OPIE.

'Let brother's picture be sent off as soon as possible, and I will take care the other shall be sent down as soon as I have time to paint one of Amelia to go with it.'

But it is time to speak of his literary talents. Charles James Fox,† Horne Tooke, and Sir James Mackintosh had the highest opinion of his mental powers. Horne Tooke (whose portrait also Opie painted) says of him that he spoke in axioms worthy to be remembered; and Mackintosh observed: 'Had Mr. Opie turned his powers of mind to the study of philosophy, he would have been one of the first philosophers of the age. I was never more struck than with

* An old sweetheart of his, whose portrait he once painted in the act of milking a cow.

† When Opie was painting Charles James Fox's portrait, worried by many and various criticisms, Fox said, 'Don't attend to *them ;* you *must* know best.'

his original manner of thinking and expressing himself in conversation; had he written on the subject he would probably have thrown more light on the philosophy of his art than any man living.'

There is a capital short 'Life of Sir Joshua Reynolds' by Opie, written for Pilkington's 'Dictionary of Painters;' and the accompanying extract from a letter which he addressed to one of the periodicals on the subject of a grand national memorial to the triumphs of the British fleet, may serve as a specimen of his powerful, glowing style. Opie proposed a huge building in which everything connected with the subject might be displayed—including statues of our naval heroes, surrounded by pictorial representations of their achievements.

'What an effect,' he says, 'might a design like this, happily planned and executed, produce! How magnificent, how instructive it might be made! How entertaining to trace down from the earliest records of our history the gradual increase of our navy! to remark the different stages of its growth from a few simple canoes, in its infancy, to the stupendous magnitude of a hundred first-rate men-of-war, miracles of the mechanic arts, proudly bearing Britain's thunder! the bulwarks of England! the glory of Englishmen, and the terror and admiration of the world! How flattering to the imagination to anticipate the pleasure of walking round such an edifice, and surveying the different subjects depicted on its walls! Battles under all varied circumstances of day, night, moonlight, storm, and calm!—the effects of fire, water, wind and smoke mingled in terrific confusion. In the midst, British Valour triumphantly bearing down all opposition, accompanied by Humanity, equally daring and ready to succour the vanquished foe! Discoveries, in which we see delineated the strange figures and still stranger costume of nations till then unknown, and where the face of Nature herself is exhibited under a new and surprising aspect. Then to turn and behold the statues and portraits of the enterprising commanders and leaders in the expeditions recorded, and compare their different countenances: here a Drake and an Anson! there a Blake, a Hawke, a Boscawen, and a Cook!'

To me these enthusiastic sentences have something of the ring of a sea-song of Dibdin's; and it is pleasant to think that the idea has been carried out in the Painted Hall at Greenwich Hospital.

His Lectures before the Royal Academy (prepared with a severity of labour which probably shortened his life), are, however, the works by which his literary fame will be handed down to posterity. Sandby tells us that Opie had, shortly before his appointment to his Professorship, delivered some lectures on Art at the Royal Institution; but though they were generally thought good, and were numerously and fashionably attended (that sour critic, Allan Cunningham, by the way, calls them 'confused, abrupt, and unmethodical'), Opie was himself much dissatisfied with them, and would not complete the intended course. He was also concerned in a scheme, in conjunction with West and

Flaxman, for establishing a 'Gallery of Honour,' under the sanction of the Royal Academy, for the encouragement and reward of all those who contributed to the higher walks of art. And he is further said to have projected a colossal statue of Britannia, to be erected in some prominent position in the Isle of Wight, as an alternative mode of commemorating the naval victories of Great Britain. Northcote, again (whom, it may be observed, Wolcot, as Opie's patron, much abused), was associated with Opie in 'a project of getting paintings into St. Paul's,' which they hoped 'would tend to raise the drooping head, or rather the almost expiring art, of painting;' and to this project the Bishop of London gave his assent.

Opie's 'Discourses on Painting' were delivered before the Royal Academy in 1807.* His scheme included six : four on the practical aspect of the subject, viz., 'Design or Drawing,' 'Colouring,' 'Chiaroscuro,' and 'Composition;' and two on the intellectual side, viz. 'Invention' and 'Expression.' The last of the series in each division, viz. those on 'Composition' and 'Expression,' he did not live to complete. I propose to give as characteristic a short specimen as I can select from each of the four which Opie delivered,† merely premising that they were enthusiastically received, and that their author was, for once, satisfied with his work, and so elated by his success that he could not sleep. Even Allan Cunningham admitted : 'A

---

* In this year he contributed to the Exhibition six portraits, one of them being that of Dr. Samuel Parr.

† That on 'Design' was delivered on 16th Feb., 1807, the others followed on 23rd Feb., 2nd March, and 9th March.

passage such as this would reflect credit on any professor the Academy ever possessed.'

In his first lecture, on 'Design or Drawing,' after insisting on the absolute necessity for hard study of anatomy, with constant practice so as to insure accurate drawing, without which, whatever may be the other merits of the work, 'when the tide of taste rises, and the winds of criticism bluster and beat upon it, the showy but ill-founded edifice must quickly be swept away, or swallowed up and forgotten for ever,' he goes on to say :

' These remarks are the more necessary, as it must be confessed that the strength of the English painters never lay so much as it ought in *design ;* and now perhaps, more than ever, they seem devoted to the charms of colour and effect, and captivate by the mere penmanship of the art—the empty legerdemain of the pencil.

' But if the English artist runs counter in this instance to the established character of his country, and prefers the superficial to the solid attainments in art, has he not many excuses ?   May it not in great measure be attributed to the general frivolity and meanness of the subjects he is called upon to treat ? to the inordinate rage for portrait-painting (a more respectable kind of caricature), by which he is for ever condemned to study and copy the wretched defects, and conform to the still more wretched prejudices, of every tasteless and ignorant individual, however in form, features, and mind, utterly hostile to all ideas of character, expression, or sentiment ?

And may it not in part be attributed to the necessity he is under of painting always with reference to the exhibition ? In a crowd he that talks loudest, not he that talks best, is surest of commanding attention ; and in an exhibition he that does not attract the eye does nothing. But however plausible these excuses, it becomes the true painter to consider that they will avail nothing before the tribunal of the world and posterity. Keeping the true end of Art in view, he must rise superior to the prejudices, disregard the applause, and contemn the censure of corrupt and incompetent judges ; far from aiming to be fashionable, it must be his object to reform, and not to flatter—to teach, and not to please—if he aspires, like Zeuxis, to paint for eternity.'

The spirit of this passage will, I think, enable us to understand how irksome mere portrait-painting must always have been to our professor ; and its precepts might be laid to heart even by the artists of the close of this nineteenth century.

In the lecture on ' Invention ' the following passage seems to me worthy of being reproduced. He observed that both the poet and the painter have ' something more to do than to illustrate, explain, or fill the chasms of history or tradition ;' they must both first penetrate thoroughly into the subject, and then mould it anew.

'Each adopts a chain of circumstances for the most part inapplicable in the case of the other; each avails himself of their common privilege of " daring everything to accomplish his end," not scrupling on some occasions to run counter, if necessary, even to matter of fact; for though most strictly bound to the observance of truth and probability, these are obviously very different from such as is required in *history;* his truth is the truth of *effect,* and his probability the perfect *harmony* and *congruity* of all the parts of his story, and their fitness to bring about the intended effect—that of striking the imagination, touching the passions, and developing in the most forcible manner the leading sentiment of the subject.'

Much would naturally be expected from Opie when he came to treat of ' Chiaroscuro,' for it was one of his strong points. West said of him : ' He painted what he saw in the most masterly manner, and he varied little from it. *He saw nature in one point more distinctly and forcibly than any painter that ever lived.* The truth of colour as conveyed to the eye through the atmosphere, by which the distance of every object is ascertained, was never better expressed than by him.' And the following fine description of Opie's idea of this recondite branch of art accordingly seems to me worthy of the painter and writer :

' Light and shade must be allowed to be the creator of body and space. In addition to this, if properly managed, it contributes infinitely to expression and sentiment; it lulls by breadth and gentle gradation, strikes by contrast, and rouses by abrupt transition. All that is grave, impressive, awful, mysterious, sublime, or dreadful in nature, is neally connected with IT. All poetic scenery, real or imaginary, " of forests and enchantments drear," where more is meant than is expressed; all the effects of solemn twilight and visionary obscurity that flings half an image on the aching sight ; all the terrors of storm and the horrors of conflagration are indebted to IT for representation on canvas; IT is the medium of enchanting softness and repose in the works of some painters, and the vehicle by which others have risen to sublimity in spite of the want of almost every other excellence.'

We now come to his last lecture, that on 'Colour,' and in it note this felicitous, nay poetic, passage:

' Colour, the peculiar object of the most delightful of our senses, is associated in our minds with all that is rare, precious, delicate, and magnificent in nature. A fine complexion, in the language of the poet, is the dye of love, and the hint of something celestial ; the ruby, the rose, the diamond, the youthful blush, the orient morning, and the variegated splendour of the setting sun, consist of, or owe their charms principally to, *colour*. To the sight it is the index of gaiety, richness, warmth, and animation ; and should the most experienced artist, by design alone, attempt to represent the tender freshness of spring, the fervid vivacity of summer, or the mellow abundance of autumn, what must be his success ? *Colouring is the sunshine of art*, that clothes poverty in smiles, rendering the prospect of barrenness itself agreeable, while it heightens the interest and doubles the charms of beauty.'

The next extract which I shall make will be the best answer to some cavillers who used to aver that Opie was unwilling to admit excellence in the works of other artists:

' Like Michael Angelo in design, Titian in colouring may be regarded as the father of modern art.
He first discovered and unfolded all its charms, saw
the true end of imitation, showed what to aim at,
when to labour, and where to stop; and united
breadth and softness to the proper degree of finish.
He first dared all its depths, contrasted all its
oppositions, and taught COLOUR to glow and palpitate
with all the warmth and tenderness of real life : free
from tiresome detail or disgusting minutiæ, he
rendered the roses and lilies of youth, the more en-
sanguined brown of manhood, and the pallid cold-
ness of age with truth and precision; and to every
material object, hard or soft, rough or smooth,
bright or obscure, opaque or transparent, his pencil
imparted its true quality and appearance to the eye,
with all the force of harmony and light, shade,
middle tint and reflection ; by which he so relieved,
rounded, and connected the whole, that we are
almost irresistibly tempted to apply the test of
another sense, and exclaim

> ' " Art thou not, pleasing vision ! sensible
> To feeling as to sight ? " '

But the too industrious artist's health was already
beginning to break down. Exactly one calendar
month passed away, and there

> ' Came the blind Fury with abhorred shears
> And slit the thin-spun life—'

the lecturer was silent after the delivery of the
foregoing lecture ; and his busy pencil at length
idle. John Opie died, childless, in the house in
Berners Street where he had lived for sixteen

years, in the forty-sixth year of his age. He had loving nurses in his devoted wife and a most affectionate sister; he had also the advantage of no less than six medical attendants, who saw him daily—frequently three or four times a day. But the exact nature of his illness seems not to have been quite understood,* and all was in vain; he lingered awhile, and died, as he had lived, a painter. His friend and pupil, Henry Thomson, R.A.,† had been called in to complete the background and robes of one of Opie's finest portraits, for the forthcoming Exhibition. It was a likeness of the Duke of Gloucester. 'It wants more colour in the background,' said Opie, in the intervals of his deathbed delirium. More was added, but he continued to express himself dissatisfied :—the delirium returned ; and he continued (in imagination) at his easel, until he breathed his last on the 9th April, 1807.

And his prophecy as to his place of burial was fulfilled : 'Aye, girl,' he once said to his sister, 'I, too, shall be buried at St. Paul's.' There he was laid on the 20th April (close to Barry), in the crypt, by the side of a yet more illustrious artist from the West-country,—Sir Joshua Reynolds. Benjamin West's remains followed in 1820. Vandyke had long before been buried near the same spot. Fuseli, and Lawrence, and Turner, followed

---

* According to his sister's account, the *post-mortem* examination disclosed 'a bladder on the brain'; but Dr. Sayer thought the patient's malady was a species of painter's colic.

† Another of his pupils was John Cawse, the well-known subject and portrait painter, of whose works the writer possesses an example. Theophilus Clarke, A.R.A., was another of Opie's pupils.

them. Amongst the distinguished men who were his pall-bearers were two eminent Cornishmen, Lord De Dunstanville and Sir John St. Aubyn, his friends, and (the former especially) his patrons.

We have seen something of Opie's career as an artist, and of his grasp as a writer: it remains to say something of his private character. The predominant features of it seem to me to be a lofty, unselfish ambition for excellence, a deep earnestness and stern truthfulness combined with a most affectionate placable disposition, a generous heart, and no inconsiderable sense of humour. He was never idle for a moment, his wife says—he painted all day long, and grudged himself the shortest holiday; but he never made sufficient progress to satisfy himself, and would sometimes exclaim: 'I shall never, never make a painter.' As in his youth, so in his manhood, he was liable to fits of depression, from one of which he especially suffered during a gloomy three months at the end of the year 1802, when commissions for a short while came in slowly. He recovered his spirits, however, at the beginning of the following year, when more work came to him, and from that time to the very last he was full of commissions. The last work he finished was a head of Miranda, and it was one of his best.

His tastes were simple, and his ambition (except as to his art) was moderate. To save 'a certain sum,' Mrs. Opie tells us, in order that he might keep a horse, and collect a good library which he could study at his leisure, was the limit of his desires.

A few words may be expected as to Opie's personal

appearance and manners. As to the former, his bold, homely, melancholy features, noble forehead and penetrating eye—the 'index' to his mind—are tolerably familiar to us from the fact of his having several times painted his own portrait—Mr. Rogers catalogues more than twenty. One of the best with which I am acquainted is, I think, that engraved in mezzotint by S. W. Reynolds, and selected by Mrs. Opie to prefix to her edition of her husband's 'Lectures;'* but that presented by his widow to the Royal Cornwall Polytechnic Society, Falmouth, is also a very fine one. There is another portrait, painted by himself when a youth, at the National Portrait Gallery; and there is one at Dulwich. And Opie was caricatured, with six other R.A.'s, in Gillray's 'Titianus Redivivus, or the Seven Wise Men consulting the Venetian Oracle.' He was always somewhat careless of his personal appearance, and frugal in his mode of life. For drawing-room society he had no liking or capacity; but, as we have seen, he enjoyed a good dinner-party, where sterling con-

---

* I fancy, notwithstanding the thin disguise of the title of the poem, that Mrs. Opie must have been thinking of this portrait when she wrote the following lines :

'To me how dear this twilight hour,
    Cheered by the faggot's varying blaze !
If this be mine, I ask no more
    On morn's refulgent light to gaze :

' For now, while on His glowing cheek
    I see the fire's red radiance fall,
The darkest seat I softly seek,
    And gaze on Him, unseen by all.

' His folded arms, his studious brow,
    His thoughtful eye, *unmarked*, I see ;
Nor could his voice or words bestow
    So dear, so true a joy on me.'

versation went on, and to which he was able and ready to contribute his quota—sometimes brusquely enough.   But on this point his friend Boaden should be heard :

'I know that, to some, his frank open conduct appeared uncalled for; nay, I have even heard it termed coarse; but the coarse man is he who says a thing in bad language, and not he who, with a noble simplicity, comes immediately to the point, and, when he has obtained conviction, in the plainest words delivers his judgment. If I were to attempt to characterize him in one word (I should most certainly use that word to the honour of our species) it would be that he was a genuine ENGLISH-MAN—for affectation he despised, and flattery he abhorred.'   It may be added that he regarded with utter indifference any attacks which might be made on his private or professional character.

His sledge-hammer style of expression had doubt-less something to do with the cessation of intimate relations which took place between old Wolcot and himself.   Opie was not the sort of man to be *patronized*, even by a ' Peter Pindar.'

Most of his great works live to speak for themselves.   Some of the finest examples are at Petworth ; and Dr. Waagen pronounces these almost equal to Sir Joshua's.   In energy of style, breadth, purity of colour, harmony of tone, and exquisite chiaroscuro, they stand very high.   His portraits especially were real and lifelike, but they were not without their defects, and, as we see them now, are much marred by his too copious use of asphaltum : Thackeray, in his 'Four Georges,' even refers to them as 'Opie's pitchy canvases.' His historical works are somewhat deficient in imagination; and his portraits sometimes lack dignity as well as delicacy; whilst his style, partaking too much of his own temperament, and even of his personal appearance, was apt to run in a sombre vein. But a brother R.A., who knew him well—J. Northcote, a friendly rival, and to some extent his imitator—wrote of him : 'The toils and difficulties of his profession were by him considered as matters of honourable and delightful contest; and it might be said of him that *he did not so much paint to live, as live to paint.** He was studious, yet not severe; he was eminent, yet not vain; his disposition so tranquil and forgiving that it was the reverse of every tincture of sour or vindictive, and what to some might seem roughness of manner, was only the effect of an honest indignation towards that which he conceived to be error.' Northcote would often exclaim to those whom he esteemed, ' How I wish you had known Opie !'

And his friend Sir Martin Archer Shee, a President of the Royal Academy, paid this final tribute to his memory :

> ' His vigorous pencil in pursuit of art
> Disdain'd to dwell on each minuter part ;
> Impressive force—impartial truth he sought,
> And travell'd in no beaten track of thought.
> Unlike the servile herd, whom we behold
> Casting their drossy ore in fashion's mould ;
> *His* metal by no common die is known,
> The coin is sterling—and the stamp *his own.*'

---

* When a lad, Opie used to say that he loved painting ' better than bread and meat.' Northcote was himself another of our West-country artists ; he was born at Plymouth, close to the Cornish border.

It may be interesting to some readers to know where the best Opies are now to be found in Cornwall; and for information on this point I am indebted to the following extract from a letter from my friend Mr. Edward Opie, of Plymouth:

'As I have mentioned where Opies are *not* to be found, I ought to state where they *are*—I mean in Cornwall, if not removed lately. Sir John St. Aubyn has the greatest number—I think seven or eight. These include two portraits of his grandfather, Sir J. St. Aubyn; one of his grandmother; one of Captain James; one of Miss Bunn;* one of Dolly Pentreath; and one—the best of all—of Mrs. Bell, housekeeper at Clowance. This last was much admired at one of the R.A. Winter Exhibitions. Lady Falmouth told me she had three, if not four, Opies. Mrs. Boscawen, you know, was an early patroness of the painter, and invited him to breakfast, when old Mr. Polwhele sent him into the kitchen. The Hon. Mrs. Gilbert has four, including a beggar; —another beggar is at Enys. Mrs. J. M. Williams, at Carhayes, has two, both fancy pictures. At Scorrier, Mr. G. Williams has two. At Penrose, Mr. Rogers's, there are two or three. At Prideaux Place, Mr. Prideaux Brune's, there are two; one being a dog's head, the other his own portrait. At Tregullow there are two, one being his mother with Bible;—there are several copies of this.'

* Opie also painted his first wife's portrait with that of the famous Conjuror Chamberlain. It was at one time in Sir Joshua Reynolds's Collection ('The lost Opie'), and afterwards passed into the hands of Sir Charles Bell.

THE ST. AUBYNS OF CLOWANCE AND THE MOUNT.

THE ST. AUBYNS OF CLOWANCE
AND THE MOUNT.

'A Wit's a feather, and a Chief a rod ;—
An HONEST MAN'S the noblest work of God.'

POPE : *Essay on Man.*

'HIS gentle and knightly family,' as Hals calls them, are amongst the few examples of eminent Cornishmen who, like the Bevills, the Grenvilles, the Lanyons, the Chamonds, the Bassets, and others, were of Norman, or at least of French, origin.

In the 'Chronicum Johannis Brompton' (quoted by John Henneker) we read :

'Vous que desyrez assaver
Le nons de Grauntz de la mer,
Que vindrent od le Conquerour,
William Bastard de graunt vigoure,
*   *   *   *
Seint Aubyn, et Seynt Omer,
Seynt Filbert Fyens, et Gomer.'

Leland says that St. Albin came out of Brittany; and Camden, in his 'Remains,' names Plaus as the place of their origin; according, however, to other authorities, St. Aubin du Cormier in Brittany enjoys this distinction. Of Armorican extraction, they were

therefore akin to Cornishmen, though abiding in
'Little Britain.' Possibly the name was not an
uncommon one; and either of the two above sur-
mises may be correct. There are now upwards of
thirty French Communes into which the name of
St. Aubin enters: to say nothing of the picturesque
little village in Jersey of that name, which fringes
the shores of St. Aubin's Bay.

Their first English home seems to have been in
Somersetshire; and here, in the middle of the
fourteenth century, we find Guy de St. Aubyn, or
Albin, settled at Alfoxton. It seems to have been
he who, by his marriage with Eleanor Knoville,
first obtained a footing on the Cornish soil; and,
according to Tonkin, it was his grandson, Geffrey,
who took up his abode at Clowance on the latter's
marriage with Elizabeth Kymyell of Kymyell, the
sole heir of Piers Kymyell and his wife, a daughter
of — as Tonkin assures us, 'an old and notable
Cornish family'—the house of Sergeaux, or Seriseaux.
Their son Geffrey has a monument in Crowan church,
thus inscribed:

> 'Hic jacent Galfridus Seynt aubyn, Et Alicia uxor
> ejus, filia et heres Johannes Tremure de launcbet,
> Armigeri, qui quidem Galfridus obiit tertio die mensis
> Octobris, Anno Domini, Mill'imo ccccº; Alicia obiit
> Anno Domini Mill'imo ccccº; quorum Animabus pro-
> picietur deus, Amen. Jhu mercy, lady help.'

Since the time of the first Geffrey, the St. Aubyns, for
nearly thirty descents, have dwelt at their pleasantly
situated seat* at Clowance, 'the ancient house of

---

* There is a view of Clowance House in Borlase's 'Natural History of
Cornwall,' 1758.

an ancient gentleman,' as Norden calls it ; though the present mansion dates only from the early part of the present century.

From the days of Richard II., the St. Aubyns have frequently filled the post of High Sheriff of Cornwall, and have also served their country as Members of Parliament and Justices of the Peace. For several descents they have been Baronets, until at last the name of ' Sir John St. Aubyn, Bart., M.P.,' has become in Cornwall a ' household word.'

Of the earlier members of the family I have found little of interest, unless, indeed, it be the remarkable physique of one of them, Sir Mauger de St. Albin, who lived at Barnton ; in Risdon's ' Devonshire,' it is stated that he was a man of enormous strength and stature, as is evidenced by a huge stone thrown by him to a great distance, and by his very large effigy on a tomb in the church.

On their settling in Cornwall, the St. Aubyns followed the accustomed (perhaps the almost inevitable) practice of intermarrying with the old county families—the Tremeres, the Trethurfes, the Trenowiths, the Grenvilles of Stow ; and, in later times, with the Arundells, the Godolphins, the Pendarveses, the Killigrews, the Bullers, the Bassets, the Prideauxes, and the Molesworths.

Of the fruit of one of the pre-Reformation marriages—namely, that of Thomas St. Aubyn (who was Sheriff of Cornwall in 1545) with Mary, fourth daughter of Thomas Grenville of Stow, we have a touching little notice in the MSS. Lisle papers preserved at the Public Record Office.

Thomas is writing to his sister-in-law, Honor Grenville, Viscountess Lisle; and the following passage occurs in his letter:

'My daughter Phelyp is departyd on Crstmas Day, Almyghtie (God) pardon her soule; and my wyffe hath take grette discōfort therbye; but, I thank our Lord, she doth take it better way, and thankyth god of his sending.'

From this marriage of Thomas St. Aubyn with Mary Grenville, descended his grandson, Thomas, —the St. Aubyn of Carew's days—of whom that historian of his native county wrote thus:

'Saintabin, whose very name (besides the Conquest roll) deduceth his first ancestors out of France. His grandfather married Greinvile; his father, one of Whittington's coheirs: which latter couple, in a long and peaceable· date of years, exercised a kind, liberal, and never-discontinued hospitality. He himself took to wife the daughter of Mallet; and with ripe knowledge, and sound judgment, dischargeth the place which he beareth in his country.'

I find nothing further of general interest touching the family until we come to the stirring times of the Civil War—a conflict in which Cornwall took, as is well known, a distinguished part. Until that period the St. Aubyns seem to have been a thriving and distinguished family, serving their country in the various capacities already mentioned, and 'gathering house to house, and vineyard to vineyard.' Their possessions were in almost every part of the county: for instance, Lysons (who was indebted to the fifth

Sir John St. Aubyn for the loan of Borlase's MS. folio of notes on Cornwall) says that, amongst other properties, ' The manor of Godolphin is still held of Sir John St. Aubyn, as of his manor of Lambourne, by the payment of a gammon of bacon ;' and, that the manors of Berippa and Penpons were in the possession of the St. Aubyns ; also a moiety of the manor of Gaverigan in St. Columb Major, the manor of Argallez or Arrallas in St. Enoder, of Trelowith in St. Erth, of half of Treninick in St. Gorran, Kimiel and Butsava in Paul, and Mayon in Sennen ; they were also impropriators of the great tithes of Crowan, and patrons of the Vicarage ; and they held a moiety of the advowson of the rectory of Duloe. The revenues of the nunnery of Clares, which formerly stood near the junction of Boscawen and Lemon Streets, Truro, came (according to Hals) into the possession of Sir John Seyntaubin and others ; and again, the Priory of Tywardreath, so Davies Gilbert tells us, ' was the joint property of the St. Aubyns, and the Pendarveses of Roscrow.'

To return to the family at the time of the great struggle between the King and his Parliament. Most of the Cornish gentry sided, as is well known, with the King, and behaved with such marked valour and success as to elicit from Charles the well-known letter of thanks which still hangs in many of the churches in the county. One of the St. Aubyns of the day,* however, seems, according to Hals, to

* John St. Aubyn, grandfather of the first baronet ; it was he who purchased St. Michael's Mount from John Basset of Tehidy in 1657 or 1660, and died in 1679.

have thrown in his lot with the Parliament ; he was at the siege of Plymouth, in 1644 ; and was present at the defeat of his party at the battle of Braddock Down, near Lostwithiel.

Hals tells us that, after the rout of the Round-heads, ' it was resolved by Essex's council that he should desert his army, and, privately by night, in a boat, go down the river to Fowey, and from thence take ship for Plymouth ; which expedient was accordingly put in execution, and the General Essex, the Lord Robartes, and some others, the next day got into Plymouth, being the 31st August, 1644. On the same day Sir William Balfour, with two thousand five hundred of the Parliament horse, with divers officers, viz., Colonel Nicholas Boscawen, his Lieutenant Colonel James Hals, of Merther, Henry Courtenay, of St. Bennet's in Lanyvet, *Colonel John Seyntaubyn, of Clowans*, and his Lieutenant Colonel Braddon, Colonel Carter, and several other officers and gentlemen of quality, early in the morning forced their passage over St. Winnow, Boconnock, and Braddock Downs, though the body of the King's army, which lay encamped on the heath in those places, maugre all opposition to the contrary ; from thence they rode to Leskeard, from thence to Saltash Passage, and from thence to Plymouth safely the same day, amidst their own garrison and confederates.'

Whether from conviction, or from a wish to be well with either party in the State—whichever might succeed—it seems pretty clear that another member of the family, Thomas, espoused the cause of the Royalists. His monument in Crowan Church so describes him; and in the spring of 1882 I saw, on the walls of the principal staircase at Clowance, his portrait — hard, but apparently faithful — in Cavalier costume.

Of the second baronet I find nothing to note, except that he was Sheriff of Cornwall in 1705.

But the third* Sir John St. Aubyn, the sturdy little Cornish baronet—of whom Walpole said, 'all these men (his opponents in Parliament) have their price except him'—claims more of our attention than, perhaps, any other member of the family. He was born on 27th September, 1696, and we get a glimpse of his early life, when at Exeter College, Oxford, in the following extract from a letter written by his friend and fellow-collegian, Borlase, in 1772, to a lady in London. The MS. is amongst that collection at Castle Horneck, which formed the subject of an interesting articlet in the *Quarterly Review*, vol. 139; and the following extract describes the homeward journey of the two young fellows. A hundred years ago this must have been a somewhat formidable undertaking; and we almost regret that the chronicler did not furnish us with more details than he has done:

'1772 * * * Sometimes,' writes Borlase, 'we met with a landlord in men's clothes, but for the most part we discovered that the men had dropt

---

* The first baronetcy dates from 11th Dec., 1671.

† I quote very fully from this article with little reluctance, because the writer is believed to be a gentleman who is not only master of the subject of which he treats, but who also enjoys peculiar facilities for elaborating it. 'I do not *count* what I borrow, but I *weigh* it,' said Montaigne in his essay on ' Books.'

their prerogation, and we found the supreme
authority over the inns lodged in gowns and
petticoats. Ordered by Sir John not to write one
word of the pretty black-ey'd girl at Bridport, but to
go on with the particulars of our journey. I think I
am at liberty to tell you of a misfortune which
happened to me at Launceston. As we were passing though that fatal town (I am heartily sorry I
have forgot what day of the month 'twas), but, however, as we were passing through, whom should we
see at the door of an inn but our landlord's daughter!
Whether Sir John was dry and thirsty or not I can't
tell, but we all agreed to take our pint at the door,
and being men of no little gallantry because just
come from town, we were talking very smartly, as
you may imagine, to the girl who filled the wine,
when all of a sudden, my unfortunate eyes happened
to fix upon a green ribbon that hung playing to-and-
fro with the air a little lower than it should. As I
was the only person that discovered it, I told the
lady I was apprehensive she would lose that pretty
ribbon if she did not withdraw. I was then on
horseback, and, to my great confusion, had not the
presence of mind to alight and take care of it myself,
upon which Sir John has so teased and bantered me
that I have had no rest ever since. I beg you would
write Sir John, and let him know that such a misfortune deserves rather pity than upbraidings. And
now, Madam, I suppose you are almost as tired with
our journey as we are, or (to go as far as possible
with the comparison) as three of Sir John's horses,
which we left upon the road.'

The writer of the article goes on to say :

*　　　*　　　*　　　*　　　*

'We must now turn away for a moment from the pleasant scenes at Ludgvan, and follow Borlase's friend of college days as he enters the chapel at St. Stephen's—the youngest member, perhaps, of that distinguished assembly. Born in the year 1700, Sir John St. Aubyn was only just of age when, in 1722, he was returned to Parliament for his native county. Different indeed, yet in one respect alike, had been the destinies of the friends since we left them after their journey in the beginning of the year. Parting, the one to mix in the affairs of State in times the most perplexing, the other to the peaceful seclusion of his country parsonage ; each had, nevertheless, marked out for himself a path of mental activity. That the confidence of his country, though entrusted to so young a man, had not been misplaced, may be judged from an extract in the correspondence before us. Thus, a gentleman writing from London, March 2nd, 1726, observes : "Sir R. —— [Sir Robert Walpole] this Session has met with a strong opposition in the House of Commons ; Sir John St. Aubyn has gained a great reputation in that House, and the opinions of our politicians in relation to war or peace are as different as their faces."

'A year or two later an incident in Cornish history gave him an opportunity of making himself more than ever beloved at home. In 1727, when, as Hume tells us, "the Courts of France and Spain were perfectly reconciled, and all Europe was freed from the calamities of war, the peace of Great Britain was

disturbed by tumults amongst the tinners of Cornwall, who, being provoked by a scarcity of corn, rose
in arms and plundered the granaries of the county."
At this time it happened that Sir John had just completed a new pier at the Mount, to facilitate the
exportation of tin, which was shipped in large quan-
tities at that place.*   The consequence was that the
tinners congregated in considerable numbers; the
place became a rendezvous for malcontents, and
fresh riots broke out.   Very serious consequences
were apprehended, and what might actually have
happened none can say, had it not been that the
magnanimous spirit and unselfish patriotism of the
young statesman showed itself in a measure of local
policy which doubly endeared him to his countrymen.   He "forthwith advanced a considerable sum
of money to the tinners, by which they were saved
from starving, or the necessity of plundering their
neighbours."   "Constant in his attendance and application to the business of the House of Commons,"
writes Borlase, in a note attached to the St. Aubyn
pedigree, "he soon learnt to speak well, but spoke
seldom, and never but on points of consequence.
He was heard with pleasure by his friends, and with
respect by others."   In 1734 he seconded the repeal
of the Septennial Act, in a speech which will be
found in the "Handy Book of British Eloquence."'

* He rebuilt the pier in 1726-27. In 1811 there were fifty-three houses
on St. Michael's Mount, whereas before the year 1700 the place had so
decayed that there was, it is said, only one cottage, and that inhabited
by a poor widow. The present baronet has spared neither pains nor
expense to enlarge and beautify the domestic buildings of the Mount,
under the professional guidance of his relative, the well-known West-
country architect, James Piers St. Aubyn; and Sir John has also much improved the causeway which gives access for foot-passengers at low tide.

And here we must leave the *Quarterly* Reviewer for awhile, in order to give a sample of Sir John's oratorical powers. I quote from the report, in the *Gentleman's Magazine* for 1734, of his speech of the 13th March, on seconding Mr. Bromley's motion.

Sir John began by vigorously sketching the characters of those monarchs who were fond of ' Long Parliaments,' and thus referred to the Parliaments of Charles II., who, he said, ' naturally took a surfeit of Parliaments in his Father's time, and was therefore extremely desirous to lay them aside. But this was a scheme impracticable. However, in effect he did so, for he obtained a Parliament, which by its long Duration, like an army of Veterans, became so exactly disciplined to his own Measures, that they knew no other command but from that Person who gave them their Pay.

' This was a safe and a most ingenious way of enslaving a Nation. It was very well known that Arbitrary Power, if it was open and avowed, would never prevail here. The people were therefore amused with the Specious Form of their Antient Constitution ; it existed, indeed, in their Fancy ; but, like a mere Phantom, had no Substance nor Reality in it, for the Power, the Authority, the Dignity of Parliament were wholly lost. This was that remarkable Parliament which so justly obtained the opprobrious Name of " Model," from which, I believe, some Later Parliaments have been exactly copied.'

He then went on to describe the evils of Long Parliaments, saying :

44—2

'But this must be the Work of Time. Corruption is of so base a Nature, that at first sight it is extremely shocking. Hardly anyone has submitted to it all at once. His Disposition must be previously understood; the particular Bait must be found out with which he is to be allured; and, after all, it is not without many struggles that he surrenders his Virtue. Indeed, there are some who will at once plunge themselves over Head and Ears into any base Action; but the generality of mankind are of a more cautious Nature, and will proceed only by some leisurely Degrees. One or two perhaps have deserted their Colours the first Campaign; some have done it in a second. But a great many who have not that eager Disposition to Vice will wait till a Third.

'For this reason, Short Parliaments have been less Corrupt than Long Ones; they are observed, like Streams of Water, always to grow more impure the greater Distance they run from the Fountain-head.'

The independent speaker finished with this spirited peroration:

'The Power of the Crown is very justly apprehended to be growing to a monstrous—I should have said, too great—a Size, and several Methods have been unsuccessfully proposed for restraining it within due Bounds.

'But our Disease, I fear, is of a complicated Nature, and I think that this Motion is wisely intended to remove the first and Principal Disorder. Give the people their antient Right of frequent new

Elections; That will restore the decay'd Authority of Parliament, and will put our Constitution into a natural Condition of working out her Cure. Sir, upon the whole I am of opinion that I can't express a greater *Z*eal for his Majesty, for the Liberties of the People, or the Honour and Dignity of this House, than in seconding the Motion which the Hon. Gentleman has made you.'

It should be remembered that such sentiments as these were uttered to an audience—not of his constituents, whom he might have felt bound to please, but to a thoroughly corrupted House of Commons, at a period when '*not* to be corrupted was the shame;' and in the presence of a powerful Minister, whom few men of the day were either strong or virtuous enough to dare to thwart. The chubby, youthful-faced portrait of the little Sir John hangs in the dining-room at Clowance : childish the face may be; but, as if in apology for his small, juvenile presence, he points with his right hand to the Mount, to indicate that his principles were as firm and unshaken as that ' hoar rock.'*

The *Quarterly* Reviewer (from whom we again quote), after concluding his observations on Sir John's speech in 1734, goes on to say :

' In the same year a curious incident occurred in the neighbourhood of his seat at Clowance, with which Sir John was only indirectly connected in

---

* It may be noted here that the family portraits are at present distri-buted between the Mount, Trevethoe near St. Ives, and Clowance ; but the majority are at the latter place.

his capacity of Justice of the Peace, but which was
ultimately attended with very serious consequences
to himself and his family. A certain Henry Rogers,
by trade a pewterer, having some fancied claim to
an estate called Skewis, seized the manor house,
and, surrounding himself with a band of cut-throats,
organized a rebellion on his own account, and bade
defiance to the country round. Having beaten off
from his house, not without bloodshed, first the
sheriff, next the constables, and finally the military
themselves, the villain succeeded in making good
his escape. He was subsequently arrested at Salisbury, and brought to Launceston for trial, where
the grand jury found five bills of murder against
him, and Lord Chief Justice Hardwicke publicly
returned thanks to Sir John "for his steady endeavours to bring him to justice."*

'The terror, however, which this ruffian caused
in the neighbourhood can scarcely be realized nowadays, and the menacing letters received by Lady
St. Aubyn so preyed upon her mind, that they brought
on a "sensible decay," or, as we should call it now,
a rapid decline, from the effects of which, in 1740,
she died.†

'With the death of his wife, Sir John's interest
in country life came to an end; and leaving his son
to the care and instruction of his old friend at

---

* A well-known engraving of Rogers's portrait is familiar to the
collector.

† This lady was Catherine, the pretty daughter of Sir Nicholas Morice
of Werrington. The country story runs that her fortune was £10,000,
which was conveyed to Clowance in two huge wagons—the whole of
the amount having been paid in half-crowns !

Ludgvan, he set out for a foreign land. Meanwhile, however, the parliamentary horizon was rapidly clouding over; a crisis was clearly imminent; and, on his return to England, it was to find that, for the present at least, his sorrow must be drowned in more work, in a redoubled attention to those duties which his early reputation now pointed to him to fulfil. And thus, as the Walpole Administration draws on to its close, the figure of Sir John St. Aubyn—the "little baronet," as he was called—comes prominently to the front as one of the most vigorous, as he certainly was the most conscientious, of the opponents of the then unpopular Prime Minister. On the subject of the vote of thanks, including an approbation of the manner in which the Spanish War had been prosecuted, which was carried by a small majority in the House of Commons early in 1741, he writes (April 9th) as follows: " I believe ye Folks in ye country are very much puzzled abo^t many of our Proceedings, and I don't wonder at y^r doubts about that unseasonable vote of Innocence; especially when ye Opportunity was so fairly given, wch ye Nation has been so long expecting us to take ye advantage of." But the country party the while felt that no opportunity must be lost, and no vigour spared in the attack. Contrast the tone of the following extract from a letter dated May 5th, and note how the space of one single month had served to fan the flame. Sir John now inveighs against "such Insolence in Administration, such wantonness in Power, wch surely nothing could produce but that mistaken

vote of Innocence, wch so lately happen'd. And yet,"
he continues, "this is ye Man ag^t whom we want evi-
dence to advise his Removal, when at my very door there
are such glaring Proofs, which, in less corrupt times,
would deprive Him of his Head." Day by day the
enemies of the Ministry acquired fresh strength:
the elections were against the Court interest, even
Westminster returning two members hostile to it.
Walpole tottered on the brink of ruin, and had it
not been that, during a short adjournment of the
House in 1742, he resigned his office and was
elevated to the peerage, he might, as we know, even
have been committed to the Tower.

'No sooner had Parliament reassembled than a
measure was brought in by Lord Limerick, and
seconded by Sir John St. Aubyn, to inquire into
the conduct of the last twenty years. This was
lost by two votes; but another, also proposed by
Lord Limerick on the 23rd of March, for an inquiry
into the conduct of Robert, Earl of Orford, was
carried, and a Select Committee appointed by
ballot. And now came Sir John's political triumph.
To this committee he was appointed by every vote
in the House of Commons, to the number of 518.
"An honour," says the MS. from which we quote,
"neither then nor before (as far as the Records of
Parliament can reach) ever conferred on any member, as Mr. Speaker Onslow on the spot observed
to Sir John's great commendation." When the
committee was appointed he declined the offer of
the chair, and Lord Viscount Limerick was chosen
chairman. The following is an extract from a letter

of Sir John's, dated from the Secret Committee Chamber, June 22nd, 1742: "We are now," he writes, "winding up our bottoms as well as we can under yᵉ disabillitys which we have been fetter'd with, nothwithstanding which, we shall show the world enough to convince if not convict. I am sorry there has been so much unconcern in yᵉ Gentlemen of our country; I wish I could say in some an unconcern only. We have had, and I wish we mayn't for ever now have lost, yᵉ only opportunity which may happen to retrieve yᵉ Honour and establish yᵉ National Institutions of yᵉ Country. . . . The Town is in high spirits at present, upon the accounts we have from Germany and Italy. This turn is not owing to yᵉ merit of yᵉ new Administration, but to yᵉ Vigour of this Parliament, which has had It's free Operation during this Inter-Regnum of Power, and whenever that happens, England must have Its due Influence upon yᵉ Continent; and if she had acted as she ought for some years past, what might have been brought about, when yᵉ bare expectation of her acting has produc'd such great events?"

'"About this time," says Dr. Borlase, "Sir John being offer'd to take place as one of the Lords of the Admiralty, he was ready, he said, to serve his King and country, but would take no place unless upon the express condition that his freedom and independency in Parliament should remain unquestioned and uncontroll'd. These were not times to endure, much less shake hands with such inflexible Virtues;

as he coveted no place, he never had one, ' though capable of any.' "

' On the 31st March, 1744, when war was declared with France, the inhabitants of Mount's Bay became alarmed for the safety of their trade. Two things were required ; a stationary armed vessel to protect their shores and fisheries from privateers (for three of the principal fishermen had already been taken prisoners), and a cruiser to convey the exports and imports necessary for working the mines. For the part he took in obtaining these advantages, Sir John received the thanks of the gentlemen of the neighbourhood, assembled as usual in their Parliament at the Bowling Green at Marazion. St. Michael's Mount he had restored from a ruined monastic cell to a comfortable dwelling-house ; but he never lived to visit it again, dying of fever, at Pencarrow, on his way home in the year 1744, at the early age of forty-four ; "to the great regret of all who knew him ; and to his country's loss of a most faithful friend."

" The dignity of this ancient family," writes Borlase in the brief memoir attached to his pedigree, " owes much to this gentleman ;" and Dr. Oliver, of Bath, in a letter of sympathy on the occasion of his death, speaks of him as "one who had bravely withstood all the temptation that honours or profit could lay in his way, and dared to stand almost single on the field of Purity, while thousands fell on his right hand and ten thousands on his left, the easy Prey of corruption."   Farther on he adds, " Let us thank Heaven who lent us the great, good man so long, and neither wonder nor murmur at his being taken from us so soon, especially when we consider how little Influence his Example had upon Earth." There is something in a character like his which renders it worthy of the admiration and the love of generations; nay, of centuries, far beyond his own.'

The year before he died the following verses appeared in the *Gentleman's Magazine* (vol. xiii.) in allusion to the firm patriotism and self-reliant character of our hero:

THE CORNISH MOUNT :—A PARALLEL.

' " Si fractus illabatur orbis
    Impavidum ferient ruinæ."
                              HOR.

'Oft have I seen, from fam'd St. Michael's height,
The ocean's rage, with wonder and delight;
Whilst foaming waves the lordly bulk surround,
Lashing its bulwarks with a hideous sound:
Thetis in vain the lofty pile assails;
But all her force and clangour nought avails;
The pile majestic scorns the pond'rous shock;
Her basis is an Adamantine rock.
Just so (in worst of times) its *owner* stood,
Serenely great and resolutely good.
His virtues early to the world were known;
He makes his country's int'rest still his own.
Nor Courts, nor tyrants can his soul affright,
Who dares to vindicate his country's right.
On him Cornubia's happiness depends;
The best of patriots and the best of friends.
Guard him, kind Heav'n, to bless his native shore,
When truth shall stand, and traytors be no more.'

The friend of Pope,* I cannot help thinking that

---

* Writing to Dr. Borlase, in May, 1744, Sir John St. Aubyn mentions that 'I doubt your friend Mr. Pope can't last long. He sent to desire Lord Oxford and myself to dine with him t'other day, and I thought he would have dy'd then; he has a dropsie which has almost drowned him.'

the poet may have had the unassailable integrity of his Cornish acquaintance in his mind when he wrote the last line of the couplet which I have prefixed by way of motto to this chapter.

Of the fourth baronet it will suffice to record that, having taken the degree of M.A. at Oriel College, Oxon, in 1747, he became a member for Cornwall in 1761, and continued to sit for the county for eleven years. His monument in Clowance Church sums up, sufficiently for our purpose, his character and his career :

'To the memory of Sir John St. Aubyn, Baronet, who, by his descent from a long line of worthy ancestors, and a father distinguished by honest zeal and prudent moderation, was recommended to the important trust of representing in Parliament the county of Cornwall ; and justified the confidence of his electors by unshaken constancy of principle, uniting with the dignity of his public character the domestic virtues of tenderness and friendship. This monument was erected by his disconsolate widow. He was born the 12th of Nov., 1726. He died 12th Oct., 1772.'

But the fifth baronet of the same familiar name will demand somewhat more of our time and attention. He was the son of the last-mentioned Sir John St. Aubyn, was born on the 17th May, 1758, and was educated at Westminster; where, when a lad of seventeen, he had an amusing escapade. He and another hopeful young gentleman, his schoolfellow, joined in a bond for raising money to enable them to obtain the delights and luxuries which the discipline of the school and the extent of their pocket-money denied. The inevitable day came for repayment of the moneys advanced. It was in vain that 'infancy' was pleaded against the suit of the London money-lender; the precocious financier was ordered to pay back the sums he had borrowed, and interest at four per cent. A lad of so much enterprise was evidently designed to make some figure in the world, and we accordingly find him, when only twenty-six years old, contesting the county in 1784. He made another unsuccessful attempt six years afterwards; but, nothing daunted, once more essayed to obtain a seat in Parliament, and on this occasion succeeded in securing his election for Penryn. He afterwards sat for Helston from 1807 to 1812.

But it does not appear that he took any very prominent part in political life, his tastes leading him rather to the pursuit of the arts and sciences; and accordingly we find that he was elected a Fellow of the Royal Society, of the Society of Antiquaries, and of the Linnæan Society. In 1804, in conjunction with others, he proposed to establish, at the Royal Institution, at a cost of £4,000, a mineralogical collection and an Assay Office, on a large scale, for the improvement of the study of mineralogy and metallurgy; but the scheme failed for want of funds, although Sir Humphry Davy, Lord Dartmouth, and one or two more took great interest in the matter, and contributed valuable collections of minerals, etc. Here it may be mentioned that Dr. Wm. Babington dedicated to Sir John* his 'New System of Mineralogy.' It was, in fact, a catalogue of the Baronet's own collection, much of

---

* Thos. Hogg's poem of ' St. Michael's Mount ' was also appropriately dedicated to him.

which had previously belonged to the Earl of
Bute.

As evidencing his fondness for art, it may be observed that he was from first to last the discriminating
friend and patron of his fellow-countyman, John Opie,
R.A.; and it may be added that he was one of the pall-
bearers at the artist's funeral. To Opie he entrusted
the painting of his portrait (mezzotinted by W. Bar-
ney), which now hangs in the Town Hall of Devonport. In this town the family of St. Aubyn has
long held large possessions, the value of which the
fifth baronet is said to have increased three or four-
fold, although he is said to have embarrassed the
family estates for many years by the singular provisions of his will. When Sir John's collection of
engravings and etchings were sold at Phillips's
Auction Rooms, in April, 1840, the sale attracted
the presence of most of the principal connoisseurs in
the kingdom ; and to give some idea of the vastness
of the collection, it may be added that the sale lasted
for seventeen days.

It is not surprising to find that, with such tastes
as his, Sir John St. Aubyn found London a more
congenial place of abode than Cornwall. In the
metropolis, therefore—at 63, Portland Place—or in
its vicinity—as at Short Grove, Saffron Walden, or
at Woolmers, Hertford—he lived ; and, close to
London he died—at Putney, on the 10th August
1839—at the good old age of eighty-one. He was
noted for his beneficence, and for his refined and
courteous manners ; and these virtues and graces are
suitably recorded on his monument at Crowan. On

the occasion of his funeral, advantage was taken of his popularity (especially amongst the Freemasons, of which body he was a prominent member) for his body to 'lie in state' at St. Austell, Truro and Clowance; and his remains were followed to the grave by between 20,000 and 30,000 persons— a multitude as numerous as their sorrow was sincere.

It has not been my practice to refer to any of the living representatives of the families whose histories I am endeavouring to sketch, but it can hardly be out of place on this occasion to observe that Sir John St. Aubyn, the present baronet, has also been for more than a quarter of a century a Member of Parliament for Cornwall; and that, to say the least, he is not likely to tarnish the lustre which surrounds the names of the past St. Aubyns of Clowance and the Mount.

TREVITHICK,

THE ENGINEER.

> 'I exult,
> Casting reserve away, exult to see
> An intellectual mastery exercised
> O'er the blind elements ; a purpose given ;
> A perseverance fed ; almost a soul
> Imparted—to blind matter.   I rejoice,
> Measuring the force of those gigantic powers,
> That, by the thinking mind have been compelled
> To serve the will of feeble-bodied Man.'
>
> WORDSWORTH'S '*Excursion.*'

TREVITHICK,

THE ENGINEER.

'Soon shall thy arm, unconquered Steam, afar
Drag the slow barge and drive the rapid car.'

DARWIN.

T would not be unreasonable to inquire how it can be necessary now to write an account of Richard Trevithick, seeing that only nine or ten years ago two elaborate volumes on the subject were published by his son Francis.* But, apart from the propriety of including so remarkable a man in the *fasciculus* of our Cornish worthies, it may be observed that the very amplitude of the ' Life ' to which I have referred renders it inaccessible to the general reader ; and moreover it is (as the talented civil engineer who wrote that valuable and interesting work himself observes), almost as much a technical history of the development of the steam-engine as a memoir of him who was so intimately associated with its rise and progress. Our purpose is biography ; and, unless I

---

* A work to which I beg to acknowledge my indebtedness for the main facts of this notice.

am grievously mistaken, this aspect of the subject will be found full of interest.

The steam pumping-engine is to a mine what the heart is to a man : were its action to cease, or to be inefficiently performed, the mine would be flooded, and would cease to be. It is therefore not to be wondered at if, so soon as men ceased to find the precious ores in granules on the surface, washed down by mountain streams from the denuded veins which seam the hillsides, attention should be directed towards finding the coveted treasures in the bowels of the earth itself. But here a difficulty met the searchers. As they sunk their pits they often tapped the sources of streams, which, gushing out, at once put an end to their quest. Rude expedients were at first employed to remedy this; wooden pumps, worked by the hand, and such-like feeble attempts at getting over the difficulty. But it was not until 1702 that, according to some accounts, the first steam pumping-engine was erected in Cornwall, by Savery. Newcomen, whose name will always be honourably associated with the improvement of this invaluable machine, very soon was able to increase its efficiency, and erected one of his best engines in 1720, at the mine-works of Ludgvan-lez, near Penzance. By 1756 there were *several* steam-engines at work in Cornwall; but their defects, especially as regards their low power, and their extravagant consumption of coal, were inconveniently felt. It was at length perceived that the solution of the difficulty lay in a diminution of the size of the boiler, and an increase in the elastic force of the steam ; and for

the accomplishment of these objects we are mainly
indebted to the subject of this memoir, as well as,
in some degree, also to his father.   The circumstances which surrounded them were by no means
encouraging.   Coal, of course, had to be imported,
and also iron plates for the boilers ; and the latter
it was necessary, in those days, to make of small
size, on account of the indifferent condition of the
Cornish roads, along which (as no heavy wheeled-
traffic was practicable), the burdens had to be transported from the ports to the mines, and *vice versa*,
on the backs of mules.   Now-a-days the huge
boilers are moved entire, and there are few more
gladsome as well as picturesque sights to be seen
in Cornwall than the transit of a gigantic new
boiler through the streets of one of the West-country
towns.   It means that mining enterprise, which has
flagged of late years, owing to the increased impor-
tation of foreign ores, and has caused deep depression and cruel poverty in many a Cornish home, is
awakening once more ; and the teams of thirty or
forty horses, with their noisy conductors, and the
ponderous mass which slowly toils along the weary
road, are hailed with shouting and songs.   We see,
then, of what vital interest to a mining county, such
as Cornwall, must ever be all that is connected
with that seemingly prosaic structure, the steam-
engine ; and how full of interest, to Cornish folk
at least, should be the story of any Cornishmen
who have been prominently connected with its development and history.   Such certainly were the
Trevithicks, especially the younger.

Though in later times they settled in the western part of the county, the family seems to have sprung, in the sixteenth or seventeenth century, from Trevemeder, a ' town place ' in the seaboard parish of St. Eval, four or five miles north-west of St. Columb Major, a parish which contains some of the finest cliff scenery in Cornwall, at the far-famed Bedruthan Steps and Sands. Some of the family monuments are still to be found in the church, which lies two miles south of Trevemeder.

The elder Trevithick, who, like his more illustrious son, was christened Richard, was born in 1735 ; and that he was a man of sound judgment and much force of character may be surmised from his having been appointed, when only thirty years of age, manager of some of the leading Cornish mines, in days when mine-managers were expected to be their own engineers. In 1760 he married Ann Teague, one of a family (said to be of Irish extraction) distinguished for many a long year past in the annals of Cornish mining. By her, a woman of large and portly figure,* he had a tall stately family of four daughters and one son, all of whom were, I believe, born in an unpretending house amongst the mine-heaps which lie between Dolcoath and North Crofty, in sight of the noble hill of Carnbrea crowned with its old castle, and still more antique remains of ancient Britons.

* On her wedding finger-ring (the internal diameter of which was ⅞ths of an inch !) her husband had rudely engraved the pretty old English posy :

'God above
Increase our love.'

An example of the elder Richard's inventive skill as an engineer was given when he repaired, or rather, almost reconstructed, about 1775, Newcomen's old Carloose, or Bullan Garden engine ; especially by adding thereto a strong top of new form to the boiler, a drawing of which is given in the Appendix to Price's 'Mineralogia Cornubiensis,' 1778. The old boiler-tops were scarcely more than kettle-lids, and were actually weighted down in order to keep them in their places ; indeed, there is a tradition that the first Cornish boilers were nothing more than stone fire-places ! In effecting this improvement Richard Trevithick, senior, was assisted by one John Harvey,* the founder of the celebrated firm of Harvey and Co., of Hagle Foundry, of whom we shall hear more by-and-by.

But about 1777 Watt, the celebrated 'low-pressure' engineer, appeared on the scene with his improvements in the steam-engine ; travelling into Cornwall for the purpose of obtaining orders, erecting his first engine at Wheal Busy, and exciting the most angry jealousy on the part of all the local mine-managers and engineers—and notably our Richard : who, however, had the magnanimity and good sense at length to acknowledge and to adopt many of his illustrious rival's improvements.

---

* A very remarkable man. Being anxious to ascertain how castings were made, in order to substitute cast-iron pumps for the bored wooden tubes formerly in use in the Cornish mines, he went 'up the country' for the purpose; but was refused admittance into any of the foundries, until he hit upon the expedient of dressing himself in rags and feigning to be half-witted, whereupon he gained employment as a sort of messenger to the workmen, and thus got an opportunity of acquiring the much-desired information.

The old man, who was a pious Methodist, a ' class-leader,' and an intimate friend of John Wesley, died when sixty-two years old at Penponds, near Camborne, on the 1st August, 1797, and, I believe, was buried on the summit of Carn Brea, but no monumental stone marks the spot. The whole of his life was spent amongst mines and steam-engines, an industry which was deeply depressed at the time of his death; and Richard, the younger (who had married Jane, John Harvey's tall and buxom daughter, shortly prior to his father's decease), may be said to have succeeded to a 'heritage of woe:' not one in ten of the steam-engines which his father had contributed so much towards putting into operation being at that time at work, and our hero had almost to begin the world anew.

So much as the foregoing seemed necessary in order to rightly estimate Trevithick's position and surroundings when he had arrived at the age of twenty-six. But it will now be desirable to retrace our steps, and begin at the beginning. He was born in the centre of a group of some of our most important Cornish mines, in the parish of Illogan, on the 13th April, 1771, one of a family of five, of whom Richard was the only surviving son, and, as a matter of course, his mother's pet. One can picture the tall, sturdy lad, 'creeping reluctantly' to the little school at Camborne, where he was reputed a lazy, inattentive, and obstinate pupil, always drawing upon his slate lines and figures, unintelligible to any but himself, but, likely enough, containing the germs of those inventions which were destined hereafter to contribute largely to the success of Cornish mining, and make his own name famous. As he grew up he seems to have been more noted as a wrestler, and for his feats of strength, than for anything else, except, perhaps, for his rapid power as a mental arithmetician. He was a great hand at throwing the sledge-hammer, and could lift half-a-ton. A huge mass of iron of about this weight, which tradition says Trevithick used to lift, is still shown at the Patent Museum, South Kensington. He would climb the mine-shears —a height of fifty or sixty feet—stand, balancing himself on the summit, and then and there swing round his sledge-hammer ' to steady his head and foot.' There is a story told of his being attacked by pickpockets while walking with his friend, Captain Andrew Vivian, in London ; but Trevithick seized two of them, knocked their heads together, and then flung them away from him in opposite directions, not to return to the Tartar whom they had caught! The mark was long shown on the ceiling of Dolcoath account-house, which was imprinted by the *heels* of one Captain Hodge, who had dared Trevithick to try a fall with him, but who found himself first flying through the air, and then flat on his back on the table, before he knew what had happened !

But Richard Trevithick was endowed with something more than mere physical strength ; for, having first received some instruction in his calling from an engineer, well-known in Cornwall, of the name of Bull, he at length got to work, in 1790, at Stray Park Mine, at 30s. a month. Whilst here he was selected, when only twenty-one years of age, to report upon the relative merits of Watt's and Hornblower's engines, a fact which, surely, speaks volumes for his powers of observation, and for the solidity of his judgment.

In 1795 he erected at Wheal Treasury, when his pay was 3s. 6d. a day, his double-acting steam-engine—a model of which is still, I believe, in operation at Battersea—and in 1796 or 1797, he removed to Ding Dong Mine, near Penzance. It was about this time that he, fortunately for himself, met with Davies Gilbert, of Tredrea, afterwards President of the Royal Society, whose impressions of Trevithick are recorded in the following letter to J. S. Enys, Esq., of Enys:

'Eastbourne, April 29, 1839.

' MY DEAR SIR,

' I will give as good an account as I can of Richard Trevithick. His father was the chief manager in Dolcoath Mine, and he bore the reputation of being the best informed and most skilful captain in all western mines; for as broad a line of distinction was then made between the *Eastern* and *Western* mines (the Gwennap and the Camborne Mines) as between those of different nations.

' I knew the father very well, and about the year 1796 I remember hearing from Mr. Jonathan Hornblower, that a tall and strong young man had made his appearance among engineers, and that on more than one occasion he had threatened some people who had contradicted him to throw them into the engine-shaft. In the latter part of November of that

year I was called to London as a witness in a steam-
engine case between Messrs. Boulton and Watt and
Maberley. Then I believe that I first saw Mr.
Richard Trevithick, jun., and certainly there I first
became acquainted with him. Our correspondence
commenced soon afterwards, and he was very
frequently in the habit of calling at Tredrea to ask
my opinion on various projects that occurred to his
mind—some of them very ingenious, and others so
wild as not to rest on any foundation at all. I cannot trace the succession in point of time.

'On one occasion Trevithick came to me and inquired with great eagerness as to what I apprehended
would be the loss of power in working an engine by
the force of steam raised to the pressure of several
atmospheres; but instead of condensing, to let the
steam escape. I, of course, answered at once that
the loss of power would be one atmosphere,
diminished power by the saving of an air-pump with
its friction, and in many cases with the raising of
condensing water. I never saw a man more
delighted; and I believe that within a month
several puffers were in actual work.

'DAVIES GILBERT.'

Thus was born the *high-pressure* engine, with which
the name of Richard Trevithick will for ever be
associated; and in a few months many of these
machines were at work, notwithstanding Watt's
allegations that they were dangerous to public
safety. Indeed Trevithick, writing to Davies Gilbert,
observed that 'James Watt said, . . . that I deserved

hanging for bringing into use the high-pressure engine.' Trevithick never afterwards reverted to the low-pressure model. And here it may be observed that Mr. Michael Williams considered that this invention, in conjunction with Trevithick's improved cylindrical boiler, doubled or trebled the work done by the old Boulton and Watt engines. The saving to the Cornish mines thus effected by Trevithick has been estimated at nearly £91,000 per annum.

He was now in full swing of work; much to the surprise of his father, was engaged in twenty different mines; and was everywhere recognised as a worthy successor of his father, and as the chief Cornish engineer in the county.

It was at this time, too (1797), that he married Jane Harvey. A tall man, 6 feet 2 inches high, broad-shouldered, as most Cornishmen are, with a massive head, bright blue eyes, and a large but shapely mouth, with a firm but kind expression. His bust was presented to the Royal Institution of Cornwall by Mr. W. J. Henwood, and his portrait— by Linnell, in 1816—is preserved at the National Portrait Gallery at South Kensington.

The young couple took up their abode at Moreton House, near Redruth, close to the residence of Murdock, the inventor, in 1792, of the gas-light. Watt lived not far off, at Plain-an-Guarry (the Playing-place), but the two rival engineers did not visit each other. Watt and his engines were patronized by the *Eastern* or Gwennap mine-owners, but Trevithick and his inventions were adopted by the

Camborne, Illogan and Redruth or *Western* adventurers. As an instance of the strong feeling which
existed in those days between the rival mine-
engineers, Smiles, in his 'Lives of Boulton and
Watt,' states that it was reported that old Captain
Trevithick and Murdock had actually fought a duel
over the subject of their inventions.

From Redruth, after only a few months' residence
there, Richard and his wife moved to Camborne.
Whilst here, and about this time, he invented
his improved plunger-poles, the forcer temporary
pump, the plunger-pole pump, the pole-pressure*
engine, and the double-acting pressure-engine for
Wheal Druid; all of them greatly conducing to the
facilities required for removing the water out of deep
mines.† He seems, too, to have been particularly
happy in the methods which his versatile ingenuity
employed in adapting old machinery to more modern
requirements; and, though he was always busy as a
bee, he was full of fun and good-humour, and noted
for being a capital story-teller.

But Trevithick did not confine himself to the

---

* Still largely in use, in almost precisely the form in which he
designed it in 1797.

† Cf. Gregory's 'Mechanics;' Ree's 'Cyclopædia;' and Stuart's
'History of the Steam Engine;' Luke Hebert on 'Railways;' Lean's
'Historical Account of the Steam Engine in Cornwall;' Davies Gilbert's
'Observations on the Steam Engine,' in *Philosophical Transactions*,
25 Jan., 1827; 'Memoirs of Distinguished Men of Science in 1807-8,'
by Wm. Walker, junr.; R. Edmonds, junr.'s 'Contributions to the
Biography of R. Trevithick;' the *Edinburgh New Philosophical
Journal* for Oct., 1859; and *All the Year Round*, 4th Aug., 1860:—for
much valuable technical, and other, information on the subject of Trevithick's inventions.

steam pumping-engine. The improvements which
he and others had made and were making in that
most important machine necessitated improvements
in other parts of the mine. The ore must be drawn
more rapidly to the surface, and the mode of sending
it up the shafts must be improved. He was equal to
the occasion : the steam whim solved the former,
and the wrought-iron kibble (formerly a bucket, constructed of wood) the latter difficulty. About this
period an amusing incident occurred which is
worth recording, as exhibiting Trevithick's force of
character in other than merely professional matters.
His remuneration would appear to have consisted
partly of a fixed salary, partly of the profits incident
to the supply of machinery, and partly of royalties
payable upon instruments of his invention. Now
one of his engines was supplied to a mine called
Wheal Abraham, whose shareholders, on somewhat
fanciful and possibly unfair grounds, appear to have
unnecessarily delayed satisfying Trevithick's just
claims; whereupon, one night, the engineer and his
men took the matter into their own hands, and
(to the astonishment of the staff of the mine next
morning) removed the huge engine bodily.

We now approach a very interesting episode in
Trevithick's career—namely, the invention of his
'Camborne common road-locomotive.'* The idea

* Cf. *Engineering*, 27th March, 1868—'Trevithick was the real
inventor of the locomotive ;' also Zerah Colburn's ' History of the Locomotive,' p. 13 (ed. 1871); and O. D. Hedley's ' Who invented the
Locomotive ?' (ed. 1858). The second model had a horizontal instead
of a vertical cylinder. His locomotive of 1804, built at Newcastle-on-
Tyne, was specially fitted with flanged wheels for running on a railway.

of this may possibly have suggested itself to him (as doubtless other causes suggested similar ideas to Murdock, and to others before and after Trevithick) from his having to transport one of his portable engines from mine to mine, as required—sometimes at a considerable cost. To such a practical genius as his the idea doubtless occurred, ' Why not, with all this available power, make the engine move herself?' However this may be, the curtain now rises on an amusing little group in Trevithick's house ; Davies Gilbert acting as stoker, and Lady De Dunstanville of Tehidy (on whose estate most of the great Camborne Mines were situated) playing the part of engineman to a little model locomotive which ran round the table. The original working model of ' the Trevithick high-pressure locomotive,' the first working model for which was made in 1797, is still to be seen at the South Kensington Museum, in the machinery department ; but it was not till Christmas Eve or (according to other authorities) Christmas *Day*, 1801, that the ' puffing devil,'* as it was locally termed by the astonished Cornish folk, made its first performances on the roads round Camborne, Tuckingmill, and Tehidy, carrying its ten or a dozen passengers uphill faster than a man could walk. The success, though not complete, was sufficient to determine Trevithick, with his brother-in-law Andrew Vivian— who found the money and shared in the speculation —to proceed forthwith to London in order to obtain a patent (his first), which was accordingly secured

---

* Sir Humphry Davy spoke of these machines more euphemistically as Trevithick's 'dragons.'

on the 24th March, 1802. Smiles points out, in his
' Lives of the Engineers,' that a remarkable feature
in this engine was that it not only raised but also
depressed the piston by the action of the steam ; and
he also tells how, in 1803, the wonder was exhibited
to the public first at Lord's Cricket Ground, and
afterwards near the spot where the London and
North-Western Railway Station, Euston Square, now
stands. This engine attained a speed of twelve miles
an hour. When the noisy machine worked its way
along Oxford Street, all horses and carriages were
ordered out of the way ; many of the shops were
shut for fear of accidents, and the roofs of the houses
were crowded with spectators. I believe it was also
exhibited at one time on the site of the present
Bedlam. To Trevithick, also, Smiles awards the
credit of ' putting *the two things* together—the steam-
horse and the iron way,' when he invented his
second or *railway* locomotive. The controversy
as to the priority of the invention has been thus
ably summed up in the following extract from
' Locomotive Engineering,' by Zerah Colburn, C.E.
(vol. i., pp. 32, 33 ; 1871) :

' As a true inventor, no name stands in so close
connexion with the locomotive-engine as that of
Richard Trevithick. It was he who first broke
through the trammels of Watt's system of condensa-
tion and low, if not negative, pressure ; it was he
who first employed the internal fire-place and
internal heating surface ; he was the first to create
or promote a chimney-draught by means of exhaust

steam ; the first to employ a horizontal cylinder and cranked axle, and to propose two such cylinders with the cranks at right angles to each other ; the first to surround the cylinder with hot air ; the first to draw a load by the adhesion of a smooth wheel upon a smooth iron bar ; *and the first to make and work a railway locomotive-engine.* Trevithick and George Stephenson were contemporaries ;* the first locomotive seen by the latter was constructed by the former ; and a personal acquaintance was afterwards established between them. Although irrelevant to the present purpose, it may be added that Trevithick patented the screw-propeller, and specified several forms of that instrument, and various modes of applying it, in 1815—years before those to whom the invention is more commonly ascribed had turned their attention to it.'

The history of steam locomotion by rail was thus conveniently summarized by a writer in the *Times,* on the occasion of the George Stephenson Centenary, 8th June, 1881 :

'It may be mentioned that there were iron railways before Stephenson's time. The earliest account is of a timber tram-line laid down near Newcastle in 1602. Lines were made of iron at Whitehaven in 1738. In 1776 an iron railway was laid down near Sheffield, by John Curr, but it was

---

* Trevithick was born April 13th, 1771, and died April 22nd, 1833. George Stephenson was born June 9th, 1781, and died Aug. 12th, 1848.

destroyed by the colliers. Ten years later the first considerable iron railway was laid down at Coalbrookdale. The first iron railway sanctioned by Parliament—with the exception of local lines used by canal companies—was the Surrey iron railway, worked by horses, from the Thames at Wandsworth to Croydon, laid down in 1801. *In the year* 1802 *Trevithick and Vivian obtained a patent for a high-pressure locomotive engine.* In 1813 William Hedley, of Wylam Colliery, constructed the first travelling locomotive engine in a colliery; and in the following year* the first locomotive constructed by George Stephenson travelled at the rate of six miles per hour.'

Notwithstanding, however, this practical success, from a pecuniary point of view Trevithick's position was far from flourishing. It is true that he was engaged, not only on his Cornish work, but also at Pen-y-darran in South Wales, at Coalbrookdale, and at Newcastle-on-Tyne; and it is also true that the exhibition of his 'Catch-me-who-can' engine, as Mr. Davies Gilbert's sister named the railway locomotive, working on a circular railway of about 100 feet in diameter, drew crowds of Londoners to witness its performance. But the shilling admission fees did not come in fast enough to counterbalance the legal difficulties which our engineer had to contend with in the working of ill-defined Patent Laws; and the breaking of a rail caused the engine to overturn—thus putting an end to the exhibition.

* Viz., not until 1814—twelve years after Trevithick's locomotive.

Ill-health, too—typhus, gastric, and brain fever supervened; bankruptcy and imprisonment were the result; and, to anticipate a little, poor Trevithick was driven from London, after an unsuccessful application had been made to the Government for remuneration for his truly national services. He was not only, as his biographer contends, the real inventor of the blast-pipe; but, up to 1808, had constructed two road-locomotives (one for Camborne and one for London), railway locomotives for Coalbrookdale and Newcastle, and a tramroad locomotive for Pen-y-darran; to say nothing of his steam-dredger engine, his travelling steam-crane, his brilliant though ineffectual attempt to construct a driftway under the Thames at Rotherhithe,* etc., etc.

The following extract from the ' Catalogue of the South Kensington Museum ' gives the official account of Trevithick and his patents :

'*Inventor and constructor of the first high-pressure steam-engine, and the first steam-carriage used in England;* constructor of a tunnel beneath the Thames, which he completed to within 100 feet of the proposed terminus, and was then compelled to abandon the undertaking; inventor and constructor of steam-engines and machinery for the mines of Peru (capable of being transported in mountainous districts), by which he succeeded in restoring the

---

* Brunel, who afterwards constructed the Thames Tunnel, at Wapping, is said to have formed the highest opinion of Trevithick's inventive skill in this operation. (It had been previously attempted by Dodd.) Trevithick very nearly lost his life when the water flooded the driftway, owing to his insisting upon seeing all his men safely out before him.

Peruvian mines to prosperity; also of coining-machinery for the Peruvian mint, and of furnaces for purifying silver ore by fusion ; also inventor of other improvements in steam-engines, impelling-carriages, hydraulic engines, propelling and towing vessels, discharging and towing ships' cargoes, floating-docks, construction of vessels, iron buoys, steam-boilers, cooking, obtaining fresh water, heating apartments, etc.

The following is a list of his patents :

NOS.	DATES.	PATENTS.
2599	(1802)	Steam Engines for Propelling Carriages.
3148	(1808)	Ship Propeller.
3172	(1808)	Iron Tanks for Ships.
3231	(1809)	Iron Docks, Ships, Masts and Spars, Buoys, Steam-arm, etc.
3922	(1815)	Screw-propeller.*
6082	(1831)	Surface Condenser.
6083	(1831)	Heating Apparatus for Rooms.
6308	(1832)	Superheating Steam.

But this list by no means exhausts the whole of his inventions, for he was so fond of talking of them before they were matured that many were found sharp enough to seize Trevithick's ideas, and then to reduce them into some practical and remunerative form for themselves.

Sorry reward this for such incessant industry and varied inventive skill as induced . Hyde Clarke to write as follows :

'In the establishment of the locomotive, in the development of the powers of the Cornish engines, and in increasing the capabilities of the marine

---

* Trevithick's claim to the invention of the screw-propeller was disputed.

engine, there can be no doubt that Trevithick's exertions have given a far wider range to the dominion of the steam-engine than even the great and masterly improvements of James Watt effected in his day.'

The *Quarterly Review* for October, 1867, has an article on ' George Stephenson and Locomotion,' in which George Stephenson is described as ' the father of railway locomotion; ' and yet two pages after (p. 499) the writer of the article mentions, with greater accuracy, Richard Trevithick (or, as he spells it, 'Trevethick') as 'the first who put together the two ideas of the steam horse and the iron way.' Alas for our Cornishman! such is fame! It has been shown above that Trevithick not only first put together the steam horse and the iron way, but that he first worked the steam horse on the turnpike road ; and to *him* therefore is due the chief credit for there being 'not a line or a locomotive which does not bear testimony to his genius, his sagacity, and his perseverance ; nor is there a traveller upon a railway, who saves time, money, fatigue and anxiety . . . who has not reason to think of *Richard Trevithick* with gratitude for the benefits which he has conferred, and with admiration for the intellectual triumphs which he achieved.'

Fortunate it was for him that he was a remarkably good-tempered man, most simple and frugal in his habits, and richly endowed with that ' friend of the brave '—Hope !

His freedom from debt and imprisonment seems

to have been at length due to the sale of one of his
patents for iron tanks (for ships) and iron buoys, to
Mr. Maudslay, founder of the now eminent firm of
London engineers of that name.   Trevithick had
pressed his proposals on the Admiralty for a long
time in vain; and at last, with characteristic im-
petuosity, settled the matter for ever, it is said, by
calling the Navy Board to their faces 'a lot of old
women.'

Mrs. Trevithick now joined her husband in
London, but not until after prolonged importunity
on his part; and her reluctance is scarcely to be
wondered at when we think of the difficulties which
then existed in making the journey from Cornwall
to the metropolis.   She had to post all the way,
three hundred miles, with four children, one of them
a baby, and probably with no servant.   Besides
which, her brother, Mr. Henry Harvey, of Hayle,
represented to her that Trevithick's position in
London was hardly sufficiently assured as yet to
warrant her making the move.   Conjugal love,
however, at length prevailed over every other consideration; and on her welcome arrival, a touching
little incident occurred.   She found her two last
letters, unopened, in her husband's pocket; and on
her reproaching him with this seeming forgetful-
ness, which she attributed to his being so thoroughly
immersed in his multifarious engineering schemes,
he confessed that he had not dared to open them,
lest her arguments against their reunion should have
prevailed over his wishes.   It was well for both that
the faithful wife came to town: for soon after-

wards, had she not ransacked London for a doctor, whilst her husband lay almost dying in a sponging-house, it is unlikely that he would have survived to return to his native county. To Cornwall, however, he at length returned, in broken health and spirits, in 1810, to find that his mother had just died. Trevithick went home by sea, a six days' voyage, and, as we were then at war with France, the *Falmouth Packet* in which he sailed was under convoy. They were chased by a French man-of-war, from whom they luckily escaped; her commander little dreaming that his small craft (which seems to have owed her safety chiefly to her captain's knowledge of the coast) had on board her the man who had laid proposals before the Government for fitting vessels with high-pressure engines and launching them against the French fleet equipped at Boulogne for the invasion of England.

Trevithick's first idea of steam navigation appears to have arisen in 1804, though his specification was not dated till 1808 ;* and in this, as in almost every other important step in his life, he relied very much on the sound judgment and sympathetic advice of his friend Davies Gilbert. Paddle-wheels, however (the original mode of propulsion), were found cumbrous to ships, especially in heavy weather; and this led Trevithick to the invention of the screw-propeller, a design for which he laid before the Navy Board in 1812, but without effect. The patent was

---

* Earlier attempts were made in 1788 and 1803. The first remunerative steamboat for passengers seems to have been the *Comet*, which ran, in 1812, between Glasgow and Helensburgh, on the Clyde.

not dated till the 6th of June, 1815; nor was success
assured until after the busy engineer had left his
native county on a voyage to Peru, which seemed
to hold out promises of proving an El Dorado
for him. His son and biographer, taking into
consideration the numerous marine inventions and
appliances of his progenitor, claims for his father,
and not without much show of justice, that he may
be regarded as the originator of our present iron
steam fleet.

But, in fact, the man's versatility in his profession
seems to have been unbounded. In 1813 he was
the life and soul of the arrangements for constructing the Plymouth Breakwater; then he turns his
attention to the manufacture of agricultural engines,
and constructs the first steam thrashing-machine,
which was until recently at work at Trewithan, in
Probus, but now occupies a place of honour in the
South Kensington Museum of Patents, together with
a boiler of curious construction by him.*   This invention, like some others of Trevithick's, seems to
have been almost still-born; yet it was destined, as
we now know, to re-appear as a powerful factor in
the development of agriculture.

His next great stride was the new ' pole-puffer-
engine ' of 1816, in connection with which squabbles
arose between the engineer and his relations, Henry
Harvey and Andrew Vivian, both of whom were
said to have been moved to jealousy by Trevithick's
having arranged to get the castings for the first of

* ' The next step was to call in the aid of Steam to Agriculture.
Steam is almost an Englishman.'—*Emerson.*

these engines (viz., that for Wheal Herland, near Gwinear) made at Bridgenorth, instead of at Hayle. The first trial of the new engine, when at length set up, seems to have been somewhat of a failure, owing to the inaccurate way in which it was made. Here is an eye-witness's amusing account of its starting:

' I was a boy working in the mine, and several of us peeped in at the door to see what was doing. Captain Dick Trevithick was in a great way; the engine would not start. After a bit, Captain Dick threw himself down upon the floor of the engine-house, and there he lay upon his back; then up he jumped, and snatched a sledge-hammer out of the hands of a man who was driving in a wedge, and lashed it in, in a minute. There never was a man could use a sledge like Captain Dick; he was as strong as a bull. Then he picked up a spanner, and unscrewed something, and—off she went! Captain Vivian was near me, looking in at the doorway. Captain Dick saw him, and, shaking his fist, said, "If you come in here, I'll throw you down the shaft." I suppose Captain Vivian had something to do with making the boilers, and Captain Dick was angry because they leaked clouds of steam. You could hardly see, or hear anybody speak in the engine-house, it was so full of steam and noise; we could hear the steam-puffer roaring at St. Erth, more than three miles off.'

Another altercation on the subject of this engine took place at a meeting of the Wheal Herland adventurers, when Trevithick said: ' I could not help threatening to horsewhip Joseph Price for the falsehoods that he, with the others, had reported. I hear that he is to go to London to meet the London Committee on Monday. I hope the Committee will consider J. Price's report as from a disappointed man. It is reported that he has bought very largely in Woolf's patent, which now is not worth a farthing, besides losing the making my castings, which galls him very sorely.'

The final result was that the Wheal Herland engine proved a great success.

'Every engine that *was* erecting is stopped, and the whole county thinks of no other engine,' wrote its engineer; and that Trevithick had 'the courage of his convictions' may be judged from his saying: 'I have offered to deposit £1,000 to £500 as a bet against Woolf's best engine, and give him 20,000,000 (lbs. "duty"), but that party refuses to accept the challenge.' Indeed, Mr. Francis Trevithick claims that '*This engine performed the same work as the Watt engine, with less than half of the daily coal.*'

It would, in fact, be difficult to exaggerate the importance of Richard Trevithick's contributions to this branch of applied mechanics; and had he been as prudent in his management of his business affairs, and as sharp in looking after his pecuniary interests as he was brimful of talent in his scientific inventions, it would never have been necessary for the late Mr. Michael Williams, M.P.,* to write of him that

* Trevithick, before leaving England for South America in 1816 being pressed for money, sold a half share of his patent in the high-pressure steam expansive pole-engine to Messrs. Williams, of Scorrier, for £200. He remained abroad for ten years.

' he was at the same time the greatest and the worst-used man in the county.'

Such was Trevithick's position when he had reached the age of forty-five. Sanguine, impetuous, and brilliant—no sooner finishing one invention than commencing another (nay, sometimes before he had thoroughly completed the first)—a benefactor of incalculable extent to the prosperity of his native county, but so unsuspecting and so indifferent to his own, that he turned at length to the New World for the appreciation and reward that he had failed to secure in the Old.

The circumstances which led to this determination are somewhat curious. A desire having been felt amongst several wealthy Spaniards in Peru to re-work certain of the old gold and silver mines which required draining, Don Francisco de Uville, of Lima, a Swiss gentleman, was sent to England to search for the best steam pumping-engines for their purpose. The names of Messrs. Boulton and Watt were so famous, that, almost as a matter of course, he first consulted them ; but they discouraged the project, mainly on the grounds that the rare atmosphere of the Cordilleras would interfere with the efficiency of the steam-engine. Thus rebuffed, and much dejected, he chanced to see in the window of a shop, near the spot where the 'Catch-me-who-can' had been ex-hibited, a small model of one of Richard Trevithick's engines, which he at once secured for £20, and hastened back with it to Peru. Arriving there, he at once put its powers to the test, and was delighted to find that Boulton and Watt's doleful prophecies were not fulfilled. Accordingly he forthwith returned to England with the model, which bore Trevithick's name engraved on it, in search of the engineer who had constructed the wonderful machine, and had the good luck to find on board the same ship as that in which he made the voyage a cousin of Trevithick's —a Mr. Teague—who at once put the Don on the right track. Satisfactory interviews ensued, large orders for engines were put in hand—pumping-engines, winding-engines, sugar-rolling engines, and crushing-engines, to the tune of some £16,000. The anticipated profits were £50,000 a year, and Trevithick was to be paid, not in money, unluckily for him, but in shares, which were to secure to him an income of £10,000 per annum.

At length the engines duly arrived at Lima, and were landed under a salute from the guns of the batteries. But things did not work well. The men sent out were unaccustomed to the use of wood-fires, and they failed to carry out all Trevithick's instructions, whereupon he himself resolved upon going to the rescue ; and accordingly he sailed from Penzance in a South Sea whaler, the *Asp*, on 20th October, 1816, intending to land at Buenos Ayres and work his way across the South American continent—an undertaking which, in those days, it need scarcely be added, was of a most formidable character, and no doubt, therefore, was all the more attractive to the remarkable man whose career we have been considering.

On his arrival in Peru, he was received with

almost royal honours, and, at once getting to work, soon set matters to rights; for by the early part of 1817 there were four engines at work, including that used for coining at the Mint. An immediate collapse of the whole undertaking would probably have been the result but for the timely arrival of 'Don Ricardo,' as he was styled by the natives. Amongst the difficulties to be overcome in this enterprise may be mentioned those of transit, and these may be estimated from the facts that the Cerro de Pasco Mines were 170 miles from Lima, that the roads were for the most part mule-tracks only, and that the site was 13,400 feet above the sea! No wonder that, on his eventually triumphing over all these difficulties, thoughts were seriously entertained of erecting a statue to him in solid silver, and that, according to Mr. Walker's memoir, he was made a Marquis and Grandee of Spain. But the whole scheme was unhappily doomed to failure. Deaths and dissensions took place amongst the shareholders; Uville died in August, 1818, and the whole brunt of the management fell upon Trevithick. He now, too, foolishly engaged in other undertakings whilst his hands were already sufficiently full, and lost large sums of money in a speculative process for extracting silver by smelting instead of by amalgamation. Then a war of independence broke out, and poor Trevithick had the mortification of learning that the Royalists had actually destroyed his machinery, and flung it—where he had so often before threatened to fling *his* enemies—'down into the shafts.'*

* Some of the remains of the machinery were seen lying about on the mountain-sides in 1850.

This was the death-blow of the affair, and he immediately set to work on a fresh venture, namely, the
raising of the cannon from a Russian ship which had
been sunk near Callao. By this he readily made no less
than £2,500, but—will it be believed ?—he forthwith
lost it all by an imprudent speculation in a pearl-fishery
at Panama! Some of the money would have been
particularly acceptable to poor Mrs. Trevithick,
whom her thriftless husband had left at Penzance
unprovided for; in fact, he omitted (doubtless from
sheer thoughtlessness) to pay, as he had promised to
do, the house-rent a year in advance for her. Another
curious instance of Trevithick's utter incapacity for
understanding business matters appears in the following anecdote. Being very hardly pressed for
payment of some account due from him, he snatched
the bill from his creditor, and writing, ' Received—
Richard Trevithick,' at the foot of it, handed it back
to the poor man with an angry exclamation, in his
strong Cornish dialect, of ' There! will that satisfy
you ?'

A strange episode in his career now occurs.
Bolivar actually pressed him as a soldier; but Trevithick soon ' tir'd of war's alarms,' and the President readily allowed him to return to more congenial
pursuits, sending him on some special mission to
Bogota—yet not before Trevithick had signalized
his connexion with the army by inventing a most
ingenious carbine with an explosive bullet. Whilst
in South America he also became, for the nonce, a
surgeon, and actually amputated both legs of a poor
fellow crushed by the fall of some of Trevithick's

heavy machinery. The man was very proud of what
he had undergone, and used to boast of his capital
stumps.

Having previously paid a short visit to Chili,
Trevithick (who had now lost all his property)
finally left Peru in 1822, on the above-named special
mission; but, distrustful of Bolivar's promises and
hearing of something more to his advantage, as he
considered, he made his way to certain rich mines
that he had heard of in Costa Rica instead. Thither
—to that region of snakes, miasma, and earth-
quakes—we must now follow him.

There were known to be rich mines of the precious
metals near Quebradahonda, in the interior of the
little tract of mountainous country which forms part
of the narrow belt of land connecting North and South
America; but the difficulties of access in 1826-27
rendered them almost valueless, and Trevithick and
his party conceived the idea of approaching them
from the Atlantic side, by a route which should be
practicable for steam conveyances—namely, by way
of San Juan (now Greytown) and the rivers San
Juan de Nicaragua and Serapique. Rafts and boats
were constructed for the descent of those streams,
and fearful hardships and dangers befell the explorers
—who were bent upon accomplishing a somewhat
similar task in Central America to that which Lander
had performed a few years before in Western Africa.
Three weeks were spent in accomplishing their
object — during which the little party subsisted
on monkeys and wild fruits; and more than once
Trevithick, an indifferent swimmer, but who managed

to buoy himself up by bundles of sticks which he placed under his arms, was nearly drowned. He had however, at length the gratification of reaching San Juan—the first European who had made the voyage from Lake Nicaragua to the sea.

By some means or other he contrived to reach Cartagena (de las Indias) on his homeward journey, disconsolate enough no doubt; but what befell him on his way is best told in the following letter:

'Stanwick, Cumberland, 27th November, 1864.

'SIR,

'I read in the public prints that in a speech made by you in Belle Vue Gardens you referred to the meeting of Robert Stephenson with Trevithick at Carthagena, which, if your speech be correctly reported, you attribute to accident. The meeting was not an accident, although an accident led to it, and that accident nearly cost Mr. Trevithick his life; and he was taken to Carthagena by the gentleman that saved him, that he might be restored. When Mr. Stephenson saw him he was so recovering; and if he looked, as you say, in a sombre and silent mood, it was not surprising, after being, as he said, "half drowned and half hanged, and the rest devoured by alligators," which was too near the fact to be pleasant. Mr. Trevithick had been upset at the mouth of the river Magdalena by a black man he had in some way offended, and who capsized the boat in revenge. An officer in the Venezuelan and the Peruvian services (Mr. Bruce Napier) was fortunately nigh the banks of the river shooting wild pigs. He heard Mr. Trevithick's cries for help, and seeing a large alligator approaching him, shot the reptile in the eye, and then, as he had no boat, lassoed Mr. Trevithick, and by his lasso drew him ashore much exhausted and all but dead. After doing all he could to restore him, he took him on to Carthagena, and thus it was he fell in with Mr. Stephenson, who, like most Englishmen, was reserved, and took no notice of Mr. Trevithick, until an officer said to him, meeting Mr. Stephenson at the door, "I suppose the old proverb of two of a trade cannot agree is true, by the way you keep aloof from your brother chip. It was not thus your father would have treated that worthy man, and it is not creditable to your father's son that he and you should be here day after day like two strange cats in a garret; it would not sound well at home." "Who is it?" said Mr. Stephenson. "*The inventor of the locomotive,* your father's friend and fellow-worker; his name is Trevithick—you may have heard it," said the officer; and then Mr. Stephenson went up to Trevithick. That Mr. Trevithick felt the previous neglect was clear. He had sat with Robert Stephenson on his knee many a night while talking to his father, and it was through him Robert was made an engineer. My informant states that there was not that cordiality between them he would have wished to see at Carthagena.

'The officer that rescued Mr. Trevithick is now living. I am sure he will confirm what I say if needful. A letter will find him if addressed to No. 4, Earl Street, Carlisle, Cumberland.

'There are more details, but I cannot state them in a letter, and you might not wish to hear them if I could.

'I am, sir,

'Your very obedient servant,

'JAMES FAIRBAIRN,

who writes as well as rheumatic gout will let him.

'P.S.—I forgot to say the name of the officer is Hall.

'To E. W. Watkin, Esq., M.P.'

On recognising Stephenson, Trevithick is said to have exclaimed, 'Is that Bobby!—I've nursed him many a time.' The younger engineer had £100 in his pocket, and generously gave his senior half of it to facilitate his return to England, which Trevithick shortly afterwards accomplished, by way of Jamaica, in the autumn of 1827, landing at Falmouth on the 9th October, after a weary, anxious absence of eleven years. His health does not seem to have been much injured; but his belongings were simply the clothes he stood upright in, a gold watch, a pair of dividers, a magnetic needle, and a pair of spurs. A friend had to pay his passage-money before he could leave the ship which brought him home.

But he had the happiness of finding his wife and their family of four sons and two daughters all well. The Church bells rang out a merry peal of welcome; and he was entertained at the houses of all the principal people in the county. A great deal was said of the handsome remuneration which was due to him for having been the means, through his many inventions, of saving Cornwall half·a million of money,—but little or nothing seems to have come of all the talk; and when he claimed £1,000 from each of the leading mines which had adopted his machinery, they seem—so far as I can ascertain, with one exception only—to have repudiated them. The exception to which I refer was a compromise of his claims by the Messrs. Williams, of Scorrier, in respect of certain mines in which they were interested, for the sum of £150. Nor was his petition to Parliament, dated 27th February, 1828, setting forth his many truly *national* claims for consideration, and containing an interesting summary of his inventions (but unfortunately too long to reproduce here), more successful.

Trevithick was now verging upon sixty years of age, and found that he had to begin life anew. His first endeavour was to form a company to work his mines in Costa Rica, but neither he nor his friend Gerard could succeed in doing this either in England, in France, or in Holland ; and, if the report be true that he refused a cheque for £8,000 for his share in the mine-grants, he must have lived to repent it bitterly. However, his busy brain was soon at work again with inventions. First an iron ship and a gun with friction-slides; then a recoil gun-carriage, in which he utilized the recoil somewhat after the manner since so effectually accomplished by Moncrieff; then we find him suggesting a mode of making ice by steam. Next he invents a chain-and-ball pump for draining the Dutch marshes ; and, soon after, we hear of his being employed by the Government of that country to examine into sundry important engineering works which they had in hand, whilst poor Trevithick had to borrow £2 from a friend to enable him to get over to Holland for the purpose. It may be mentioned, to show what a good-natured fellow he was, that he at once gave 5s. out of this to a poor neighbour who had had the misfortune to lose his pig.

During a great part of this period of his life Trevithick was at Hayle Foundry, engaged in the construction of the great draining engines for Holland ; but he, nevertheless, found time for further inventions, notably for applying tubular boilers, a super-heating system, and surface-condensers to marine engines, to say nothing of his proposals to make the same water act over and over again by alternate expansion and contraction, so as to avoid the objectionable necessity for using salt water in the boilers. By his method marine engines occupied only half their former space ; were half the weight ; and consumed half the fuel that they formerly did : and it would scarcely be too much to say that his genius rendered the first voyage across the Atlantic practicable. In connexion with this subject, he took out his eighth and last patent in 1832.

Perhaps his latest project was as original—not to say Utopian—as any that even his fertile brain ever conceived. It was to erect a perforated, gilt, cast-iron column, 1,000 feet high, to commemorate the passing of the Reform Bill. One novel feature in it was the air-elevator, which worked in a tube in the centre of the column, and shot the traveller from the base to the summit, on arriving at which he was to secure a glorious bird's-eye view of London.

But the end was approaching. He had been in indifferent health in the spring of 1830; and, although his son does not state the causes of his father's death, there is too much ground to fear that poverty and misery at least accelerated it. He was at work in April, 1833, in Messrs. Hall's factory, at Dartford, Kent, probably on one of his marine engines, when, on the 22nd of that month, somewhat suddenly—for his relations knew nothing of his illness—the great engineer died. He was penniless, and was indebted to charity for his grave, and to the mechanics of Messrs. Hall's factory for becoming the bearers and the only mourners at his simple funeral.

Unless a tombstone has lately been erected, Richard Trevithick furnishes another example of one of Cornwall's most illustrious sons being without a monument to mark where he lies. Is this creditable to the county, or the country, in which he was born, or to the age which he so much enriched by the versatile power of his genius?

Since the above was written,—and also since the date of a letter which I sent to the Cornish papers in June, 1881, calling attention to the facts above referred to,—endeavours have been made to procure some fitting record in Cornwall in honour of Trevithick's memory; and an influential meeting on the subject was held in London on 20th April, 1883.

VIVIAN,

THE SOLDIER.

VIVIAN,

THE SOLDIER.

'See ! through the battle's lurid haze,
How Vivian, as the trumpet blew,
Led the last charge at Waterloo.'
H. S. STOKES : *Rhymes from Cornwall.*

HE nest of the Vivian family was Truro ;
here our hero was born, and here resided
his father, John Vivian, who may be
called the founder of the copper trade
in Cornwall, and who subsequently became Vice-
Warden of the Stannaries : but the present seat of
the Vivians is Glynn, the ancient residence of the
Glynn family, from which place the subject of the following remarks, Richard Hussey, first Baron Vivian
of Glynn and Truro, derived the former of his titles.
He derived his second name from his grandmother,
who was a Miss Hussey, of Okehampton ; his
grandfather was the Rev. Thomas Vivian, of Com-
prigney, Kenwyn ; he was vicar of Cornwood, Devon,
and was a man of some literary ability.

Well do I remember, when I was quite a youngster, an autumnal visit in 1842 to the well-wooded

valley which Glynn overlooks, and through which
rushes the Fowey, a lovely trout-stream, when the
' fiery finger ' had been laid upon the leaves of the
myriad-tinted oaks in its glades; and when Death
had just claimed the owner of that noble mansion.
On the grand staircase hung the great picture by
Shee,* representing the lithe figure of the tall,
bronzed hero advancing in his hussar uniform, dis-
mounted and bareheaded, fresh from the ' rapture of
the fray ;' whilst in the background was a servant
holding a spirited white charger. I thought then,
and think so still, that I had never seen a more goodly
presence.

Vivian's mother was as much distinguished for
her beauty and vivacity as his father was as an
upright man of business, and able administrator of
the Stannary laws. She was a daughter of the
Rev. Richard Cranch, vicar of St. Clement's, near
Truro, an early friend and patron of Sir Joshua
Reynolds ; and, accepting her own admission,
must have had a sufficiency of admirers. 'What
a fine creature she was !' said Dr. Wolcot ('Peter
Pindar '). ' I once told her in jest that she *must*
be my wife, for I had never been so deeply in
love before.' ' It is out of the question, my dear
doctor,' she replied ; 'it is impossible. I am *five
deep* already !' The charming buxom profile of the
good old lady, who died in 1816, might until recently
have been seen on her cenotaph at St. Mary's

---

* Engraved by Meyer. A copy of the print hangs in the Museum of
the Royal Institution of Cornwall, a building which now occupies the
site of the Vivians' Truro residence and Copper Office.

Church, Truro;* as well as a medallion portrait, on his marble tomb (with an epitaph), of her eldest and illustrious son, the subject of this notice.

He was born at Truro—probably at the house to which reference has just been made—on 28th July, 1775; and when about eight years old was sent to the Truro Grammar School under Dr. Cardew. Here, however, he did not long remain, as we find him from 1784 to 1787 at school at Lostwithiel, from which place he went direct to Harrow.

Another three years of his life were passed there; and in 1790 he entered at the old West-Country College—'Exeter'—at Oxford; but he only kept two terms. His education seems to have been completed by a visit to France in 1792.

The time had now come for Vivian to choose a profession; and in this important matter one hardly knows whether to admire more the liberality of the father, or the instinctive sagacity of the son. Mr. Vivian wished his heir to follow a pursuit in which distinction had been gained both by himself and by other members of the family, and an attempt was made in this direction. Our hero was accordingly articled to a Mr. Jonathan Elford, a solicitor, of Devonport, with a view to Vivian's becoming a 'counsellor, learned in the law;' but the attractions presented by the lives and the uniforms of the officers of a garrison town were an all-powerful opposing force; and, besides, Vivian could urge family precedents for a military career; for was not his great-uncle, Colonel

* Sir Joshua also immortalized the fair Betsy Cranch by a portrait of her, painted in her prime, in 1763.

Hussey, amongst the heroes who fell with Wolfe on the heights of Abraham ?*

Accordingly, an ensign's commission in the 20th Regiment of Infantry was procured for him on 31st July, 1793. In the following year he got a captaincy in the 28th, and was present in all the affairs of that time between the French and British armies in the Low Countries ; his regiment suffering severe losses at Geldermalsem. In 1795 he returned to England ; and shortly afterwards made an attempt—the second unsuccessful one—to get with his regiment to the West Indies. But the war god had other and higher services in store for Vivian ; and the winds and the waves drove back the transports to the British shore.

For the next two years (1796-98) Vivian was doing garrison duty at Gibraltar. This sort of pursuit must have fretted so high a spirit as his, and probably led to his exchanging into a cavalry regiment, the 7th Light Dragoons, or 'Queen's Own' Hussars ; —now, at least, he thought he should be sure to see service. Nor was he disappointed ; for in 1799 he took part in the unfortunate Texel Expedition, under Sir Ralph Abercombie, one result of which, however, was the capture of Helder on the 28th August in that year.

To Vivian the piping times of peace during the next four or five years gave an opportunity for turning his thoughts from war to love ; and in 1804 he married his first wife, Eliza, daughter of Philip Champion De Crespigny, of Aldborough (with whom, so the story goes, he ran off from a boarding-school).

* Hussey was a name early celebrated in the annals of England ; *e.g.,* a Sir William Hussey was Lord Chief Justice in the reign of Edward IV.

She was descended from an old French family, refugees from the Edict of Nantes ; and the fruit of this marriage was two sons and three daughters.

The Peninsula was destined to be the scene of Vivian's next exploits; and in 1808 we find him landing with Sir John Moore at the once busy port of Corunna. He was engaged in most of the cavalry affairs during that brief campaign, and led the rear-guard during the historic retreat in January, 1809, collecting the infantry stragglers to the number of about 600, forming them, and so repulsing a pursuing enemy, almost as weak and winter-stricken as themselves. For his skill and valour on this memorable occasion he obtained the thanks of Sir G. Paget. He also received high commendation from that gallant hero and graceful gentleman, Sir John Moore himself, whose masterly tactics were recognised by his generous antagonist Soult's placing a monument to his remains on the Corunna ramparts, —celebrated in the ode with which we have all been familiar from our childhood.

After an interval of repose for about three years in Ireland, during which he was made Aide-de-camp to the Prince Regent, and attained the rank of a Colonel in the army, in 1813 Vivian was ordered to take part in the Peninsular campaign ; and, in the August of that year, he landed at Bilbao—'the beautiful ford '—that scene of so many conflicts between the French and the Allies. He was now appointed Colonel on the staff, and had the command of a brigade of cavalry ; and in the latter capacity he was present at most, if not all, of the important cavalry affairs in that campaign—gathering laurels at Orthes, Vittoria, and in the Pyrenees.

Vivian particularly distinguished himself in the following year at Croix d'Orade; of his conduct on that occasion there is no better description than that which is contained in the following extract from the Duke of Wellington's despatches to Earl Bathurst:

'Toulouse, 12th April, 1814.

'I have the pleasure to inform your lordship that I entered this town this morning, which the enemy evacuated during the night. . . . The continued fall of rain and the state of the river prevented me from laying the bridge till the morning of the 8th, when the Spanish corps and the Portuguese artillery . . . crossed the Garonne. We immediately moved forward to the neighbourhood of the town; and the 18th Hussars, under the immediate command of Colonel Vivian, had an opportunity of making a most gallant attack upon a superior body of the enemy's cavalry, which they drove through the village of Croix d'Orade, and took about one hundred prisoners, and gave us possession of an important bridge over the river Ers, by which it was necessary to pass in order to attack the enemy's position. Colonel Vivian was unfortunately wounded upon this occasion, and I am afraid that I shall lose the benefit of his assistance for some time.'

For this affair he bore on his coat of arms (amongst other allusions to his brave deeds) a flying pennon inscribed with golden letters, 'Croix d'Orade.'

The wound referred to by the Duke was from a carbine-shot in the right arm.

It is curious to contrast the Great Duke's appreciative eulogy of this brilliant exploit with Napier's sour version of it in his ' English Battles and Sieges in the Peninsula' (p. 453, ed. 1873) : 'In this operation a single squadron of the 18th Hussars, under Major Hughes, being *inconsiderately* pushed by Colonel Vivian across the bridge of St. Martin de la Touch, suddenly came upon a regiment of French cavalry. The rashness of the act, as often happens in war, proved the safety of the British ; for the enemy, thinking a strong support must be near, discharged their carbines, and retreated at a canter. Hughes followed ; the speed of both parties increased ; and as the road did not admit egress .by the sides, this great body of horsemen was pushed headlong by a few men under the batteries of St. Cyprian.'

When the late Chaplain-General Gleig disputed a statement of Napier's relating to the battle of Vimiero, the latter writer fell back on the authority of the Duke of Wellington, which, of course, Napier preferred to that of Gleig, adding tartly, that 'the two authorities may be weighed by those who are fastidious.' A similar process may be recommended as to Wellington and Napier's authority touching Vivian's share in the affair at Croix d'Orade. It may also be well to add the significant fact that the 18th Hussars presented Vivian with a sword of honour on the occasion.

The year 1814 was further memorable in our hero's annals. The Transitory Peace was signed ;

Vivian was promoted to the rank of Major-General; returned to England; and was appointed to the command of the Sussex Military District, taking up his residence at Brighton. On thus giving up his connexion with the Hussars, his brother officers presented him with a piece of plate worth 250 guineas.

The curtain rises upon the eventful year 1815— the year in which Napoleon's ambitious career was to be at once and for ever checked by the Iron Duke on the field of WATERLOO.

Vivian, now a Knight Commander of the Bath, was the first major-general sent in command of a brigade of cavalry to join the army assembling at Brussels; and did 'yeoman's service' during the few days which preceded the great battle, notably covering the retreat (as at Corunna) of the army whilst falling back from Quatre Bras on Waterloo.

It would of course be out of place here (even if the familiar histories of the great battle, given by Siborne, Alison, and Hooper, had not also made it unnecessary) to attempt any description of that world-renowned fight. But Vivian's share in it demands more than a passing notice; and this I have drawn up from the authorities whom I have mentioned, as well as after having made a visit to the field of battle; and from other sources.

It may be premised that, at Waterloo, Vivian commanded the 6th Brigade of Cavalry of the British and King's German Legion. It was composed of the 1st, 10th, and 18th Hussars, numbering, according to

Siborne, 1,279 sabres. They were at first stationed on the *extreme left* of the first or main portion of the British line. The 10th and 18th regiments were in line in rear of the road to Wavre, and withdrawn a little from the crest of the ridge, the right of the 10th resting upon a lane. The 1st Hussars were also in line, and formed the reserve. The extreme left of this brigade was completely *en l'air* (*i.e.*, unsupported), upon high, open, and flat ground. A piquet, consisting of a squadron of the 10th, occupied the village of Smohain, and their vedettes were within half-carbine-shot of some of the French cavalry. Vandeleur's brigade of light horse was on Vivian's right.

But the frequent and furious charges of the enemy made it necessary, as the anxious, bloody day wore on, to strengthen the Duke's left centre ; and accordingly in the sheet of Siborne's Atlas representing the field at a quarter before eight p.m., when the Prussians had begun to arrive, Vivian's cavalry appear as then occupying the *middle* of the much-weakened British force, close at the rear of the Brunswickers and Nassauers. This change of position was effected on Vivian's own responsibility, and to the great satisfaction of the Duke ; for when these fresh troops took up their position, the British cavalry had been reduced to mere skeletons of regiments. It is not difficult to fancy how long the day must have seemed to the fiery Hussars, who had not yet struck one blow, and who were anxiously longing for the opportunity of displaying their own valour, and of avenging the deaths of their slain comrades.

They were not to wait much longer, as we shall presently see; for, twenty minutes later, Vivian, instead
of being at the rear of the British army, was at its
head, sabring the Imperial Guard:—'Oh the wild
charge they made!' It must be borne in mind that
the crisis of the battle had arrived; and Napoleon, like a desperate gambler, had risked his all
by sending his masses of reserves against the at-
tenuated British regiments, with instructions, *at all
hazards*, to force the centre, in the rear of which
Vivian had placed himself, in a most trying position
for cavalry, exposed as they were to the fire of the
French tirailleurs. His first impression, on contemplating the destruction which he saw around
him, was that he had come, once more, to cover a
retreat of the Anglo-allied army: and, indeed, but
for the exertions of himself and others—actually using
the flats of their sabres—the contemptible Dutch-
Belgian troops, who formed Wellington's second
line, would have probably fled from the field, and
have left a hideous and fatal gap in the British line.

But Adams's infantry brigade had swept, like a
triumphant wave, the front of the Allied line, and
the moment had arrived when a daring charge by
fresh cavalry against the shattered Imperial Guard
and the French cavalry reserves round La Belle
Alliance, was all that was wanting to secure the
impending victory. Vivian was the happy man
upon whom this glorious task devolved. He moved
out to the rear of Alten's division, and thus clearing
himself from the British infantry, advanced directly
to the front by the right of Maitland's brigade of

Guards. His orders from the Duke were not to attack till the infantry came up to his support, unless he was '*confident of success.*'

At this juncture, Sir Hussey Vivian—encouraged by the cheers of his comrades, heard above the fierce trumpet-blasts, by the ringing of scabbards as the swords leaped forth, and by the victorious omen bestowed by a crimson gleam of the rapidly setting sun, which now pierced and incarnadined the smoke and clouds—charged in echelons of regiments; the 10th, headed by himself, leading: and with that regiment he dispersed and drove in the cavalry posted in the front and on the left of the squares of the Old Guard. No sooner was this done, than, galloping to his left, he led on the 18th, also in person, against the Cuirassiers of De Lorte, who were on the right of that veteran body; the 1st Hussars of the German Legion following. In a few minutes the dazzling helmets of the French Cuirassiers and the spears of their Lancers were seen scattered in every direction! At the same time the 2nd King's German Legion, which Wellington had moved up to support Vivian, successfully charged a body of Cuirassiers on the right of the 10th; and although this corps was in its turn assailed by fresh Cuirassiers, and thrown into disorder, it quickly rallied, and soon drove the French off that part of the field. The squares of the Guard were thus laid bare, and the artillery in the intervals opened a heavy fire on the British horse; but Vivian, dashing on, captured the guns, twenty-four in number, *before any foot-soldier on his left arrived*. Then, seeing the Osnaburgh red-coats coming up to his support, he ventured to attack the squares themselves. Such was the ardour of the men, that a squadron of the 10th, having re-formed after taking the artillery, and Vivian himself leading them, charged one of the squares with unparalleled vehemence. That attack was, after a short struggle, at first repulsed by the steady fire of the veteran French grenadiers. The French square, nevertheless, fell back after the shock, still keeping up a rolling fire on its opponents, who never ceased to cut at them till they too were lost 'in the crowd of fugitives. About this time Vandeleur's brigade came up. It charged upon Vivian's right, defeating a body of French infantry, who were formed in square, and who were endeavouring to restore the battle in that quarter; but the rout was now complete.

Wellington, encouraged by the rapid and beautiful style in which Vivian's brigade advanced, and by the brilliant success of the attack, now ordered, amid the enthusiastic cheering of the troops, the long-looked-for general advance of the whole line. That this was, as Siborne well describes it, 'a march of triumph rather than of attack,' is matter of history. The battle of Waterloo was won; and the British General's prediction was verified, in the words of Scott, that 'England should tell the fight.'

That night Vivian and his exhausted Hussars, satiated with their bloody victory, bivouacked in advance of the main body of the English at the little village of Hilaincourt; while the fresh Prussian troops followed up the retreat of the flying French.

One or two episodes in this memorable achievement have been recorded by Captain Malet, in his
' History of the 18th Hussars.' As at Balaclava,
there came an order which

' Some one had blunder'd :'

the leading half-squadron, in the final charge, was
wheeling in precisely the wrong direction, which
Vivian perceiving, at once rode up to rectify, exclaiming, says Malet, ' with emphasis, and a good
hearty d——, that it was *towards* the enemy he
wanted them to wheel !'

Again, after the 18th regiment had been led to the
charge, Vivian, on returning (with his arm in a
sling, the result of the wound at Croix d'Orade)
to lead on the 10th also, was intercepted by a
straggling French cuirassier, who cut at the English
General. Taking his reins, however, in his right
hand, which was barely able to grasp them, Vivian
not only parried the blow with his sword in his left
hand, but also contrived to wound his antagonist in
the neck. This unequal combat might possibly
have ended fatally for the gallant Cornishman, had
not his German orderly galloped up at this moment,
and cut the luckless Frenchman down.

Vivian's own account of the affair, as contained in
the following extract from a letter written by him
soon after the battle to Mr. Pendarves, will probably be read with interest :

' St. Benir, in part of the Château, 23rd June, 1815.

' . . . About six o'clock, however, I learnt that the
cavalry in the centre had suffered dreadfully, and

the Prussians about that time having formed to my
left, I took upon myself to move off from our left,
and halted directly to the centre of our line, where I
arrived most opportunely at the instant that Bonaparte was making his last and most desperate effort ;
and never did I witness anything so terrific—the
ground actually covered with dead and dying,
cannon-shot and shells flying thicker than I ever
heard even musketry before, and our troops some of
them giving way.   In this state of affairs, I wheeled
my brigade into line, close (within ten yards) in the
rear of our infantry, and prepared to charge the
instant they had retreated through my intervals (the
three squadron officers of the 10th were wounded
at this instant); this, however, gave them confidence, and the brigades that were literally running
away halted on our cheering them, and again began
firing.   The enemy on their part began to waver ;
the Duke observed it, and ordered the infantry to
advance.   I immediately wheeled the brigade by
half-squadrons to the right and in column over
the dead and dying, trotted round the right of our
infantry, passed the French infantry, and formed
lines of regiments on the first half-squadrons.

'With the 10th I charged a body of French
Cuirassiers and Lancers infinitely superior to them,
and completely routed them.   I then went to the
18th, and charged a second body that was supporting a square of Imperial Guards; and the
18th not only defeated them, but took fourteen
pieces of cannon that had been firing grape at
us during our movement.   I then, with the 10th,

having re-formed them, charged a square of infantry
(Imperial Guards), the men of which we cut down
in the ranks; and here the last shot was fired.
From this moment all was *de route.*

'Whether the Duke will do my brigade justice or
not, I know not; but Bonaparte has given them
their due in his account. We are the cavalry that
he alludes to, where at the end he says, "At eight
o'clock," etc.; and the Colonel of the 3rd Chasseurs,
who lodged the night before last in the house I
occupied, last night told the proprietor "that two
regiments of British Hussars decided the affair."*
The third regiment (1st Hussars) I kept in reserve.

'Of course, our loss was severe. All those returned missing are since ascertained to have been
killed.

'I never saw such a day, nor anyone else. I
expect and hope that every soldier will bear a medal
with "Mont St. Jean" on it. I would rather do so
than be adorned by the brightest star that any
potentate could bestow on me. . . .

'To Wynne Pendarves, Esq.,
    'No. 11, Queen Anne Street, London.'

For his services on this occasion Vivian received
the following decorations: viz., the Order of Maria
Theresa from the Emperor of Austria; the Order of

* Gourgaud, Napoleon's aide-de-camp, as well as other French military critics, ascribe their loss of the battle of Waterloo mainly to the
charge of Vivian's brigade on the flank of the Old Guard, after the
repulse of the middle guard. 'These three thousand cavalry,' says
Gourgaud, '*prevented all rallying.*'

St. Wladimir from the Emperor of Russia; and that
of Hanover from the Prince Regent.

In his despatch dated 'Waterloo, 19th June,
1815,' the day after that great and glorious victory,
the Duke says that the British army ' never, upon
any occasion, conducted itself better. . . . There is
no officer nor description of troops that did not
behave well.   I must, however, particularly mention, for his Royal Highness's approbation———'
Here follows a list of heroic and illustrious names ;
amongst which Truro men especially, but also all
Cornishmen, and all Englishmen, ever read, with
glowing pride, the name of our own hero, Major-
General Sir Hussey Vivian.

A brother-officer of Vivian's (Colonel Taylor, of
the 10th Hussars) wrote the following lines on the
occasion :

> ' From the left flank, in column, winding far,
> Speeds with a whirlwind's force the swift hussar ;
> Tho' to their thund'ring hoofs the plain resounds
> Still cautious discipline their ardour bounds.
> Who, with a hero's port and lofty form,
> With waving sabre onward guides the storm ?
> While through the tangled corn and yielding clay
> His spurs incessant urge his panting grey*—
> 'Tis VIVIAN, pride of old Cornubia's hills,
> His veins the untainted blood of Britons fills.
> Him follows close a Manners,† glorious name,
> In him a Granby's soul aspires to fame,
> Or such as erst, when Rodney gained the day,
> Ebb'd from his kinsman's wound the life away.
> " Front form the line !" cries VIVIAN ; still its course
> The head maintained ; the rear with headlong force

---

* He rode on this occasion a milk-white troop-horse of the 10th
Hussars.
† Colonel Lord Robert Manners.

Speeds at the word, till troops to troops combine,
And each firm squadron forms the serried line.'

His subsequent connexion with the Waterloo campaign may be briefly summed up in the statements that he led the advanced guard of the British army all the way from Waterloo to the gates of Paris; and that, on the restoration of Louis XVIII., his brigade formed part of the allied army of occupation in Picardy—services less brilliant perhaps than those which have just been described, yet certainly most useful and important.

But the reception accorded to ' the Warrior of the West' by his native town, after the battle of Waterloo, should not pass unnoticed. Towards the latter part of July (the 27th was, I believe, the day) Vivian returned home for a short time ; and when it was known that he was approaching Truro, which was *en fête* on the occasion, numbers of the inhabitants went out to meet him, and, taking the horses out of his carriage, dragged it in triumph through the streets. Several of the townsfolk had assembled at Mr. Vivian's house, to greet the victorious hero on his return. Amongst them was the writer's mother —then quite a young girl—whom the tall, strong man lifted up in his arms as if she had been an infant, and embracing her, exclaimed to those around him, ' There ! believe me, that's the first kiss I've had since the battle of Waterloo !' His speech to the populace on this occasion could not be reported, for the air was rent by their shouts ; and I should judge, from the contemporary accounts, that a similar enthusiasm prevailed on the occasion of the

public dinner which was given to him at the Truro
Assembly Rooms on the 31st July.

The army returned to England in 1818; and with
it Vivian, who now found himself, for the first time
in twenty-three years, unemployed. Great reduc-
tions in the military establishments, of course, took
place; and on the 10th September, 1821, the 18th
Hussars was, amongst other regiments, disbanded.
On this occasion he was presented by the *soldiers*
with a silver trumpet purchased out of the proceeds
of the sale of horses which had been captured by the
regiment during the Peninsular campaign.

It seems hardly necessary to dwell upon the facts
of his having been despatched in 1819 to Newcastle-
on-Tyne, and thence to Glasgow, for the purpose of
quelling riots which had broken out at those places;
it will suffice to mention that the service was
promptly and efficiently performed.

The University of Oxford in the following year
accorded to him the high honour of the degree of
D.C.L., which, however, for some reason, he does
not seem to have taken until fourteen years afterwards. In 1820 he was elected a Member of Parliament for his native town, and represented it for five
or six years.

In 1827 he received a Colonelcy of the Life
Guards; and in the following year he was created a
baronet—a coat of arms full of heraldic allusions to
his distinguished career being at the same time
granted to him.

For the five years, 1825-30, Vivian represented

Windsor in the House of Commons; but the failing health of Lady Vivian, and his appointment to the command of the forces in Ireland, caused him to retire from Parliament. It is said that during this period he was offered the post of Secretary-at-War, but that he declined it on account of his preference for the more active duties of his profession. Whilst in Parliament he seldom failed to speak on all military questions; he also took part in the debates on Catholic Emancipation (of which he was a supporter), and on the distress which prevailed in the country in 1830. Polwhele thought highly of his fluent eloquence; and I am told by Mr. H. S. Stokes that Vivian was remarkably successful in his addresses to election mobs. In this year he attained the rank of Lieutenant-General; and about the same time William IV. made him a Grand Cross of the Royal Hanoverian Order of Guelph.

In 1833 (the first Lady Vivian having died) Vivian married a second time; the lady of his choice being Lætitia, third daughter of the Rev. J. A. Webster, by whom he had one daughter, Lalage. Four years afterwards he again entered Parliament, this time as a representative of the Eastern Division of Cornwall; having, however, been previously made a Privy Councillor in 1834, and having filled, with distinction, for four or five years the historic post of Master-General of the Ordnance.

Little remains to be told of his history. On his retirement from the above post, he was created a peer, and took his seat in the Upper House as

Baron Vivian of Glynn and Truro, the patent being dated 11th August, 1841.   His last-earned honour he did not enjoy for more than a year; for, on the 20th August, 1842, he died suddenly at Baden-Baden.

On the 13th of the following month the little town of Truro presented a doleful contrast to that which it bore some twenty-seven years before, when her brave son returned in the full flush of victory.   All business was entirely suspended in order that the townsfolk might receive, at the town quay, Vivian's mortal remains; they were brought up the river from Falmouth, and carried to the church, which was draped in black.   He was buried at St. Mary's Cemetery, in the same vault with his father and mother, against the eastern wall of the enclosure; but no inscription marks the spot.   His epitaph which was in St. Mary's Church (now the new cathedral), need not be inserted here, for his career has been described in the foregoing pages, and it will be perhaps sufficient to quote the description of his character as summarized by Dr. Wolcot—no lenient critic :

'An excellent officer, and, better still, a kind, brave, honourable, and good man.'

INDEX.

H

THE END.

Elliot Stock, Paternoster Row, London.